# Sealed Letters

## 1850-1917

# Dora Openheim

# Sealed Letters

## 1850-1917

Translation by
Clifford E. Landers
2016

"-Cartas Lacradas-1850-1917"
Dora Openheim- Rio de Janeiro -Record-2013
All rights reserved in Portuguese- to Brazil
Editora Record- Ltda.
Rua Argentina-171-20921-380-Rio de Janeiro,RJ
ISBN-978-85-01-09471-1
13-0140,CDD 949.565
CDU : 94(495.622)

1- Memories - Correspondences-2- Jews- 3-Salonica- History- 4 Family Baron Maurice de Hirsch- 5-Constantinople - The Oriental Express 6-Holocaust-7- Nineteenth Century- 8 Europe -1850-1917-9 JCA- Jewish Colonization Agricultural -10-Bank de Paris et Pays Bas-Paribas-11-Oscar Straus-12 Lord Rosebery-13 Montefiore levy

Grateful acknowledgement  is made for  the permission in the use of the rights of the Archive   number 350A on the Royal Archive of Belgium, as all the photographs.

A CIP Record of this book is available from the Library of Congress

This English translation, by Clifford E. Landers-
Publishing in first edition  October- 2016

## WHY AM I TELLING YOU THIS ?

*I visited new Europes and was greeted by different Constantinoples,*
*as I sailed into Because it is absurd to be telling you this story ,*
*after having said …*
*I would talk about my voyages.*
*the ports of Pseudo-Bosphoruses.*

*It baffles you that I sailed in ?*
*You read me right, the steamer in which I set out, came into port as a*
*sailboat.[…]*
*That´s impossible you say…That´s what happened to me…*

*"The voyage I never did "*
 *The book of disquiet- Fernando Pessoa*

*To my grandchildren*

*Carolina, Theodora, Stefanos and Felipe*

*For all their smiles...*

# CONTENTS

## Part Three

# Europe and Ottoman Empire

*The path of the letters- the Grand Voyage*
*1865-1917*

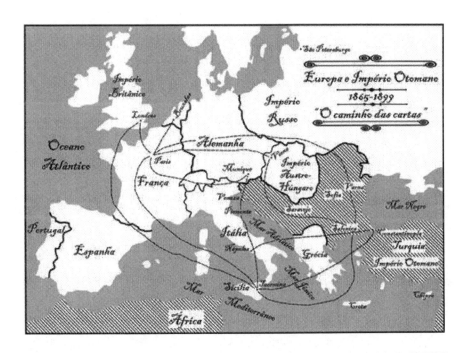

# INTRODUCTION

## 1970- 2005

*"The backstage of this book,*
*the obsession to understand the letters,*
*and all coincidences of life"*

For many years it has been my desire to write about Anna Varsano, her daughter Michaela and her husband Alberto–about their letters, their memories, their lives intersecting with other lives, with the history of the Jews since the Diaspora, who for centuries transported in their trunks the weight of survival.

In August 1970 I chanced upon one of those trunks, because fate plays tricks on us, I became involved with the life, thoughts, memories, and secrets of Anna Varsano.

I never had any contact with her, never heard her voice, but she penetrated my soul in a powerful yet subtle way. She ignited my imagination with detailed descriptions on every page of her diary, albums of postcards, photos of her family, drawings and small pieces of cloth pasted in yellowed notebooks.

It began during my honeymoon. The high point of the trip was to be Greece, more precisely the city of Salonica, or Thessaloniki, as my Greek husband's birthplace is called. There I would meet his family, his maternal grandmother, aunts and cousins. My sole concern was to please and to be accepted, a foreigner who didn't speak the language and professed a religion all but proscribed in those lands .And thus was my first contact with Salonica and its history.

The home of Katina Mavrofridis, my husband's maternal grandmother, was a large, magnificent old house from the early twentieth century, sold shortly before to one of those construction companies avid to "modernize" the city. I felt a twinge in my heart when I saw it, knowing it would soon be reduced to dust, taking with it a part of the city's history. The two-story neoclassical-style dwelling had housed the Mavrofridis family since 1923, when as Greek citizens from the time of Byzantium they had been expelled from Istanbul. And in that house they married their five daughters and welcomed their grandchildren.

The grandfather, Anthony Mavrofridis, a merchant marine captain who passed away in 1963, was regarded as a man of character and few words. Meeting his family and his five daughters, I understood: women of strong personality, they did the talking for all. Mery, my husband's mother and the eldest daughter, had emigrated to a "savage country"–Brazil–in 1954. She followed her husband, leaving a comfortable home and taking with her only her diploma from normal school, three small children, and an enormous will to remake her life. They penetrated deeply into the interior of Minas Gerais, dragging behind them language and suitcases, learning Portuguese from customers and neighbors, pedalling a sewing machine until late at night... Thus she graduated her three children and raised a fourth, born in Brazil.

She returned to Salonica only once, after her father's death, and reunited with the sisters in a picture frame. When I met the other four sisters, that summer afternoon in Salonica, I saw attractive women of varied physical types. Helena, the American, lived in Boston and reminded me of Esther Williams. Zoi, a brunette with green eyes, had come from England and had absorbed the refinement of the British. Thekla, tall and elegant, was married to a much older retired admiral. Angelica, younger, almost the age of my husband, a brunette with abundant eyebrows and blue eyes, had married one of Aristotle Onassis's pilots.

Katina, the mother of these beautiful women, was sixty-seven and possessed incredible vitality. In a matter of seconds she communicated with me through gestures and mimicry while moving among the grandchildren and sons-in-law who were packing belongings, and she still managed to set before us a dinner fit for the gods. All without missing a single word of the dialogue of the daughters lounging on the sofa in the parlour, fanning themselves with magazines, their faces flushed from the inclement August heat. I thought I'd be under a microscope and be examined from head to toe..

But if they did so, I truly didn't notice it, for there was so much to talk about, so many questions, that I was grateful for the course in English forced upon me by my parents. But I never stopped promising myself that one day I would speak Greek...
Summer reigned absolutely, cicadas hummed in the garden, and the hours slipped slowly by. Days of feasts, dinners, strolls in the square, and, of course, the departure... In a few days the house would no longer exist. Only the memory. The grandmother, in excellent humour, was auctioning everything. She would stride through the parlour, banging spoons together and requesting attention.

"Who wants this samovar?" And no one replied. "And this dresser?... Come on, children, where am I going to put all this on that little *kotetsi*? The new apartment is a matchbox!"

The only thing my husband was interested in was his grandfather's binoculars. He had them in mind since the passing of the old man, whom he called *"Capitán* Pantellis." But none of the cousins had any memory of their grandfather. Nor had they accompanied *"Capitán* Pantellis" in action, giving orders, docking and dragging the leg shattered in the Second World War. For my husband, however, even the smell of wax on the wooden floor brought back childhood memories.

Everyone took a nap after lunch, it was the law. Only my husband and I, accustomed to Brazilian ways, didn't manage to do so. And it was on one of those afternoons that he decided to venture into the attic. According to his grandmother, there was nothing there but dust and empty boxes. But curiosity won out. When he had lived in the house, he was forbidden to go into the attic... A dangerous place populated by bats and ghosts... No place for a child.

He went up and stayed there. For hours... We awoke, the teakettle whistled, and one by one the aunts asked about their nephew. I pointed to the ceiling and went on reading my magazine. The grandmother, at the foot of the stairs, shouted something in Greek, for him to get out of the dust...

I went up, if only to entice him with coffee.
The attic was very hot, and the only light came from a few broken roof tiles. Piles of old newspapers, books, and boxes. I worried about fleas getting into my clothes and cobwebs in my hair...
He was standing in front of a panel with collages of icons, peering through a small crack lit by a weak beam of light. He was trying to remove one of the boards from the panel. He ripped away the collage, revealing the worm-eaten wood underneath.
And I saw it too. A room on the other side... A bed, a trunk, a table and chair... Some clothes hanging on a kind of line... The grandmother shouted from the foot of the stairs.
"Don't mess around up there, come on downstairs. Don't break the wall. Don't touch the icons... It doesn't belong to us," she chided. "It's theirs... the Varsano family's... Our neighbors next door... and all of them are gone... They never came back for any of it..."

The aunts and cousins came up. The wall was opened. No one there knew exactly what it was about. I remember it as if it were now. My legs shook–I, who had read *The Diary of Anne Frank* as an adolescent and grown up hearing stories from my Polish Jewish grandmother about the ghettoes, the yellow star on one's sleeve, death camps, massacres. I was overcome by strong emotion, tears of pain and loss; it was as if part of my own family had lived there, the memory of my grandparents. The memory of a people hiding like rats, for survival. In that place, at that moment, the truth of what I had heard in Brazil, a country blessed by distance from wars and persecution, became clear.

Everything matched the accounts. People walked in, unable to cough in an unbeatable atmosphere. The compassion of a neighbour, running the risk of being taken away as enemies of the Reich, an escape from envy and calumny, the traps set by others, hunger, disease, and human misery.
Gradually, I managed to touch things. The trunk with no contents, the empty pockets of the hanging clothes. Under the bed, a box lined with a faded blue cloth held papers, notebooks, and a small candlestick bearing the star of David.

We took the box downstairs. Katina, in tears, told how she and her husband hid them there, trying to save them... Not understanding Greek, I missed a good bit of the narrative and was able to recover it only some days later, translated by cousins and my husband.

When we were leaving, I asked them to show me the box again. Katina Mavrofridis agreed.

"It's yours, if you want it. It's no use to any of us, it's from your people, part of your history..."


I arrived in São Paulo, on September 7, 1970, in my new home, my new life, taking with me a box packed with memories, the story of Anna Varsano and her descendants.

The sewing box , kept in a closet for some months, seemed to call out to me. First I arranged the correspondence by date and leafed through the photo albums and the thick notebooks without much understanding. The drawings and photographs fascinated me. I began reading Anna Varsano's diary. Four thick bound volumes and handwritten manuscripts in sepia ink, in a language that looked to be Italian. Among the pages were memorabilia of images, dried flowers, papers, clippings, drawings, small pieces of cloth, some sewn, other glued or even held by thick, rusty pins.

What could I understand of all that at the age of eighteen ?

As the descendant of Ashkenazi Jews from the north of Europe, I knew nothing about Salonica and its history, or that hundreds of thousands of Jews lived there, or anything of the importance of the city since the time of Alexander the Great. I also understood little of life and its subtleties, as mine had barely begun. But the box held an attraction for me, and I wanted to know who the people were who lived with me in that closet.

I sought out books on Salonica and, on other trips there, contacted the Molho family, the oldest booksellers in the city, who provided me with veritable gems of history, mimeographed notes, historians' and travellers' accounts of the city's customs and daily life.

I began reading the contents of the box with the help of friends for the translations. I organized the letters by date and spent nights and weekends reading and rereading Anna Varsano's diary and recognizing the characters through descriptions and photos, the places where they lived, through old postcards.

In short, I fell in love with them. In later years, crossing oceans and seas, I visited the places described, looking for their perfumes, their customs, languages, the recipes of the period, exploring the life they lived... From 1850, in Taormina, Sicily, until the eve of the great fire in Salonica in August 1917.

In 1973, when the city was preparing to mark the thirtieth anniversary of the end of the Second World War, I was in Europe working for some days and decided to revisit Salonica.

I recall it was still cold, the end of April, and rainy. I was sitting with my husband's aunts, having tea, the television on, when they suddenly gestured urgently for silence. The reporter was interviewing, in Salonica, the few remaining Jewish survivors who returned to live in the city after the war. Among them, a very elderly lady, living in a hospital for the mentally ill since the end of the war. The curious fact was that she was not mentally ill, and never had been, but was terrified of being free and not finding any of her family still alive. She worked and lived there, without contact with life outside; her name and the hospital were mentioned. I caught a taxi and went there.

Anxious and touched, I tried to explain my doubt. The doctor in charge showed me an old document...In the file, with the date of admission November 20, 1945, was a photo that, to me, was identical to those in the album in the blue box.

She was who I was looking for! Her name: Adele Varsano Allatini, daughter of Michaela Varsano Montefiore and Anna Varsano's granddaughter. I couldn't lose the last thread of life that came from that box... And I was able to embrace her... I stroked her thin white hair, and she looked into my eyes, murmured something in a mixture of Spanish and Greek, and kissed my hand.

Once I was back in São Paulo I became anxious to return one day and take back with me the box from the Varsanos... And to the surprise of everyone, including my husband, who didn't understand my involvement with a story not my own, I flew again to Salonica at the end of that year.

Adele opened the box with her small, trembling hands.
A yellowed newspaper clipping bore the headline:

### HUGE FIRE DESTROYS THE CITY OF SALONICA!

*On the fifth of August, 1917, at 3:30 pm, a large fire erupted in immense flames, destroying almost the entire center of the city; more than 3,000 acres were reduced to ashes. The Vardar wind, which comes from the north and blows strong at this time of year, spread the fire, which for three days and nights reduced to ashes the entire area from Vardaris Square to the Hippodrome, and from the Promenade to Kassandrou Street. More than 2,000 houses belonging to residents of the Jewish community were consumed by the fire. Commercial buildings, factories, hotels and clubs, as well as 34 of the 62 synagogues in the city, more than fifty Jewish institutions such as primary schools and crèches, libraries and cultural societies, vanished in the rubble. The new Stern store, considered the jewel of European Turkish architecture, collapsed... along with the model school of the Alliance Israélite Universelle.*

Adele immediately understood everything.

Trembling, she took my hand that afternoon, and those that followed. Her deliberate speech merged memories and languages. She used her still alert eyes to make herself understood. I recorded what I could, hampered by the buttons on the "modern" Grundig tape recorder, moved by her vivid memory, her candid and affectionate way of speaking, moments of fear, furtive glances looking for the enemy, pauses for breath, songs... and tears.

She had never read her grandmother's letters, or even opened her diary, had never really had the courage, perhaps from fear or respect, she said. She still had a clear memory of her grandmother Anna Varsano writing by candlelight in her bedroom, and she, still a child, lying on the large iron bed, pretending to sleep, waiting for her grandmother to return to her bed and hug her... And now, with clouded vision, she told me she would no longer be able to read all that. She could barely make out the headlines in newspapers!

When I said goodbye I mentioned taking her from the hospice, but she wanted to die there, without leaving her hiding place.

Adele caressed the box, kissed the photos, and offered it to me, in exchange for the promise that I would one day write a book, telling how, in the city she loved, there had once existed a family called Varsano. And that I would tell the story of her grandmother. That I would write about her beloved Thessaloniki, her Salonica. A divine city, blessed, for in it lived the God of three religions. A city free of prejudice and persecution, where its inhabitants blended their languages, their customs, their aromas in every district and block.

"Now everything's over," she murmured, looking to the sides with a frightened gaze. "They came here..." She continued speaking almost in my ear, clutching my hands. "They came into the city with their cars and tanks, demanding to know the name of every Jew in the city.

They deceived us, said the yellow star was so we could provide services, work for them, in exchange for our freedom, in exchange for food...

In the beginning we believed, afterwards we were forbidden everything, and those animals in gray uniforms with swastikas, clicking their boots, swept house by house seeking out one by one every Jew in the city. They had all our names, it was Rabbi Korech who gave them the list, close to fifty thousand of us. They took us from our houses, left us with nothing, and imprisoned us in ghettoes.

They closed our pasta factory, put my husband to work building highways, and he never returned.

"Daniel, my son, and I stayed in the Hirsch ghetto, and one day Katina Mavrofridis, my neighbour, managed to go there and find us. She gave me black clothing, a crucifix, bread, oil, and some cereals, and also her own papers. She told me she had another identity card, issued in Constantinople, when she was forced to leave there. And that she would have no problem proving who she was if she were caught.

"She asked me if I knew how to pray in Greek. I remembered the prayers in the Church of Saint Demetrius, next to our house. And in minutes she taught me how to pass for Christian.

"'Make the sign of the cross like us, Adele... This way: *Hagios o Theós...*' And I did, once, twice, three times, until she said it was right. ' And if they ask for your papers, look the person in the eye, pretend not to understand anything, display the crucifix, and make the sign of the cross. Like this, with three fingers. Don't forget.'"

Adele made the sign of the cross three times to show me while she recounted this, her eyes filled with tears, continuing in a low, hoarse voice:

"After fear, the worst thing was the hunger. I would go outside the ghetto, passing through the Reich barrier as Katina Mavrofridis, in search of food. The entire city was looking for food. I knew my son Daniel would never be able to leave there; he would be caught immediately. They ordered men to lower their trousers. My son was circumcised..."

Adele sighed deeply and closed her eyes, remembering the scene.

"Later they took him away, first to Freedom Square, with thousands of Jews, young and old, without water, without anything. They remained there for days. No one could approach them. I wanted to break through that enclosure and get him, but I knew that Daniel would find some way to escape. He was always agile, a Maccabean athlete who ran track for his club, a worker who carried heavy loads in the factory, entire sacks of flour!

"And he did! My son, in a heavy rain, ran, flew like Pegasus, and hid in the Mavrofridises' house. *Capitán* Pantellis, soon afterwards, boarded up the rear of the attic and put icons on the wood.

He left a crack for passing the plates, water, and the vessel for faeces and urine, and placed an armoire with a false back full of books. Katina went into my house through the rear–the front door was sealed up with wooden boards.

And once inside, she looked for my belongings. They had taken anything of value, leaving everything turned upside-down. She found this box, a coat of my husband's with the yellow star, and filled a suitcase with the few clothes she found thrown everywhere. She took everything to the attic.

" Katina Mavrofridis  told me days later, when I came back from the mountains looking for food. I had to search for something to eat, fruit of some kind to strengthen my Daniel. Up in the mountains I even went beyond the ancient walls, in the cold and rain, with no food, I became too weak to walk the entire distance, and I delayed three days, stumbling and sitting down... A shepherd in a small cave fed me hot bean soup and apologized for having no corn for the bread.

However when I arrived, with a few quinces, figs, and wild greens in my bag, my legs were trembling.

"Katina was crying, every candle to the saints was lit. She explained that she had begged Daniel not to leave there. But the third night, with no news of my whereabouts, he couldn't bear it any longer and asked the Mavrofridises to be allowed out of the hideaway. The Capitán called for calm, spoke, whispering up against the wall of icons, and nervously begged him to stay quiet, for everyone in the house was in danger.

There was no way to persuade him. Terrified, and fearful the youth would make noise pushing aside the armoire and thus alert the German patrol stationed across the square, he waited until dark and took Daniel out. He left by the rear, jumped the wall, and disappeared as silently as a rat.

"He went looking for me in the mountains and never came back." Adele sighed deeply, her expression one of pain. Tears poured from her eyes, further clouding her vision.

"I found out they caught him and took him away on the trains. Where did they take my son? Only God knows!"

I wanted to find out how she had been saved, and why she was there, in that sanatorium, almost thirty years after the end of the war.

"The Mavrofridises still wanted to hide me," she explained. "But they were also in danger of being shot. I hid in the basement of Hirsch Hospital. I didn't even realize at first the risk I was taking. They, the black-booted killers, were occupying the hospital. I stayed there, underneath them, hidden among old steel beds and dirty mattresses. For months I could hear their boots going from one side to the other, and like a rat I fed myself, gathering potato peels from their garbage, hiding at dawn. I didn't forget the sign of the cross and Katina's crucifix. I have it with me as an amulet even now.

"One afternoon in October 1944, everything upstairs became quiet. There was no longer anyone walking around, just shouts of joy and music; I heard throngs of people coming up from the city screaming: 'Is Salonica free?'

"Not understanding what was happening, and thinking I had lost my mind, I peeked out through the cracks and saw the people in the streets, lefting my hiding place, prepared to be shot.

"People surrounded me; I was skin and bones. Greek people hugged me, gave me food, clothing, medicine for me to regain my strength. Doctors came and admitted me here, in the sanatorium. I was taken care of, and later worked helping out in the kitchen, cleaning, in the infirmary, and I never again left here.

"'Crazy Adele' was the nickname they gave me—'*Adele i trelli*' is going to die here! I don't have anyone anymore, and here I have all of them. Salonica must not still be the same city where I lived, and my friends are no longer here; they've gone to heaven... It's all going to remain in my memory. It's better that way... I can dream about all of it, the way it used to be..."

Mute, I felt my heart beating furiously. I didn't know what else to say. She dried her tears and sobbed. I kissed her brow, stroked her white hair, and embraced Adele, who was trembling.

I picked up the box and said goodbye.

"You promise me the book?" she asked for the last time, wiping her nose on a handkerchief and essaying a smile tinged with doubt.

I replied yes by nodding my head, unable to speak.

Moved, made my promise...


I struggled for years and decades to free myself from that virtually impossible commitment, always finding excuses. But I found no peace, and my subconscious finally prevailed.

More than a hundred years had gone by, and many leads no longer existed. The letters, the maps I drew in my imagination little by little became the route I followed. A time I never lived but had to describe.

The photo album, the postcards, and Anna Varsano's diary, always with me during all those years, took me to distant places. To Salonica. Then to Istanbul, the timeless Constantinople, the *polis* founded by Constantine, up to the period of the decline of the Ottoman Empire. Years later I journeyed to Taormina, in Sicily, and sought out *Mongibello*, the Varsanos' first home, then to Naples, Munich, and Planegg, always following the path of the family's letters and postcards. I sought out biographical details of each person mentioned in the diary and the letters, struggling to learn the languages and to understand the words written by them. I searched for people and visited the places from which they had been written, with the dream of finding vestiges of memories and documents.

I found some in Istanbul, much help in Salonica, in archives in Paris, London, and Munich, in the Inventories of the General Archives of the Kingdom of Belgium, in Eton College in London, and in lyceums and schools in Esneux and Brussels


It was quite some time after my last encounter in the sanatorium that I managed to return to Salonica; Adele Varsano no longer lived there. The hospital had been demolished, and no one could tell me where Adele was buried. I looked in vain for a tombstone in all the cemeteries. None bore her name.

I returned home with the list of questions I would have asked Adele. In my solitude, however, I had to answer them all in my own fashion, and it took me many years to understand the meaning of the words written there. Gradually, year after year, I made my way into their lives. When I could spare the time, after a day working in a clothes factory and reviewing the children's lessons, I would open the blue box and take out my old notebooks, annotating and writing, spent many a night answering the questions page by page.

A world of emotions surfaced, and people totally unknown to me became part of my daily life. I loved them, heard and spoke to them in thought. Many events and mysterious coincidences led me onward when I was ready to give up on keeping my promise. We left behind the time of the mimeograph, of carbon copies in the Molho Bookstore in Salonica, and entered the Xerox era; I had some years earlier put aside my notebooks, my file cards, and entered age of the computer and the Internet. I sought out help to clarify the mysteries and doubts, listening to stories of people who lived through part of that era or who carry in their mind the memory of their ancestors.

To all those who helped me with their memories, and to the coincidences of life.
I offer my thanks, as listed in the Acknowledgements at the end of this work

At the end of 2005, weaving together all the data and happenings, I was at last certain History truly held a story to be told.
And today, finally, after thirty-five years, from my home in São Paulo, a place distant from where it all happened, I can finish writing this book, *Sealed Letters*, keeping my promise to Adele Varsano.

Salonica- September 1970

São Paulo- December 2005

*"The Vardaris wind came, and with it the fire.*

*It came whistling loudly. Came with the fury of an assassin.*
*Gigantic flames licked at every house and the people passing by...*
*And it wiped out everything it encountered, killing, destroying, street by street...*
*"It was on Saturday, August 4, 1917, the eve of my wedding...*
      *"Everything turned to ashes!*
*"That night, giving no quarter, the wind, guiding the flames like tentacles, head toward the White Tower.*
*The minarets of the mosques fell one by one, our synagogue      crumbled, as did the immense Church of Saint Demetrius.*
      *In a matter of hours, everything in the area was a pile of embers. "The next morning, my fiancé was found dead in the rubble of the Vardar orphanage.*
*"He was trying to save the children...*
*"When the fire arrived at the Promenade, Daud took me to the sea."*
*"I stayed in Nico's caïke for a night and a day, unable to do anything to ameliorate that misfortune. "And for more than three nights, barely sleeping,*
*I walked through the city in flames reflected in the waters of the sea.*
*"Of my home, or my family, of everything I had*
*ever experienced, all that remained was this box of memories,*
*our beloved gardener Daud, and I..."*

*Memories of Adele-*
*Sanatorium of Salonica-1973*

Salonica-Promenade

The Great fire -August 1917

# Part I

# I

## *ADELE REMEMBERS*

*"Last days before the Great Fire "*

Salonica, Ottoman Empire, August 3, 1917.

The sun was doing the last spectacle that August afternoon.

In the silent garden, only the cicadas was humming , predicting another hot week to come . From the Grand Mesquite, like a clock, comes the voice of the muezzin, calling for the Ottomans to pray:

" Allah ú Akbar..."Allah is Great...

Adele outside, gathered the clothes from the line and in seconds a warm wind, strange for the time of year, shook the crowns of the nearby cypress trees. The fresh sea breeze from the Promenade merged with the scent of roses and basil.

"Finally comes the good wind ," she murmured.

Soon it would be night, and like every Thursday in the Vardar district, the neighborhood women stoked their ovens with wood and charcoal. The perfume from Adele's garden mingled with the smell of baking from the neighbouring houses.

On Thursdays the women of Vardar cooked together, their wooden rolling pins rapidly unfolding the paper-thin phyllo dough in a constant rhythm. . The sound of their labour recalled the working of a loom.

In the kitchens, daughters, mothers, and grandmothers gathered, some laughing, others complaining, mixing time-honored family recipes with seasonings and spices, each to her own taste. Some added a pinch of faith, others envy, or hope; many, of superstition and secrets, as they prepared the Friday night Shabbat meal.

In that district the sweets go by various names: *pastelas*, *rondachas*, *mordopites*, or *köl böregui*. The name did not matter, nor where people came from. The city held as many different races and languages as there were recipes and spices.

The women would wake up before daybreak on Friday and don aprons and turbans. Humming songs in Judeo-Spanish, they would relight the fire, braid new loaves of bread, and prepare sugar-and-cinnamon sweets.

"This is the best time of the day!" Daud's hoarse voice interrupted Adele's reverie. Lost in thought, sheets bundled against her chest, the girl was startled to see the aged family retainer behind the jasmine bushes.

She had been pensive, sad. Everything in Adele's life was happening too fast, too painfully. First, the death of her beloved grandfather, *Dottore* Alberto Varsano. Once the perfume factory closed, he had faded away into melancholy and infirmity. Then her brother Victor.

After arguing with grandmother Anna, he had left and vanished, taken the train, without sending word to Adele. Victor hadn't returned, not that summer or ever. . The house became large and empty without the pianist, without Victor and his music.

Anna Varsano's search for a husband for her only granddaughter began a period of secrets. Women would come and go, whispering, sipping countless cups of mint tea or eating almonds sweets. Finally, the suitor arrived, crowning her grandmother's efforts.

But in May, on the long-awaited day for Adele's final fitting, Anna Varsano, her adored grandmother, perhaps from the emotion of seeing her granddaughter in her wedding dress, collapsed as if struck by lightning.

The scene wouldn't leave Adele's head. She and Daud carried the unresponsive body down the stairs from the atelier to the garden, intending to take her to Hirsch Hospital. But Anna Varsano no longer breathed. And there, under the white tents of the Promenade garden, a place she adored, the scene of so many memories and laughter, of hot sunny days and long perfumed afternoons, lay her grandmother, lifeless and serene.

"Such a hot wind… Isn't it strange for this time of year, Daud? It looks like we'll have an early rain," Adele commented as she gazed at the horizon.

"May Allah hear you, my sweet girl!" replied the old gardener as he moved away, taking a basket full of roses into the house.

Almost seventy, stooped and melancholy of late, the Moroccan, wearing the same long *entari* and the frayed and faded *tarboosh*, had become a weary old man since Anna's death. He had been with the Varsanos since 1883, when Adele's grandfather, *Dottore* Alberto Varsano, had emigrated from Sicily to Salonica. They had come on the same ship and together had experienced adventures and misadventures, poverty and wealth, quests and journeys.

The city that received them and thousands of Jews was the Promised Land, the Mother of Israel. For centuries Salonica, part of the Ottoman Empire, had taken in those persecuted by the Inquisition, and there they built their lives.

. The gardener Daud was best friend, faithful counsellor, servant and protector. Together, more than two brothers, he and *Dottore* Alberto, had constructed everything around them. Grandmother Anna's home, the atelier, the worthless lands that had become a beautiful garden—all of it Daud's work, in his simple way of going unnoticed, his temperament, his sensitivity and lack of selfish ambition.

It had all begun with the garden. As a child, Adele had listened at table to countless heated discussions about the *attar* of roses, the essence of perfume. But those days were gone. *Dottore* Alberto and her grandmother Anna no longer existed.

The large house was now silent and gloomy; only Adele and the Moroccan gardener remained.

As Daud slowly disappeared into the bushes and the long shadows of sunset, Adele's gaze followed that beloved figure.

She considered Daud one of the two most important men in her life. The first, beyond any doubt, had been *Dottore* Varsano, her grandfather, a man of countless lessons and stories, who had taught her the poetry and fables of La Fontaine, which she memorized in French and later declaimed at the Lycée. Fables with morals, fables shared and discussed by the two grown-ups there: *Dottore* Varsano, the learned one, a pharmacist educated in Venice; and the simple mixed-race Berber born in a crude hut in the Atlas mountains.

The Moroccan couldn't read any language, but from a single listening to *Dottore* Varsano's lessons, Daud would memorize what Adele and her brother Victor were studying in school.

"*Voilà... pedakia mou...* Well, my children..." Daud spoke in a hoarse voice, summoning them to the essays read aloud in the garden.

Mixing accents and languages, he would begin:

"*Atténtion. Atténtion*, Victor and Adele!

Start together, in unison:

"*Nuit et jour à tout venant*
*Je chantais, ne vous déplaise*
*Vous chantiez, j'en suis fort aise*
*Eh bien! Dansez maintenant...*"

Only now did Adele realize that, though illiterate, Daud had studied with her and knew everything and had also taught her a great deal about life. The idea for roses had been his, and he had taught her grandfather how to grow them, identify them, tend to them. He had built the first shed for the *Dottore*, the oven and boiler where they distilled oil from the petals and where, later, the perfume formula was created. Even the unforgettable Rose du Soir, the best known fragrance manufactured by her grandfather, bore the touch of the gardener's blessed hands.

Victor, Adele's older brother, laughed at her. He told their grandfather that she didn't think, but he did, he was more intelligent. He was constantly declaring in Greek, "I am the *Mégas* Victor" and chasing her around brandishing a book: "I'm the great Victor... the Great One... the *mégas*..."

And when the *billets* from the Lycée would arrive at the Varsano house, with the grandchildren's progress report, the *Dottore* would summon Anna and Daud. Adele would sit in her grandmother's lap to escape Victor's pinches, snuggle there, feeling the warmth of her bosom, the rustle of her silk dress and the perfume of her damp skin.

"Granny Anna... What a wonderful woman! How I miss her," Adele lamented.

Adele loved the atelier, the room of dreams, as Anna called it.

She remembered her grandmother moving among brocades and silks, wrapping ribbons around the iron mannequins, sticking in pins and assembling models, smiling at clients, her white teeth contrasting with her olive skin. Anna would spend most of her day in that room.

Illuminated by the skylight, everything there had a chalky white aura. Influenced by what she had seen in the *hamams*, the city's public baths, Anna had told the architect: "I want my atelier to have a round ceiling like the sky, with sunlight filtered through small glass plates in the dome." She spent most of her time there, humming and nodding. Combs and hairpins adorned the abundant, shiny hair that was the envy of her customers.

That was her world, a realm that the grandfather seldom entered.

Anna would go downstairs only for lunch in summer, served on the terrace of the Promenade garden. Usually the *Dottore* had guests for those leisurely lunches, with conversation about politics and recollections; when the visitor was very formal, it was like torture to Anna, who was anxious to return and finish what she had started in the morning.

She enjoyed receiving visitors, yes, but never at three in the afternoon "with the sun at its highest point and my face damp," as she put it. Anna hated the sun. The terrace had been lined with gauze to keep out the afternoon heat. When a guest stayed longer than expected, Anna would give a discreet signal; Daud would cross the garden with a concerned expression and after bowing ask her permission to interrupt: "there was always a very important lady waiting in the atelier." The *Dottore*, dozing off, would be startled to find someone about to leave.

Adele laughed as she recalled the scene. She remembered the building of the new house, Anna's long-time dream, following numerous lunches with a famous architect from Livorno.

That night, Adele went in search of her grandmother's albums. She had to find the thick velvet-bound book, which had always been a mystery to her. It was where Anna wrote every night, while Adele, in the high iron bed, watched as she spent hours there, her back turned, the candlelight flickering on the wall; sometimes she seemed to murmur, or weep softly. And when she finished she would look at Adele, who pretended to be asleep.

Adele wanted to discover her grandmother's secrets before leaving the house forever. She would take with her in her new life the sewing box that had been kept locked in the closet. It would be like embracing her grandmother again, hearing her advice, feeling she was alive once more. Now she would read the letters, caress the small cuts of fabric, the sketches of clothes, everything kept during a lifetime, small souvenirs mixed with newspaper clippings. The collections of postcards and photos, some marked with her perfumed lipstick, others stained with tears, would recount Anna's life from when she had lost her mother in Sicily. There was much to be read in a short time.

Adele thought about her grandmother's counsels. One night when she was still little, Anna affectionately explained that an album of that kind wasn't intended to be read by anyone and served only to bring closer those who had already departed. Someday Adele would have one just like it, and in hours of nostalgia, distress, or even joy, it would be shared, and one day, perhaps, read again.
She hadn't understood what her grandmother meant. She was too young."A diary is a secret and discreet friend, my love. In it you write your most intimate memories, everything good or bad you've ever done, and it will contain the true you."


Anna was gone, and now the atelier was empty.
Her perfume impregnated everything she had touched. Her soul was there, on the terrace with its vista of the sea, from the White Tower to the port, in Daud's secret garden, surrounded by jasmine-covered trellises, and in the large dining room with the silver candelabras and engravings that once belonged to their ancestors in Toledo.

Adele admired the sunset as it turned the sea to gold. The crest of Mount Chortiarthis hid the rising full moon of August. From the mosques in the distance came the muezzin's call to evening prayer. Lanterns twinkled like tiny stars.

Like magic, Salonica was alight in its ritual of summer nights, enveloped in the perfume of basil and roses.

∽

On Friday morning ,the Vardaris wind seemed to have returned to the north .In Adele's room, stuffy from the direct sun on the windows, the curtains no longer swayed. Far off, the blue sea, the gilded domes of churches, the minarets of mosques, and the tiled roofs of synagogues reflected a city unlike any other.

The chimneys of the Allatinis' factories discharged clouds of prosperity, and the sound of hammering from the Modianos' construction sites mingled with the happy shouts of children on their way to school. Itinerant peddlers trumpeted their wares in the streets: Turks, figs and seedless raisins; Greeks, steaming cream-and-cinnamon *bougatsas*; and Haim La Vaca, the melon vendor, going from door to door selling the sweetest fruits in the city.

The *hamalitos* of the Sibi market, elderly but strong as Samson, easily carried loads like ants, bound for the port or the train station.

The men left for work wearing summer clothes. Women beat carpets and jabbered away in Judeo-Spanish, known in Salonica as Ladino, the age-old language surviving from the Inquisition. As the Vardar neighborhood prepared for Shabbat, there was noise, aromas, and color. Afterward, calm and silence.

Beneath her window the strident calls of old Avramicos, the itinerant peddler, roused Adele from her bed. Early every Friday, she would go with her grandmother to see him. Tall, thin, with a white beard, wearing the *agnieri*, a threadbare coat with fur collar. The coat's lining was a repository for clasps, pins, ribbons, buttons, bobbins.

Anything not found on his tray would surely be in his *agnieri*. The old man came up the street calling out in Greek, his voice shrill and carrying:

*"Carulaaaakia, siiiritaaaakia…massuraaaakia…*
clasps… pins… bobbins…!"
The children followed him, shouting:
*"Skiatro! Skiatro!*
Scarecrow, Scarecrow!"

The sun blazed ,spitting August fire.

Adele, looking out the window, tried to relax, her body still aching from the work of the previous day. At eight o'clock, she would try on her wedding gown, the final fitting. It had been ordered hurriedly, based on sketches from the best seamstress in the city— Anna Varsano, her late grandmother. The great store Stern, the best in the city, stocked with *vêtements* from European Turkey, had agreed to execute the design of the gown. The wedding would take place in two days.

The following Sunday, August 6, 1917, at twilight, before the full moon lit the Salonica sky, Adele would be led to the altar by the man to whom she would vow love and fidelity until the end of her days. The wedding would take place in the Sicilia Hadash synagogue. And she must be beautiful and happy, just as her grandmother had dreamed.

Anna Varsano, her grandmother, had planned everything.

She had met her granddaughter's suitor through an old friend.

The young man, Michael Dervis, was the son of a manufacturer of *tarbooushs*, the felt red hats. He was assuredly the best prospect. A gentleman, well brought up, with strong features, a comfortable life, a citizen of the world, as Adele's grandmother proclaimed.

"Think about it, Adele, you're 25, and here in Salonica that's inconceivable... It's very hard for a woman your age to find a suitor!"

Good fortune was knocking at the Varsanos' door, sweeping away the tedium of recent summers, without Victor at the piano, without his noisy, talkative friends, strolls in the Promenade or Lumière films from Paris at the Olympia or Pallás theatres. .

The friends had disappeared when Victor left for Paris at beginning of that September ,all became silent inside the house.

๕

The idleness of the long summer days bothered Anna. She distracted herself with music and fantasizing about the life of her two grandchildren.

They were all that remained to her, after the tragedy in England.

Adele felt a tremor as she remembered her brother Victor, the last day she had seen him. A horrible day; after an argument with her grandson, Anna had never been the same. Victor, his eyes blazing with fury, had packed his bags and, without saying goodbye to Adele, headed to the train station. For several days and nights Anna had been confined to her bed, weak and dishevelled, refusing even a spoonful of soup. Adele never understood what had caused the fight. Jealousy on Victor's part or overprotection by their grandmother?

Perhaps, she thought, the hot temper of both. It was never made clear. Anna avoided the subject. Vaguely, blame was placed on the young woman, called Lucienne, with whom Victor had fallen in love. But she believed that in time he would forget her and all would be as before.

Adele recalled the day when her brother had arrived and placed the girl's portrait on the night table beside his bed. Everyone had admired the beauty of the *mégas* Victor's first sweetheart. They met her at a piano recital in Brussels, she was an orphan adopted by a family of bankers. Like him, she had studied music in Paris, and she was beautiful in Adele's eyes. She was smiling in the photo.

Definitely, Adele thought when she saw the portrait, she must be quite rich. Her lacy dress exposed the neck, adorned by a magnificent necklace of rectangular gems.

Victor left for good, but the picture of his loved one remained on the night table. His grandmother, despite vehemently opposing the relationship, never removed the picture from his bedroom. Adele discovered her *Nonna* late one night, holding a candlestick and sitting on her grandson's empty bed, gazing at the girl's portrait. She seemed to be talking to her, weeping and begging her forgiveness.

Some days after Anna's death, a letter arrived from a French agency specializing in locating missing individuals, hired by Anna much earlier. The letter listed the whereabouts of the two disappeared persons. Mademoiselle Lucienne de Hirsch, or rather Baroness Lucienne de Hirsch, was married to Edouard Balser, a banker, lived with relatives in Belgium.

Anna Varsano would have sighed in relief were she still alive. But there was not a word about her grandson Victor, only a terse "disappeared." Victor never again wrote or returned to Salonica, nor did he reply to Adele's letters, and he wasn't to be found among his friends in Paris. It was as if the earth had swallowed up Victor Varsano Montefiore! He disappeared from their lives forever. And the memory tormented Adele.

That slow, airless morning, one of the most important in her life, none of this would leave Adele's mind.

"Victor and his hot temper, Victor the *Mégas*, did it to scare his grandmother," the old gardener told her. "Don't worry: one day he'll come back to us…"

Daud told her the water in the *kazani* was warm. Only he knew how to prepare the bath. He would divide the water in basins and drip essence of rose into one crock, vinegar with rosemary leaves into another; in the final rinse her hair would emerge perfumed and shiny. He had learned the secret in Morocco, from his mother, who gathered rose petals and looked after a plantation near the Dédes plain.

"My mother used to say roses should be picked very early, before the sun could hit them, when the flowers were still only half-open," Daud said.

Adele grew up hearing him talk about roses. "The best are the *damaskinas*, Missus Anna," he would say. "The ones from cuttings from our rose bushes that came from Göksu, not the ones from the Modianos' garden," he stressed. "These new ones, which you insist I plant in your garden, are large and pretty but have weak perfume and only serve as decoration!"

In the bath, a sense of comfort took hold of Adele. The fragrance of roses, so familiar to her, imparted a feeling of love and security. It was as if everyone were downstairs waiting for her, to have breakfast. Her mother, her brother, her father, *Nonna* ..Yayá Anna always in a hurry to get back to the atelier, and her *Nonno*, *Dottore* Alberto, arguing with Daud.

She could still remember them recounting her favourite story: about the small vial of perfume. She heard Daud saying in his hoarse voice:

"Someday I am going to get a cutting, and then, Effendi Varsano, you will have the best fragrance in the Ottoman Empire! You will be able to bottle it in a crystal flask like those in the French Pharmacy, and be very, very rich!"

*Mabrouk Effendi Varsano, Mille Mabrouks!!*

᪣

# II

## TAORMINA

*"Know'st thou the land*
*where the lemon-trees bloom ?"*
*Goethe*

Taormina, Sicily, spring 1865

In September 1865, Anna Cohen married Alberto Varsano.
Summer in Taormina astonished foreigners

.Alberto came from Venice with a wooden trunk stuffed with jars, essences, potions, and books. His elegant bearing and educated manner gained the attention of various merchants when he entered shops in the upper part of the city requesting information. His speech was impeccable and no one would suspect that the foreigner, a Venetian with an Austro-Hungarian inflection, was a Jew. He wore an olive-colored topcoat that accentuated his dark green eyes. Wandering about the city, he might be one more northern noble there to contemplate the beautiful scenery.

Like many others who showed up in search of opportunities, he could be considered a bourgeois in rebellion against the new order that was unifying the Italy of Victor Emmanuel II.

Anna took care of the jewellery store of her father, Raffaele Cohen, a goldsmith practicing the craft learned from his grandfather, who in turn had mastered the secrets with ancestors, a closely guarded ability for more than fifteen or twenty generations. They were the *Oropes*, the jewellers of Toledo, Spain, fleeing the Inquisition.

Raffaele's shop was narrow, on a side street leading to the *Piazza di Sant'Agostino* in the high center of Taormina. The *Piazza* was the city's great attraction, and from his shop nearly hidden by the clock tower, Raffaele could see the activity, and further on, the sea meeting the sky. Across from the shop, an imposing stairway provided access to the Palazzo Sgroi. That morning the *scalinate*, passageways with steps linking one level of the city to the other, were crowded. Women, almost all in black, climbed and descended the steps, carrying baskets of bougainvilleas to decorate the city.

It was a festival, San Giorgio's Day, and the businesses soon closed their doors. Time for a bountiful lunch in the city, with houses emanating the aroma of fresh bread, rosemary, and oregano. Raffaele had left early to deliver an order near the Palazzo di Corvaja. Then he had returned home, at the foot of the Greco-Roman theatre, where his aged mother Rachelle and Anna, his only daughter, lived with him in a small white house.

Anna, who had lost her mother at an early age, nicknamed the house Mongibello, the last house on the street that led to the crest of the hill. The steep climb turned into a mere path, and Mongibello emerged among cypresses, the abyss and the sea, and the Greco-Roman theatre, the relic of ancient civilizations. As a young child, Anna played in the immense amphitheatre. Barefoot, she would ascend the hill, scampering over the ruined steps, feeling infinitely small before those monumental arches. She loved the contact of her feet with dilapidated stones, smoothed from time and warmed by the sun.

She had barely known her mother.

Rachelle Cohen, her paternal grandmother, had always taken care of the house and of young Anna. Rachelle Cohen was a different woman, who hardly spoke and never left the house, even for celebrations or funerals. Her speech, heavy with accent, always spoken in a very low voice, wasn't the language used in the neighborhood or the one her granddaughter learned at school. And when Anna didn't understand her, she would squint her clouded eyes, smile, and say, "One day, my dear one, you will understand..."

Rachelle never let Anna play with the children from nearby houses; fearfully, she would peer out from behind perpetually closed blinds at the movement in the street. Since Rachelle's good friend Esther and her family had left Taormina, Anna no longer heard her grandmother sing in Ladino.

She loved hearing her grandmother sing "*morenica a mi me llaman*" as she braided her long hair, or "*el sueño de la hija del Rey*" while preparing the favourite Shabbat recipe, chickpeas sautéed with garlic, eggplant on the brazier, sprinkled with olive oil, and roasted potatoes with Sicilian lemon and oregano.

Little Anna would sing with her grandmother while old Rachelle cooked or sewed. On Fridays, in late afternoon, the eve of Shabbat, Rachelle slowly bathed and changed into a brown dress, strung two strands of gold chain around her neck, and replaced the kerchief with a mantilla of black lace and gilded beads. On the dinner table stood the candlesticks with new candles, and she removed from an old trunk a thick book with a black cover and worn, yellowed pages. Standing in a corner of the room, murmuring incomprehensible melodies, she would rock her body back and forth. Her young granddaughter, attracted by the candlelight, wanted to take part in the ritual. But her grandmother, with a serious gaze and an index finger to her lips, signalled that the girl must respect that moment.

With the passage of time, Anna came to understand: that was not a moment for celebration, not there, in near darkness, at sunset amid deep silence. With time, she could see the reason for fear, for secrets, bitter memories, the loving embrace when her grandmother closed the book. It was a moment for recollection, gratitude, petition...

It was the start of Shabbat in Taormina.

Afterward, the candleholders were cleaned and wrapped in cloth embroidered with threads of gold, and Anna used the moment to peek into the chest. Inside were two small wine-colored velvet bags and another book, whose pages were bound with strips of cloth. To her, it was a treasure to touch things kept hidden in a hollow in the false bottom of a cabinet.

The little girl always believed that was the book from which her grandmother took her fantastic stories:

*"Cuando en 1492 los reyes católicos Fernando e Isabel desterráron de España, de Sefarad..., a los Hebreos..."*She would relate in a faltering voice.

That was how Anna grew up.

Anna was never seen speaking with her classmates, and had her grandmother prevailed, she would never have left the house to study.

"In all these generations, no woman has ever done that! And just where? In that temple of conversion?" she said, distressed. "They"–referring to the nuns at the school–"will make you into a convert, and even then you'll never find your place... None of them found their place when they became New Christians..."

Anna never mentioned her embarrassment at being different at school. Nor did she question the reason for more homework on Sunday than her classmates, who had no homework other than going to Mass and looking marriageable. Anna was even initially forbidden to attend theology classes. But she persuaded the sisters by crying in the office of the mother superior. She wanted to be thought of as an equal. She believed that by gaining permission she would learn a little about the religion itself and where all the hatred, all the persecutions came from and why they, speaking a strange language similar to Spanish, had for centuries been living in Sicily and not in Toledo. What crimes had they committed? What had her people, the grandparents of her grandmother, done to live like that, forever in hiding and fearful for hundreds of years?

Anna had difficulty understanding why what she heard at school never coincided with what she was told by her grandmother. And because she distrusted the new versions, she would never achieve a good grade and wouldn't go to heaven!
Anna Cohen had grown up between heaven and hell in Taormina. Her proud carriage, long-limbed body, and dark complexion highlighted her untamed and delicate beauty. Her walk was sensual, a subtle swaying of the hips and a toss of her abundant hair. She knew that behind her back they called her Anna *spagnola*, the Spanish woman, and that even as she was disdained she was also the envy of the class. As time passed, she realized that *spagnola* fitted her. Not that being Sicilian displeased her, just the opposite. That was her place and she was proud of her homeland.

Raffaele and his aged mother didn't consider Sicily their land. They were always prepared to leave... Like birds of passage .
Such feelings made Anna insecure. Nothing there was hers. She wasn't part of that place. She was a foreigner.

School days came to an end, her fellow students married, had children, and Anna's routine continued unchanged. She felt an emptiness, the desire to see them again, even if only for a few seconds and from afar. She would go down from Mongibello on Sundays and, almost hiding, watch them coming from Mass at Sant'Agostino. She always thought how much simpler it would be if she had been born into one of those families. The family of Francesca Galladoro, or Maria Cavallaro, or even poor Giuseppa Arrigò, the plainest creature in the class. Their families had found suitors for them before the age of fourteen. And in my house, she thought, the subject isn't even mentioned. As if she had all of eternity to live and good fortune would come knocking at her door.

"It can wait," her father said.

Nothing mattered more to Raffaele Cohen than to live honourably and not to get rich... For that would attract everyone's attention and be dangerous.

When Garibaldi's soldiers, in his last campaign, amassed regiments near Mongibello, her grandmother had for the first time opened the windows and hung up her famous faux sausages stuffed with garlic and day-old bread.

"An old trick from the time of the Inquisition," she explained. "So there can be no doubt that a family like the others in the neighborhood lives here."

Also, for the first time, Anna saw her freedom to leave the house curtailed. When she asked her grandmother why... she heard these verses in Ladino:

*"Hija mía, mi querida*
*No te eches a perdición*
*Más vale un mal marido*
*Que mancebo de amor."*

Anna's life now was limited to going from home to the jewellery shop and back to her grandmother in the kitchen.

One morning, she realized that the aged woman was no longer able to light the fire, and so she began assuming the housework. Rachelle had always done the cooking, invariably in wonderful fashion, and in recent months, sitting in a corner of the kitchen, she tried to pass along to her granddaughter her secrets and recipes, dictating and patiently explaining the details learned from her mother. If she forgot something, she would fetch the black book from the chest, leaf through illegible pages, and resume her explanation.

After a lifetime spent almost without speaking, she was never so talkative .Rachelle's customs were passed along to her granddaughter: to observe the rules of never using pancetta, the impure meat of the pig, as they did in neighbouring houses; to respect the domains of cooking, of milk and meat; and to know which foods Jewish law forbade. Anna carefully wrote down the recipes: rice with garbanzos, with saffron, or with *piñones*, rice with *spinaka*.

Thus, day by day, Anna learned the secrets of breads that rose, bell peppers and eggplants that came out sweeter. Of tomatoes, fresh fish, olive oil, and lime. And every day there was a new aroma in Mongibello.

Rachelle was in a rush to teach, to pass to her only granddaughter her books, her candleholders, the mantilla with gilded beads. Anna no longer left her bedside. She remained there, day and night, next to her grandmother, holding her hand, trying to feed her spoonfuls of soup, warming her chilled feet with blankets, fondly smoothing her sparse white hair.

On a cold December afternoon, strong wind rattled the windows of Mongibello. It was the last day of Hanukkah when all the lights of the menorah were extinguished. In her bed, Rachelle was ready. Extremely pale and panting, her hands trembling, the old woman brought the embroidered mantilla to her lips and with great effort offered it to her granddaughter.

"It's for you, dear Anna," she whispered. "This is your inheritance... All that I can leave you... It's our history, from my mother... From my grandmother..."

And, the words scarcely uttered, Rachelle Cohen closed her eyes forever.

❧

Anna fell in love with Alberto Varsano before she ever heard his voice. She noticed the foreigner the morning of the festival of San Giorgio.

Sitting in the shade of the oleanders in the Piazza di Sant'Agostino, the young man remained there for hours, gazing at the horizon. The piazza was empty at that time of day, so nothing obstructed her view from inside the shop. From the bench in the piazza the landscape was magnificent and she knew that every foreigner was enthralled by it.

The piazza overlooked the sea, protected only by an iron railing with large amphorae from which, in springtime, hung anemone, blue iris, and white narcissus.

The vantage point afforded a clear image of Etna to the south. Below, at his feet, the foreigner could see part of the Plain of Giardini and purplish-red flowers circling the road leading to the sea.

Further down, among the curves that led to Cape Schisò, he could glimpse the waters of Naxos.

To the left, he would see the majestic columns and arches of the Greek theatre. And behind it, the abyss where cypresses met the sea.

She went on looking at the stranger until her view slowly became obstructed. Movement unusual for that time of day filled the piazza. The area was about to serve as stage for the Ópra di Pupi, the puppet *teatrino* that would be staged there, next to the bench where the foreigner sat. The people of Taormina, from the wealthiest citizens to the poverty-stricken beggars in front of the city's churches, cheered, laughed and cried together, reliving part of the history of Sicily.

At night, the street lights in the piazza would be extinguished when the curtains of the small stage opened. Wooden Harlequins and Columbines with porcelain faces, gentlemen and heroines would tell the story of epic battles between Christians and the villainous Saracens, Ottomans, and other infidels. Ariosto's *Orlando Furioso* or Tasso's *Jerusalem Liberata* would be staged. Anna adored Orlando, Rinaldo, and Bradamante, the heroes, and always cheered during the *Feroce Incontro* between Orlando and Don Chiaro.

At home that afternoon,, Anna served lunch before the Ópra. Raffaele had no interest in the presentation as such, but it was an opportunity to see the jewels the aristocratic ladies of Taormina were wearing and, in this way, find ideas to offer his clients.

Anna and her father arrived early at the piazza, seeking a good spot; they didn't want to miss anything. Raffaele observed the women's golden necklaces with coral or amber and wondered:

"Since when is that considered a jewel?"

The golden piece on the heaving chest of *signora* Paternò, beside Anna, did not possess half the art of a simple chain: the difference was drops of amber that, in the candlelight, accented the metalwork. Anna was restless. Raffaele traded places with his daughter, and as she got up she noticed the gaze of the foreigner. She felt her cheeks turn red. There he was, at her side. She had not yet heard his voice, but she could feel his breath.

The next morning, life in the city returned to normal. In the empty piazza, the disassembled *teatrino* was all that remained of the spectacle. The city was still sleeping when the doorbell of the jewellery shop rang. It was the foreigner. His heavy eyebrows framed a deep, provocative gaze that made Anna's heart race. He felt flustered at the sight of the woman with a tapered nose, pink lips and golden skin sitting at the shop's table, amid tools and scales. He asked for Levy, the cobbler. Yacov from Messina had recommended him. Anna, shaking, didn't understand what information he desired. The shop belonged to Raffaele Cohen, the jeweller, not Levy, the shoemaker!

In fact, Levy and his family had left for Salonica, following the unpleasant episode in which Garibaldi's men, in the name of the Redshirts, had carried off his stock of boots. But she told the foreigner that her father could explain the story better.

*If I tell him everything*, she thought, *he'll turn his back, say thank you, and never return.* Her father must be at home by now, judging by the distance between the Palazzo di Corvaja and Mongibello.

She stood up and, leaning on the counter, pretended to look for Levy's address.

"I'm very sorry, sir," Anna said with a smile, "but I cannot find it! Maybe my father can give you the information... If you wish, you can find him at Mongibello..."

Alberto could not take his eyes off the girl, who seemed even prettier than the night before. Her tanned neck was carelessly displayed by her slightly open blouse, and her full breasts contrasted with her narrow waist. Her loose and untidy hair gave her a wild, sensual look.

Blushing, Anna began to braid her hair.

"And what is *signor* Raffaele's address? Is it far from here?""Well, if you'll wait a few minutes for me, I can show you the way," she said casually, gathering up her things. "I was just closing up!"

Alberto helped her to place the heavy bars on the door and offered to carry the basket of vegetables she had bought earlier.

On the way, in silence, Anna felt a frisson at her irresponsible attitude. What would her father think when she showed up with a total stranger?

Foreigners, though common in Taormina, were rare at that time of year. German aristocrats had begun buying property in the city as a refuge from the cold. In season, between January and April, one would frequently encounter a grand-duchess, prince or barons in their coaches ascending the steep streets in the direction of Castelmolla.

During Carnevale they vied for places in the hotels and *pensioni*, and the small Theatro Regina Margherita opened its doors for celebrated balls.

Anna took a deep breath when she spotted smoke in the chimney. Her father was cooking *melazane ripiene*. Giovanni Bagaglio, the fisherman, had left a beautiful slice of *spadone*, the enormous swordfish, so there would be a way, if her father agreed, to invite the foreigner to join them at the table. Alberto rested the wicker basket at the front door of the house, apprehensive lest he cause misunderstanding between father and daughter. The old man looked through the kitchen window, drying his hands on the cloth around his waist:

"Why did you bring him here, Anna? What does he want?" he asked in a hushed voice.

"I didn't understand very well, Pappá," she replied, fearful of her father's reaction. "I did understand that *signor* Varsano came from Venice and is looking for Levy, the shoemaker."

"What did you say? He's a friend of Levy's? What is his name, Anna?" he asked, as if testing his daughter.

"Varsano, he's *Signor* Alberto Varsano from Venice," answered the girl, emphasizing the foreigner's name.

Raffaele Cohen looked through the opening again, as if doubting that at his door was a Varsano from Venice.

"But of course, Anna, have *signor* Varsano come in!" he said, taking off his apron and raising his voice so it could be heard outside.

The girl quickly unlocked the front door. Seeing her smile, Alberto breathed in relief.

At the end of the summer of 1865, Anna Cohen became *signora* Varsano.
Her father smiled in contentment. After all, Anna, already a woman at 18, could not have had a better fate. Alberto Varsano had fallen from heaven; in all of Taormina, she would never find a Jewish suitor, much less a pharmacist from Venice, a *vero Dottore*.

On the day of her wedding, Anna wrote in her diary:

"I always thought my life had no direction, that I would forever be an old maid like Nedda… One fine day I met my prince from Venice, and today we are marrying.

"My beloved *Nonna*, I know that from there in heaven you approve of my half of the good lemon, whom destiny sent me."

❧

# III

## MICHAELA

## LEMONS AND INDIAN FIGS

Taormina, summer 1882.

Raffaele Cohen's jewellery shop had almost no new clients.

The development of the city brought tourism and wealth, along with competition and fashion. The Hotel Timeo, inaugurated by musician named Richard Wagner, transformed the city, largely because Otto Geleng, a Prussian baron enchanted by the scenery, had painted Taormina and exhibited his canvases in Paris.

The baron could not convince critics, who thought such a paradise was a mere artist's fantasy. A kindly man indifferent to his material goods, Baron Geleng paid for the critics to become acquainted with those landscapes and in exchange upon returning they would write in all the major newspapers a description of their breathtaking visit to that Eden.

Taormina became known throughout Europe as the best *villa saisonnière*, attracting in both winter and summer a cast of famous names like Goethe, Krupps, Nietzsche, and von Gloëden. Some spent the day painting watercolours; others, in high hunter's boots, would climb in groups, protected by parasols, laughing and conversing in various languages.

The noise would often awake young Michaela from the lethargy of summer, when she would sleep later. Only the *très chic* foreign ladies, so different from the women of Taormina, let curiosity overcome laziness. Michaela would peek through the blinds to watch the movement of foreigners near the window, admiring the demeanour, the clothes of the unknown women who often paused there, recovering from the steep climb to Mongibello. She followed every gesture, absorbing everything.

The foreign ladies, always well dressed, carrying damp handkerchiefs, would whisper, casting mischievous glances at the men waiting patiently for them on the other side of the road, laughing frequently. *How good it would be to live like them*, Michaela thought.

Observing them closely, however, she saw they were not all that beautiful, no more so than her mother. Anna Varsano had always been the perfect woman to her daughter, the best and most beautiful she had ever seen. Even now, almost 18 years old, Michaela had not changed her opinion.

The old jeweller realized that his granddaughter was now a grown woman of marriageable age. But these were new times: 1882! Women wanted to study, to work outside the home. Despite her father Alberto's reluctance, she had taken a job in a pottery studio. The daughter of a *Dottore*, he felt, should be a teacher. He hadn't sacrificed so much money and so much sleep keeping up with her studies, going through Latin declensions, memorizing Cicero's denunciations of Catiline, Baudelaire's verses in the original, excerpts from Dante's *Inferno* and from Goethe, to see her end up in a pottery studio. But she had overcome the obstacles with dignity, learned French and German with the nuns and was an excellent student of algebra, chemistry, botany, and world history.

Her greatest pleasure came from the occasional classes in painting and drawing that Sister Antonina di Luca, a beautiful young Carmelite nun, taught on free afternoons substituting for crabby old Mother Jolanda, the Latin teacher.

Evil tongues commented that Antonina, granddaughter of the powerful Sebastiano Curcuruto, owner of the lands around Castelmolla, had been responsible for the death of Francesco di Stefano, a young mandolin player hired to serenade by the *inamorati* among the city's upper aristocracy. The forbidden romance between the two young people had become known, and when they were found talking in the Giardino della Fontana Vecchia, Curcuruto's workers had dragged the youth to Misericordia Point and thrown him into the abyss.

Antonina was cloistered in the convent. Years later, she received permission to have dealings with the outside world, giving classes substituting for the elderly nun.

Poor sister Antonina, if called upon to clarify some doubt, had to do so only with gestures and by nodding her head. The schoolgirls, mindful of doing nothing to harm the beautiful and gentle sister Antonina, would repeat in unison the Latin declension *rosa, rosae, rosae, rosam, rosa... rosa!* Out of the corner of their eye, they looked at one another, call attention to the tree where the mother superior was hiding to spy on the class.

Michaela knew from the start that she would never be a teacher. A Jewish woman would not be accepted at any school in the region. Only if she became a Christian and wasn't pretending, as she sometimes did. As her mother had also done in school. Anything not to be seen as an enemy, forbidden to take part in religion classes or wear the crucifix in school. Her father didn't consider that a pretense, merely a means of survival. She wanted to be an artist, and for such she would have no need to hide her religious origins. There was no longer an Inquisition, or persecution, and all that mattered was what people made of life, Michaela argued.

"Are you saying, Michaela, that today each person is judged merely by what he achieves, and even if he's a Jew he's well received?" the old man asked, winking at Anna.

"That's right, more or less, grandpa!" she replied, laughing. "Take what happened today at the studio," Michaela said, elated to work at a ceramics studio in the style of the famous Caltagirone ceramics works, and, moreover, as a disciple of the Bongiovannis themselves!

She wanted to prove to her grandfather that the world had changed and nothing was unsafe as in the times he and his ancestors had lived through.

"Imagine, with so many girls from well known families, they chose a Varsano to pass along the secrets of Caltagirone!" she continued. "Yesterday, *signor* Bongiovanni told us to leave the studio in perfect order because we were going to have an important visitor, a baroness from Bavaria. She was very impressed with my work! She went from table to table and stopped to look at my plate, the one I was finishing painting, and then she told another lady, in German, 'Beautiful. I really like this work!'

"I kept my head lowered, pretending I hadn't understood, but inside, grandpa, my heart was racing and I felt my cheeks catch fire! The baroness then asked someone to translate for me what she had said. I raised my head and answered: 'No need, baroness, I'm grateful for your praise!' The lady and her entourage, and even *signor* Bongiovanni himself, were surprised that in a remote place like that an artisan in a ceramics studio understood and spoke a little of another language! And the best part? She, a blueblood, became my friend!"

Raffaele frowned.

"Why are you making such a fuss, Micha? What's so special about being a 'friend' of a baroness? And you boast about a simple friendly word of praise!"

"Let me tell the rest, grandpa!" the girl answered impatiently. Alberto left his laboratory, at one side of the kitchen, and moved closer, curious to hear the story.

"Out with it, Michaela," said Anna.

"Well," Michaela continued, "that same lady ordered an entire set of my lemon plates! With one condition: that on one side I paint the family coat of arms, with azure over the yellow on the edge. Then, she even gave me her card and a sheet of stationery for me to copy the design of the coat of arms," she said.

"Afterward, as she was leaving, she asked my name. When I said Michaela Varsano, she thought for a moment and replied: 'Hmm, Vaaarsaanoo, Varsano, Varsano! Very well, Fräulein Varsano, continue your *worrk*, and *bitte* sign your name on the plates in the same paint as the coat of arms.'" Michaela laughed as she imitated the baroness in Italian with a German accent. "Then she said goodbye, touching my head."

Everyone shouted "Brava!" and applauded the new artist Michaela Varsano!

Alberto proudly winked at his wife and resumed work in his laboratory at the side of the kitchen, as he did when he returned from the pharmacy, as well as on Saturday nights and Sunday afternoons.

✌

After years in Taormina, waiting for an opportunity to set up a pharmacy, he saw that his money would never be sufficient. Shops in the center of the city had increased in value, all to cater to the new source of survival: tourism.

Ever since marrying Anna he had worked at *signor* Galliani's Santa Maria Pharmacy. The owner did not have a pharmacy degree but enjoyed great power and prestige in the city. His fat cheeks were always red from grappa, while his two sons fought over the cash register. According to the merchants who frequented the Café Scala, neither was of good character, and they understood nothing of their father's business.

After dinner every night, Alberto did research: a cream for one case, an unguent for another. He had struggled for years to ameliorate the problems of sick people who resorted to the pharmacy, obtaining success with a cream of his own formulation that did in fact cure most of the strange eczema plaguing the region.

His research, as well as a large part of the medicines from his kitchen laboratory, he kept to himself, and everything done there he gave to the poor, who were unable to pay the pharmacy's prices. But the greatest problem was materials, expensive and rare in the area. He depended on Altanario Managò and his boat from Messina to take or bring orders. The materials didn't always arrive complete; that week even tincture of iodine had been lacking. In fact, for ten years Sicily had experienced difficulty in obtaining pharmaceutical products, unlike his family's pharmacy in Venice; herbs and exotic roots from the Orient were delivered to his father, balms and leaves from which were extracted medicines known for their quality. But in Sicily, such materials never found their way to *signor* Galliani, who always had some excuse to avoid extra expenses for the *Dottore*'s researches.

"What do you want that for?" Or: "There's no such thing…" the fat owner would repeat, flushed from grappa.

Alberto would spend his own liras, and the pharmacy's reputation benefitted from his formulas. On Saturdays, Altanario would dock and, through the fisherman Giovanni, always bring something from the list. Giovanni was among those who believed in the *Dottore*'s prescriptions. The fisherman would go up to Mongibello with his basket filled with fishes, and in the middle carefully place the vials that Alberto had ordered.

"*Dottore?*" he would yell from the lower part of the street. "*It's heeere!*"

Though exhausted,, the pharmacist would arrive home in the late afternoon heat, excited to continue his work in the laboratory. Raffaele had built a new kitchen where an old fig tree, planted by grandmother Rachelle, once stood.

"The poor tree," she lamented, "it died, and with it our tree of life."

But in its place a space was built for the women in the family. The house gained a wider front, and each one in the family had a favourite corner. On one side, they cooked and laughed. In the front parlour the old man was always occupied with something that needed repair, and in a corner of the old kitchen, the son-in-law mixed potions intended for the poor.

There, no one, not even a German aristocrat, a woman who had fainted under the arches of the Greek Theater, paid a single lira. With the sun at its zenith, the lady had turned quite pale and fallen unconscious. Alberto was summoned and managed to bring her around. Afterward, returning to his laboratory, he prepared a potion and sent her the vial, prescribing a twice-daily dose until the end of summer.

The next morning, the pharmacist received an elegant envelope with the Hirsch family letterhead, along with a letter from the baroness, thanking the *Dottore* and asking what she owed for his services. Alberto carefully crafted his reply and went through several drafts. As he finished addressing the envelope, he stopped: Baroness Clara Bischoffsheim de Hirsch auf Gereuth.

"Good heavens, where do I know that name from?"

He did know that name, perhaps the same name as on Michaela's plates. But her face, even when pale, was familiar. From where? The light-colored eyes, the nose, the small and delicate mouth wouldn't leave his mind. Suddenly, he exclaimed:

"That's where I know her from, the correspondence box!"

He dashed to the cabinet and returned with the box of letters.

Ever since his brothers, Victor and David, had left Venice to settle in Salonica, he had kept the letters, postcards, and newspaper clippings they sent telling of their new life in the Ottoman Empire. Alberto spread out the contents of the box, rereading each letter, every page.

A newspaper article from September 1874, sent by Victor, read:

*"Today, the city of Salonica and the Jewish community had the honour of a visit from His Excellency, Baron Maurice de Hirsch, and his most noble wife, Baroness Clara de Hirsch. The illustrious visitor is the representative of the Sublime Porte of the Ottoman Empire, at the inauguration of the projects for construction of the railroads that in the future will make Salonica the hub of commerce linking Occident to Orient."*

In another clipping, there she was. An oval-shaped portrait of the great philanthropist Baroness Clara de Hirsch, on a postcard commemorating her visit.

"Found it!" shouted the pharmacist, amid curious looks from Anna and Michaela. "Look... On this postcard is the Baroness who fainted in the ruins of the theatre! What a small world... We already knew her even before we could guess that one day she would knock at our door!"

"Pappá," asked Michaela, " the lady in the photo is the same one who ordered the plates in our studio! Now I understand why, after I gave my name, she turned and said, 'Tell me, *Signorina* Varsano, how many of your community live in Taormina now?'"

"And what did you answer, Michaela?" asked Raffaele.
"At first I didn't understand what she meant by community. 'Maybe today,' I said, 'only two families; my grandfather's and ours!'"

Michaela asked her father to read aloud her uncles' letters from Salonica, and, as if in a storybook, she began putting together passage after passage, like loose pages. It was the first time she had heard her father speak of his brothers Victor and David so intimately. Victor told of his work with a family named Modiano. He earned the confidence of Levy Modiano, a man highly respected in Salonica.

The Modianos were planning to construct a villa designed by the famous Italian architect Vitaliano Poselli, and Victor would be the overseer of the works. The house would have three stories, numerous rooms, and a garden overlooking the sea…

"Well," Michaela said, "I remember Uncle David writing that he wanted us to go there. He'd found a place for you to open your pharmacy. Why didn't you want to, Pappá?"

Alberto fell silent, sensing Anna's disapproving sigh. It was she who slowly read the other letter.

*Salonica, December 1880.*

*My dear brother Alberto*

*Here in Salonica opportunities are many. There is no shortage of work, and we do not suffer discrimination; just the opposite, our community is highly respected by both Turks and Greeks. We are very close, and many of us from Italy are getting rich overnight, As is the case of the Allatinis from Livorno, who bought the steam-driven mill from a Frenchman and now have immense landholdings around the city, building schools and houses for the needy.*

*The Modianos and other families from our homeland build, buy, and sell. Everyone here expects to prosper from the new railways Baron Hirsch is constructing.*

*All the products of Anatolia will arrive here and be resold to the whole of Europe! Tobacco, carpets, cotton, silk, lumber, figs and raisins will find a market here in Salonica, and many from our community will be the retailers…*

*Come to Salonica, here we have nothing to hide, here we are free…*

"Now I can connect the facts," commented Alberto pensively.

David, Alberto's younger brother, lived in his memory, embracing him upon his departure from Venice, the last time they had seen each other. He remembered David's smile as he waved at him from the moorings of the Canal Grande.

Against the sun, his brother reminded him of the Adonis described in his books. Tall, broad-shouldered, with curly hair, at 16 already a man. He insisted on not adopting his father's profession in his old pharmacy in the ghetto.

His ambition was to be a lawyer. But his father was unable to pay for his youngest son's studies. Tired and ailing, he had lost his pharmacy, and everything he managed to salvage was now packed and stored. All of it so Alberto, his first-born, would have a start in life following graduation.

Forty years of the elder Varsano's work had disappeared the night the waters of the canal invaded his house, his pharmacy, his life.

To help the family and pay for Alberto's schooling, David went to work in Murano, in a *cristalleria*. He would blow glass for hours, and during his free time, using leftover molten glass he had permission to create and produce small objects, which he sold on Sundays.

On those days David would put on his best clothes and go to the Piazza di San Marco to offer his pieces. What he saved helped him buy books to study, which he devoured during Murano's humid late hours, lit by the stubs of candles from the chapel of Santa Filomena.

He knew Cicero's Catiline orations in Latin and memorized Homer's verses in Greek, and on his way to work would declaim them on the guard walls of bridges. This made him feel less alone, less unhappy, less poor in his exile in Murano. Whenever he was in Venice and saw a group of men in judicial robes, he would draw near to listen. Afterward, he would walk along the canals, discoursing:

*"Lex est commune praeceptum... virorum prudentium conjuntum... delictorum... etcetera..."*

It was in that letter that David Varsano related, twenty years later, having become, in Salonica, the clerk of the largest firm of attorneys in the Ottoman Empire.

He was 36 now, and with his experience could soon open his own firm. He had met Baron Hirsch, responsible for the railway that would become known as the Orient Express, which in the future would link Paris to Constantinople, Venice to Salonica.

In David's words, it was one of the greatest engineering feats of the century.

As right-hand man to the lawyer Grassi, David participated in diverse arbitrations in proceedings of international law. He wrote, read, and understood Turkish, Greek, French, and German. With the learning he had acquired by arduous study day and night, he had won the confidence of his master and the representative of the port, enabling him to administer the majority of the concession contracts. Among his assistants a young man named Emmanuel Raphael Salem stood out, a person with dreams, very industrious and, David said, a kindred spirit. Just like David years before, he declaimed the Catiline orations and the verses of Homer, not on the guard walls of Venice but at seaside on the Promenade in Salonica.

The bells of San Nicolò had rung twelve times, but Raffaele couldn't fall asleep. In his mind were scenes of past and future, of regret and repentance, of uncertainty and dreams of happiness and prosperity.

The postcards his son-in-law Alberto had received for those twenty years, and that he had not seen until that night, would not leave his mind.

Was the news true? He couldn't believe it.

Silently, old Raffaele left his bed and returned to the living room to reread the letters, in private. He too had his box of memories. Lately, only the shoemaker Levy sent him news. Once or twice a year he would receive a postcard or letter, but since 1881, nothing.

In one of the letters Levy told how good it was to be in Salonica: "In our Mother of Israel we don't have to hide our race or our religion. The Turks don't care what language we speak or who we pray to, as long as we pay our taxes on time, live peacefully, and don't mix with them.

"Imagine, here we speak Ladino like our ancestors! We sing aloud the songs that there we sang softly, remember? I'm just a poor cobbler, I was never lucky enough to learn a profession as artistic as yours. If you come here you'll have so many orders for gold chains that you'll never be without work! Women here wear lots of jewels, whether Jews, Greeks or Turks!"

Raffaele had always read Levy's letters with suspicion.

How could anyone under the yoke of the barbarous Turks be free and happy? he thought. Surely Levy was an idealist, or maybe blind, he reflected. Or a liar, whose pride would never allow him to tell the complete truth, trying to convince me that there in the middle of nowhere we'd have a better life!

The shoemaker said he was still living in a single room with his wife and their two children, in the Sibi district, and that thanks to the benefactors of the Sicilia Hadash synagogue, his two sons were studying at the Alliance Israélite Universelle school.

They had classes in Hebrew, Greek, French, and Turkish, as well as Halakhah and Talmudic Law. They were learning the Tamin melodies, the liturgy for every festival, the history of the prophets, the proverbs and much more. In one of his last letters, Nathan, Levy's older son, also wrote to Raffaele, telling of the preparations for his bar mitzvah, his coming of age and his vows upon reaching the age of thirteen. Like the majority of the Alliance students, Nathan didn't pay the school. It was maintained by an international organization that used funds from institutions supported by rich Jewish families in Europe and America.

Dr. Moses Allatini, its director, had transformed the Alliance into an open school that, besides Jewish students, received Greek and Turkish students from well-to-do families who paid a high tuition. Those families sent their sons there to study in what was recognized as the best French *lycée* in the city.

So many years had gone by, and Raffaele had never spoken with Alberto about Levy's letters. At times Raffaele wanted to believe, but he felt it impossible to live under the dominion of the sultans, terrible masters who cut off heads and persecuted more than the Inquisition itself.

No… Never! Why should he flee again? It was already hard enough to be here, he thought

.

He learned, through generations, that to survive in a land not his own it was necessary not to stand out, to be humble, and, especially, to conceal his religious principles.

He would survive better if he resembled the local folk. Raffaele lived in Taormina, and that was enough for him. He wouldn't change, or run away, learn to hide or speak a different language. He had always tried to be a good Sicilian, for that was what he considered himself.

He lived in Sicily, not caring who was the king giving orders or collecting the taxes. Bourbons or Savoy, none of it mattered! If the taxes went to a new king named Victorio Emmanuele, to Raffaele it represented no change at all.

He always repeated what he had heard one day, that all those battles, the campaigns of nationalists, of Garibaldi's Redshirts, the patriotic uprisings, the dances given in homage to the French, the English, the Piedmontese and all the others who came to save Sicily, the visits of unifiers, the speeches in the theatre, the discussions of the Ballaròs, the Sturzos, the Carusos – in sum, all that happened in Sicily, and there in the Piazza di Sant'Agostino in the last few years, would lead to change.

And Raffaele would look at the ceiling and say,

"Yes… Things need to change in order to stay the same…"

And nothing had changed for Raffaele. He had never stormed a barricade, never discussed politics or religion, always trying to remain as invisible as his mother and his grandparents had been their entire lives.

⮵

Alberto, in his room, also couldn't sleep. He looked at Anna, sleeping beside him. Despite the years, she remained a beautiful woman. Her still youthful skin and her loose hair shone, in the position in which she lay, her eyes closed. Outwardly, Anna appeared happy and accepting of the life she led, but deep down felt she deserved a different life. The man who in her eyes had been a prince come from Venice to rescue her from poverty and monotony hadn't succeeded in changing in twenty years... And perhaps he would never dispel the routine that was Anna's life.

Anna was also awake. She was intrigued about why her husband never commented on her brothers-in-law's letters with those invitations so full of promise. Alberto had never spoken about them because he knew she would never leave Taormina. Not without her father, and Raffaele made it very clear that he didn't want to flee again.

Alberto sometimes dreamed of returning to Venice. Crossing the Piazza di San Marco with moonlight illuminating the church's velvet-bronze portico, like a private sky of golden stars. To feel the warm breeze and the sea-smell from the canals, see the city once more in four seasons, hear the lament of the mandolins; even the rhythm of the gondoliers' oars would not leave his ears. He would take Anna to his secret places, together they would caress the bronze gates gleaming in the sun. They would cross bridges, visit palaces...

And they would go to the Lido... His heart raced as he recalled his country. He had forgotten Venice, forgotten his afternoons in the old Jewish cemetery, that silent, distant and abandoned spot with its nearly intact gravestones, the wistful afternoons he spent walking in the shadow of immense cypresses. He had forgotten the Ghetto, he had forgotten his mother and his father.

One day he would take Anna there, to his Venice.

# IV

## *MONGIBELLO*

Taormina, autumn 1882.

Baroness Hirsch returned to Bavaria at the end of summer free of her sickly, pale appearance, permanently transformed by Taormina. The Sicilian climate and sun, the long morning walks, the olive oil, lemon, fruits, fish and fresh vegetables helped greatly. But she insisted on thanking the pharmacist Alberto Varsano for the potions he created. She had rigorously followed the prescribed treatment, though secretly doubting the results.

She had previously tried prescriptions from the best professors in medical schools in the Austro-Hungarian Empire and even France and England.

She had been of fragile health since childhood. When her father became a senator in Belgium, the young Clara Bischoffsheim had not lacked for treatment from the greatest medical centers of Europe. But nothing had proved as effective as the Taormina prescription.

She felt well, happy, more feminine, strong. Her skin, once pale and lifeless, became rosy and glowing. And it was in this condition that she arrived in Munich. As she descended from the train, many did not recognize the woman who approached smiling. Among them, her husband Maurice.

"My dearest," he whispered. "You look attractive, I almost did not recognize you!" Clara smiled and shyly caressed Maurice's hands. They gazed at each other with empathy and emotion, just as in the past.

In the carriage, Helga, the lady's companion, sat next to Gustav Held, the Baron's faithful amanuensis, who looked at Clara incredulously from beneath the brim of his hat. And there was another person, a stranger to both men, seated on the bench next to the door. The young woman smiled shyly at the Baron, then lowered her eyes.

"Oh, Maurice ,my excuses... Let me introduce you... The young lady is *Signorina* Varsano, daughter of the pharmacist in Taormina, of whom I spoke so often in my letters!"

The Baron made a reverence and smiled."I take immense pleasure in meeting you, *Signorina* Varsano," said the Baron, tipping his hat and kissing her hand. "I was quite *currious,* once Clara described your virtues. I hope we can repay the confidence your family has placed in us, by our sponsoring your studies..."

Michaela smiled and looked at Clara, raising her eyebrows questioningly, asking for assistance. She didn't know what to say. Or rather, she hadn't understood half of the baron's grandiose words. Clara quickly intervened so Michaela wouldn't feel embarrassed in the presence of two strange men.

"Dear," she said quietly, "to speak with Michaela in German, pronounce your words clearly and very slowly; otherwise she won't understand you! She still needs some study in order to carry on a conversation... But soon, if she accompanies me everywhere, she'll be speaking like an authentic Bavarian..."

Baron Hirsch smiled at the Sicilian. He would do anything to see Clara remain healthy and happy as she was at that moment. If the girl was one of the causes of that happiness, then she was a blessing and would be welcome in their home. He smiled at Michaela and in a heavily accented Italian tried to communicate:

"I hope you will be *verry* happy here in our home, as we, Clara and I, are now to receive a new daughter!"

A new daughter? Or the daughter they once had and lost so prematurely before Lucien was born?

Nothing could make Clara more complete than having a daughter with whom to share moments of solitude and joy! After all, the baron thought, neither I nor Lucien can fill that void, and in any case it's a woman thing...

Michaela, sitting there, focused her attention on the landscape around her. She knew to live in a place like that she would have to learn much more than just to speak German correctly. And that was also the Baron's thought as he observed her closely. Beyond any doubt, the Sicilian was a beautiful woman, with strong features, a tapered nose, black hair tied in braids, and enormous lashes that framed her expressive green eyes. But she was a poor girl from the other side of the world. Poor in every way! She wore a dress so simple that, in Maurice's eyes, accustomed to the luster and elegance of the ladies who surrounded him, it bespoke the rusticity of a village woman.


And to think that her mother Anna had painstakingly sewn it, using the best alpaca fabric she had! The lace-up shoes, almost hidden by her long skirt, slightly worn—nothing the young woman wore did justice to her beauty. Her long tanned hands, nearly uncared-for, showed clearly her modest circumstances. He told Clara that now such things would be less important... She must be sent to a good school and become someone.

The journey with the young Sicilian woman was an experience in patience for Clara de Hirsch, always accustomed to treating those around her simply as servants, giving orders, requesting reports or demanding something of them.

She found herself, after a few days, worried about how to take care of someone who had never seen the world beyond Taormina. But little by little her concern lessened. Together day and night, the two came to know each other and formed a bond of love, friendship and mutual respect. They travelled through all of Italy, from Sicily to the Alps, on ships and trains. They went to Naples and visited Vesuvius, where Michaela proudly demonstrated her knowledge of the history and legends of the site.

In Rome, they went to the Coliseum, the Baths of Caracalla, visited churches and cathedrals. They stayed at the luxurious Albergo Plaza, where beautiful women paraded in the grand amber-colored ballroom in rustling taffeta and silk dresses, flowered hats, and unusual accessories.

Michaela had never seen such elegance. She could not take her eyes off the ladies, and when she would turn her head, there was Helga, reprimanding her: it was not considered good manners for a young woman to turn like that to observe others.

In Venice, Michaela felt at home. From so many nights of hearing her father describe the charms of the city, when she walked along the squares, bridges, and canals everything was familiar, as if she lived there. She sensed what her father had lost when he left such a magical, fascinating, and historic city.

The Baroness was amused to see the young, almost savage woman mingling with the noble castes of Italian aristocracy. She would imitate the gestures of her mistress in the restaurant of the Lido Grand Hotel or in the cafes of the Piazza di San Marco, sitting primly. Gradually she became transformed into a lady. Back in her room in the hotel, she would stand before a mirror, rearranging her clothes. She would remove a petticoat, trying to place it inside another for effect around her hips, and transform ribbons and sashes from her dresses into bows to adorn collars and blouses.

Poor Michaela. Her wardrobe was so limited. Anna, after yielding to Baroness Hirsch's insistent invitation to sponsor her daughter's studies, had had only a few days to sew certain clothes and alter others. Nothing her daughter could take would be adequate for such a luxurious journey, much less for being presented in a castle in Bavaria.

She also knew that even if Alberto were rich and bought the best weaves from *signor* Rinaldi's shop, it would still be too little. But she prepared her daughter's wardrobe as best she could. With great creativity, she cut and trimmed, draping and basting over Michaela's body. Mother and daughter shared much laughter at the end of each phase, with a fashion almanac in hand, trying to absorb and copy every detail.

The week had rushed by like the wind. The next day, the house would be turned upside down. The Varsanos were to have a special guest: the baroness was coming to Shabbat dinner, and everything had to be in order.

The lace tablecloths had been washed, bleached, and starched. All the china in the house was clean and gleaming.

Michaela scrubbed the floors with pine water and vinegar. She brought from the field beside the ruins everything she could find. She arranged bouquets of delicate anemones, cut lemon branches and gathered a basket of Indian figs that grew wild on the slopes of the Greek Theater.

Raffaele did the shopping that morning: at the outdoor market at the Catania port he bought ripe tomatoes, a new bottle of olive oil, and a string of garlic. He chose the tenderness eggplants, the most perfect zucchini flowers, the freshest eggs, and hulled rice.

Alberto came from the pharmacy to help his father-in-law with the purchases carrying the baskets, and the two climbed the hill to Mongibello.

Anna had seasoned a leg of lamb in a marinade that Sicilians called *salmoriglio* but to which she added a secret ingredient her grandmother had taught her: condiments from her ancestors in Spain; a spicy paste made of hot bell pepper, ground caraway, cumin and a few cilantro seeds .It imparted an unforgettable flavour.

When Clara de Hirsch arrived at the small white house, she could smell the aroma of spices in the oven. She dispensed with the services of Helga, who returned in the same carriage to the Hotel Timeo with instructions to come back after nine o'clock to fetch her. And she breathed in relief. Clara finally feel free, without ceremony, among people who truly liked her, who esteemed her as a human being rather than a fortune in a strongbox! What a difference it made to be received with love...

Michaela had prepared a simple but original decoration, with flowers and lemon branches for the dinner table and, in the center, a nest with eggs of an almost golden color. Raffaele made *huevos haminados*, a recipe that came from his ancestors. In a special copper kettle the eggs cooked over low heat during the night, covered in onion skins. It was always the principal attraction at Shabbat dinner. Clara savoured every detail.

At the head of the table, candles glowed in the silver candleholder that had once belonged to grandmother Rachelle, along with the lace mantilla and the book with a black leather cover. To the side, wineglasses and a small dish with clove, cinnamon, and cardamom. On a walnut sideboard was a tray with melon, Indian figs, and orange slices sweetened with almond paste. All was so different and new to Clara. She knew only the Ashkenazi traditions, never had been inside a Sephardic Shabbat .

When the Varsanos and Raffaele Cohen toasted Clara, she regretted not having spent more time with that wonderful family during her four months in Taormina. In parting, Michaela showed her the clipping from the Salonica newspaper and the portrait in an oval frame, drawn many years before.

"Good heavens! Where did you find that? I remember that moment, but I had never seen the portrait," exclaimed the Baroness. Alberto answered, telling what had gone through his head the afternoon he had attended her in the amphitheatre.

"I was intrigued for days by the certainty that I knew you. Forgive me for such an expression of intimacy, Madam Baroness, but you lived among us even before we met!"

Raffaele took his old mandolin from the armoire and, with Anna, sang in Ladino "El Sueño de la Hija del Rey."

The baroness would never forget that Shabbat in Mongibello.

Michaela wrote Anna regularly.

The letters were delivered by Antonio, the postman, who climbed the hillside to Mongibello waving an envelope and shouting, "*Signora* Varsano, it's from Michaela!"

The three of them would sit at the dining table to read and reread the news from the girl. She greatly missed home, the laughter, stories told in the kitchen, the warmth of their hugs, their perfume… Anna recalled every moment of the departure, Michaela in her room, her trunk ready, her smile both happy and fearful. The carriage arriving to fetch her, the jealous gaze of the governess Helga, Clara's wave. The new hat, and Michaela turning to see one last time the three who remained behind.

Raffaele had other memories of his granddaughter's departure. The night of Shabbat he had given the baroness a small bag of lemon seeds from Sicily. It was an odd gift, but she insisted she wished to plant them on her lands. The old jeweller had no idea where she would do so, because in Bavaria there were no lemon trees… And for his granddaughter he took from his coat pocket a small velvet box and asked that she open it only upon arriving at her destination.

Discreetly, Anna watched the legerdemain of her aged father, who was concealing something from her. When the carriage disappeared at the end of the hill, she insisted on knowing what the secret was between grandfather and granddaughter.

Raffaele laughed at his daughter's curiosity.

"Anna, you're acting like a jealous little girl! Let Michaela tell you. She will one day…"

The envelopes with Clara's monogram arrived, relating how Michaela was adapting well in school but was suffering the cold of a Bavarian winter. The baroness had provided a new wardrobe, with heavy clothes and an overcoat of marten fur, a cherry-colored cape for use in the elegant soirees. Michaela wrote that she was learning to dance the waltz and that she must be well prepared so that when Lucien, the baroness's son, came from Paris he would have a lady for the spring dance season. They could go to the balls in Vienna or to those given by the king of Bavaria, Ludwig II. The Hirsches received invitations to all of them.

"Who knows," wrote the Baroness in a letter, "my son may one day turn his attention from art and collecting coins and manuscripts and take an interest in human beings. He is quite introverted. When he gets to know Micha, I am sure they will become good friends. Your daughter is open and transparent. I love her like the daughter I never had and ask God that when Lucien does become interested in a woman she will have something of the qualities and dignity of our Micha. Unfortunately, the women who approach him are only interested in money and status…"

The days passed slowly for Anna; however much she occupied herself with household tasks, there was always time to think about her daughter and imagine her daily life in a faraway land. At the end of the afternoon, when the girl would normally be returning from the pottery studio, Anna would become distressed, peeking through the windows at passersby in the street.

*No*, thought Anna in her loneliness, *she won't return today.*

There were nights when Anna even cursed having yielded her daughter to the entreaties of Clara de Hirsch. And blamed Alberto, for having been enraptured by the prospect of giving Michaela a better opportunity, a future, a more comfortable existence. When for the first time Anna had found a real friend, someone who understood her thoughts and looked into her eyes with love and admiration—all of that had been stolen from her. Alberto couldn't fathom what went through his wife's mind, sensing only that day by day Anna was sadder and more distant, profoundly melancholy. She no longer took any interest in leaving the house, not even when the puppet opera came to the city at year's end. And it was as because of those grave signs that Raffaele decided to try to change her life.

One morning, the jeweller asked his daughter for assistance. He was unable to create new designs, he argued, and she, with her good taste and imagination, could help him. It was not long before she was involved in her father's work. Passersby could scarcely recognize the place as Cohen's jewellery shop, everything now shone with a different aura, attracting the foreigners who came to see the Clock Tower.

Anna conceptualized and created designs, seeking out different stones and beads, and was at her father's side mounting and polishing piece by piece.

It was high tourist season in Taormina. Movement in the streets and stores had intensified. Anna, the new goldsmith in Raffaele Cohen's jewellery shop, added a display window to attract passersby to his small entryway. Her torrent of ideas led her to search for new materials. An iron backing, covered with a scrap of honey-colored velvet, sewn and attached, cut, polished and mended, became a magnificent necklace with three strands of matte gold. Each link of the necklace formed interlocking braids with polished gold and enormous tear-shaped crystal pendants.

"This is crazy," grumbled the old man. "Who's going to buy gold with worthless stones?"

"It's the fashion, *Pappá*. These days women wear low necklines and the jewels are large, exaggerated," she explained. "It's to cover wrinkles in the neck! Simple chains and charms don't perform magic anymore," she said, lowering the neckline of her blouse even more, much to her father's alarm.

"Foolishness," he grumbled. "*La moda*, who invented it? Who can understand the minds of those women?" he said, smiling behind his moustache. He not only had faith in Anna's ability but also sorely needed her advice and her presence in the shop. In a matter of minutes she had managed to transform in her own way everything that her father had intended to do. With Michaela living in such a cosmopolitan place, Anna would have access to the world of the women who came to Taormina in the summer to parade their extravagances at his door.

She should be prepared, to know long ahead of time what they desired, what they would spend their money on...

In one of her letters Anna asked her daughter to send almanacs the baroness no longer used and, if possible, a more detailed description of everything having to do with the court. The clothes, the houses they lived in, the flowers, the jewels, and even the attitudes and customs of the people there.

Clara de Hirsch, reading the letters, took Anna's request seriously and began to collect everything that might interest her.

The spring of 1883 was just beginning in Taormina when Anna received in the jewellery shop a visit from a foreigner who brought her news and a package from Bavaria. The man arrived accompanied by Anjù, the receptionist at the Hotel Timeo, who acted as interpreter. The German explained that the box was a gift from Baroness Hirsch; it was heavy and must contain a lot of things, the interpreter commented, with a curious gaze.

There was also a request from the baroness for *Dottore* Varsano to fill a prescription for her. Anjù's chest swelled like a turkey as he explained what a certain count wanted. Then, putting on his monocle, he cleared his throat and read the address on the other envelope.

"This is to be delivered to *Signor* Raffaele Cohen, please."

Anna was surprised and didn't know how to say thanks. She asked how soon the medicine was needed.

"The Count will be here for three more weeks, *signora*, and will then go back to Bavaria. He is staying at the Hotel Timeo."

The foreigner, still mute, took his leave by handing her a card.

Sighing, Anjù left the heavy box on the counter, and with a polite bow, said goodbye. The foreigner's name printed on the card read Count Frederick von Bucovictz.

He was quite different from the other nobles who had visited the jewellery shop, a very tall man, very thin, with arms as long as an octopus. His eyes, blue and sad, and his well trimmed reddish beard contrasted with his dark blue double-breasted blazer, covered with medals. She didn't know what all those things hanging from the man's clothing signified, but he seemed to be a general or some such. She looked at the box and imagined Michaela tying those strings and ribbons. Anna took a deep breath and caressed the box. She could feel her daughter's scent. Curious to open the heavy box at home, she closed the shop earlier than usual and left. She would stop by the Santa Maria Pharmacy first to ask Alberto's help.

"Poor Alberto," she sighed. "He already has back pains from so much carrying! And he kills himself working..."

In addition to the pharmacy and the small laboratory at home, the pharmacist had dedicated himself in recent years to researching an emerging new field: perfume and cosmetics. He had prepared an essence of lemon flower that was much sought-after by tourists in the summer. Later he was successful with almond balm, which alleviated pains in the breasts of nursing women. Ever since his eczema cream had proved effective and cured many in the city, *signor* Galliani's pharmacy had become famous in the region. Orders came in from Messina and Palermo, and even foreigners arriving in the city knew of the pharmacy and its products.

In vain, Alberto sought to obtain the commission for his prescriptions and formulas. *Signor* Galliani would laugh and change the subject, and every year promised a major settling of accounts to compensate the pharmacist.

But that day never came.

# V

## *THE EDICT*

Taormina, June 1883.

Alberto didn't wait for Anna at the door of the pharmacy as he usually did. They met at the *scalinata*. His breathing was ragged and he was very pale. She smiled when she saw him. She waved two envelopes at him, but he was serious and dispirited.

"Guess who these letters are from!" she said, taking his hand. Trembling, Alberto withdrew his arm and hastened his pace.

Others greeted the couple but received no response from the pharmacist.

When they arrived at the top of the Catania Port garden, she grabbed his coat.

"For heaven's sake, Alberto, what's gotten into you? What's going on?"

Without answering, he continued walking rapidly toward the rail of the Bella Vista as if wishing to reach the end of the world. The dark-red sun, disappearing on the horizon, imparted a strange aura, and Alberto, who had always been erect and strong, was now like a feeble old man whose unsteady legs sought out one of the benches in the garden. His head remained in his hands for long minutes, until his body began to shudder and, like an explosion, he released a mournful cry and sobbed. Motionless, he continued in that state for a time that to Anna seemed endless.

When the sun finally vanished and lights illuminated the city in the distance, she sat beside Alberto and gently stroked his back.

"Forgive me, Anna... You're the last person in the world that I would hurt, but I'm going through a difficult moment... I–" he continued, taking her hands, "I did not want to worry you, but today... Today... Since this afternoon, I'm no longer the pharmacist at Santa Maria."

Her eyes widened in suspicion, as if at a joke in bad taste.

"What do you mean you're no longer the pharmacist there?"

"I'm not... and won't be again!"

"Then who will be, Alberto? What nonsense are you telling me?"

He didn't answer, his mouth so dry that he was unable to speak.

"Alberto, you're the only one in the pharmacy's laboratory! Only you know how to develop the formulas and prescriptions! Then who will do it?"

"I already told you, Anna!" he replied. "I won't be a pharmacist there or at any other pharmacy anywhere in Italy!"

"I do not understand, Alberto. You're Alberto Varsano, who graduated in Venice, known in all of Taormina for your formulas for eczema, for breast-feeding… the syrup… You study all the–"

"No, Anna," Alberto replied, placing his index finger to seal her lips. "I'm not and won't be again… This afternoon," he continued, "a group of strangers came into the pharmacy. From Messina. They went into *signor* Galliani's office… As soon as they closed the door, I heard a loud conversation with a lot of laughter, and after a time," he continued, now in a calmer tone, "*Signor* Galliani opened the door, shouted to his wife to bring a bottle of grappa and some glasses… I thought it was a meeting of old friends and went calmly about my work…"

"And then? What happened after that?" she asked, growing impatient.

"They stayed there for a few hours, laughing loudly, talking, toasting some event…"

"Yes, and then, Alberto?"

"Then Cesare Tiopanni, the notary, came in with a thick book under his arm. He looked into the laboratory where I was working, pretended not to see me and didn't answer my greeting…"

"But he never had anything against you! Wasn't it his grandson whose asthma you took care of this winter?"

"Yes, and that's when I began to think something very strange was happening," said Alberto, lowering his voice. "*Signor* Tiopanni went in and shut the door. After a time, *Signor* Galliani called me in a rude manner: 'Come here, Alberto! We have visitors who want to talk to you! Right now; they're in a hurry!' As I was in an iodine-stained apron and my hands were smeared with lanoline, I changed clothes, washed my hands, and knocked at the office door. I heard the notary finishing a sentence:

'Well, in that case… he has no right to anything… it's just a matter of signing the documents…' When I went into the room there was a book on the table and a page with various signatures and stamps. *Signor* Galliani said,

'This is *Signor* Francesco Anetto, this is Giovanni Pavoni, and his partner *Signor* Rubino Brandolini.

You already know *Signor* Cesare Tiopanni.' And he winked at the notary. 'These gentlemen,' said Galliani, 'are the owners of the largest pharmacies in Sicily and today they're closing a major deal with my pharmacy!'

"Anna, I thought it was a matter of furnishing raw materials to fill prescriptions in the laboratory. And that they were going to supply us with what had always been so difficult to acquire. That's why I was idiotically surprised and happy!"

"And so, Alberto?" Anna asked. "What was happening?"

"Good,' I told them, 'excellent!' I turned to *Signor* Galliani and said: 'This comes at a good time! It will help solve my problem in the laboratory. I'm very happy...'

" At that moment, *Signor* Galliani turned to me, with bloodshot eyes, his voice became hoarse with rage, and he began yelling: 'Your problem, Varsano, what problem?' He went on bellowing like a lunatic, red with anger, pointing his finger at my nose. 'The problem is that you've been telling everyone in town that the formula for the eczema cream is yours, and the nursing prescription too... and even the lemon water. That wonderful perfumed prescription was invented by my daughter!' And, banging the table hysterically, he went on: 'No! No, gentlemen! Don't be fooled by the noble, honest look on his face! That man is an impostor... and besides everything else, a Jew!' he shouted, beating his chest, his cheeks burning. 'Me... I myself taught him our formulas, which he was always out to steal!"

As he told this to Anna, Alberto again felt the nausea that he had experienced in the office at the pharmacy. His heart was racing, and he couldn't move. His body felt heavy, and for the first time in his life he experienced raw hatred, rage... He had left the pharmacy trembling like a madman, and out into the street. Tiopanni, the notary, had come running after him, with the book.

"*Dottore* Varsano, forgive me, but it's my job as notary," he said, panting and opening a page of the book. "Please read this while I get a pen and inkwell. You have to sign here!" he said, pointing to the line below the stamp.

"But, *Signor* Tiopanni, for God's sake, what's happening? What was the problem? Why so much hate on the part of *Signor* Galliani? What did I ever do to him?"

"It's not hate, *Dottore* Varsano. Don't be offended by what you heard. All Taormina knows your value as a pharmacist, everyone knows you did everything in the pharmacy, but this is the business world. And in business, things must always be in writing and signed..."

"But, *Signor* Tiopanni," said Alberto, not understanding, "what am I to do now?"

"Listen, my boy," said the notary, handing him the book. "Sign now, as you have no right to anything. *Signor* Galliani is selling the pharmacy to those gentlemen from Palermo and wants to guarantee that, with the success of the formulas he has, he'll get a better price!"

"That *he* has? What formulas does he have? Good Lord, you know very well who developed them! Everybody knows it was me... I worked in that laboratory for twenty years and in all that time he never once set foot in the place, never opened a medicine cabinet, or filled a single prescription!"

"Yes, my friend, we all know, myself included, but he was craftier. He registered the formulas in his own name, and unfortunately you have no right to anything," said the notary, handing him the books. "Sign here... This is a notification that you are aware of the terms to be imposed on you..."

"What will become of me, *Signor* Tiopanni," asked Alberto, his voice quivering.

"What's going to happen, what terms are these?"
Clearing his throat, the notary began,.

"First, the clause that terminates your work responsibilities at the Santa Maria pharmacy; second, you cannot, before the year 189, exercise your profession in any competing pharmacy–that is, in any pharmacy in the unified territory of the Kingdom of Italy. *Dottore* Varsano," he continued, "there's no way out in this case. I'm very sorry.

By law, you must sign this document and acknowledge the fact... Try to start a new life!

All I can do is wish you good luck..."

It began to rain more heavily. The couple hastened their pace, climbing the hillside hand in hand.

He felt a sense of relief and even freedom at that moment. His shoulders were looser, and he looked at his wife with a mixture of collaboration, friendship, and love. When Anna tried to leap over a water-filled ditch, he clutched her by the waist and took her into his powerful arms, cradling her body as if she were a little girl. She rested her cheek against her husband's warm, wet neck. She kissed his damp hair, his ear, and finally his lips, passionately, as never before...

It rained heavily that night. The next morning, he wouldn't let Anna get out of bed. It was a weekday, but for the first time in twenty years Alberto did not leave for work. It was also the first time Raffaele awoke concerned. Neither of them had touched the soup he had left on the stove the night before. Nor had he heard a noise of any kind. But on the sideboard in the dining room was an envelope addressed to *signor* Raffaele Cohen.

"Good morning, Raffaele!" said Alberto, smiling at the old man.

"May I ask what happened with you two yesterday? I stayed up late and fell asleep, but from what I see— Today's not a holiday, or am I mistaken?" said the old man doubtfully.

"It almost is; we decided to make it a special holiday, and today no one will work! Today's a special day, *signor* Cohen," said Alberto, humming a melody. "We're going to celebrate!"

Anna, in her room, didn't know how Alberto was going to tell her father what had happened. She had no desire to be present during the conversation. Her husband would know how to deal with the subject in his own way, very diplomatically, without worrying the old man unnecessarily. When she came out of her room, the two men were sitting at the table. Raffaele, looking serious and nervous, was holding an envelope. Alberto rose and went to fetch his correspondence box.

When he returned, he called for Anna to join them at the table.

"Come, dear, we have to decide about our future."

He opened the box, took out a package of letters and a small leather bag with money.

"Well," he said, "here are the opportunities, the invitations, the incentives from my brothers, and *here*, our reality, what we've managed to save. It's not much, but I think it would be enough for our trip and to rent a place to stay for a few months, maybe even a year..."

"Trip? Where are we going? What trip are you talking about?" Anna asked.

"Let your husband explain," interceded Raffaele.

"Anna…" Alberto breathed a deep sigh. "You know about everything, and I've explained to your father the ban I received. I can't work anymore… I can't fill a prescription or prepare medicine of any kind, either here at home or anywhere in Italy! Think about it, Anna. What am I going to do? What do I actually know how to do? Only that… Only to formulate, fill prescriptions, do research… Where am I going to do that? It's against the law! I lost my license for ten years and I'm not going to go on with my hands tied!"

"But, Alberto," said Anna, furrowing her brow. "Of course you can do other things; we have the jewellery shop, you can help Pappá, and I know how to sew, I can pick up some orders… I can cook," she continued, "I can get a job in the hotel they're opening in the city, or in the kitchen at the Hotel Timeo!"

"Enough, Anna!" shouted Alberto. "For the love of God, just listen for a while… I need to leave, don't you understand? Don't you understand that I can't work here? And I need to work… So many things to be achieved, so many things still to do…"

Alberto sighed and fell silent for several moments, then softly caressed his wife's hands.

"Dear Anna, understand! In these twenty years I haven't achieved anything… Just this," he said, hefting the small leather bag.

"But are you going alone? What about us? And me, Alberto?"

"Let your husband speak, Anna!" the old man shouted, nervous by now.

"Raffaele," intervened Alberto, startled by the old man's reaction. "I need to talk to you… I and I alone am to blame for all this. You're the best friend and father that I've ever known in my entire life. We've never had grievances, just the opposite, I've always had your help, your affection… All this time you've worked happily to help maintain this house, which isn't mine but which shelters us to this day. You dedicated yourself to raising Michaela. You gave her guidelines of morality and honesty, taught her the good principles that are so hard to find nowadays!" he said.

Raffaele remained immobile, his head bowed, and didn't reply.

"You know you're an important part of our lives! I can't leave you here, without your daughter, without your granddaughter, without a family, without anyone… We can't go and leave you behind," Alberto continued. "And if you don't come with us, I will never be able to be the breadwinner in this family, never be able to prove I'm capable!"

The old man took a deep breath, his eyes watery, his gaze on the still unopened envelope in his hands. He was seeking a solution but said nothing.

"Anna," said Alberto in a calmer tone, "I'm thinking of going to Salonica. I would go first, find work, set up a house and send the money for you both to come. It will only be a few months, I'm certain of that; soon we'll be together again… and Michaela, when she finishes her studies, will join us there. As my brother David said, in Salonica, the Mother of Israel, we'll have opportunities we don't have here!"

Raffaele took a deep breath before finally nodding in agreement.

The following week the pharmacist, carrying his old luggage from Venice, would take the steamship *Victoria*, heading for a new life.

# VI

## PASSAGE TO SALONICA

From Taormina to Salonica, Summer 1883.

After weeks between the Ionian and the Aegean Sea, pitching with the Meltemi wind at the end of summer, the ship docked at the port of Salonica.

Seen from the port, Salonica seemed like a gilded Nativity scene. It was much larger than Alberto had pictured it. The bustle made it resemble Venice, the Grand Canal. Fishing boats, ships, dockworkers nicknamed *hamalis* unloading enormous boxes off their backs, merchants, vendors, people coming and going from the vessels...

From the deck, Alberto tried to get a feel for the geography of the city that was receiving him, perhaps forever... *Who knows?* he thought. From his vantage point he could observe the construction underway along the docks, which rose smoothly to the center of the plateau of a very high mountain. On the shoreline to the far right was a circular tower and a fort. And further ahead, another cluster of boats. He was impressed by the number of whitewashed minarets. At that moment, the reality struck him:

He was in the Ottoman Empire...

Upon disembarking, he merged into the surrounding multitude. He heard Greek, Turkish, a little French, Ladino, small bells, the noise of the breakwater, smelled the sea air, the fish, the sweat of the porters, along with the perfume of fresh fruits.

The men were wearing striped caftans and odd hats shaped like red berets. Alberto headed out for the street. Alongside the gate, a building with an enormous chimney bore a red plaque: "Saias Brothers Mill."

Alberto felt lost for a few moments, standing there with his heavy trunks beside him, but he didn't move from the spot. His legs swayed as they had shortly before, at sea. The nearby vendors offered trays with figs, tobacco, and salted seeds, some calling out *pepitas de calabaza*, others *pepitas de melón*...

One of them approached Alberto, who was dragging the heavy trunks with his pharmacy vials.

"*Señor... Signore*," the seed vendor called out, tugging at his coat. "*Los hamalitos... los hamalitos*," he said, pointing to the right. "*Señor... los ratones... portefaix... portefaix*," trying to make himself understood in all languages, and again gesturing toward a group of men sitting on crates and coiling rope. "Hey, *hamalitos*, haulers! Don't you want to work?" cried the seed vendor.

The three men leaped from the crates and came toward Alberto. They were very thin and, seen from up close, old and wrinkled. They had dark, furrowed skin, long white beards and turbans of rags wrapped around their heads. They wore long pants, held by strips below the knees, and two of them were barefoot.

"No, sir," Alberto replied, gesturing with his hands. "I don't need them. They're too old to carry this much weight!"

The vendor laughed.

"You don't know them. I can tell right away that you're not from here. In this city, old men work, they're strong! All our *hamalitos* carry heavy loads. Want some advice, *Señor?*" said the vendor, winking conspiratorially. "Stick with them, because in a few minutes the port will be empty, and all the *hamalitos* will be hauling the cargo from the mill to the Sibi market." He ended the phrase by extending his hand to Alberto, expecting a coin.

As he put his hand in his pocket, Alberto felt a frisson. He was in the Ottoman Empire, treading the soil of the ancient Greece of Philip and Alexander in the historic city of Salonica, the Mother of Israel, as the Jews called it, and without a single Turkish piaster! And he had no notion of how much his money was worth there!

The *hamalitos* asked Alberto for the address. They gestured, speaking Ladino. He requested a moment to think. He took from his pocket the most recent letter from David. It bore a commercial letterhead and the address of the lawyer Grassi.

At that hour David would no longer be working, he thought. Would he be at home? He searched his pockets looking for the last letter from Victor, then gave up; he must have stuck it in one of the trunks. He didn't know where to go.

The porters had taken on the load. One of them bent over with his head between his knees and the other slipped the burden onto his back, protected by cushions of rags. The nape of the neck and the top of the head served as anchor. The old man was tied to the cargo and, like a camel, rose carefully, flexing his knees and head. In this way, almost doubled over, the poor men circled the foreigner, awaiting a decision.

Alberto saw he had no option. He asked one of them, "*Albergo? Hotel?*"

The three looked at one another, and one of them snapped his fingers, asking, "*Piasters? Lire... Drachmas?*"

"Oh. Yes, not many." And he indicated a signal, a few, with his thumb and index finger.

And so Alberto Varsano, pharmacist from Venice, followed two aged porters. The third one, running ahead, carried only a coil of rope and whistled a song.

When they were near the factory of the Saias Brothers, the large chimney of the mill sounded a deafening and frightening whistle. The *hamalitos* turned around to see the startled expression of the foreigner, who staggered, unable to keep his footing.

The three sprites pointed to the chimney and yelled: "*Barou... Barou... Barou...*"

The day grew brighter, and sunlight invaded Alberto's room. He awoke startled. He had lost count of the hours since signing the register at the Grand Hotel d'Angleterre.

The Greek doorman, dressed in a comical green uniform, resembled attendants in Venetian hotels. The difference was that here they all wore a fez on their heads. Alberto had a vague memory of how he had arrived there, crossing the seaside avenue to the busy square the Turks called Mezazeri. All he recalled was discomfort, faltering and unsteady legs, his head spinning, and a horrible feeling of nausea.

It was the small old men, miniature Samsons out of some fable, who guided him. How much had he paid them?...

Alberto leaped from the bed and ran to look for the small bag in the pocket of his overcoat. His money was all there! Then who had paid them?

His documents were not with the coins. He nervously went through the pockets of the overcoat, inside and out. His head ached as if he had drunk an entire bottle of wine the night before. The floor under his feet was swaying as if he were still on the ship. *I could never be a sailor*, he thought as he washed his face in the small basin by the window. In the armoire mirror he saw his image after the days of travel.

He had aged. Thinner, dishevelled hair, unshaven, he was grateful he hadn't gone to meet his brothers looking like that. He seemed, a thousand times over, a failure...

The ticket was second-class and the ship, with many more passengers than its capacity, had no space for so many children and their mothers, who were heading for the Orient to reunite with their husbands. Except for the crew, few men were on board, most of them old and sick. The rest of the passengers were women dressed in black, taking care of their children, seeming more like widows than wives. Many were no older than his daughter Michaela. Alberto heard on the deck that many of the husbands had left to work on the new railroad, others to try their luck in smuggling tobacco, carpets, and spices.

If not for Daud, the Moroccan, he wouldn't have been able to find a chair to sit in during the entire voyage.

What an interesting person that fellow Daud was. I didn't even get a chance to thank him, Alberto thought. The ship would leave for Constantinople that morning. If he hurried to the port, he could try to find him, to say goodbye, to thank him. Maybe even leave his brother's address, a reference. Perhaps one day the Moroccan would return to Salonica, and then he could repay the favour...

Hastily, forgetting his documents, he passed by the reception desk, where he was stopped:

"Mr. Varsano," a youthful Greek said to him, "are you planning to ... go out? Did you have a good night? Just look at you," continued the young man cheerfully. "You appear in excellent shape, not even like the same person who arrived here yesterday... You mustn't go out without your documents... It's dangerous, I'll get them for you," he said, dashing to the counter.

When he returned holding the papers, his tone changed and he whispered into the foreigner's ear. He looked around, speaking quietly, as if divulging a secret.

"Wherever you are, don't be without these documents, and keep them away from the sultan's men... The sultan's, understand? Stay away from men in uniform and from places outside the city gates, it's dangerous!"

The pharmacist could feel the man's breath on his cheek, a mixture of spearmint and cinnamon. His smile was sincere, and his eyes shone as he spoke an Italian laden with French words.

"Excuse me, Mr. Varsano, you owe two Turkish piasters to the hotel. I paid the porters with my own money. Don't worry about paying now; when you have it, just let me know."

Alberto went down Sabri Pasha Street, breathing the cool morning air, taking long steps, heading toward the sea. He tried to get his bearings. To the right, entering the Promenade, was the road to the port, and if he turned to the left he would go to the White Tower.

He quickened his pace.

The port was crowded at that hour of the morning, and Daud should be finishing up cleaning the ship's deck. He did so every morning, in every port where they moored, and the routine here would be no different. Alberto tried to get near the gangway, but a large number of people were lining up to go on board, and he was being pushed back.

From a distance he tried to distinguish the Moroccan's head among the others. There he was, hanging from the outside ropes of the steamship. He seemed more like a monkey, leaping from side to side.

"Daauuudd!" Alberto shouted, cupping his hands. "Daud!"

He spent a good deal of time watching the incredible movements of his travel companion. His newest friend. The cat-man, a Negro with broken nose and an ivory smile, the color of his turban...

ༀ

# VII

## MEMORIES OF *DAUD*

Salonica, 1883
*From Messina to the Aegean Sea...*

Daud had talked with Alberto on the deck of the ship every night. He would secretly bring leftovers from the kitchen and, after all the passengers scattered about the corners were sleeping, would squat beside the pharmacist to relate stories from his life and his adventures. The Moroccan must have been ten years or so his junior but physically seemed even younger.

He enjoyed talking. Daud had an ability to assimilate languages and would converse with Alberto in Italian, in a mixture of sounds and accents ranging from French to Arabic, from Turkish to Spanish, in his rich, hoarse voice, guffawing. An ebony-colored Moroccan with a noble demeanour, he was the most unusual person Alberto had ever met. Daud told him what he knew about his father, a very tall and lanky black man, who left his tribe, from far away, and had gotten lost in the Dédes plains, at the foot of an enormous mountain range called Atlas. He fell in love with Daud's mother, a Berber girl with olive skin, green eyes, and straight black shiny hair. Even though neither spoke a word of the other's language, they ran away together. Some members of his mother's tribe set out in pursuit of the couple. When they were found, months later, his father was stoned to death and his mother was taken back, beaten, shunned and pregnant, later to be cast out without so much as a blanket.

The sailor had learned a lot during his wanderings in the world. After leaving the small village in the Atlas mountains, he had done a bit of everything. He was more a gardener than a sailor. He had grown up on a plantation of pink roses Damaskinas. Beginning in childhood he took care of the planting, picked flowers, separated and carefully bagged the petals. Every harvest season, he said, a large number of Frenchmen would come looking for that precious commodity. Only now, after having traversed the globe, had he discovered where it went.

"They go into tiny crystal vials in the form of intoxicating perfumes!"

As a boy, Daud had taken to his mother the remains of discarded petals, which she would carefully prepare in water that had been distilled for days in a copper vessel. It was rose water, the attar of roses. She kept it as a treasure, and every year, after the harvest, she would fill a few more centimetres of her clay pot with that golden perfumed oil.

When he left his land to go with an expedition of foreigners and met the French explorer Pierre Savorgnan de Brazza, his life had changed entirely. Daud was illiterate, a Berber good only for cleaning his master's boots.

Count De Brazza, a nobleman born in Italy, was a special kind of man. A Francophile, he believed the territory of Africa was the ideal place to promote French culture. When his first expedition, in 1871, passed through Daud's village, it was almost bankrupt. De Brazza was on his way to Fez, then to Tangier, and finally to Paris, where he would raise funds for a new expedition, this time through the vast territories of the Congo River.

The count had grand dreams. He would find gold, build missions and schools, and, finally, achieve his vision of founding a city with the name Brazzaville!

During the Tangier expedition, Daud began to know and understand his master. Count De Brazza dressed like his Moroccan servant on the journey, looking more like a ragged Bedouin than a noble explorer. But as they approached villages and cities, he once again became a gentleman. He would put on his best clothes, take interminable baths in his copper tub, and trim his beard with a pair of silver scissors. Daud learned to attend to the details with perfection and soon was able to turn a scarecrow into a prince. He knew how to cook, how to pitch and strike the tent as if by magic.

De Brazza came to care about his Moroccan servant more than five years, frequently laughing at his mistaken phrases, and, like a good teacher, demanded efficiency in the learning process. When they arrived in Tangier the count, who had only to cross to Gibraltar to complete his mission, changed his plans and set off to the east, following the long road to Tunis. He had a hunger for knowledge and even more of a hunger to teach. He was practically a megalomaniacal idealist, tormented by the dream of becoming a great explorer and taking back to France the laurels of his work.

In those five years Daud learned almost everything that a true European gentleman should know. He imitated his master's genteel manner, was deferential and tidy, ate with silverware, and even spoke self-assuredly. He also knew his place. Always. When the explorer's financial situation finally became serious, and even his magnetism could no longer persuade his business-rich compatriots to bankroll his plans, De Brazza was desperate.

"Ignorance!" he shouted nervously as he entered the hotel room.

"The English, gentlemen," he said in a passionate voice, "sponsored the voyages of Livingstone, Stanley, and all the other great explorers... Why not us, the French?" Beating his fists against his chest, he proclaimed, "*Vive la France!*"

For De Brazza there was magic to achieving a donation, a loan, a partnership, between puffs of cigar or hookah. And Daud, impassive as a statue, would stand with crossed arms, always posted at his master's back. Count De Brazza seriously considered taking Daud to Paris, but the idea seemed utopian. It would be inexplicable for an antislavery liberal, a cultured and progressive humanist, to arrive in the City of Light with a dark-skinned Berber, illiterate and with calloused hands!

And so Daud followed his destiny...

∽

# VIII

## NEWS FROM ALBERTO VARSANO

Salonica, October 20, 1883.

The plane trees in the public garden were golden when Alberto's first letter arrived in Taormina. Anna was leaving the house for the jewellery shop, and the mailman Antonio was climbing to Mongibello, as always, his cheeks flushed and his breathing laboured.

"It's from *Dottore* Varsano!" he shouted, waving the envelope. "And there must be something else inside."

Anna went to meet him, descending the hill in a run.

The envelope contained a letter and a postcard.

She read and reread the letter countless times until her heartbeat returned to normal and her hands stopped shaking. He missed her greatly, Alberto wrote... He told a little about his trip, about someone named Daud, his effort to locate Victor and David. He hadn't expected Salonica to be so large and so prosperous! It was a city quite different from what he had imagined.

He had gone to the office of the lawyer Grassi the afternoon following his arrival, looking for David, and not found him. In his place was a young man who received him as if they had known each other for years. He was Emmanuel Raphael Salem. The poor youth, David's kindred spirit, described so often in the letters sent to Taormina. Salem seemed to know everything about Alberto. He knew the names of Anna and Michaela, that Alberto was a pharmacist, knew about his life in Venice as well as in Taormina.

Only he didn't know that Alberto was coming there, or his motive. Not even David, who had always told him everything about his family, could imagine that one day it would be Salem who received his brother's visit.

Salem considered David Varsano his older brother and teacher. They had been working together for more than twelve years, and there were no secrets between them. The young lawyer was one of the first people Alberto met in the city who dressed in European clothing. A well-cut coat complemented a very white, starched shirt with wide cuffs and gold cufflinks bearing the crescent-moon design that was the symbol of the Ottoman Empire. Sensing the eyes focused on his wrist, Salem said with a sly smile:

"Don't get the wrong idea, we haven't become converts yet. This is just for the benefit of the sultan's men!"

Alberto learned that his brother David was working in Constantinople and from there would go to Bavaria with attorney Grassi; they would return only at the beginning of December. Also that he was still unmarried.

His time was devoted entirely to work. When there was a party or social event, he would put in an appearance solely out of obligation. He lived alone in a large rented room in a two-story house on the Promenade, the street that ran along the oceanfront, the most cosmopolitan and desirable area of the city.

It was the district where the consulates of several countries were located. The wealthiest Turks, he explained, lived in the high part of the city, in a pristine and manicured place called *Baïri*.

Well-to-do Jews, industrialists or bankers, had built a new neighborhood in recent years, Hamidie. And the Greeks lived in the Christian neighbourhoods, near the Church of St. Demetrius, converted into a mosque and renamed to *Kasimiye Camii*, or around the Church of St. Nicholas, known in Turkish as *Fakir Aj̈ Nicola*.

David had not chosen his residence as a function of community, race, or religion, or even based on cost or financial situation, but he had fallen in love with the space and even more with the pleasantness of the landlady. Everything there reminded him of his land, his Venice.

Salem went on describing the city and David's place of residence. His bedroom was lit by large windows that opened onto the sea. And he had a special landlady who took care of him with dedication and friendship.

When Alberto agreed to fetch his belongings from the hotel and await David's return already lodged in his room, Salem finally stopped arguing.

"Now," he said, "the *Dottore* is acting like a true Varsano," and laughed. "Intelligently and economically! Why spend your savings on a hotel if your brother can lodge you?"

Salem had the key to the room. He was a trusted friend, even in David's absence. Emmanuel Salem described his recent meetings with Victor Varsano, Alberto's middle brother.

"We have often had coffee together. He loved spending hours with a hookah, smoking, playing backgammon; he was a dreamer… And he dreamed really big!"

Victor harboured grand ambitions and had departed the city after trying to establish himself on his own. He had been doing very well, working with Levy Modiano, an Italian from Livorno, a member of a wealthy family held in high esteem in the city because of its charitable activities. Victor was construction head of the Villa Ida but became dissatisfied with the slow pace of the project. It would take at least four more years for completion, with everything, even the smallest details like window locks, imported from Italy. All designed by the great architect Poselli.

When a shipment of materials arrived, carts would haul it from the port to the construction site in Hamidie. The architect would meet with Victor and the owners to discuss and verify each detail.

The garden, with rose bushes and jasmine, featured an iron framework with Lalique stained glass, installed in the corner of the grounds. Ancient plane trees and carefully preserved cypresses gave the impression that little was lacking for the family to establish itself there. *Signora* Ida Modiano participated regularly in the meetings. The villa bore her name and was to be as lovely as she—according to what was said, the most beautiful woman in the city, an opinion shared by Victor.

Victor fell in love with Ida like a schoolboy and did everything possible to see that all was to her liking. He noted her observations and even against the architect's opinion fought to see them realized.

One day, Victor sketched on the ground a road and a small pond, almost in the shape of a heart. He set some of his workers to digging, brought small white stones from the dry riverbed, and lined the trench to form a light-colored carpet. He filled it with water from a spigot, bucket after bucket. The pond was as transparent, as limpid as a mirror. Victor asked the gardener to plant tufts of lavender cotton around it. He imagined Ida sitting under the Lalique glass reflected in the water.

Venetian's work, he smiled and immediately made it clear to the couple that Victor Varsano had brought to fruition a surprise that that he, Vitaliano Poselli, had conceived.

Victor never returned to Hamidie. How grandiose were his dreams! Ida Modiano was a married woman. She loved her husband and was both the most beautiful and the richest woman in Salonica. He had gone several months without a job; his savings were enough to last half a year or more. He lived in a room in Vardar, in the home of Elia Covo, a religious man, head of a family of four women and two men. Victor was not long looking for work.

A nephew of Covo's arrived from Astrakhan carrying woollen and furs, and after some days sold everything, making a profit of two thousand percent. Victor asked Covo how much he would need to start such a business.

"Well," calculated the old man, "to make a hefty profit you need at least three hundred Turkish liras!"

That was a fortune to Victor, who had probably a hundred liras and some gold florins. He could borrow another fifty from David, sell his watch, and that would be enough to get started. The venture would require heavy clothing and boots for protection from the cold. In Joseph Bechara's store he bought sugar and coffee and a few other items for the long journey.

Days later, Victor went to the Hachette bookstore, the new French branch in Salonica represented by the bookseller Molho.
Since leaving Venice, Victor had never again touched a book. His thick and calloused labourer's hands could barely manage the silk-paper sheets of the maps he sought. He felt shame at being singled out by the bookseller. Given his appearance, his greasy hair and worn-out clothes, it was hard for anyone to believe he was truly interested in something so rare and specific.

The seller managed to find a second-hand book that described the region Victor was going to visit. He began to plan his journey, but he needed more details.

He hung around the docks, met fishermen, listened to sailors, adventurers, smugglers, and itinerant peddlers. Each told of a different exploit he had experienced or heard of.
Then, he sought out Covo's nephew.

Moise Covo, fat and extremely pleasant, good-natured and calm, explained to Victor that he was looking for a partner. He had no desire to go back there himself. A lucky stroke, which sufficed to give the Venetian all the indications of what he should and shouldn't do, along with half the money necessary for the investment, and send him on his way to Astrakhan.

David had never again received news of Victor.

After many months, a group of men from the Vardar neighborhood who had also attempted to smuggle furs returned from Sebastopol saying they had called off the trip because they were warned of a serious outbreak of malaria and typhoid fever attacking that side of the Caspian Sea.

❧

Along with the letter in which Alberto related his first impressions of Salonica, a postcard arrived.

Anna was unsure whether it was a joke or a provocation on the part of her husband. The photo was of a horribly ugly, fat, poorly dressed woman and read "Souvenir of Salonica."
On the back, Alberto had written:

*My beloved Anna,*
*When you come to Salonica,*
*you should dress like this, like most of the women.*

Anna examined the photo of the large-breasted woman countless times. She looked more like a Saracen villager from the Ópra di Pupi. Now of all times, when she was assiduously perfecting her knowledge of couture and had page after page of the best fashion sketches to do! Now, when she had no time to sleep and stayed up late at night looking through the books on fashion that the baroness and Michaela had sent! And she would go to Salonica and look like that? It had to be a joke on Alberto's part...
"*Costume de femme juive,*" she said aloud. "What bad taste!" Her husband's jest in sending the card set her to thinking about the future. When would she go to meet him in Salonica?

The photo of the *femme juive* stuck to the mirror encouraged her to dedicate herself more and more each day to her work so she would never become that woman.

On the other side of the world, Alberto Varsano had no idea of the efforts Anna was making to become a famous dressmaker. She created models with small pieces of cloth, consulting the "Great Bible," as she nicknamed the heavy volume that Clara and Michaela had assembled for her. The two women visited the best shops in Bavaria, collecting samples of fabrics. The baroness patiently selected them for quality: on one page she glued remnants, laces from the north of France, silks and brocades. On the next page: taffeta, satin, organza, and muslin. With the material in her hands, Anna pictured what the women tourists would be wearing when they arrived in Taormina the following season .She saw clearly that the silhouette was new, no more crinolines, the bosom would be cinched in, more flattened, the hips slimmed, and merely a *basque* to effect a lifting of the posterior, what the French termed *portelón*.

And on the final pages of the thick book, *"the last cry,"* so nicknamed by Michaela. The greatest success among the women was an English trend. A silhouette in which the top of the dress imitated the shoulders and sleeves of a masculine dress-coat.

There were sketches of famous fur coats from Revillon House and advertisements of bathing attire and corselets, illustrated pages of shoes and hats, and a separate chapter of jewels and needlework... Together, it represented a treasure to Anna, her tie to the world.

*"Sayo-bustikó* and *entari.* Those clothes of the women of Salonica! What fantasy if he thinks I'll ever wear them?" Anna continued, grumbling aloud, her eyes locked on the photo on the mirror. "Poor Alberto; other than the pharmacy, he doesn't pay attention to anything," she said, pointing out the photo to her father.

Raffaele put on his glasses and approached the mirror.

"My poor son-in-law. How could he think he'd please you with such ideas? Just look at those gold chains the woman's wearing! Not even in Toledo, in the days of my ancestors, was that attractive," commented old Raffaele, laughing.

Anna wrapped herself in white cotton cloth and gradually pinned the shape. She looked at herself in the mirror, front, side, back, out of the corner of her eyes, assuming the pose of an empress. And raising her eyebrows.

She lowered the fabric of the neckline, adjusted the bust.

*"Voilà!* An authentic French model!"

Father and daughter laughed until they cried.

After the *Dottore* left, she had used their bed only to hold the patterns of cotton basted during the day. In time, that wedding bed, witness to their love, had become a mountain of white patterns, cheery skeletons floating on top of one another, awaiting the right moment to magically transform into colourful, real apparel and finally be worn by a personage. Exhausted, late every night Anna would lie down in Michaela's bed. She would hug her pillow and fall asleep, her eyes swimming with tears.

IX

## THE CHESTNUT ROASTERS

*"Kaïnar... kaïnar... kaïnamos – kestane... pis-mis kestane"*
*"Chauds, chauds les marrons... buillis et rotis les marrons."*

*... Chestnuts... nice and hot...*

Salonica, Ottoman Empire, October 20, 1883.

Alberto waited anxiously for David to return.

The city was transformed. The plane trees had turned red, then the leaves dried and fell. The cool breeze became damp and cold, and the smell of the city, of the flowers, the Mediterranean pines, the sweet ripe fruit now yielded to the aroma of chestnuts roasting over coals, sold by Turks on every street corner.

A melancholy chant, a cadence echoed throughout the city: "Hot, very hot... Roasted chestnuts, toasted... Chestnuts... roasted chestnuts... *Kaïnar... kaïnar... kaïnamos... Chauds, chauds les marrons...*"

And, little by little, cold raindrops transformed the golden afternoons into long and silent nights.

David's room reflected his soul. His paintings, objects, clothes, his meticulously arranged volumes in an improvised bookcase–everything bespoke the personality of a brother Alberto barely knew. Everything there reminded him of his father's library in the old house in Venice, in back of the pharmacy.

For one of his sons to have access to those thick volumes, there was always a lecture forthcoming. Care, attention, respect, for many of the books contained divine thought, knowledge, wisdom. Looking through his brother's books, among treatises on law, history, and philosophy, he found some that were especially personal. Yes, before him were books he had read in childhood. The Greek classics, everything he had learned from Plato and his Republic, from Aristotle, from Socrates, from Pindar's poetry…

He started looking in the volumes for underlining and notes made more than thirty years earlier. They were there, in his handwriting, page after page… "Know thyself… Know thyself!"

*De Rerum Natura*, the work by Lucretius, his companion, which had taught him in Latin the nature of things, had explained in verse that the universe is infinite, demonstrated the difference between *anima* and *animus*, and that the soul is born, grows, and dies with the body. That in death it escapes like smoke and disintegrates more quickly than the body.

"That is it!" he murmured incredulously. "Titus Lucretius Carus wrote some years before Christ, and I still wonder whether I believe in him or in those who preach about heaven, hell, and burden us with all the treatises in the name of God."

He ran his fingers along the crumbly black leather spine. It bore no title, but he knew it intimately.

*So, that book had come from Venice with David!* The book proscribed to Alberto. Their father had forbidden him to read it and had hidden it in an old trunk.

"It is heresy… Spinoza is a heretic!" he shouted, looking deeply into Alberto's eyes with fury and fear. "Do you want to attract another Inquisition? Do you want to bring into our house the heretic, the excommunicated, with ideas contrary to our own beliefs? A person who does not believe in the most sacred words, the immortal soul, in our God the way we feel him, who rejects our God-fearing, humble principles?"

His father's words still echoed in his brain.

"Doubts? Doubts... A Jew does not have doubts! Doubt is the greatest of sins, the blade of the whirling sword. Doubt comes from the devil, from our mortal enemy! Don't you remember what have learned when studied for your bar mitzvah when made your vows?

*Es lehav ha cherev ha mis hapeches,*" he said in Hebrew.

"It is the fatal weapon of doubt, for anyone who doubts God and his teachings... The path will be hard. The path may appear one way by day, but be different at night. A man with doubts cannot find his path!"

His father had hammered those words into his memory. He felt the senior man's presence beside him, his smell of ether, his deep and poignant gaze.

Alberto had read part of Spinoza's *Ethics* in his youth. He had not finished it. And now he was free and alone, with no fear of committing a sin. He sat on David's couch holding the book in his hands, and even his own shadow fluttering on the walls frightened him. He saw his father, bald at the temples, the old yarmulke, the long white beard, shortly before his soul left his body. Was it immortal?

Was he still exacting from him the lessons and teachings of the Hebrew codes of the Torah, the Talmud, the Psalms, Proverbs, those works so difficult to understand, the endless writings of Maimonides? And just how much of Spinoza had he read and understood? He looked for marks or notes at the bottom of the page and discovered his handwriting, in pencil and almost illegible, in The Nature of Affects, where the philosopher defined humility.

There they were, in Ethics III: his mark on those pages. He had underlined and written references and the differences between "virtuous humility" and "vicious humility," but sections of it were illegible.

Alberto looked through his writings, and an underlined passage caught his eye. Now, almost thirty years later, he understood better. Now he possessed the maturity to understand what his father had never read.

"Humility is a sadness," Spinoza said, "born of the fact of the human being considering his impotence or his weakness."

"Humility, then, was a state of the soul, he thought. His father, his poor father, had preached his entire life that humility was a virtue.

But if that virtue is a sadness, it cannot be considered a virtue!

And what is virtue ? he asked to himself. There was.. the answer with his calligraphy..

*"Virtue is a force of the soul and therefore must always be a cause for happiness."*

"And when is humility considered a virtue?" Alberto had written at the bottom of the page. And the answer was on the next page.

"When humility is merely a shield. When we encounter something stronger and know impotence and delimit our own strength."

Alberto increased the flame of the lamp in order to read his writing.

In the corner of the next page he had written:

"That way of knowing one's own strength, one's limits, is a virtue, a greater power for the soul. It is the appropriate knowing of oneself."

He felt his cheeks burning and his heart racing...

"That's it!" he exclaimed. "It's the Delphic maxim!"

He was closing a circle:

*Know thyself*, from Plato. Then Pindar: *Be how thou hast learned to know thyself.*

Next," *Werde der du bist*, "or Become who you are, from the book by Goethe that he had read in Taormina and whose subtle teachings lived on in his memory.

Alberto clutched Spinoza's book to his chest. Benedictus de Spinoza had given him a lesson, an opportunity to understand all of that, to be proud of what was, and to better himself by becoming that which he had always been, but with self-knowledge.

For the pharmacist, that would now be the only chance to rethink his principles, to be himself, a humble man, neither coward or pessimist, to be the true Alberto Varsano...

He didn't realize the time, having been engrossed since nightfall. He heard someone knocking softly on the door. He rose and opened it. There was a basket, a steaming casserole, and a loaf of braided bread .Perhaps a gift from the landlady Marika Karakassos, confusing his presence with the return of David.

Alberto ate the soup, thickening it with pieces of bread. He felt his body warm up and laughed at himself. He was cold, but with so much to think about, he had forgotten to turn on the coal-burning *sobah*. The room was damp and chilly.

Winter in Salonica would be harsh, but no more so than his Venice. Remembering his room, perpetually mouldy from the sea air of the canals, the hot bricks his mother placed under the woollen blankets to warm the children's feet, and the soup served at dinner with thick pieces of bread, he breathed deeply.

"Venice!" he exclaimed.

He could now recognize everything that for years his parents had done for him in that house, that dark and sad place, during the long winter months. His poor mother, who baked bread, starched his shirts, and cleaned the pharmacy.

His beloved mother, always unaffected, dressed in an apron, her head covered with a kerchief, wrapped in traditional knitted shawls, devoid of vanity, detached from everything.

The old house, the stone stairs, the floor redolent of wax, windows stuck shut. He missed his mother.

He looked at the English watercolour hanging on the wall.

He lay down on the couch, extinguished the lamp, and, closing his eyes, saw images, strolled through squares and canals, crossed bridges, and finally fell asleep.

# X

## MANDOLINS, DREAMS... AND A NIGHTMARE

Taormina, December 1883.

Raffaele Cohen's shop offered many new pieces in November of that year.

The jeweller had never displayed so many necklaces, chains, and rings. It was the worst period for business in the city of Taormina because the olive harvest took the younger ones into the fields, and all that could be heard in the empty city was the Clock Tower in the Piazza di Sant'Agostino, the wind and the lamentation of mandolins.

The small entrance of the jewellery shop remained closed, but inside, father and daughter would work until late every day, in a frenzy, and then leave to sleep in Mongibello. No one could imagine that from one moment to the next they would respond to a call from a distant and unknown place called Salonica, pack their trunks and sail on the first ship.

But until that happened, Raffaele and Anna would be partners in a wonderful undertaking. They had nothing to lose. She had transformed herself into what she should always have been, true *materfamilias*, an insatiable creator, hungry for justice; in Raffaele's mind his daughter seemed like a different woman, a woman on her own.

That evening, criticized by her father, she answered in a different way, a bit angry, ironic, and rebellious.

"No one lifted a finger to defend Alberto, no sign of solidarity when those vultures took away his license! All I heard was hypocritical questions: 'What now, *signora* Varsano? What will your poor husband do?' 'If you need anything, you can count on us.' Hypocrites!" Anna shouted. "We don't need anyone... I want to pretend that we survived their false generosity just as they benefitted from the genuine generosity of my husband! Night after night in that laboratory, trying to cure the illnesses of this city. *Povero* Alberto!"

*Generosity or ingenuousness?* Raffaele thought but said nothing, so as not to further incite his daughter's ire.

"The people of the city aren't to blame for anything," he said, trying to calm her. "They're all cowards and nowadays those who have money give the orders... They're admired, respected, flattered."

"And that's exactly why we're going to get rich, Pappá! I want to make as much money as I can, to restore part of the dignity that was stolen from Alberto!"

The old man, startled by his daughter's idea, turned and asked with an ironic smile:

"Have you by some chance found a rich lover? Maybe a Russian prince or German noble like those who devour you with their eyes when they come into the shop?"

"*Acqua in bocca, Pappá...* Don't talk that way..."

Raffaele didn't reply, lowering his head. Anna approached her father, kneeling beside the chair where he sat.

"Look deep into my eyes, *mio caro*. Please, Pappá... I never again want to hear you mention what I do to attract those rich idiots. You know very well... It's a way of penetrating that circle, of being accepted by them as a  famous dressmaker, the most respected one in Taormina."

"Are you dreaming, Anna?"

His daughter's discourse was making Raffaele nervous.

"You, daughter? Have you ever thought that with that name, Anna Cohen Varsano, in this city you're going nowhere? That there are other competent dressmakers here with names of well-to-do families, who won't let you be recommended to the tourists?"

"*Caríssimo*, you still don't know who I am and what I'm able to accomplish? Me, *signor* Cohen..." she said, rising, her cheeks red with fury. "Know what I really want? I want to dress those rich women who come to Taormina for Carnevale in the Teatro Regina Margueritha. I'm going to cover them in silk and velvet, real or faux jewels, I'm going to be so famous that I'll even sew the wedding dresses for Galliani's granddaughters."

Raffaele wanted to get that absurd idea out of his daughter's head, but the more he tried to dissuade her, the angrier she became.

"I, I myself, Anna the *spagnola*, from the Sacred Heart of Maria... The time has come for the *spagnola* to avenge herself for the humiliations I suffered from my classmates, like the Inquisition itself... They were bluebloods! Who accused me of being a Jew, and said we Jews had crucified Jesus Christ. The ones who dressed like angels, who fawned over the most pious nuns, who punished me... I couldn't study theology, couldn't set foot in the school chapel..."

"And did you–" Raffaele tried to calm his daughter. "Did you ever miss ... learning their religion... or going to Mass?"

Anna didn't answer. Then, very close to her father's ear, she whispered:

"The two of us, Pappá, are going to disappear from here. And when we return, women will fight over a dress from the atelier of *Signor Rossetti et Madame Lambert!* The finest apparel... *Fabrication Française!*"

"But who are they?" the old man asked, no longer understanding anything.

"The two of us, Pappá. You and I will be managers of the house of couture from Paris. Rossetti et Lambert will open their doors in Taormina, in the old shop of the jeweller R. Cohen..." she said, wrapping an old blanket around her body and leaving the room as haughty as if she had slipped into the most beautiful dress at the ball.

Anna left the room, searched through Alberto's old laboratory and found ammonia, mixing it with hydrogen peroxide. She prepared an infusion of red-onion skins. In front of the mirror, she cut her hair short. She sewed the long tresses onto a black velvet ribbon.

Next, she poured the prepared liquid onto her cropped hair. She felt nauseous. Her scalp burned, but even so, she used what was left to lighten her eyebrows. Then prepared a second batch for her father. Carefully, she worked it strand by strand into Raffaele's sparse hair while he sat impassive as a statue. She trimmed his moustache and shaved off his beard, leaving only an odd goatee. Finally, she covered his head with a black velvet beret.

Now he looked identical to the foreign intellectuals who gathered in Zamara's cafe in late afternoon to discuss music or literature.

Raffaele couldn't believe what he saw in the mirror. He raised his shoulders, straightened his vest, tipped the beret in a gesture of deference to Anna. His dyed hair and goatee made him appear at least thirty years younger. He looked at his daughter beside him, with her hair short, mussed, the color of flame. He stared at her as if he had seen her go crazy. He embraced Anna tightly and burst out laughing in a way he had never before. He laughed until he cried. His body shook and he sobbed. Between laughter and tears he asked:

"*Poverina mia*... I still don't understand... "

"Who ordered that Nazarene crucified?"

"Nor do I, Pappá," answered Anna softly, caressing the old man's trembling hands, "but I must confess that the Nazarene, the one they call Jesus, to me isn't God or the son of our God. To me... yes, a great Cabalist, a spiritual master, perhaps a messiah or the greatest Jew ever... and I like him, Pappá . A lot!"

Rafaelle embracing Anna like a little girl said into her ears..

"Do not mind *poverina mia*... It is always about religion...Religion..religion!  Those people here ...they are always changing  History to win. For what ? Hate, war, all the worst.."

" Have you ever asked the nuns if they heard that this man, this one called by them Jesus was a Jew like you are? "

"Did you told those good ladies that if they love  him, for what he was one day, they have to respect us. All the Jews in the world are another Jesus without the Croce, but condemned  to  persecution for a sin .Who killed this man?

Anna awoke late the next morning. Her body ached. She had a fever. And her eyes avoided the light.

She remembered what had happened the night before...

A tremor ran through her body. Staggering, she went to the mirror. Her hair was still long and black; only her face was livid and haggard.

"Thank God..." She exclaimed.

"It was just a nightmare."

XI

RONDO À LA TURK

Planegg, December 1883.

It was snowing.

Baroness Clara de Hirsch reread Anna Varsano's letter several times. It left her feeling melancholy the rest of the day. She remained seated in her elegant parlour, staring into space, until nightfall.

Incredible that a woman like Clara, born into one of the wealthiest families in Brussels and married to one of the most influential men in Europe, should be there that evening, motionless, her thoughts transported to such an insignificant place as that small white house at the top of Mongibello.

Clara Bischoffsheim recalled one of her best moments and the affection of the Varsano family on Shabbat, in Taormina.

It had been a long time since she felt the warmth of a family. Actually, she had never felt anything like it. She remembered her childhood in Antwerp, her mother and how she had been raised by her. There was much respect, but never what she recognized now, reading the letter from Taormina, collaboration between mother and children, affection, or what the Italians called love. In the relationship between Anna Varsano and Michaela existed a rapport in the way they looked at each other, caressed, said things that she had never experienced. She laughed with her, embracing her and kissing her cheeks, braided her hair, praised her work and her beauty.

Clara had never witnessed a scene like that. Love, affection, attention...

In the Bischoffsheim home, everything was a topic of conversation and discussed, there was a code of nobility, a bell jar enclosing her parents and her siblings, an unending competition to be the best, to be noticed, to win praise or the reward of a smile. But the burden of meriting it was huge.

She remembered her mother, to whom nothing was worthy of notice. From a new dress to a floral arrangement on the dining room table, everything would be deemed ostentation, a way of demeaning the less favoured. When something pretty or novel appeared she would shake her head in negation. To her, it was an affront to those who had nothing.

The privileged situation in which they lived in Belgium, as owners of banks, a father in politics – all of it was a heavy weight for her mother, a woman who had always been unpretentious, pious, born and raised in the old ghetto of Frankfurt.

To her, the way to demonstrate love was by helping others.

There were small things in the house in Mongibello that Baroness Hirsch would have liked to have in her own home; not material objects, for Clara had never known any lack of them. Perhaps more love and less onus of responsibility, more sharing between mother and children, the freedom to run, to put on a dress and hear her mother praise her beauty, as she had seen happen with Anna Varsano as she sewed a dress for her daughter, her eyes shining with joy. In her family, Clara had never seen anything of that nature. Never heard a compliment. Her father treated her as if she were one of the men in the family, and in order to stand out among them, all industrious and good students, the trait was ability. That was how she was seen by everyone.


Until Maurice had crossed her path.

She wasn't deemed beautiful. She was 19, merely an intelligent, well balanced young woman. When Maurice chose her instead of her younger sister, considered the most attractive, Clara was surprised.
She had never told anyone, but now she was certain he had chosen his bride by intuition. Dowry for dowry, it would be the same picking any of the senator's daughters.

But she was considered, for her time, a different kind of woman. She was not concerned with embroidery and trousseaus. She didn't read novels or spend her time on frivolity like most women. She was the private secretary to her father, Senator Bischoffsheim, often his counsel, and the most competent of all the siblings. As for business, she knew everything about the topics discussed, from legislation to philanthropy. She was knowledgeable but still feminine and delicate.

That was how Clara had grown up. Remembering magical moments in her life, which were few in her youth, waltzes, ballroom gowns, she smiled. Maurice had shown up to rescue her, she thought; the days were numbered until she married a different type of suitor, becoming merely a petty and undistinguished woman living a monotonous life in some large house, taking care of children and grandchildren.

She looked around the living room in Planegg.

This was not her home, it was the Hirsches', a pied-à-terre for their constant travels. Maurice never stayed in the same place for more than fifteen or twenty days. One time he would be in Vienna, close to Planegg; another time, in Eychorn; in spring, he loved Beauregard. And Paris, where he had a circle of friends, the bank, numerous festivities, political and social works. In springtime he would go to the Riviera or Grasse, tend to obligations in Constantinople, where they had lived for a period, and then London, where the meetings with aristocracy took place and where he attended the horse races, always accompanied by Clara.

Her father, the senator, had said that Maurice was a reckless investor.

"He'll end up either a millionaire or a beggar!"

Clara felt weary at times, or melancholy, from so much coming and going, but after all Maurice would never be happy confined to a single place. He was a man of note, in addition to being intelligent, witty, and *charmant*. Everything he had planned in the years before marriage he had achieved, he had the mastery to run several businesses at the same time, all of them large in size and responsibility. He earned money for the pleasure of earning, like a gambler, and he lived large, spending on himself, on his family, and the needy. He loved feeling useful, taking an interest in everything. After all, he would say, unless the heart beats with emotion, life becomes monotonous.

She was happy, yes… She had a good son, sensible and loving, and even going months without seeing him, because of her life of perpetual travel, the brief times they spent together were enough for mother and son to share wonderful moments.

Lucien was her only child. But now there was Michaela…

The young Sicilian, happy, smiling, with her rustic manners, her expressive gaze, talkative, pure in heart and soul, had turned into a beautiful *signorina*, delicate and extremely well bred. She was intelligent, able to calculate accounts in a way that amazed Maurice. She now practiced waltzes and played some of them on the piano. She spoke German and French well and was quickly learning English. The young woman had a future, if she found a good husband.

Baroness Hirsch could smell the fragrance of lemon blossoms invading the room and, smiling at her own thoughts and sensations, finally returned to her true world of Bavaria. Mongibello was very far away. The Planegg castle was already dark, before four o'clock in the afternoon; it was Helga's free day. The remaining servants were probably in the kitchen busying themselves with preparations for dinner.

Clara folded the letter from Taormina, hiding it in the lace of her blouse. She didn't want Michaela to see what Anna had written. Not now, but in time, when everything was all right. Nothing in the world could make her want to see the happy Sicilian suffer from the news. For the Hirsches, she had become a blessing in that large, empty house. Even Maurice, after some months of reluctance, had a special affection for "Micha." He liked her delicate gestures, her laughter and her sincerity, as well as the intelligent way she handled his affairs.

After some time, she moved freely about the house, helped with small tasks, and would sneak into the kitchen to prepare a surprise from her land, lamenting the lack of olive oil, lemon, and basil... This was another world, she complained, yearning for tomatoes. On the long days of summer, when sunset came late, she would look at the immense lake and breathe deeply, trying to inhale the zephyr from her Sicilian sea.

But in Planegg the breeze came from tall pines, the horizon held snowy peaks. Chilly and with no hint of salt, the gentle and silent breeze filled her soul with melancholy.

Every morning she went into Munich, in the carriage from the baron's house, to study German with other foreigners, the daughters of ambassadors or representatives moving to Bavaria. She also learned to ride and paint, took music lessons, literature classes, and began reading the books in the library. Later, Clara felt she should also take lessons in philosophy and Greek at the school of Master Kastelli, famous for having taught the empress of Austria, Greek history and mythology, to love Corfu and all those wonderful visions of a place called Bonrépos, where Sissy spent the better part of the year.

Every Thursday the waltz instructor and the pianist opened the Hirsches' ballroom in Planegg in preparation for the dances. Clara watched the transformation of her protégée day by day. She was beyond any doubt a beautiful young woman, intelligent and diligent, but her best qualities were good taste and sensitivity. This no school could teach; it was a gift. She was like that, had been born that way, even if she was a villager... As soon as people discovered that attribute of hers, they would ask for her suggestions and advice.

The baroness took her to the best dressmakers, and with a single glance the Sicilian would express her opinion about what to buy. She would raise her eyebrows when she disapproved. The two women had a code. When Michaela smiled at her or blinked, almost mischievously, behind the back of the saleswoman, Clara would order the purchase delivered. Michael felt more secure and free shopping with her and had never again faced the disapproving looks of Helga, her lady's companion.

Helga was a good person, loyal and very responsible but nothing more. There was no emotion in the relationship. "Madam, your tea; your carriage is ready; it's time for your medicine." With Michaela there was joy in living. Helga, poor woman, lost her role and naturally became more sullen than usual. She no longer accompanied the baroness to tea at the palace of Sophie de Alencon or, in the Habsburgs' pantry, learned of the latest happenings of the family, like the secrets of Emperor Franz Josef's relationships with a singer, one Katherine Schratt.

It was on one of those afternoons that Michaela met Gisela, the daughter of Empress Elizabeth.

Sissi, as the empress of Austria was affectionately known, was suffering from depression of late, almost constantly away from Vienna dealing with her health on the Greek island of Corfu. She was rarely with her family in Austria or her sisters and cousins in Bavaria. And Princess Gisela was beautiful, married and unhappy, as was commented in the kitchen, had all but been raised by her aunt Sophie, Nene to her intimates.

In that milieu so different from Taormina, Michaela was living a dream but knew exactly her place. Often, when interrogated out of curiosity, she made a point of recounting with great simplicity her life, where she came from, what she was doing there, living with Clara de Hirsch. The baroness had frequently advised Michaela to always tell the truth, but given certain facts, to omit details.

"You have no need to proclaim to the four winds who you are. Always maintain an aura of mystery... It's enough to say you were born and raised in Sicily! They're going to adore you, they're going to think it wonderful to have such an exotic friend! And don't say anything more... Not about your origin, not about religion... They're never going to understand what you're doing here!" This was the baroness's affectionate advice as she helped Michaela undo her braids.

There were those who looked down their nose when they heard Micha's background, but not Gisela; just the opposite – she sought her out more every day. The odd thing was the princess's dependence on the plebeian's taste. Everything the Sicilian wore or made was imitated by her. The little that Micha had, for she accepted nothing, she gave to her friend.

The previous winter she had knitted a cherry-colored woollen sweater. Still not content, she had decorated the neck with wine-colored ribbon, accenting the cuffs with lace from one of the baroness's old dresses.

"Even the ribbon in your hair is something different for a princess," commented Clara with a complicitous smile. "Goodbye to the cherry-colored sweater.

What will the next one be, Micha?"

"A stake ? Tomorrow I'm going to wear the green one ,with the necklace of my grandfather's citrines!"

"You're not crazy.... Don't even think of giving her your necklace! Your grandfather would die of disappointment."

"No, of course not! I won't trade it for anything she offers me. But if she really likes it, when she goes to Taormina this spring, the count can commission my grandfather to make one for her. Just imagine him receiving an order from the daughter of an empress. *Dio mio!*"

Sissi did not imagine how much Gisela missed having a mother, her advice and her presence. The empress, when she visited her, stayed ensconced in the castle, keeping company with her cousin, King Ludwig II of Bavaria. They seemed like twin spirits. He was an extremely attractive man, happy and quite loquacious, but also eccentric and selfish. According to Gisela, "the two were like brother and sister, and when she was with him, my mother turned into another person." She would become happier, smile, forget her beauty concerns, the hair that fell below her waist and had to be brushed five times a day. Her bouts of depression would go on for days without her answering or saying anything. But with Ludwig she always improved markedly. Together, the cousins would spend entire afternoons strolling through the palace gardens, or detailing the decoration in yet another room.

Michaela needed to get away from Gisela's problems. And with each passing day she saw that diving into her studies, reading, would be her path to becoming a cultured, well educated woman and admired. After all, she would never aspire to be a princess. She had already seen enough of the unhappiness of that family.

So she became an exemplary student, the most attentive one in her classes in Greek, philosophy, and history.

On those days, she would shut the door to her room and study tenaciously, knowing that, in the future, everything she learned would be useful and of help to her parents. Michaela also knew she was not one of them, a rich woman, a noble; she had no illusions. She was merely living a dream that would end one day, when she returned to the little house in Mongibello. But until then, there was much to enjoy and learn with Clara and Maurice.

The Hirsch castle in Planegg, Bavaria, was a world apart.

It had been planned and constructed by Baron Hirsch's own father and later remodelled during the time Maurice worked as economic adviser to Sissy's cousin King Ludwig II.

Step by step, Michaela understood that the Hirsch family fortune went back two generations. Maurice de Hirsch was known throughout Europe as a banker extremely adroit in business, a man who had no fear of taking risks and chasing new ideas, but also as a great philanthropist concerned with alleviating the poverty, as well as the racial and religious persecution, of his coreligionists. Everything he possessed had been achieved through his own merit.

A part of his profits was invested directly in institutions around the world, in furtherance of his fellow man; his point of departure was always those in need.

Gradually, Michaela began to participate in the Baron's world, called upon for her opinion on various family matters as if she were part of it. He would relate a case, asking her to help him analyze it and find a solution. He always used a parable or proverb to show her the way.

And in so doing made Micha think and grow.

One June afternoon, returning from a meeting, Maurice came into the house livid. Michaela was on top of a ladder in the library when the baron summoned her.

It took her some minutes to understand what he was saying:

"Poor Ludwig! Poor Elizabeth!" he exclaimed, frightened.

"Micha, please call Clara and ask her to come to the library. There is a matter of extreme urgency that I need to discuss with her."

The baron appeared very nervous and worried. He sat at his desk, his head lowered and his features taut. He was talking to himself when she entered.

"I said it, not once but countless times! Ludwig is taking a huge chance... Spending enormous sums of money," Maurice de Hirsch repeated. "Spending, making loans... Thinking of nothing but parties, competing with his cousin, who thinks only of herself... Ludwig is doing everything to undermine his position, he's becoming a megalomaniac... Paranoiac. He's taking Bavaria's economy into bankruptcy! I myself lent him thousands of pounds sterling, because of our friendship, because of his father Maximilian, because of my father..."

Maurice de Hirsch breathed deeply, trying to calm down. Clara didn't understand what he meant.

"Our bank, Clara, financed an industrial complex here in Bavaria. A plan to develop industries on the English model," said the baron unsteadily. "What did the lunatic do? He spent it... Spent it on castles, lakes and parks! Pomp and extravagance to impress his cousin and those false collaborators. Those leeches!..."

The baroness looked at Maurice de Hirsch in alarm. He was unsettled. She had never seen him like that, with his cheeks sweating and pale and his hands trembling. He wouldn't stop talking and gesturing...

"I think they're going to kill him, Clara. There's a conspiracy, and what's worse, I don't have anyone in the palace today who can back me to save him. I just found out today what Count von Holstein is planning to do..."

"But what has happened, Maurice?" asked Clara, not understanding.

"I was pressured. I have to keep quiet... I can't even get to Ludwig to warn him. No correspondence gets through to his chambers. First, they're demonstrating that he's insane... Poor soul.

Soon they're going to do something bad to get him out of the way. I feel his days are numbered. In desperation I tried a way to protect him, but... I don't know!" he said, sighing, his head between his hands.

"But the worst, I've already done! Early today I sent a letter to the leading newspapers of Europe denouncing the plot. That way, I think Ludwig will gain time, as well as a degree of safety, because I don't believe 'they' will have the courage to kill him once the papers report on the situation."

"What now, Maurice? What are you planning to do? Are you afraid?"

"I...?" he answered slowly, gaining time to think. "No! Our names aren't linked to anything he may have done; just the opposite, we were always creditors..."

"Even so, what could happen, Maurice? Do you think Bismarck is going to take revenge against you?"

Maurice de Hirsch sighed and drummed his fingers nervously on the desk.

"Times won't be pleasant for us if that comes to pass... I wouldn't like to be here when the government changes. If, at least, Schrenk were alive this wouldn't have happened! I don't sympathize with their ideas, they are no liberals... And I'm not certain whom they're going to designate. If he's removed or killed... I don't believe they would bring in Otto from Greece... Maybe Leopold, I don't know... And, besides," he went on, looking at everyone in the room, "we have no reason to continue here... Our center of business is London... Paris... And you, my dear Clara... Don't worry, there you'll be closer to our son. To our Lucien. So it's time for us to think about definitively closing down Planegg and moving everything to our other residences."

Clara agreed with a nod, and her thoughts went immediately to those who worked there, to her special kitchen, to the visitors, the mendicants, to the task of making endless lists for the move, leaving behind what belonged to the House of Hirsch. After all, the house also had other heirs... She thought of Mirla, the cook; Josef, the cobbler; Helga, her governess, who had her entire family nearby and in all certainty would not want to go with her. She remembered Michaela!

Yes, the Sicilian was part of her family now. She would accompany them whatever their destination... It would be better for the little Sicilian to be able to live in a more cosmopolitan center and be more independent. Perhaps London rather than Paris... In London she would not feel any social difference, would be received anywhere and might even find a good marriage...

After some weeks, the castle of Baron Moritz von Hirsch auf Gereuth was in an atmosphere of moving. Definitely, they were closing Planegg.

Clara chose the furniture to be dispatched. Her standing desk, in her possession since her childhood in Brussels, the canvases that she and the baron had bought during all their years together, two large rugs from Constantinople, a gift from the Grand Vizier. Pieces from her trousseau, her porcelain, crystal, and silverware from the house.

There were so many houses to furnish; they could ship it to Rue de l'Élysée or part to Beauregard. Or even to Saint Johann where the hunting lodge was, or Eychorn, where it would be nearer Planegg, on the Austro-Hungarian border.

Something for the house in Berkeley Square, which was part of her inheritance, or the Baron's new mansion in Piccadilly... The Bath House. But it was for the pieces at Planegg that had come from her dowry that Clara felt the greatest attachment.

The Baron chose his table, a grand piece carved by Jacob Desmalter in 1850; his chairs with the family coat of arms; and the ebony-and-crystal clock with figurines of nymphs acquired in Paris directly from the mansion of Balthazar Lieutaud.

Maurice had a genuine passion for that clock. Sitting over the fireplace, it was always the focal point of his conversation. When he needed to reflect or catch his breath during a discussion, he would leave the table and go straight to the dancing nymphs, caress them, and then use his index finger to move the clock's gilded hands ahead a few minutes.

They asked Michaela to choose what she would like to take.

"Take where?" she asked Helga, confused.

"We don't know. The baron is making a list of what will be packed," she replied, whispering. "No doubt they're going to establish themselves in London, at the baroness's home in Berkeley Square, close to one of their banking houses. "You know, Micha, her family's businesses. Bischoffsheim & Goldschmidt Bank," she said. "But the baroness surely won't stay there all the time; she'll probably look for a place with a more pleasant climate during the winter. London is horrible, girl!" She went on grumbling: "Horrible... Damp, foggy...You'll see... You're going to detest England ..."

Michaela didn't ask Helga anything further. She didn't want the housekeeper to think that up to that moment she had been told nothing about what was to become of her in that change of residence.

The Baron had spent the last few days ensconced in the library, working until late at night. Clara was helping him, separating documents, papers, and portfolios into towering piles. During the day there was a lengthy agenda to be taken care of.

Entire families of poorly dressed peasants, small merchants, refugees from Russian pogroms came into the Baron's house speaking softly, with long beards and black hats, dark and threadbare overcoats, dragging dusty trunks.

And from there, without a sound, they descended to the hunting pavilion, into the special galley, as the basement of the house was known, where a kitchen operated daily. The baroness provided a hot bath, clean clothes, and meals for all.

The person in charge of the kitchen was a woman who had fled the Czar's pogroms and who, because she had no family or anywhere to live, had stayed on with the Hirsches. She did the cooking and cheered the children by singing old Yiddish songs from her childhood. She prepared borscht, a soup made from beets and sour cream; *simis*, a stew of sweet carrots; and *latkes*, grated potato balls. The samovar always held water for tea, and there was a large basket of honey cookies.

In fall and winter, because of the cold and snow, the shoes and boots of the penniless wanderers were cleaned and hung over fireplaces. Yosef, an aged cobbler, a poor man who had seen his family burned alive by the Czar's men, was now among those under the Hirsches' protection. He lived in the hunting pavilion and was called upon to repair the shoes of those peculiar visitors. The old shoemaker would hum his favourite song in Yiddish while the guests waited with shoes or boots in their hands. He would hammer the tacks, apply polish, and nod to the rhythm of the music, making everything shine again.

"Wear them in health… Shalom..A good journey," he would say as he handed over an almost new shoe.

"Be happy in America! "

"America... the promised land!"

Michaela was accustomed to seeing groups of refugees sleeping in the improvised beds in the hunting pavilion. They were all in transit, frightened, terrified. And with a dream to be realized, that of emigrating to America.

The Baron provided documents, tickets, money, and directed each of the groups to a city, a town, a farm—and all were going to America. Far away from the massacres, the oppression, to a safe place distant from persecution and abuse. He filled ships, buying the freedom of each of them, paying for the transport, security, and installation of the groups in strange and faraway lands..

Part of his profit from banks, from his stocks, his railroads was intended for poor and persecuted Jews.

Michaela had learned this from him: in life, money is useful for helping those in need. And with Clara she had seen love for one's fellow man. Many nights she had witnessed the baroness cross the grounds in the snowfall to make certain their guests were comfortable, whether there was enough wood for the fireplaces, covering the elderly and the children with blankets.

Affection for those completely unknown people who after a few days would depart, never to return or have a chance to offer their thanks.

Clara wanted neither thanks nor goodbyes. That was the other side of the Hirsches of which few in Bavaria were aware, as they had no knowledge of the special kitchen for the needy. It was another world, one which Mirla, the overseer of the pavilion, blessed with her small happy eyes and her calloused hands, lighting the fire and cooking every meal in accordance with Jewish precepts.

Michaela moved easily from one group of visitors to another. One group was the Orthodox Jews who lived their religion, Talmudic Judaism, and because of this had no rights in the lands of the Czar and were stoned, terrorized, robbed and plundered by their own neighbors; these people had to be rescued from that endless nightmare. Another group was those who knocked at the Planegg door seeking funds for their reforms. They were the new philosophers and intellectuals whom Mirla called *schnorrers*, professional Jewish beggars who lived off richer Jews. They were glib, intellectual, always promising to repay the "loan" as soon as their books, articles, or ideas were published

One day she heard that many of those intellectuals, when they attained notice or position, were ashamed of their origins. As Heine had become the genius of German literature, but with outsized ambition and as a literary progressive, he formed with a philosopher named Marx and others a school of Jewish thinkers who were at the same time anti-Semitic.

"You can never trust those high-born, discontent young men who speak eruditely but have heads full of shit," said the baron at the table, commenting on some interview by a *schnorrer.*

"They think I'm going to support these false secular intellectuals who spend their time in that 'I am, but I'm not' ambiguity! If they had learned to do something, they'd be more useful and would save us a lot of problems. They were always careerists on the way to baptism! They leave here with their pockets full of money and go on to philosophize and write poems, dogmas, publish articles in newspapers filled with hate and venomous attacks against not only enemies but also against the very friends who helped them achieve a position! And do you know for what?" he asked, incredulously.

"Just to please French intellectuals by saying what they want to hear. Those clichés like 'Religion is the opiate of the spirit.' No! How does it go? Ah… *Die Religion … Sie ist das Opium des Volkes …* 'The opiate of the masses,'" said the Baron, correcting himself, his eyes shot through with rage.

"And they…those *schnorres* ..they write ,all those *faux* Jewish called intellectuals, oblivious to the danger such thoughts cause us! They speak of work without ever having set foot in a factory."

Among the groups that visited Maurice de Hirsch were those received for purposes of business. And the baron would issue an alert: "Today we're hosting authorities, so treat them with diplomacy and a degree of pomp." There were also men who spoke different languages, wore strange red hats and entered in groups, spending many hours opening large spreadsheets and plans on the enormous table in the mirror room.

On one of these visits it was Michaela who served tea.

This must be something special! A round silver tray, crystal teapot and cups, and the serving ritual: raise the spout of the teapot above chest level and let the hot liquid foam into the cup.

"That way the spearmint tea keeps its aroma and remains light," explained Helga, her coat over her arm as she was leaving for her free day. "Oh," she continued, "don't forget the walnut scones. They especially like those!"

They're very important visitors, Clara had warned the night before.

A group of lawyers, engineers, and bankers was there to renew with Baron Hirsch contracts for concessions of the new railway. In the group, which came from Constantinople, were the counsellor and representative of the grand-vizier, Mehmed Said Pasha.

Michaela was charged with serving tea to those gentlemen, freeing time for the baron, who was engaged in the library with a group of bankers from Vienna sent by Emperor Franz Josef himself.

The Sicilian had learned how to please the Ottomans by serving tea in the Turkish manner. She prepared each steaming cup with the spout of the pot very hot and delicately served each guest in turn. But as she served the next-to-last visitor, she was startled to see that the hands that received that cup were identical to her father's. When she raised her eyes, her own hands shook before the man, who also had the same features, the same eyes, the same profile, the same frame... The cup fell to the floor.

Panicked, she kneeled, trying to pick up the pieces and dry the hot liquid on the carpet. The man, bending down at the same time, took her hands and gently asked her not to worry about the incident.

At that moment, the doors to the room opened and everyone rose to greet the baron.

Michaela, still on her knees, remained paralyzed, expecting a reproving look. She heard the introduction by Count Frederick:

"Sir, I introduce you to the great attorney Maître Grassi and his assistant David Varsano, who came directly from Constantinople as soon as they became aware of your call."

Michaela, behind the chairs, felt her heart race... David Varsano, David Varsano! Had she heard correctly?

David Varsano is his name, she thought; then that man who resembled her father, who had the same eyes and hands, was her uncle David!

The baron continued listening to the presentations of the delegation until he suddenly noticed something different in the room. He approached Michaela, who was holding the broken shards in her hand.

"Micha," he said affectionately, "leave it, please! Where's Helga? She can take care of the tea. It's not your job," he said, speaking softly. "Excuse me, gentlemen," he said, "I forgot to introduce *Signorina* Varsano, our guest and friend..." As soon as he spoke the last sentence, it struck him and, turning to David, he asked, "You told me your name, forgive me, but I didn't hear it very well!"

"Varsano," replied the lawyer, smiling. "My name is David Varsano."

"David Varsano from Venice?" asked Michaela, her voice caught in her throat.

"Yes, *Signorina*," he answered, turning to her almost incredulously. "Have you heard of me?"

"Yes, sir. Your name, David Varsano, I... I've heard of you, I've known of you for a long time... My father is Alberto Varsano from Venice!"

The Baron was confused by the conversation, not fully understanding Michaela´s speaking almost intimately with a stranger.

Maurice extended his arm to help Michaela up and whispered, "Then you two know each other?"

Micha smiled at David.

"He's my uncle David, about whom my father has always spoken! It has to be him, I recognized him as soon as I saw him... He looks just like my father!"

David Varsano had met his niece even before dreaming of a reunion with his brother. That night, all the visitors in the Constantinople delegation returned to the hotel, except for David. Clara de Hirsch insisted he stay there, in the family wing, more specifically in the room belonging to their son Lucien.

After dinner, Clara discreetly told David what had happened to Alberto in Taormina. She also related how Anna had asked her to keep certain details secret, to spare Michaela worry. She knew only that business there was not going well and that he was going to Salonica to start over.

"Good heavens," exclaimed David after listening to the Baroness. "My poor brother... And I wasn't there to receive him... Salem must be going crazy trying to let me know..."

The next morning, he would ask the baron's secretary to send the telegram he had written to his office colleague.

*Salem take good care Alberto — we are in Bavaria.*
*Meeting Hirsch — return 28th*
*Signed, D. Varsano.*

It snowed heavily that night, and David's heart pounded from the emotion of the reunion. Lying in the large four-poster bed, he was unable to sleep. He looked at the bedroom walls lined with colored damask silk, a room filled with furniture painted a delicate blue. It was beyond a doubt a most beautiful place to sleep, but he couldn't manage to close his eyes. He stared at a canvas in front of his bed but was unable to discern it very well. He turned up the lamp and leaped out of bed, startled. It was a view of Venice.

He went to it, the lamp in his hand, as if doubting what was plainly there before him. He read the signature: "W. Turner."

What an incredible coincidence, he thought. It's the same Englishman I met in Venice. Turner... It really was he, the man who spent weeks sitting on the *Nera* wall of the Grand Canal, the one who traded one of his watercolours for a pen and inkwell from my tray! That had happened many, many years ago...

David fell asleep, remembering the movement of the skilled hands of the Englishman, who had used the inkwell to mix a white watercolour pastille with a little salt water, and as if by magic, using that mixture, had detailed the sky and the lapis-lazuli shadows, the transparencies, the railings, the windows, and the clouds reflected in the Canal.

As if by magic, under the curious eye of the young peddler, that English gentleman named Turner had brought to life that landscape of dreams.

❧

# XII

## *VIA  EGNATIA*

Salonica, December 1883.

Alberto loved Venice... It was impossible to forget it.

Salonica was not what a Venetian would call a beautiful city. But for a foreigner like him it held a special magnetism, an amalgam of dignity and strength, human misery and sensitivity. The races and languages, the creeds and customs, a history so scarred by time—all of it visible in the faces of the inhabitants. Salonica was like a book written and rewritten each day.

It had been a palimpsest for Greeks, later for Romans, Byzantines, Crusaders, Venetians, Ottomans—in a word, all those who in different centuries marched over the same stones of the Via Egnatia and left there a little of their soul, riches, principles, beliefs, and blood.

That same Via Egnatia, which the Turks called *Zadé Yol*, had witnessed Philip of Macedonia and his son Alexander the Great, as well as storms, earthquakes, fires, bravery and pageantry, massacres and festivals.

And it was on those same stones that Alberto trod that December day in 1883, the sun shining despite the cold wind of winter. That day the markets had closed early. There was a tacit truce among the three religions, and the city seemed like an immense kitchen. In each neighborhood wafted a different aroma.

Dottore Varsano left to look for the home of Levy, the shoemaker from Taormina, his father-in-law's best friend. Raffaele insisted on some news of him and had already written three letters reminding him.

"Have you found my friend Levy?" With the markets closed, this was the perfect time to locate him. The address was the Great Talmud Torah synagogue, on the right-hand side of the main port. It shouldn't be too difficult; eventually, all roads lead to Rome, Alberto thought, taking heart.

He left the Quartier Consulaire like an explorer without a map or destination, venturing into unfamiliar neighbourhoods and streets. He traversed the whole of the Syndrivani, bordering the sea, where Greeks in their best clothes were returning from family celebrations. He crossed Sabri Pasha Street, jammed with fruit vendors, trays of steaming sweets, and children playing with wooden Hanukkah dreidels. And from there, entered the Turkish blocks.

In his short time in the city he had learned the areas were divided. Salem had shown him on a map of the city. There were Turkish residences in several parts of Salonica, always in neighbourhoods removed from the center, in *Kuçük Selianik* or Little Salonica, also called *Yedi Kulê*; near the gates of Cassandra; in the extensive *Kalamaria* area; near Vardar in the eastern part of *Kulê Café*; and above the region of the tanners and dyers.

The homes of the Ottomans had two stories and a balcony, jutting out and covered by a trellis, as well as large windows. Muslim women, protected from the gaze of others, peeked through the trellises. Ottoman houses were easily identified by the religious motifs, painted red with the lower portion in black, to ward off evil spirits. At each corner, under the overhang of the roof, was inscribed at verse from the Qur'an in gold letters.

The properties of the *bëy*s, the rich, were called *bëhcimar*, with abundant orchards and domestic animals. The Turks esteemed flower gardens, the *gülbahceler*, cultivated with pride and visited by neighbors on holidays.

There were cypresses... The Turks admired the dignity and bearing of the cypress as much as did Sicilians, a fact that had not escaped Alberto when he described the city to Anna.

Night was falling when he found Levy's house. He almost doubted it was the right place. From the door, it looked like a cafe, packed with people sitting on benches, chatting, smoking hookahs, playing backgammon, the women separated on the opposite sidewalk, and in the center, near a plane tree, a musical group.

A violinist and three women were playing tambourines, singing, and dancing *chalghidjis*: the music of Jewish festivities. Alberto saw a bride, in a lace mantilla, in a circle of women, dancing with a twisted handkerchief in her hands.

And everyone sang in unison in Ladino:
*"Buona la Tagnedera..."*

Other women served trays of pita bread and steaming tortes. Two boys dressed in gray robes and carrying copper platters, offered coffee to the guests. Alberto looked for Saul Yakov Levy, the shoemaker.

Levy was just as Raffaele had described him: a long, thin face, blue eyes, aquiline nose, and a slight humpback. His sparse white beard came to a point.

The pharmacist identified himself and the cobbler moved, began to cry.

"God sent you," the old man said in a hoarse voice. "Yesterday, at the Sicilia Hadash synagogue, I prayed for Raffaele and all his family, that they might know as great a happiness as I am having with the wedding of my Nathan! And just look who God sent us! Come in, *signor* Varsano, and let's toast my old friend Raffaele and my little Anna!"

Levy introduced Alberto to the guests.

"This is Saul Moise Molhou, this is Yehuda Matarasso, here, David Abravanel and his son-in-law Yakov Avram Botton, our friends from Vardar, and this is *Dottore* Alberto Varsano, the pharmacist from Venice, son-in-law of my best friend Raffaele Cohen. I know a lot about you," said Levy, smiling at Alberto, who had become the great attraction of the party. "Gentlemen, a toast to the bride and groom! And to our new friend in Salonica, *Dottore* Alberto Varsano, the most famous man in Italian pharmacies!"

Alberto was introduced to the merchants of the Aun Kapani market present there.

"This is Nissim Abravanel, in dried fruits, Yeshua Carasso and David Solomon, in hides, Mordochai Benveniste, who works with tobacco, Judah Rousso, who sells the best essences and oils, and here is our famous Rafael Bendavid, in cereals... And this gentleman is the son-in-law of my best friend in Sicily," he repeated.

"The *Dottore* is a famous pharmacist from Venice and soon he'll be opening his pharmacy here, in our beautiful and prosperous city..."

Alberto sensed everyone looking at him as they toasted, and suddenly his cheeks felt on fire. In a second, there came to mind what had happened to him in Taormina and his actual situation. And everything said about him seemed so strange that he had the sensation of having told a huge lie.

He was sweating, despite the cold. Embarrassed and ashamed, he didn't know how to answer so many curious questions about his work.

The musical group was still playing when the full moon appeared and illuminated the circle where the bride and groom were dancing. But the attraction of the party seemed to be Alberto. Many approached to offer advice about how and where he should establish himself.

Bendavid, in cereals, was discussing the matter with Rousso:

"I think the best thing would be for him to visit Angel's pharmacy."

"Have you been there?" Rousso asked Alberto, who shook his head. "It would be worth your while to see it. It's the best pharmacy in the city, and two years ago the owner, Maïr Angel, brought a fantastic formula from Italy, a salve for eczema and got rich off it! It can only be called miraculous. It became famous for having cured the sultan's skin sores. I furnish walnut oil to him."

Alberto felt his heart race and his mouth go dry.

Tomorrow, very early, he told himself, I'm going to meet this famous Angel.

In Maïr Angel's *droguerie*, the busiest in Salonica, a poster advertised the properties of *Pommade de Milan*, an excellent product for treatment of chronic eczema.

Alberto planned to spend up to ten Turkish liras to analyze its formula, but that wasn't necessary... The touch, the color, the smell of tar and verbena identified the formula, which he had tested for close to fifteen years of his life, perfecting it, monitoring its use with every sick person, and it had been sold, perhaps copied, stolen!

Nothing the *Pharmacopoeia Internationalis* had published since 1865 in its compendiums and translations was unfamiliar to him. That was his formula.

"*Ladri*," he said under his breath, leaving the jar on the counter.

"Monsieur," asked the clerk, with a worried expression, "is this not the Pommade de Milan that you requested?"

"No... Thank you... I– Actually, I was looking for a Sicilian salve."

Almost to the door, he had second thoughts and went back to the counter.

"Do you fill prescriptions?"

"Yes, sir, we have them ready in three days."

Alberto took paper from the counter and a pen and, writing with flourishes, prescribed the salve for himself:

*Sig. Alberto Varsano*
*Rue Longeant le Quai, 23 – Thessaloniki, Ottoman Empire*

*Tintura di iodo–grami 10*   *Verbena–grammi 8*
*Acido salicilico–kgr 18*   *Ossido di zinco–grammi 6*
*Fiori di golfo–grammi 1*   *Vasellina–grammi 20*
*Catrame–grammi 5*
*S.W.E.*

He fanned the sheet with the wet ink and handed it to the clerk, speechless at seeing for the first time a customer write a prescription.

"Are you a doctor?" he asked from curiosity.

"*Sì*," Alberto replied, smiling at the young man. *Or I once was*, he thought about saying.

He left the pharmacy, promising to return for the medicine the following Wednesday

That afternoon he wandered the streets. He still had a few coins in his pockets to spend; the rest were safely hidden in the leather bag in David's room. He sat in a café crowded with men talking, arguing, playing backgammon, smoking hookahs, Turks on one side, Greeks on the other, Jews speaking Ladino, Italian, and French. The Greeks were the majority. They discussed business, drank spearmint tea or coffee, bought sunflower seeds or salted chickpeas, spending hours that way. Everyone respected one another, and the rule was cordiality and mutual good manners.

Salem had told Alberto a bit of history and local customs With so much mingling of races and creeds, it was best to explain to a foreigner what was good or bad in each situation he might encounter. This was a world apart, with customs coming from the Byzantines, the Greeks, who feared the Ottomans, dominant since 1453. Everyone still felt the terror of someday experiencing again the horrors and brutality committed in the name of the Ottoman Empire, as had happened in 1821, in the most recent uprising for Greek independence; thousands, including women and children, were punished in a manner so cruel and inhuman, at the order of then governor Yusef Bëy, that many of the Turks themselves, disgusted by the massacres, questioned whether the orders really came from the sultan. Whether killing innocents, gouging out their eyes, severing hands, feet, and ears, cutting off young boys' genitals were acts approved by Allah

Since then, the empire had decided to be more circumspect and avoid political issues in order to escape censure by the sultanate's creditor nations. It had become necessary to put an end to slaughter, thus calming the suspicion of the European governments that financed the magnificent works of Abdül Aziz.

The sultanate and the Ottoman Empire had nowhere else from which to borrow; the loans were coming due and they already owed English and French banks the "modest" sum of two hundred million pounds sterling.

Nearly all of Greece had been independent since 1821, except Salonica and Macedonia. It was a whim of the sultan. Everyone knew it was only a matter of time. The Greeks would never give up. During all those centuries they had never forgotten their own language, preserving the same way of life from the Byzantine era, the same songs, the same faith, despite prohibitions and persecutions; for them everything was just a question of time.

The Greek families used their homes as a refuge and opened their doors only on festival days, Christmas, Easter, and on their namesake saint's day. The Greek portion of the city held intellectuals, musicians, doctors, professors, judges, lawyers, merchants, and industrialists, but the great majority consisted of groups of artisans who, remaining united, succeeded in growing in partnership and developing new artisans.

The women took care of their homes, would go out to church on Sundays and, like the Turkish women, the more attractive young females would cover their faces with a *yashmak*, a veil white as gauze that covered part of the face, hiding it for fear of being kidnapped or raped.

Also, they never wore green or red, so as not to draw the attention of the Muslims, for those colours were sacred to the Turks.

Alberto felt great sympathy for the Greeks. They made a point of making themselves understood. They spoke every language and were playful and good-humoured. They would whistle, imitate the singsong intonation of the Jews' accent and form jocular sentences in the mixture of languages they spoke. A word in French, others in Ladino. Italian, Greek.. Deep down, they even seemed like brothers of the Sicilians, he thought.

*"Bonjour Yako... donde vas a ir?... Ciao, Ade Yassu!"*

Alberto laughed when he heard these words. He looked at the men who were speaking. They nodded, and one of them observed:

"That is Salonica Monsieur… we are a mixture, a Babylonia, but we love our city! What about you?"

Standing up, Alberto left a coin for his coffee, put on his Ottoman hat and smiled at the young men.

"Someday I'll understand everything you are saying, and that is when I'll begin to love this city!"

After a delay, David Varsano, the great lawyer in Grassi's office, would arrive from Bavaria on Wednesday. That was the message Salem had left with the landlady, Marika Karakassos. By all indications the delay was because of a snowstorm that clogged the rails to the north of Graz. Frequent avalanches and accidents occurred at that time of year, he had explained to Marika. But he would not be delayed by more than a day; Salem would come to fetch Alberto and they would go to the station the following day.

"A good man, Salem," commented the widow, "a perfect gentleman, intelligent and dedicated."

Alberto agreed. He admired Salem, who seemed to possess integrity, elegance and breeding rare in men of his age, he thought

That morning, Alberto awoke startled. He suddenly realized that David's room, which he had occupied all that time, was in total disarray.

The wooden floor had dust in its cracks and the rug hadn't been beaten in a long time. The iron bed against the wall was unmade, and the sheets were very worn. On the table, the remains of fruit and food the landlady had been offering him.

From the shutter of the front window hung a cord with Alberto's shirts, and his trunks blocked the other corner of the room. The books that Alberto had taken from his brother's armoire were still on the couch, and on the floor, a stack of folded quilts served to support the rest of his clothes.

He didn't know where to start, what to straighten up first. He would need the landlady's help.

Marika was Greek, the widow of a certain *Capitán* Pantellis.

In her youth she must have been a beautiful woman; she had strong features, thick eyebrows still black, and an expressive gaze.

She lived in that house, a large two-story structure beside the sea, always dressed in black with a veil covering her hair and a Byzantine cross around her neck. She must be around sixty. She moved with some difficulty climbing and descending the stairs. Spending the day on duties downstairs, discussing and giving orders to Cassandra, preparing the meals, she would go upstairs to the large parlour only at nightfall.

One day Marika was surprised to hear a noise coming from David's quarters, and, knowing he was travelling, went at once to see who the guest was.

That was how they met. She invited him into the parlour after recognizing him as the brother of David Varsano, her lodger.

Alberto learned that she was the landlady, that the room was paid until the end of December, and that when his brother was in town she provided the evening meal and took care of his clothes.

Cleaning was the responsibility of Cassandra, an old woman with ravaged hands who lived in the rear on the ground floor and took care of the residents. When the landlady wasn't around, she would stay in her tiny room, scratching her lice-infested head and singing Byzantine songs in a shrill voice.

Those cold, humid days, Mrs. Karakassos had advised her guests that Cassandra was sick with a high fever and cough. That night, Alberto could no longer stand the poor woman's incessant coughing. He knocked at Marika's door and asked for the keys to the rear.

Cassandra, burning with fever, was clutching an icon. "It's *Hagios Nikolaos*, St. Nicholas, the saint of her devotion," Marika explained to Alberto. "She is very devout. He saved her from the Turks, from at least three of the Evil One's massacres. And will save her again... I'm sure of it."

Alberto dashed upstairs and opened his pharmacy trunk.

He brushed iodine on her back and made compresses with alcohol. The landlady brought towels, wrapping the old woman's body, which trembled from the cold.

That continued well into the night. Marika, sitting in one corner, observed the foreigner, almost a stranger, who affectionately took care of a poor old woman ready to commend her soul to God. She prayed...

Cassandra spent the night holding onto the hands of the pharmacist, her eyes half-closed, exhausted, her cheeks sunken and her brow damp. At dawn, a ray of light fell directly on her face. She squeezed Alberto's hand and said in a soft voice:

"You look like Him! Thank you, sir," and continued in Greek, "*Efharistó Kyrie mou*. Thank you, O my Lord."

Alberto's gaze met the light-colored eyes of St. Nicholas, the icon on the old woman's chest.

The icon's eyes stared at the pharmacist, and at that moment, smiled at him.

The train station was located in the eastern part of the city, next to the Vardar port. Alberto kept pace with Salem's lengthy strides, walking beside him and listening to his comments and stories about the buildings and squares they passed.

When they got to Syndrivani Square, the lawyer paused and took his watch from his vest. It would be best to use the new *tram à cheval* to arrive on time for the trains from Vardar, he said.

"It will be a new experience for us!"

A comical situation arose during the men's wait at the arrival and departure point of the city's new means of transportation. In front of the Café Menelaos a crowd was observing the approach of the horse-drawn carriage as it drew near, making a loud din.

A group of nomad Turks positioned themselves in front of the pedestrians, shouting: "*Dür burda sejtan araba geliyor!* Get out of the way, the devil's carriage is coming!"

From the waterfront avenue came the sound of the driver blowing his cornet to warn that the tram was passing. The passengers from the stop at the café climbed into the large coach, among them Salem and Alberto.

And it was that way along the entire route, from Syndrivani Square, traversing Egnatia, to the Vardar Gate.

Alberto had no idea how long it had been since he had smiled or laughed out loud so much. He repeated to himself the refrain of the Turks in the street: *"Dür burda geliyor… Dür burda geliyor!"*

"What a strange and funny city this is," he commented to Salem. He was already speaking even Turkish!

The train bringing David from Bavaria linked Salonica to Mitrovica. Considered a great work of engineering, it followed the Axios River, entering the mountains of Bosnia in a run of more than 360 kilometres. The work of Baron Hirsch himself, the rail line was a prize for Salonica, making it possible for the merchants of the city to reach Venice in three days, or Paris in four.

From Salonica, the Baron's works extended in a maze of lines, passing through Alexandroupolis and tremendously impacting commercial, political, and financial relations between the Ottoman Empire and Europe. The city celebrated the arrival of a train from the other side of the world, bringing new things, important people who dressed differently, with unfamiliar customs. With them came newspapers, books, boxes with riches of all kinds, cloths, foodstuffs, and other items destined for the new consumers, who bought as if in Paris, having ordered by mail through catalogs.

However, all of it was intended for only a small portion of the population, mostly Jewish bankers, builders, industrialists, and businessmen, and many of them lined up beside the platform, accompanied by their servants and a few *hamalitos*, waiting to claim their orders.

Alberto craned his neck to see over people in an effort to catch sight of his brother leaving the train, but hundreds around him were trying to do the same. Men in brown uniforms coming from the Balkans, the Turkish militia with red fezzes on their heads, checking documents, crying children, people hugging one another, other asking for information.

Salem, impassive, put his hand on Alberto's shoulder for him to stay calm and come down from his tiptoes. David, who was accompanying the delegation of counsellor Said Salim Pasha and the lawyer Grassi, would only descend from the special car when the station was nearly deserted.

It was David who recognized Alberto and called out to him. He knew his brother would be at Salem's side and, at that moment, understood why Michaela had been startled upon seeing him at the baron's home. Physically, they were one and the same. David was Alberto a few years younger. Nevertheless, side by side they became identical. The same physique, the same height, the same eyes, and the same expression—the sole difference the pharmacist's greying hair.

David's room was already lit when the two arrived with the luggage.

As if by magic, everything was in order.

The two beds were covered with snowy white sheets under sheepskin blankets. The table that had always been against the wall was in the center of the room, set with dishes and silverware, and the small coal-fed heater warmed a pot containing a fragrant white-bean soup.

The brothers embraced vigorously, shared a piece of bread and toasted with the remainder of wine in the last cask of the widow Karakassos.

There was much to talk about that night!

# XIII

# MORETTAS AND BAUTTAS

*"Black masks and White masks"*

Taormina, winter 1883.

After writing to Clara de Hirsch, Anna felt relieved. She spoke of her husband's disappointment, his leaving Taormina, and even her recent dream. Or her nightmare? She wanted to do something to offset Alberto's disappointment, and she would fight and work day and night before leaving to be with him. The tourist season was about to begin, and she wanted to take advantage of the opportunity. To do so, she would need material.

Anna journeyed to Messina to buy the best weaves of velvet, silk, satin, needles and thread; she also looked for a cobbler who made velvet shoes. Afterward she knocked at a house asking for one Munaò, an artist who made flowers of silk and brocade. He had a delicate air and a very genteel voice, and in talking to Anna demonstrated great sensitivity and good humour. He gave her ideas, spoke of colours, needlework, and showed her how to starch and dye lace. They became friends.

Munaò was not in a hurry; while he chatted and showed Anna the secrets and delicacy of the fripperies, he prepared a bowl of fresh bean soup for his new customer. Sitting at the kitchen table, Anna observed Munaò as he simultaneously cooked in one pan and dyed materials in another. Even near the stove, with all that wood burning, she shivered from cold in her old cloak. It didn't do justice to her, he remarked later, and in Messina would be worn only by impoverished olive pickers.

"Buy an alpaca one and line it with sheepskin," the artist advised her as she was leaving. "You're a *bella donna*, you have to take advantage of your fame in Taormina and go around like a countess!"

It was night when Anna ascended to Mongibello, in a coach loaded with rolls of cloth and even iron mannequins covered with oakum and cotton, identical to those she had seen in the baroness's magazines. And boxes, many containing waistbands and corsets, boas and feathers. She was happy. Calmly, she thought of the many things she could do with all that. It was a beginning; it would be her new life, her catharsis, her revenge. And she found herself smiling, beside the cart driver.

She had spent a fortune in Messina; half the amount the countess had sent Raffaele in the envelope. But she felt no guilt, only confidence in herself and enormous strength. Her mind was teeming with ideas. And she owed that wonderful sensation to her father!

When, one late November night, Anna told old Raffaele about that strange dream, he saw that she was ready. Anna would succeed but lacked the money to begin. That day, Raffaele handed her an envelope embossed with a coat of arms.

"Anna, do you remember the day that German count showed up at the shop with a box from the baroness?"

"Of course," she said. "It was the same day everything happened to Alberto at the pharmacy."

"And do you remember the envelope he handed you, addressed to *Signor* Cohen?" the old man asked with an impish smile.

"Do I remember? Absolutely, not! You made such a secret of it that it seemed like a case of a man in love," she said, laughing.

"Enough of that, Anna! You find it odd that a Baroness also writes to your father? I understood the letter completely because she writes in our language, even better than you! How self-centred you are! Could no one have the slightest special consideration for an old jeweller?"

"That is not exactly what I said, Pappá," she replied, caressing the old man's head. "I just didn't understand what reason the Baroness could have sent you a letter, so privately... Is it by any chance some secret?"

"It was– Well, do you remember the small velvet box that I gave Michaela before she left for Bavaria? And how curious you were to see what was inside? Remember?"

Anna made the moue of disdain that Raffaele knew so well. Since she was little, whenever she was dying of curiosity to know something that was secret and she felt left out, she would take a deep breath and turn up her nose, lifting her eyes to the ceiling.
The mere gesture, after so many years, brought back to her aged father old memories, of little Anna roaming indomitably about the ruins of the Greek Theater, her legs scratched by thorns, her hidden report cards, the proscribed novels that she had read... The day her clothes had been stained with blood and she had been forbidden to play in the *Giardino*, and afterward... She had become a woman, an adult, there was no more discord, no secrets to keep; just the opposite, it was she who taught, who told him everything...

"I've wanted to tell you about it for a long time," he said.

"That day when you began measuring the green taffeta for a party dress for Michaela I realized my granddaughter was a young lady, and that I had never made a jewel for her. I was still seeing the little girl, and not a young woman who would leave Mongibello for school, then go to work at the Bongiovannis' atelier, and... *finito*... Thinking about it, I had never given her anything... She never even had a grandmother to spoil her a little... We didn't give her anything, Anna," he continued, his eyes welling with tears.

"Think about it, daughter, what were her dreams? She never told us... She was always smiling, washing all those tubs of clothes, humming in the kitchen. And happy! So different from the girls who come into the jewellery shop with their mothers, always demanding, liking nothing or wanting everything! They leave with a disdainful expression after having torn out their mother's heart and a fistful of liras in exchange for a simple nod of the head... And repay it with a counterfeit smile. I feel like— Well, I'm not their father!"

"Yes... So, Pappá... You were talking about the green fabric," Anna insisted, interrupting the old man's reverie. "Go on!"

"Well... The day of the dress, I went to the shop and started to show a necklace. I was imagining how to match the dress with the necklace, the way you were always explaining to me. Remember? If the dress is low-cut, the stones are larger, highlighting the neckline, if the cut is high—"

"And then... what happened?" she asked impatiently.

"I looked in our safe for stones I could use. There was almost nothing that would do... Some amber strands, too dark for the green dress... Pearls... they wouldn't go with it either... Some crystal teardrops... what was left over from *Signora* Paternò's necklace... Very heavy for such a delicate neck... And the diamond from your grandmother's ring... But nothing really matched... The next night, when you were asleep, I stole a piece of the green fabric and the following day went to see Pistelli, that cross-eyed man who used to furnish stones to Caruso, remember him?"

"Yes, and then?"

"I gave him the piece of material and asked if he could look for citrines, four turns cut into rectangles, all identical, in that hue..."

"And...? Did he find them?"

"I was almost certain that Caruso had something similar in his safe. And everything turned out almost exactly as I desired. Each strand was sized from largest to smallest. I mounted the four strands by switching the position of the stones and forming in the middle a cabochon in the shape of a flower, using the large stones and placing the diamond from your grandmother's ring in the center."

"But, Pappá, you never showed it to me? It must have been lovely!"

"I can tell you it was a *capolavoro*, perhaps the best piece I've ever done, worthy of a princess!"

"Now explain the connection between the baroness's letter and the story about the dress and the necklace! I don't understand the connection!"she said to tease her father, who had been romanticizing facts lately.

"To tell the truth, daughter, I didn't fully understand the letter. I also did not understand the pile of money the count, that tall man, handed me days later in the shop," Anna's father answered, taking from the pocket of his vest a wrinkled envelope whose coat of arms was very familiar to her. And he placed in her lap a wooden box containing hundreds of coins gleaming like gold! "Read this," he said, opening the letter with shaky hands. "Read it aloud so I can understand..."

Anna cleared her throat, raising her voice to read the baroness's letter.

*To signor Raffaele Cohen:*

*When I saw your granddaughter Michaela wearing that magnificent necklace, and when I learned it was a creation of her grandfather, I could not refrain from telling you that your hands are blessed.*
*For only artists like you have the sensitivity to create beautiful things and give people joy. And this gift that I'm sending you by way of the bearer is merely an incentive for you to always go on working with inspiration. It's 365 pounds sterling, one for each day of the New Year.*
*Shaná Tová.*
*Signed, Baroness Clara de Hirsch.*

᧞

Anna Varsano worked day and night during the entire month of December 1884 on that mountain of materials and gold. She hired Giovanna Catanzaro, her next door neighbour, who had worked with the dressmaker Maria di Pietro for years, and with her, came Francesca, her sister Cristina, and three more embroideresses.

The dining room table had been turned into a workbench for cutting cloth, Alberto's laboratory easel was now a support for the fabrics, and the walnut sideboard served to pin up the patterns. The four women would spend the day dressing those lifeless mannequins.

Magnificent pieces of velvet and silk were basted, embroidered, and mounted, and quickly moved to a clothes hanger. From there to a cord that traversed Anna's bedroom from end to end. Before Christmas more than ten dresses were ready, with many more in the last stages of stitching or embroidering.

"These dresses are for the ball at the Teatro Regina Margherita, at the start of Carnevale," Anna told Giovanna. "We ourselves are going to dress the most elegant women at the festival!"

Giovanna couldn't understand why Anna created a model without knowing who was going to wear it. There was no order placed, as with the customers of the dressmaker Di Pietro, or even, she thought, anyone in the city who knew Anna as a dressmaker.

But that hadn't crossed the mind of the *spagnola*. She hadn't thought yet of how she was going to sell them, nor where and how to present them. At the moment, she concentrated only on what to make, imagining a type of woman for each design. She pictured some clients as tall and slim, possibly those English and Austrian aristocrats who were always passing by the door at Mongibello to visit the Greek Theater. She formed in her mind designs in the style of engravings of the Catalan school. Petite women in décolletage with built-in corset allowing part of the bosom to show, and the finishing touch of pearls combined with a medieval beret.

For more robust silhouettes, she used her assistant Francesca as mannequin. She copied an image of Parmigianino from the Church of San Giovanni and dressed the model in sable skirts with horizontal and vertical stitching. There were also designs for very fat women, like *Signora* Paternò, with light skin and full breasts.

For them, she used striped damask reinforced with corset, high-cut neckline, and muslin sleeves, in combination with turbans, in the best style of sultanas depicted in the wonderful Òpra di Pupi. Moreover, for older customers, like *Signora* Carmela, the elegant wife of Mayor Domenico Ballarò, she thought of high collars with starched lace and cameos of colored stones, inspired by engravings of the *Infanta* Isabella of Spain, like those in the book of Sefarad, that she had found in her grandmother's trunk.

She mounted the pieces with collars, appliqués, and the famous *tabarino* capes, much sought-after during Carnevale. "This is turning into a Paris atelier," she said jokingly, winking at Raffaele.

In an old book of Alberto's that described the renowned Carnival of Venice, Anna found the inspiration for more costumes. Using velvet, she designed small black masks: the so-called *morettas*, and also white ones, known as *bauttas*. The hats bought in Pasquale Polizzi's store, the best milliner in Messina, were transformed in the Embroiderers' able hands into pieces identical to the "*perfumers*" of De Longui canvases, the beautiful golden nymphs of the *settecento* school that Alberto so enjoyed admired.

There was so much ready that it would serve fifty clients or more... But where to find them? That was what Anna asked her father. "Certainly not here, at the top of Theater, in Mongibello, Anna! You must go downtown and set up a display window, like those in the baroness's almanacs," he advised.

A few days after the new year, with the city preparing for the invasion of the *forastieri*, the grand duchesses, countesses, baronesses, and all the upper European aristocracy fleeing the cold and coming to Taormina, Anna conducted an experiment.

She closed the jewellery shop for a few days and removed her father's table and tools. Seen like that, empty, the space seemed large and bright. Except that the walls were very dirty and the floor was stained and scratched.

Anna asked Giovanna's husband Angelo Catanzaro, the official painter of the city's churches, for help in improving the space. After a few days, he handed her the key. It was impossible to believe. It looked like a theatrical set. The walls were so velvety they seemed like cloth. The high ceiling had been faux-painted, identical to the vaults of churches: a light-colored sky that gave the impression that the roof of the building was transparent. Alberto's old Venetian mirror hung on the rear wall, reflecting the movement on the street. The floor had been scrubbed and waxed, and the cracks and holes filled with sculptor's cement.

From her house, Anna brought lamps, two chairs, and the dresser, which she covered with a dark-blue tablecloth. Finally, she installed a huge clothesline with iron cables like those used to suspend bells, carefully bolted to the ceiling by *Signor* Catanzaro. The line ran from the left side of the street door to the rear; on the right side, Anna placed her iron mannequins displaying various designs. And the remaining dresses were hung on the clothesline. The clothing floated in a *dégradée* of colours like a rainbow, from garnet red to the lightest shades of pink, from yellow to dark green. In the rear the blues and silvers reflected in the mirror. The marvellous combination left Francesca and Giovanna speechless for a few seconds.
"*Ma chè bello, ma chè splendido,*" they told each other amid smiles and tears of emotion. After all, they were part of it!
Raffaele, when he arrived at the door, stopped. He stood for some minutes observing, raised his head as if wishing to speak with someone in the clouds, and finally murmured something. No doubt he was giving thanks to God; everything there was something to be grateful for, so beautiful that success was sure to come.

And so it did. When Anna installed the mannequin by the door, covered in a hunting outfit with that strange yellow hat where, instead of the expected feathers, there was a stuffed bird with exuberant plumage, it was as if she herself were there, nude, standing in front of the store... The effect was the same.

The first passerby stopped, called to the second, who called the third, and the store was soon packed with the curious and people knocking on the window asking to come in.

Anna and Raffaele would write to Alberto days later about that Sunday afternoon in Taormina.

It was so magical and special, Raffaele wrote, that all the bustle of the Piazza di Sant'Agostino diverted to the little street, to the new Cohen & Varsano Atelier di Moda.

Even the waiters from the Café Zamara came, wanting to see what was going on. The entire city was talking about it; nothing like it had been seen before!

At the opening of the Masked Ball at the Teatro Regina Margherita, her heart racing, Anna could count how many ladies were wearing her costumes and how many gentlemen sported her rich capes. To Raffaele, surely the most exotic and richest clothes there were those made by Anna and constituted the majority at the festivity.

The next morning, she wrote a long letter to Michaela, who reported the success in detail to Clara. Some days after the end of Carnevale, Anna calculated her profits.

"Taking into account November to March and April... it's a fine profit!" she exclaimed as she examined her ledger. And, counting once again a large pile of money, she told her father, "And we still have a few meters of cloth. Now, Pappá, I have just forty days to get ready for Easter! With the schedule of engagements and weddings to prepare for in May and June, I'm going to be doing a great deal of sewing... and afterwards comes summer! Trousseaus for the women tourists! Anjù's guests at the Hotel Timeo... We'll have a lot of work."

Raffaele raised his heavy eyebrows and smiled with only the corner of his mouth. Anna knew that expression, a mixture of concern and disappointment. He never managed to conceal his feelings.

"Have you committed to new orders, daughter?" asked the old man, closing the book. "Don't you have enough already? Can't you see you're becoming poisoned by the idea of success? What will you do when Alberto's next letter arrives asking you to meet him in Salonica?"

Anna turned to her father, her index finger over her lips.

"*Acqua Santa in Bocca*, Pappá! Don't even mention it... I can't think about such things right now... I just hope it doesn't happen so soon!"

And saying this, she left the room like Etna erupting.

Anna asked Giovanna's husband Angelo Catanzaro, the official painter of the city's churches, for help in improving the space. After a few days, he handed her the key. It was impossible to believe. It looked like a theatrical set. The walls were so velvety they seemed like cloth. The high ceiling had been faux-painted, identical to the vaults of churches: a light-colored sky that gave the impression that the roof of the building was transparent. Alberto's old Venetian mirror hung on the rear wall, reflecting the movement on the street. The floor had been scrubbed and waxed, and the cracks and holes filled with sculptor's cement.

# Part II

# XIV

## *AVE SICILIA*

Salonica, February 1884.

Anna Varsano from Taormina became a different woman.

When her letter arrived in Salonica, just after the festivities of Purim, the Hebrew carnival, and all the families were celebrating in their homes, for the first time Alberto was fearful. He read his wife's letter and realized he had never really known his Anna.

She had become a different Anna, a free woman, independent and the master of her desires. The Anna that resided in him, was the one with whom he had always shared a life
Like Persephone, condemned to live in darkness.
But now he thought of his Anna with long black hair, smooth skin tanned by the sun, who perhaps would not return…
Anna the Sicilian and Sicily were a single soul.
On one hand, she was strong like the fusion of amalgam from Etna. She possessed a sacred fire, a light all her own, unafraid of the dark. On the other, she was fragile and delicate. She knew her strength could be short-lived like the sweet pinkish flowers of the walnut trees that covered the valleys of Sicily for only a few days.
Like Persephone, who had emerged from her silence, from her isolation in the depths of the earth, Anna for the first time felt the taste of freedom. And like Persephone when she fled from Hades and his prison, nature had paid homage to her, covering with ephemeral flowers the mountains, the valleys, even the deepest ravines, and Anna smelled the perfume of spring for the first time.
Spring had come to Sicily, and to Salonica as well.
To Alberto, they were two different springs. He remembered Anna and Sicily and felt like a blind man. The sight of Sicily at that time of year was breathtaking, a spectacle described by Theocritus, Homer, and great poets, but Alberto had never paid attention to it.    The beauty and profusion of that spectacle had never touched him before.
Nor had he observed and admired his wife in a different way…

"It's only when we sense the danger of imminent loss that we value what we're losing. Only an idiot wouldn't have seen it earlier," Alberto commented to himself, absorbed. "I never thought of Anna like that, I never valued her strength or even imagined her aspirations... She had a tranquil life, taking care of the house, her father, us, always overflowing with love, always taking care of everything, smiling... I never asked her if she had a dream to pursue, whether I really made her happy... and now that she's by herself, in such a short time she's become the stylist Varsano! A successful woman in Taormina! She opened her own business, something I never managed to do in twenty years!"

David stared at his brother, not believing what he was hearing.

"Are you envious? Envious of your wife's success? I don't understand!"

"Not, not envious... I just can't comprehend what's happening! I feel I'm losing Anna, just as I lost forever the most beautiful sight in the world, the Garden of Hesperides that was always there, right under my nose, and that I never saw..."

David closed his suitcase, pensive, trying to understand the *Dottore*'s unburdening. He barely knew him after so long a separation, and he had never met Anna. But from what he had heard during that time, he admired her.

"You know what I think of all that?" David said after some minutes of silence. "That you should be proud of your wife... You're not losing her, you're gaining! Gaining a new Anna, one you didn't know... And you know what else I think?" he said. "That you sit there feeling sorry for yourself, while your wife goes out into the world to help you. She's not working and making a profit to humiliate you. What she's doing, what she's achieving must be coming from within her soul, because inspiration, creativity, and achievement are divine gifts, a blessing few people have!" David said, pacing about the room.

Alberto didn't reply; he rose from the bed, folded the letter, and, sulkily began to pack his bag.

"I hate seeing my older brother with that defeated look! Having a woman like Anna, who loves you, makes you a winner," David said.

"Think about it... How many women like that could I hope to find in Salonica? Maybe two, possibly three. And all of them would be married, and married well!"

Alberto stopped to think. No one had ever told him that. His brother was right. If he went on feeling that way, he would end up jealous of Anna's success and wanting for her to be condemned to storing away all her energy and drive to succeed.

David lowered the light in the lamp, arranged the cushions on the couch, and lay down.

"Good night, brother," he said softly. "We have a busy day tomorrow, and I'm sure your future here in Salonica will begin as soon as you set foot in that office. There'll be no shortage of work! And please," he continued, "when you write to Anna, tell her that I'm honored to be her brother-in-law! To be the relative of such a courageous and worthy woman! Write that, please…"

The next day dawned cloudy and a dark fog covered the sea and the White Tower. Alberto looked at the deserted street through the opening in the shutters. The wagon driver was already at the door, waiting for the appointed time to take him to the port.

David was doing the final tidying up of the room, separating shirts and bed linen for Cassandra to wash while they were away. They didn't know for certain how long they would be travelling, but now it didn't matter.

Then he hurried downstairs, carrying two valises. Alberto closed the room and descended with a canvas bag filled with rolled-up diagrams of projects.

He knocked at Marika Karakassos's door.

"We are leaving, *Kyria* Marika, here are the keys," he said.

"Won't you two at least have some coffee? All men do not eat unless they have a woman to take care of everything!"

"Thank you very much, *Kyria*, but we're already late. My brother is loading the baggage onto the cart, and the ship sails at seven o'clock… So, until we return…" he said, and with a fond gesture placed his hand on the landlady's fingers holding the door.

"Goodbye, Mr. Varsano. Make good use of the trip, enjoy my Constantinople! Ah, our St. Sophia, how I miss it! " she murmured.

As Alberto dashed down the stairs, the landlady remembered one more recommendation.

"Mr. Varsano, tell David not to forget what he promised: you'll visit my brother Alexandros…"

He gestured to her from the bottom of the stairs.

"It'll be a pleasure," he answered, almost tripping over Cassandra, who was waiting for him with a small cloth bag.

"*Kyrie*, this is for you and Mr. David... For... for the trip... To bring you good luck!"

"Thank you, Cassandra," said Alberto hurriedly, refusing to take the bag. "I cannot accept it."

"But I made it for you, *Dottore!*" she said in her strained voice.

"*Parta... Parta pedi mou*! Take it... take it with you, my son," she repeated in Greek.

Alberto took the bag and gently caressed Cassandra's calloused hands, smiling: "Take care of everything!" And pointing to the upstairs floor, "We'll be back soon..."


In the months spent at the Marika Karakassos house, and after the incident of Cassandra's fever, Alberto had come to be part of the family. Marika would knead dough vigorously while Alberto listened to her stories. She spoke the Italian of Corfu. She told how she had been raised on that island.

Her father was a wealthy textile and notions merchant who got in trouble with the police. After years of a comfortable life, his world collapsed. They left as fugitives, ending up in Constantinople, where her father fell ill and no longer had the strength to work. It was Marika's mother who provided for the family. She was a cleaning woman, custodian, and cook for houses in the neighborhood. She even washed the steps of their moorings, on hands and knees for hours in that cold and rainy weather.

At night she would return to their little house frozen, her back aching and her knees bleeding. Sometimes she didn't even have wood to burn...

"That was only the beginning of her martyrdom", Marika said, shaking her head. She went to work one summer in the *yali*, or seaside mansion, of the Karakassos family, on the Bosporus.

Marika was thirteen when she met Pantellis, the eldest son of Andreas Karakassos. It was the afternoon he fell out of a tree and twisted his ankle.

"He was eighteen, a good-looking young man with curly hair bleached by the sun, and he was very strong from so much rolling barrels." She sighed at the recollection.

And it was there in the Karakassoses' old *yali*, in the house where the family spent the summer, that she married Pantellis when she was still quite young. But she was happy for a lifetime.

The *Capitan*, as she referred to her deceased husband, was a man of integrity, honest and hard-working. He had a vineyard and made a very sweet wine from seedless raisins. He also had a *caïque*, a boat with three masts.

Marika never had any children.

"It wasn't God's will!" she said, raising her chin toward the ceiling. "God had his reasons for never giving us a child."

When Marika lost her mother, the *Capitan* took her brother Alexandros and raised him like a son. He baptized the boy and registered his name: Alexandros Karakassos. He would be his son and heir. They came to Salonica, a very busy port, and lived there for many years. And it was on that property that her brother established himself after the *Capitan*'s death, to help her run the family's businesses.

Alberto loved his conversations with Marika Karakassos. He would sometimes sit for hours in her spacious and fragrant kitchen, watching her work as she told her stories and prepared the meals. He learned words in Greek and Turkish from her and wrote down in a diary anything that she recommended as important words and attitudes. She knew everything—customs, history, and the local people. Marika's kitchen was a special place.

Cassandra used the ashes from the stove to wash clothes. Another ritual. She would sift the ashes and put them in a large bag.

Alberto didn't understand why they had to be sifted.

"Where's she going with that bag of ashes, lemon peels, and laurel leaves?" he asked the landlady incredulously.

She laughed, took Alberto by the hand, and they went into the backyard.

"Come, *Dottore*... Come see why washing clothes in these parts is so difficult... It's not like your land, where the water is soft and crystalline. Here the water is hard!" she said, referring to lime. "Grease won't come out, and clothes only get clean after a lot of work.

Cassandra uses the ashes to get the grease out of clothes."

Outside, next to the vineyard and the herbs planted by the landlady, was an enormous copper washtub over a brazier and beside it a vat called a *skaffi*, containing cold water that furnished the needs of the house. Early every morning Cassandra would prepare the *bougada* with all pomp, measuring the cups of water, separating the clothes and the tubs, overseeing everything.

In her screechy voice she would sing the song that accompanied her effort. She used the green bars of olive soap and scrubbed, scrubbed without stopping, and the effort made her tremulous melody echo as if coming from the depths of a cavern. Afterward she lined a basket with a sheet and put it into the previously washed sheets, covering them with the bag of sifted ashes, adding the lemon peels and laurel to perfume it. And she ended the day by tossing on hot water from the *kazani*, the copper vessel kept constantly heated.

The following day, everything would be washed again. The singing would begin earlier. In the morning it had a more pleasant tone. She rinsed everything, throwing on buckets of cold water and putting in blue stones that she called *lulaki*. Singing unceasingly, mixing Byzantine rhymes with words that described her actions, Cassandra went about her task.

Old Cassandra, with calloused hands and an almost toothless smile, was happy with her work. She lived with Marika, with her icons and her devoted love of St. Nicholaos, and now, as she said, of the *Dottore*, who had come to bring joy to her old age...

To her and to that house.

# XV

# THE GARDEN OF ALLAH

Constantinople, May 1885.

After some weeks spent in meetings with the counsellors of the Sublime Porte in Constantinople and discussing the final projects of the new rail line, the Varsano brothers finally succeeded in visiting the Alexandros Karakassos family, to deliver Marika's letter.

The property was distant. A young man named Constantine Kargopoulo, who liked to be called Kosti, arrived in the lobby of the hotel and asked for them. He had come at the behest of the Karakassoses to invite them for the Easter celebrations.

Kosti was the new portraitist of the sultan's court. He was the son of the famous photographer Basile Kargopoulo, portrait artist for the entire sultanate.

"Effendi Vassili," as he was nicknamed throughout the Empire, had been an eccentric Greek respected in all the Ottoman Empire for his art, his personality, and his discretion.

"My father was an uncommon man," the young photographer said. "He was the most agile person I ever saw, there behind his camera. I remember him with his head always covered by a dark cloth, knees bent, rocking back and forth, moving the tripod from side to side to better capture a shadow or a ray of light."

Basile Kargopoulo had been the only portraitist to receive the highest title of recognition for his work, "*Photographe de Sa Majesté Impériale le Sultan,*" with the right to use the *Tugra imperial*, the sultan's monogram, on his works and on the door of his studio. Now, after his death from heart attack in the first days of the year, his son had been summoned to the sultan's palace as the new imperial portraitist to replace him.

That morning, Kosti was in the front seat of the carriage transporting them to Büyükdere, the village where Alexandros Karakassos lived, a trip of several hours.

David raised the question: given the racial and religious issue, and the fact that Kosti was Greek and Orthodox, how was it possible to have such an intimate position of trust in the royal chambers?

"My father," he replied, "was not the only one; there are many other Greeks who work in the imperial court, like the sultan's personal doctor, a Greek named Spiridion Mavroyeannis, or the minister who holds the portfolio for Foreign Relations, Alexander Karatheodoris. Just as there were many Jews working as economic advisers; they were always the majority, since Suleiman the Magnificent," he emphasized. "And all of them were considered equals in the Bosporus."

He further related how Vassili, his father, the sultan's photographer, had died two months after receiving a gold medal for his art. He had photographed the entire city, the architecture, the peddlers, daily life, the *bëys*, the lesser princes and princesses, but never Sultan Abdül Hamid II himself.

"To him, in his position as 'Lord and Master, Successor of All the Apostles in the Universe,' to be photographed would be inappropriate for the greatest of all Caliphs! Luckily, I managed to do so..."

Kosti also spoke about the Karakassos family. Marika's brother, Alexandros Karakassos was today head of the family. He had a small cantina in the great Vizier Hane Bazaar, but as with all established businessmen it was merely a front, always maintained in the right measure, so as not to attract the wrath and envy of other businessmen and the sultan's men...The bulk of the hundreds of liras the Karakassos family had saved came from their vineyards and a small wine factory.

To get to Alexandros Karakassos's home in Büyükdere, after a two-hour carriage ride, they would take a boat and continue to the northern Bosporus.

The boat that had awaited them in Yeniköy docked directly at the door of their hosts' home. Alberto and David exchanged glances... It was a small Venice!

The dock, the facade of the house, its ochre walls bathed by the water, the smell of sea air and the sound of the waves beating against the stones of the berth, the brightness of the day— everything took their thoughts back to the canals of Venice...

The Karakassoses' property appeared to extend on land for a reasonable distance. Seen from the water, it seemed like a single house, with the berth and foreground of greyish stones, and on them a tall wooden structure with numerous windows and trellises. Everything was surrounded by plane trees and poplars that blocked any view of the interior of the property.


David and Alberto were not anticipating such a warm reception. It appeared the "*böylezmisafir*," or guests of honour, had been expected for some time. Marika had written a great deal about them, and they were welcomed and embraced as part of the family. And there *he* was, next to the mooring, tugging on the boat's lines. There he stood, the host: Alexandros Karakassos. He smiled as he met his guests, gesturing, embracing them. In a matter of minutes the Varsano brother already felt admiration for Marika Karakassos's brother. He had a contagious joy, strong features, a huge white moustache that contrasted with his dark suntanned skin. His smile was wide, showing snowy white teeth. He wore his hair long, tied at the back, in the style of shepherds, which gave him a wild and intrepid appearance.

. That morning he was wearing clothing very common among rural men, wide trousers held by leather suspenders and a coverall over a sheepskin vest. It would be quite difficult to guess his actual age; he must be fifty or a bit more... But he was a man jovial and virile in appearance.

In profile, Alexandros Karakassos strongly recalled his older sister Marika: the same nose, wide face, bushy black eyebrows. His frame of greyish hair only served to highlight the family resemblance.

Kosti had said during the journey that Marika's family name was the description of their features: in Turkish Karakassos meant black eyebrows, which in Greek would be Mavrofridis.

"And one day, when Turkish domination ends," he said, playing with the translation, "they can be called 'the *Mavrofridises* in Greek.'"

"*Mavrosegno*," Means like black eye brown... explained David in Italian, "understand, Alberto? Just like the name of the great Venetian general Mavrosegno, our hero, the one who did away with so many Tur...–" He stopped abruptly, remembering he was on Ottoman soil.

Helena, Alexandros's wife, was waiting for the visitors in the large living room. She was an attractive woman with soft features and creamy white skin. As was the local custom, she dressed like an Ottoman woman, her hair tied back with a colored silk kerchief. A few unruly ends contoured her face and allowed a glimpse of gold-colored locks. Her eyes were almond-shaped, which, as David would later comment to Alberto, made her appear more Asian than European.

Everything there was very new to the brothers.

A place so remote, the home of strangers. But within minutes they felt they had won over and gained a new family. The Karakassoses' house, which seemed to them like a return to the days of Venice and brought back memories of childhood: the sun coming in through the curtains, and the reflection of the oak floor, waxed and immaculate.

It was a magical moment in the brothers' lives.

On the terrace in the upper part of the house, a table was set for the guests, with pitchers of cool water, glasses of wine, baskets of fruit–all protected by awnings that swayed in the gentle spring breeze.

"The lamb is wonderful, Helena," said Alexandros in delight, coming from the kitchen carrying an immense tray.

"I hope you like lamb, Mr. David. Alexandros could not resist showing off his skills as chef. He raises the animals to serve later at Easter and the start of spring," she said, laughing. "And woe to anyone who touches them!"

Another table was set up in the garden in the shade of the plane trees. At the end of the afternoon, the hostess invited her guests to see the rest of the property. A stroll through the vineyards. She showed the library that had belonged to her father, the collection of maps that covered the walls, book spines in parchment, a French piano that she had played when younger and which now belonged to her daughter Katherina.

Katherina Karakassos, her only child, was not present.

"This is my daughter, Mr. Varsano," Helena told Alberto, showing her portrait. "I think she may be the same age as your daughter."

Alberto looked at the portrait and handed it to David.

"A pretty girl," the *Dottore* commented.

"She's in Paris," said Alexandros proudly, "finishing her music studies; my little girl is a virtuoso!"

When they left the library Helena opened a small side gate. Alexandros said, "This part of the house belongs to my daughter when she's with us. She hardly ever leaves it. She calls it her little paradise, and since she's away, we've prepared a surprise for her."

Katherina's paradise was a passageway between two walls, what Venetians call *loggia*, from which emanated an intoxicating perfume.

"It's beautiful!" exclaimed Alberto excitedly. "It really is a little paradise... And that mixture of perfumes–pardon my curiosity, but where does it come from?"

Helena smiled, and, as if anticipating precisely that question, replied:

"Wait just a bit longer, Mr. Varsano, and you'll understand," pointing to the path.

They walked to the end of the pergola and Helena opened the doors to a garden.

A sea of roses, from crimson to the palest hues, contrasted with the lavender and sandalwood trellises covered with jasmine.

"This is the surprise we've prepared for our daughter, Mr. Varsano, in her little paradise. As if here she were living inside a vial of the finest perfume."

Alberto held his breath, unable to bear losing the smallest part of that atmosphere. He could not imagine that anyone else could invent such perfume; it seemed like a dream.

His thoughts were interrupted when Alexandros offered him a refreshment and with his new friends toasted his daughter's garden.

"I noticed, Mr. Varsano, that you were very taken with the flowers," Helena told him. "To us, this is a truly special garden. The gardener who planned it is a poor man whom Nico, my nephew, found ill in one of the Black Sea ports. He gave him a job, nursed him back to health, and brought him to us. As recompense, that man, who was a sailor, offered us this garden."

Alberto shuddered. *It can't be!* he thought. It would be too much to hope for if they were speaking of the same person.

"By any chance, madam, is the man who planted this garden a Moroccan named Daud?"

Helena, startled, widened her eyes.

"Yes... How did you know? Ah, of course! Marika must have told you the story."

"No, Madame!" said Alberto, even more confused.

Helena stopped listening and left like a gale, passing between her husband and David, who were chatting.

"I wonder what got into her?" Alexandros asked Alberto.

"Forgive us, but sometimes women have such strange reactions... I believe it is the age now. They feel bad, become distressed, and dash off like that to take their medicines. Yes, it must be her age. She was so worried about receiving a so special guests like you are..."

Alberto had time to order his thoughts. The garden! Yes, the idea born on the deck of the ship that night in which the sea seemed to be made of oil and the sky of satin. The conversation with the black man seated beside him on deck, the roses, the attar, the perfume he described, a garden in a bottle, the idea had been his.

Alberto had merely dreamed of giving Anna a bottle of that perfume. Roses and jasmine, and a light touch of sandalwood. He had only been dreaming that night. Now he was sure of it!

A moment later, his heart raced as he saw Helena Karakassos emerging from the *loggia*, accompanied by a tall black man with a white turban around his head.

"*Dottore* Varsano! *Salaam Aleikum*. May Allah be with you," said the man in a hoarse deep voice, bowing. "It's *Dottore* Varsano, the pharmacist... How I've looked for you... Allah bless you!"

That spring evening on the banks of the Bosporus would change the course of Alberto's life.

Daud spent hours sitting in Katherina's little paradise, telling the pharmacist of his adventures in Sebastopol, recounting his meeting Victor Varsano, who in his raging fever, his deliriums, called out for Ida Modiano.

From the start, the Moroccan told him, Victor seemed a familiar figure to him–his features, his gaze; later, when Daud discovered the dying man was a Varsano, he did everything in his power to save him. There was no quinine available in Sebastopol, where in those days dozens were dying from typhus and malaria. Brigands had stolen all Victor's money and belongings on the road to Astrakhan.

The young man spent days and nights exposed to the cold, without boots or food, at the mercy of mosquitoes by day and scorpions by night. When Daud found him, his eyes were bloodshot and his body burned with a high fever. He managed to take him to Sebastopol on horseback, applying compresses and giving him water at regular intervals. He had hopes that Victor would survive when they arrived at the gates of the city. But typhoid and malaria had turned it into a ghost town, where only a handful of ragged wretches fought to survive in the muddy, mosquito-infested streets. Poor and starving, they offered help in exchange for a few coins.

Daud succeeded in feeding Victor by pawning the watch Count De Brazza had given him when he departed for Paris. He arranged for a room near the docks and also enlisted the help of an elderly lady who applied leeches while he roamed the streets in search of medicine. The third night, Victor's fever began to break. The old woman nodded her head and spoke unintelligible words. Daud found no aid–there were too many sick people in the city, many dead to be buried, there was no one to help him save Victor's life. Daud described the final scene.

An aged Jew was burying his dead. An act of pure compassion. He would not accept money. He had called his neighbors, old and sickly ragamuffins, and together they offered a prayer.

The black man, with his last piasters, bought a piece of grimy fabric and watched the old man wrap Victor Varsano's lifeless body in the yellowed sheet, which was then covered with shovelfuls of stones and mud. The sound of the shovels striking the stones accompanied the final prayer of the wizened old man, who repeated in a monotone:

*"Yitgadal Veyitcadash... Sheme Raba... Amen."*

Alberto remembered the Kaddish prayed in memory of his mother's soul. Remembered the sight of his father in mourning, the funeral cortege leaving Giudecca, the gondola carrying his mother's coffin through the canals, the route chosen by the rabbi to avoid bridges so they would not be stoned. The old cemetery on the Lido. The sun setting behind the cypresses, and the reflection of the water in the lagoon... the anguished sigh of his aged father... the tears welling from his eyes... the pain of separation.

Now it was Victor who was gone and would never return.

∽ঌ

The letter from Büyükdere, written in April at the home of the Karakassoses, arrived many months later in Taormina.

August was drawing to a close when Anna received the news: Victor's death, the reencounter with Daud, the days they spent with the Karakassos family, Alexandros's work, the sensitivity and friendship of Helena, her daughter Katherina, a great pianist recently arrived from Paris who had made David's heart flutter.

Alberto related to Anna that their intention was to spend only the weekend with Marika's family, but the hosts had strongly urged them to stay for the arrival of their daughter, returning from Paris to spend the spring with them.

After meeting the young woman, David asked Kosti to immediately send a telegram cancelling his commitments for that week, and the stay in Constantinople will be extended. In the letter, Alberto described what he had seen and done those marvellous days. Alexandros had loaded his boat with casks, and they had sailed to the northernmost point on the Bosporus, where it meets the Black Sea.

On that journey, the guests of honour had breakfast at sunrise on the boat, sitting cross-legged on straw mats, with Europe on one side and Asia on the other.

For the Varsano brothers it was the best meal, the simplest, and according to Alexandros Karakassos the oldest,.The breakfast that for hundreds of years had been the same for every man who worked in those lands: succulent red tomatoes, fresh cucumbers, a jar of thick honey and peach jelly, boiled eggs, olives, and a piece of feta cheese made from sheep's milk by local shepherds. An old mariner served a basket of cream bread, a specialty of Helena Karakassos's, and a tray with glasses of çay, a very dark, aromatic mint tea.

The people of Anatolia, Alberto wrote, drank a great deal of tea, and in all the places he had visited since his arrival, it was a ritual. Fluted glasses that received a hot foaming liquid poured from above and served with full ceremony. A ceremony equal to that in Venice when a glass of the best wine was served, he had commented to the host.

It was that morning, when speaking of the tea ritual and the aroma of mint that David remembered the dinner at which Michaela had served tea in the Turkish manner. He laughed at the memory. The frightened girl was cleaning the carpet with the hem of her dress when the Baron entered the room.

He told the story of the meeting of uncle and niece to Daud and Alexandros, praising Michaela. "An intelligent girl, well mannered and very pretty, just like your daughter Katherina," he commented en passant.

Effendi Karakassos, as the master was addressed by his servants, served the mint tea in small, very simple glasses. He said to the foreigners:

"These are the same ones from which we all drink, my sailors and I. They're inn glasses, but the ritual must always be the same, whether here or the Yildiz Palace…"

Kosti, ever the photographer, at each stop of the boat would set up his tripod and camera to record the settings and the scenery. They lunched in Rümeli and returned along the Asian side. They slept on the boat, four men and two sailors.

Daud did not leave the deck, and as on the satiny nights from the Ionic to the Aegean, Alberto, and the Moroccan had much to talk about. The stars seemed so low that night that Alberto had the sensation that if he raised his arm, he could touch them.

Daud did not leave the deck, and as on the satiny nights from the Ionic to the Aegean, Alberto, and the Moroccan had much to talk about. The stars seemed so low that night that Alberto had the sensation that if he raised his arm, he could touch them.

# XVI

## *TÜRKENHIRSCH*
### TURKISH–HIRSCH

*" Tout le monde ici demande une concession, l´un demande une Banque, láutre demande une route...*
*Ce finirá mal,banque et route...Banqueroute"*

*"Bon mot de Fuad Pasha"*

Constantinople, spring 1885.

In the letters from Alberto Varsano to Anna, he spoke of the life of Baron Maurice de Hirsch.

The pharmacist did not understand why newspapers wrote so much about Maurice de Hirsch. Could he be such an important character as to make headlines in periodicals from the United Kingdom, France, Austria, often defamatory, sometimes laudatory?

Lately they were all talking about a possible lawsuit involving the Baron and the Sublime Porte, the Sultan, represented by the counsel of the Ottoman Empire. The Sultan no longer respected the agreements, despite being aware that his Empire was being closely watched by the great banks of Europe.

Even under the provisions of an international decree that obliged the Ottoman government to pay interest on the principal debt, the new Grand-Vizier heading the negotiations always had a new rabbit to pull out of the hat. And in the case of the construction and exploitation of the tracks of Baron Hirsch's Oriental Railways, the Ottoman Empire's finance representative kept postponing the debt, paying neither the arrears nor the interest, changing the agreements and trying the entrepreneur's patience.

"This was sapping the baron's health and costing a fortune," David explained to him.

On the trip to Constantinople, David told Alberto, a little about the nobleman's personality.

Both Maurice and Clara had been born to bankers. Born in Bavaria, son and grandson of a financier who had been counsellor to kings Maximilian and Ludwig I. Beginning in 1805, they obtained contracts to supply horses and arms to the government of Bavaria. When the baron's father died in 1840, there occurred a drastic change in politics and in the economy.

The Era of Absolutism gave way to the Era of Liberalism, and the Industrial Revolution, begun in England, spread through the continent, effecting radical changes in the financial operations of the Hirsch family. The baron's businesses were no longer restricted to banks and to money as product.

Family friends said that Maurice had inherited the knack for business from his grandfather and the taste for hunting and sport from his father. He was truly an uncommon and admirable man.

Tall, slim, with an elegant and healthy bearing, he impressed with his style and charm; cultured and quick-thinking, when he spoke he had the gift of monopolizing the audience with his arguments.

David said he mesmerized woman with his *charmant* accent and smile. All of them, young and old, adored the Baron's stories, he said, including Michaela, who after all those years of living with the family knew well his habits and his character.

Many spoke ill of the Baron; defamed in the newspapers, he was called nouveau-riche or arriviste in European society. This story provoked laughter at home. Maurice de Hirsch told Michaela one day that: *what mattered was not his belonging to the aristocracy but the aristocracy belonging to him,* referring to the enviable position he had achieved.

Gradually, the young Sicilian came to understand what he meant by that, for he was a man who calculated every step, as in a game of chess.

The game with Czar Alexander III, who was influenced by religious fanatics like the leader of the Holy Synod and by the minister of the interior, Nicholay Ignatyev, went on for four years. The issue was not pounds or francs but human lives. The Baron negotiated the freedom of tens of thousands of Russian Jews in exchange for an enormous donation to the Russian Orthodox Church. Millions of gold francs was the price for those souls to escape the pogroms, safe from massacres, plunder, rapes, stoning, and death. It was a new Inquisition that spread like fire, uniting mobs of peasants and the czar's own police, under the banner of lies, infamy, and religious fanaticism. With cruelty in their hearts, they would invade *shtetls* and landholdings to destroy and steal everything belonging to Jews.

Additionally, the only way out, Maurice de Hirsch held, was through the work of the Jewish Colonization Association in countries of the New World, the only means for guiding those refugees and resettling them with dignity, safety, and a future livelihood. Not even his worst enemies, like Bismarck and his followers, or his greatest detractor, Eduoard Drumont, of the newspaper *La Libre Parole*, author of the anti-Semitic monstrosity *La France Juive*, succeeded in attacking him in any depth.

Drumont was a dangerous journalist, known for his snares and lies. He organized a ridiculous campaign when Maurice de Hirsch decided to close to public visits his private hunting grounds in Petit Versailles until then was used for recreation by the local inhabitants. Since Drumond had nothing else to say about him, another campaign against him in Parisian newspapers charged that the baron used only German personnel and equipment in the construction of the Orient Express.

"And that is the problem with them; if they're not competent or competitive, they're only good for mouthing stupidity like that," the Baron commented to Michaela after reading the papers.

"Now they are putting me in competition with the Rothschild. ..I never had any such idea, they are who they are; I am who I am, *the baron*, while they are *the barons*. All of them together." In addition, he twirled his moustache.

There were many facets to that man: the *bon vivant*, the disciplined and extraordinary businessman, and the great philanthropist. Concerned for his people and for all the persecuted, the despoiled, those stoned to death or burned alive, as in the latest pogroms in Russia, the poor with no perspective of a better life, without access to schooling because of religious intolerance, Maurice de Hirsch , was the savior of their lives.

He was active in all areas–banks, railroads, mining, sugar, ports, maintenance services. He could not miss a hunt, loved his racehorses, did not neglect the gardens on his properties, organized schools, donated hospitals, constructed villas, argued with chancellors, received princes and kings, wrote, organized and built a dream: agricultural colonies far from persecutions, in the fertile lands of America, where every human being had the same chance to prosper and live in freedom, as well, buying land here and there, he supported hundreds of the elderly ill .

Yet he still found time to live, for Clara, for Lucien and Michaela.

Clara, according to those who knew her, was his soul mate.

Born into a large and important Belgian family, daughter of a senator and partner in the Bischoffsheim & Goldschmidt Bank, the Bank of Paris and the Netherlands, she was raised in business, but always with an eye toward charity. It was said it was she who influenced the baron to take an interest in philanthropy, especially in causes relating to persecuted Jews.

David Varsano told Alberto about an event that Master Grassi, the lawyer, had witnessed in the years the Hirsches had spent in Constantinople building the first leg of the railroad.

During that time he had become better acquainted with the character of Clara de Hirsch. At the opening of the first lines of the railroad, the Baroness was accompanying her husband and the chief engineer, Wilhelm von Premel.

One afternoon, near Edirne a group of peasants, owners of numerous houses razed for the line to pass, sought out the baron's delegation to protest the loss of their dwellings. Clara knew that the contract stipulated that the Ottoman government indemnify the owners of lands and homes that were demolished, but was unresigned to the poverty and suffering of those individuals. She argued with the lawyers and her husband:

"I'm certain that you, like me, know that 'they' won't keep their word to these poor wretches. Personally, I think that any business that engenders unhappiness cannot work... Isn't that right, Maurice?"

So at the end, Maurice de Hirsch paid each of the peasants the amount corresponding to the construction of a new house, and slept peacefully.

That was at the start of 1874.

The baron had dedicated his time and millions of pounds sterling since 1869, and almost two decades, to the planning and building of the railroad.

David added that he was motivated by great challenges. At the very beginning of the project, considered by bankers and statesmen a courageous and gigantic undertaking, some laughed and some envied, while others lent support and many thought only of profit.

"Just think," David told Alberto, "the insanity and courage needed in those times, twenty years ago, to channel so much money and energy into a project he had conceived of called Oriental Railways! In an unknown land... in partnership with a government that had begun negotiating with the West only a few years earlier!"

One day, at a dinner in Paris, the lawyer Grassi had told David that Maurice de Hirsch had said that, since he considered himself merely a businessman, with no political ideology, he'd never thought his adventure in those dealings with the Ottoman Empire would one day turn into a *cause célèbre*. The case would become famous throughout Europe and the Ottoman Empire, involving his name in diplomatic intrigues. He could never imagine that his persistence, self-confidence, and optimism would merit, twenty years later, so much criticism and defamation, prompting the chancelleries of Europe into a state of alert.

David promised to tell Alberto about the various intrigues in which Baron Hirsch had been involved, so he could better understand the venom in the term Türkenhirsch: the cancellations by the sultans who had ruled during the project and the materialization of that web of rail lines, the suspension of payments, the Türkenlose.

And there was also the unscrupulous "father of all lies," the Russian ambassador in Constantinople, a man named Ignatyev, who had influenced Mahmud Nedim, the grand-vizier since 1875, not to honour the contract with the baron.

Ignatyev in reality was moving against Turkey, as it was not desirable for the railroad to ultimately succeed. The defaulted payments also implied the danger of a declaration of Ottoman bankruptcy by the European banks.

Alberto hadn't really understood their conversations about the world of politics, lawyers, bankers, and engineers. And he wrote to his wife:

*"Mia Carissima Anna,*

*I'm certain now that I'm more interested than ever in becoming a perfume maker. Even after David's efforts to transform me into a man versed in law, politics, and business, I'm sure I'm making the right choice.*
*My brother has tirelessly given me lessons in contracts, laws, and properties, trying to make me into an erudite man in a tail coat, and honestly, I was thinking only of my potions. While David was explaining all that, I would be entertaining myself with a flower in the vase on a table, with its perfume... It was as if my soul wasn't there, do you understand, Anna?*

*I'm ashamed to write this, but there were times when I counted the minutes until he finished so I could talk with him about something understandable.*

*Or even be by myself, with my thoughts, to write in my diary in order not to lose any details about the voyage that might serve as inspiration in the future.* "

What future? thought Anna.

Is there going to be a future for us in Salonica? she wrote in a letter to her daughter. Michaela was now part of that world, so different from Mongibello, thought Anna. And Alberto, poor Alberto, still hadn't found anything to do or even really knows how to do.

Raffaele read and reread Alberto's letters, trying to understand his son-in-law and the writing in so many languages in the newspaper clippings that spoke of the feats and defects of the baroness's husband.

Nights in Taormina were longer now. Anna would stay up until late sewing, reading books or catalogs or newspapers that Anjù lent her, left by guests at the hotel. It was her contact with the world "out there," as Raffaele put it.

Several times a week Anna would go to the Hotel Timeo, where she had a fitting room for her tourist clients arriving in the city. Many were famous because of title, wealth, or even a love affair with some illustrious aristocrat. But all had one thing in common: lots of money to spend in Taormina.

One afternoon, finishing a fitting, Anna listened to a conversation in French between two ladies from Paris. One of them with a malicious mien commented something about the baron and a certain Madame De Forest...

Anna continued pinning the clothes, but she could feel her legs tremble. Hours later, still trying to understand the conversation, by the tone and the sly smiles she was all but certain something had gone on between the two.

"Women talk too much," Raffaele said. "Imagine if poor Clara overheard a petty, poisonous remark like that. There's a lot of gossip, a lot of envy. A woman like the baroness, elegant, intelligent– I can't understand why you women listen to such slander."

One day, Anna thought, she should learn more French, if only to better understand the conversations between madams and countesses; it would also help with the correct pronunciation of dishes served in the best restaurants.

Did that also exist in Salonica?

Winter was beginning, and Michaela wrote her mother regularly after the Hirsches' definitive departure from Planegg to establish themselves in London. The Sicilian's life had changed greatly.

Mongibello was still in her memory, and she missed Anna, her grandfather, the gentle breeze, Indian figs, lemons... and the blue of the sea.

∼⑥

London, October 1885.

It was early autumn, and Michaela watched the darkening weather from her window in the Hirsches' new residence in Berkeley Square. That afternoon she had received a letter from Salonica, from her uncle David, announcing his marriage to Katherina Karakassos.

It was love at first sight, he wrote.

After the weeks in Büyükdere, Katherina had returned to Paris to finish her final semester at the National Music Conservatory.

A little more than a month later, she learned she was pregnant.

After much weeping, she wrote a letter to David. Ashamed and frightened, after waiting over two months for a reply, she took a train to return home but didn't go to Constantinople. She descended in Salonica.

From the Vardar station she went to 23, Promenade Longeant le Quai, to seek her aunt Marika's advice. When she entered the hallway, she saw the fruit basket with the correspondence. Her letters were there, on the table at the entrance, the envelopes still unopened.

David had left again, according to the old servant Cassandra. He had gone at the beginning of June, to work, and as was customary his room remained closed; only she went in, to dust.

It was August, David wrote. It was extremely hot, and Katherina showed up pale, her hands cold and trembling. Marika saw immediately that something was wrong. Cassandra brought the girl a drink of sour-cherry, damp cloths and essence of lemon to soothe her nausea. She finally went to sleep, sobbing.

Marika brought from the kitchen a basin of water with a few drops of olive oil. She prayed quietly and blessed the girl, sprinkling drops of water over her body.

"Poor Katherina," whispered Marika to Cassandra. "My poor niece, so pretty, so cultured, so happy... Oh!" she sighed deeply. "My poor brother, poor Alexandros! Oh! *Panaguia mou*... Oh, Our Lady," Marika moaned, "show me a path for my brother not to die from grief and shame."

They silently closed the door to the room and went downstairs to the kitchen. Cassandra left to take a note from Marika to Master Grassi. She was only to hand the envelope personally to Emmanuel Salem, the tall young man with straight hair.
Salem opened the envelope and furrowed his brow. He read the letter twice and looked unbelievingly at Cassandra.

"Tell *Kyria* Karakassos that I'm going to send a telegram right now and will return in late afternoon to speak with her."

"She'll wait for *Kiryos* Salem in the kitchen," said the old woman and left, muttering.

Marika felt she was to blame. Katherina's letter had been in her fruit basket for more than two months, awaiting David's return. She blamed herself for everything, for sending David and Alberto to Büyükdere... She had written dozens of letters to Alexandros and Helena telling about David and later Alberto, and how happy she was to have them near.

Now she shuddered to think she had once dreamed that David and Katherina were marrying, and that she felt happy. A pianist and a lawyer... Everyone said what a good match they were... and then... She woke up and thought: "No... he's not like us, he's a Jew, and they can't get married!" And she breathed in relief... It was only a dream.

Marika could never have imagined the letter was so important to her niece. She learned of the friendship of the two through Helena.

Helena had written Marika telling of David and Alberto's visit and Alexandros's insistence to host them for some weeks so they could get to know the region better and enjoy the company of Katherina, who was arriving for the Easter holidays.

Helena told Marika on her correspondences that, she had seen the two young people exchanging amorous glances, and at the end of her letter wrote:

"A pity he isn't one of us, for he would be the ideal husband for Katherina. An established man, well mannered, cultured and sensitive. But time will pass and she, studying in Paris, will forget this passion!"

Even Alexandros, who never worried about his daughter's future and never allowed anyone to introduce a suitor, as he considered such practice a part of Byzantium, was changing his mind. And he went back to the great Vizier Hane market, seeking among his compatriots news of some match for his daughter.

In the short time David and Alberto had been in Salonica on their return from Constantinople, Marika had already heard from them the account of the visit to Büyükdere. They spoke of Alexandros and Helena, the house, the vinery, the reunion with Daud, Victor's death, Katherina's garden. Of Katherina, David had said, impressed, "An excellent young woman, Mrs. Marika, a rare pearl who would make any man happy."

They showed the portraits that Kosti had made of all of them, especially of her niece, which David kept in his coat pocket.

Salem arrived at twilight bearing a telegram. Marika had spent the entire afternoon with her heart racing in anxiety, while Cassandra tended to her niece upstairs. The lawyer opened the envelope and read aloud to Marika: "Thank you for informing me. I am happy but concerned. Take care of her for me. I will return on the first ship and we will marry."

David arrived on the third day, and Marika had already persuaded the priest of the Church of St. Nicholaos. They were married in a small chapel outside the city, in the presence of only her aunt, the aged servant Cassandra, a Jewish friend of the bride named Revveca, and the always steadfast Salem.

The front room with the double bed was Mrs. Karakassos's gift. Salem sent a large coal-burning *sobah* and a sheepskin rug to warm the room in winter.

Then came the hardest part for Marika, writing her brother Alexandros about the wedding. She omitted certain details and shifted others, telling her brother a different story, doing everything possible to spare him suffering.

First she spoke of David, a young man who was well situated in life, a lawyer respected both in Salonica and throughout the empire. She said that when he returned to Salonica after the time with them in Büyükdere, he seemed very much in love with Katherina.

Marika Karakassos added that the lawyer, some time earlier, had received two tickets from the Orient Express Company and had gone to Paris. As *Dottore* Alberto hadn't wished to accompany him, and Baron Hirsch was paying all expenses, he had offered Marika the other ticket, knowing that her grandest dream was to see the City of Light.

She explained to Alexandros that if she missed that unique opportunity she would never again have the chance. She had therefore accepted the invitation and the company of the young lawyer, and together they went to Paris on the baron's new trains. When they arrived, Marika had asked David to take her to the National Conservatory to look for her niece. There they were informed that Katherina hadn't been in class for over ten days. They went to the house where she was staying, and a servant informed them of the girl's whereabouts. They found her in a sanatorium far from the center of the city, completely abandoned, thin, feverish, and with a fierce cough.

Marika, desperate at her niece's condition, had consulted doctors and discovered that the pianist had a very rare kind of anaemia, necessitating rigorous treatment. According to a specialist, it would be best to treat her at home, with hardy meals, sheep's liver, white beans, lentil soup, lots of fruit, and goat cheese.

After weeks, they returned to Salonica, with David taking care of Katherina day and night, overseeing her medicines and giving her fruits and compotes hourly throughout the journey. Deeply in love and fearful of losing her, David had promised he would be baptized and marry Katherina.

The baptism of the groom and the wedding revived Katherina. After weeks in David's care, her anaemia disappeared, and she could now live a normal life.

Marika asked her brother's forgiveness for not having informed him of the events, but she didn't want to startle him; she stated that the marriage had occurred in the Hagios Nikolaos chapel and that the bride was happy. She also told them not to worry about anything, as the groom had made it clear he would never accept a dowry—the couple would reside in her house until David could build in the new, elegant Hamidie neighborhood. They were already thinking about starting a family, since David was 36 and didn't want to wait.

Such was the version that was to be told *en famille* and that Michaela should keep secret.

❧

Only Alberto hadn't been advised. Neither Salem nor David could determine his whereabouts. Or his friend Daud's.

Michaela, holding the letter, was unsure how to tell the story to the baron.

He was a man free of prejudice and would understand and continue to admire her uncle. Or, if he knew the version of the landlady, would say, "That lady has a *strrrong* imagination, and David *Varrsano*, in any case, is a man, and men have their *veaknesses*."

So Michaela decided to be nonchalant:

"Oh," she said at dinner, "I received the news from my uncle David yesterday. He wrote that he's met a wonderful woman and they got married!"

"Already? And who is the lucky woman?" asked Clara, raising her eyebrows.

"Didn't I tell you, Clara?" said the baron, interrupting Michaela. "Our lawyer David Varsano married a beautiful girl from a good family in Anatolia, the Karakassoses. They make wine… And the girl is a virtuoso…"

And he calmly observed the reaction of the two women.

"You know, girls," he said, smiling, "I receive news too. I have my sources…" And he winked at Micha. "I hope that one day Lucien will fall in love with such a girl… a cosmopolitan woman."

London had transformed Michaela into a woman of responsibility, what the English called a cosmopolitan woman. A new class of women who did not marry by contract or for money—they were active, cultured, educated, and independent... yet still chaste.

After Clara, the Baron's right hand, Michaela was becoming his left hand, as he was in the habit of saying. She assumed part of the tasks of the running of the house, leaving the baroness free for her charity work, and the rest of the day, as well as many nights a week, she would attend to various business matters.

She also oversaw the restoration of the new mansion in Piccadilly, the bills that arrived from the Beauregard Castle in Versailles, the Eychorn in Moravia, the endless bills from Rue de l'Élysée in Paris where Lucien lived, the invitations for hunting season in St. Johann, and the most important thing: the reports of the future Jewish Colonization Association being implanted in the United States, Canada, Argentina, and Brazil.

There were hundreds of people to take care of, in addition to the Hirsches' numerous business and philanthropic concerns. And when it was a matter of strictly personal bills, of purchases and maintenance, decoration, gardening, the baron did not allow it out of his hands.

"This belongs to us, it's our private life," he would tell Michaela. "I don't want it to go beyond these walls."

At times Michaela wondered why Lucien wasn't more involved with his father's private dealings and "stayed ensconced at Rue de l'Élysée, inside that library, always with some excuse," as Helga commented in the pantry. Even then, despite living with the baron's family, Michaela knew him only through photographs, and sometimes she would hear news from the letters that came for the baroness. Lucien, according to the baroness, was always busy, pursuing some important piece or a coin for his collection. It was Clara who was constantly making plans.

"Well, this summer we shall all go together to spend a few days in Beauregard, or some weeks on the Riviera, and Lucien will surely find time to set aside his collections."

During the entire time she was in Planegg, Lucien had always found an excuse to delicately decline the invitation to visit them. The baron and Clara concealed any disappointment; however, in time Michaela began to perceive how they suffered at such refusals. Clara received letters from her son almost daily and would read them locked in the office, holding them to her breast and, saying goodbye, throw them into the burning fireplace. Sometimes, Michaela wondered what Lucien must be like. Even the portrait didn't help, as it wasn't recent. What was Lucien like in reality?

He had an angular face and a straight, tapered nose like his mother. As for the rest, he had his father's demeanour, his gaze hidden behind his glasses, which gave him a sad expression. She didn't know how to define him.

Once, at a ball in Vienna, she thought she had seen a man who greatly reminded her of Lucien. Michaela was so impressed by the resemblance to the portrait that she didn't take her eyes off him the entire evening. And he too, once he saw her, didn't take his eyes off her. Michaela had never told Clara about it and was embarrassed even to recall the encounter. She never saw him again. But she never forgot that ball or that man.

She had never felt attracted to anyone as she was to that stranger. He had caught Michaela's attention, of the hundreds of young men clustered in the corridors of the palace, most in uniforms bedecked with galloons. They aspired to or were already part of the elite of the Austro-Hungarian Empire, Gisela explained to her as they entered the ballroom.

Nevertheless, that man had seemed different to her, with his curly hair carelessly tied at the nape of the neck, as if he always combed it with his own hands, a masculine bearing, broad shoulders, a black velvet coat, riding pants and gaiters. He wasn't precisely ready for a ball like the other ostentatious young men; he seemed to be there out of obligation. He was by himself. Women took his arm and greeted him, and even as he was talking to them he cast sidelong glances at Michaela.

It was an unforgettable night .

That had been more than two years ago, and Michaela, looking at the portrait of Lucien de Hirsch on the Baron's desk, remembered the stranger at the ball, whom she had never again seen. Neither him nor the young man in the photograph; Lucien himself, in all those years, she had never seen in person.


It had all happened in the spring, when Michaela still lived in Planegg.

Gisela, the princess who had become her best friend, was going to Vienna for the week of waltzes of the Opera Vienna balls and wanted a lady's companion. She emphasized that Michaela must not miss the spectacle. Michaela did not  even have permission to travel, but Gisela insisted and promised she would telegraph the Baron. They took the train from Munich to Vienna. Gisela was excited and felt free, without her small children and her husband, just she, back to visit her father, the grand archduke Franz Josef, and as guest of honour to open the spring ball.

Michaela was accommodated in Princess Gisela's royal quarters in the Schönbrunn Castle, a labyrinth of fabulous bedrooms and indescribable salons. The hostess, knowing Michaela had nothing to wear, lent her an evening gown and a tiara of pearls and diamonds that added the final touch to the  coiffure and the flowers at her nape.

After long preparations, the day of the festivities finally came.

When the Sicilian looked at herself in the mirror, she couldn't believe what she saw. She looked like a princess. *My mother should see me now*, she thought. She was very beautiful in a lacy birch-colored dress, embroidered with pearls and crystal. Even had she been able to describe it in her letters, she could not have expressed her happiness.

She smiled in admiration at her reflection.

The grand moment arrived.


The trumpets and the herald announced the name of the guest of honour:"The Imperial Princess, the Archduchess of Austria, Princess of Hungary, Bohemia, and Bavaria: Gisela Luisa Maria, and her *dame* Mademoiselle Varsano."

Michaela's heart raced when the doors opened and a row of young men, dressed in uniforms with gold galloons and plumes, made way for the guests. The Princess went in front, on the arm of her cousin Ladislaw, with Michaela immediately behind her, accompanied by a young cadet. The ball began, and Gisela danced the first waltz with her father. And never went back to her chair.

Out of place and alone in that highly visible spot, slightly ill at ease, retired to the powder room to retouch her lipstick. And when she emerged, felt his eyes on her. She perceived his gaze accompanying her steps, and even when she hid behind a column he went on looking for her. When Michaela gathered the courage to emerge from behind the column, Michaela took a deep breath and, fanning her feather *éventail*, stood almost beside him.

He, distracted, still seemed to be looking for her, his attention directed toward the empty chair in the ballroom. Very close to him, Michaela was startled to see the man's resemblance to the photograph of Lucien de Hirsch on the Baron's desk. At that moment she thought of coincidence or fate, or both; surely it could not be Lucien.. But that gentleman so resembled the profile of Clara, with the same brilliant and light-colored blue eyes... And his bearing, she thought. The way of holding his hips with his coat open and moving his head, exactly like the Baron. Definitely, she thought, it could only be Lucien. No  for sure  not...Lucien  lives in Paris...

Her legs were trembling when he turned, smiled, and came in her direction. At that moment, another cadet, bowing, took her by the arm, inviting her for a waltz. She went out onto the dance floor. The back of her neck was burning with the gaze of the supposed Lucien. She danced with lightness and grace, as she had rehearsed so many times in Planegg. He, chatted in a circle of friends, smiled, and watched her every movement.

Then she lost sight of him for a time. When she finally found herself free of her dance partners, Michaela returned to the powder room, and there he was, standing guard at the door. So near her... This time she was certain she would meet him. Her heart beat rapidly and her hands went cold when, looking her directly in the eye, he greeted her with a nod of his head. Michaela responded with a delicate gesture and waved her large fan, hiding her smile. He bowed, inviting her to dance, but at that instant Gisela appeared, accompanied by her father. Not knowing what to do, they bowed to the Emperor, who was already between them. Gisela, taking her arm, whispered in her ear:

"Come, Michaela, we have to go, I want to get out of here; I'll explain later." After a couple of turns around the ballroom, with Gisela at her side, they went up to the princess's quarters. Michaela remained in the dark about the identity of that gentleman.

She said good night to her friend, who had had a bit too much to drink, and went to her room. She looked in the mirror. She was still beautiful and had no wish for the dream to end. She did not take off the gown or the borrowed tiara. She thought about returning to the ball but feared it would be improper.

Unresigned, she didn't want to remain confined in that room. She lit all the lamps, opened the doors, and went directly to the terrace, looking down at the guests as they departed the ballroom.

She hoped to catch a glimpse of him again.

The ball was ending and surely he would appear in the garden or in the line forming in the arches below the veranda, where the guests awaited their carriages. Finally, he emerged, crossing the garden, there below her feet. He was no longer alone but accompanied by a young, sparkling blonde. She felt a pang in her heart.

Motionless, leaning on the parapet, she watched him.

He was chatting with the young woman and looking around as he waited for the carriage. Suddenly, he turned and raised his head, looking toward the palace. He spotted Michaela looking at him. He took a few steps on the greensward and stared, furrowing his brow. As if not believing what he had seen, he smiled and nodded, perplexed.

When the carriage approached, the young woman accompanying him got in and he unhurriedly looked toward Michaela again. Then he entered the carriage and, with a wave of his hand, took his leave.

During the entire week in Vienna she looked for him. In the theatre the opera of Strauss, at the presentation of the imperial cavalry, in the grand parade; but she never again saw him or even found out who he was. Whether it was Lucien himself or not. She never forgot him, and that night he would not leave her thoughts.

For many nights she would dream of him…

The months passed, and Michaela never told Clara of the occurrence in Vienna. And it was indeed better that she never spoke of it.

∾

Almost two years had passed since the night of the spring ball. Much had happened in the interval, but in all that time she had never seen the baroness's son in person.

At the end of February Clara returned to London after an extended stay in the south of France, where, as she put it, she warmed her bones from the cold of winter.

The baroness travelled alone, without the baron, and after a few days in Berkeley Square, finding Michaela absorbed in so much work and responsibilities and already weary of the bad weather in London – and perhaps taking pity on the girl, who did nothing but work–sought to break her routine by inviting her on a little journey.

They would go to Paris. It would be a surprise, she told Michaela. She greatly wished to rest at Rue de l'Élysée, with no social obligations, and had made a raft of plans to spend some days with her son. The two of them, without Maurice. "Just mother and son," she said.

She hoped to meet him at the train station, but to her frustration only the coachman and the baron's secretary in France, the loyal Gustav Held, awaited her. The baroness was disappointed. Lucien had left some days earlier for Esneux, in Belgium, to visit his aunt Hortense Montefiore and had left no word of the date of his return. That was enough to give Clara de Hirsch a powerful stomach ache. Then, disconsolate and fatigued from the trip, when they arrived at the house on Rue de l'Élysée, Clara retired to her quarters without dining and left the Sicilian alone in that enormous palace, where Michaela didn't even know the way to the kitchen.

Michaela would never forget what happened that night.

She was taken to her room, unpacked her bags, and took a leisurely bath in a magnificent tub that the housekeeper, Madame Lory, had prepared.

It was too early to sleep, and through the window she looked at the park outside; the darkened sky presaged a heavy storm. Her hair was still wet and redolent of soap when she lay down, and she regretted having declined the dinner tray. It was past eleven p.m. and she couldn't manage to fall asleep in that large and mysterious mansion.

Rain beat against the windows and on the slate roof, but her empty stomach wouldn't let her sleep. She tossed and turned in bed until she finally decided to go downstairs. She pulled a woollen robe over her fine transparent nightgown. No one, she imagined, would be awake at that hour.

Michaela went down six flights of a staircase decorated with crystal maidens where candles, burning low, threatened to extinguish themselves. She descended slowly, observing everything. Her shadow projected onto the steps below, and the sound of rain on the skylight was menacing.

Feeling cold, Michaela looked for a carafe of liqueur on the tray in the library. She felt the freezing in her bones and was shivering. She added wood to the fireplace and lit the candles in one of the candleholders. Holding it, she searched for a book or something to distract her until sleep came.

But she heard footsteps in the gallery, and someone came into the library. Frightened, she put out the candle and made ready to leave.

The shadow approached. He was a tall man with unkempt hair, wearing a dark rain-soaked overcoat. Michaela's heart raced, but he was slow to notice her. Trying to accustom his eyes to the dim light, he whispered:

"Mother? You're not asleep yet?"

Michaela emerged from the shadow, like a foggy vision before him. He apologized.

"Sorry, but we haven't met. Who are you?"

Seeing him at that moment, her heart beat faster. Michaela recognized him from the ball in Vienna. It was he, the same profile, the same bearing–Lucien. There could be no doubt.

He came out of the penumbra, entering the library, and she, pulling back, was illuminated by a band of light from behind . Without moving, and attempting to close the robe, without which she was almost naked, she answered in a faltering voice:

"You must be… Lucien… I'm Michaela Varsano."

"Oh! So you're the famous Micha?" he replied, turning his back as he removed the wet overcoat and without paying much attention. "Then you must be the Sicilian that my parents talk about so much! Of course… Forgive me, I didn't expect to find you here… In my– I mean, in the library… I thought it was my mother… It could only be her with her insomnia…"

Embarrassed, Michaela attempted to leave, excusing herself.

"I'm going to my room, I–"

At that moment, Lucien stood directly in front of her, blocking her passage, and then, face to face, that they looked closely at each other for the first time. Her heart leaping, she tried to make a hasty exit by brushing past him. Surprised, without thinking, he turned his body and took her by the shoulders. Before she got to the door, he asked in a low voice:

"Wait, Miss Varsano! Please don't run away… Let me look at you again!"

A sudden gust of wind opened one of the windows, blowing out the last of the candles. The storm outside exploded in lightning and thunder, unnerving Michaela, who, disoriented by the darkness and the crash of thunder, retreated several steps and leaned against the wall of the library.

And he, seeing her full-length in the flashes of lightning, was stunned:

"Good God," he exclaimed, "it's you Michaela! The girl from the ball…"

She held her breath, and her legs trembled. Lucien, almost not believing what he was seeing, approached slowly, touched her cheek, and like a blind man trying to recognize a profile, ran his index finger along her face, as if wishing to record it. He caressed her lips and, looking into her eyes, took her face into his hands.

"Then you're real, are you ?" he whispered in her ear. "You… truly exist?"

The tempest ceased. Drops of water dripping from the slate roof continued to clatter on the terrace stones of Rue de l'Élysée.

Only the reddish flames of the coals in the fireplace gilded their silhouettes and warmed them in the immensity of the blackness. And in the darkness she closed her eyes, letting him plunge his mouth into an endless kiss.

At last they had found each other.

The next morning, day dawned with the house enveloped in the fog of deep winter. Michaela awoke startled, her head heavy, and made an effort to remember what had happened the night before. She tried retracing her steps... When, en route to the kitchen, she had stopped in the library, lit a candle, on the work desk was a silver basket with small colored candies. Her empty stomach was aching. She tried one of them, which melted in her mouth like sugared almonds; she couldn't resist and took one after another to sate her hunger.

Afterward, she examined that magnificent room in half-shadow, candelabra in hand, saw Lucien's books, his small sculptures, the colored vases that must be from some excavation. There was a tray with bottles of wine and liqueur, chalices and fluted glasses, and a box of cigars. Michaela was getting acquainted with Lucien de Hirsch's hiding place and was beginning to divine his thoughts.

She filled a wineglass and drank it in a single gulp to kill her thirst, clicking her tongue in pleasure. She laughed. She knew she was doing something wrong, but no one in the house was awake, and suddenly she felt happy, free, and in Paris!

Paris for the first time! She toasted herself before an immense canvas that covered an entire wall. It was a painting in which two young women were serving a corpulent old man. Intrigued, she laughed, not knowing why. One of the women, completely nude, was serving wine from a silver jug to the old man, who was lying down, his genitalia partially covered by a piece of cloth. Another woman, bare-breasted, was caressing the back of his neck.

Michaela felt attracted to the figures. She had never seen anything similar, not even in the books of Madame Arlette, those seminars with stories of bordellos and prostitutes whose existence she had recently discovered and loved to read about secretly—not even in the drawings in those stories had she seen anything as exciting.

It was all odd, the background of the canvas, revealed in the distance the light of a fire, which seemed to her to be that of described in Sodom . She brought the candle closer, curious to read what was written below the gilded frame:

"Rubens, Peter Paul, 1577–1640.

" *Loth et ses filles... Loth and His Daughters...*"

Michaela still remembered what she thought at that moment.

She saw that it was all quite old, painted over two hundred years earlier. And how, ever since that time, there were artists with the imagination to excite a woman. This was probably where Lucien brought women, intending to impress them with figures that had nothing to do with virgins. Her chalice full, she toasted again:

"*Vive la France! La douce France... Vive...* That Rubens fellow can really paint!"

Then she tried another open bottle and another liqueur... She whirled around the room and, tired, sat down, glass in one hand and a book chosen at random in the other. She felt lightheaded, as if on a ship buffeted by waves. She remembered having looked at Lucien's portrait and kissing the picture frame, pressing it against her chest, and then, driven by memories of the ball in Vienna, she must have dozed off.

I must have drunk a lot of wine and liqueur without realizing it, she thought. But the dream was so real..."Good heavens," she said aloud holding her aching head. "It was all so real, I can still smell the *vetivér* perfume, the taste of his kisses." *It must have been a dream*, she thought.

What had really happened, if she didn't even remember how she had made her way up all those stairs to her room?

A clock chime sounded nine times. She had missed the breakfast hour. Clara must be waiting for her .She washed and arranged her hair, put on face powder to cover the dark circles under the eyes that betrayed a night poorly slept, lipstick, and a little of the miraculous peach-colored liquid that brought sunlight to her cheeks.

Ready, she descended the stairs majestically illuminated by the light of day, her heart racing, thinking of how she had climbed all that t Michaela found her way to the breakfast hall by following the sound of a spoon cracking the shell of a boiled egg.

The baroness cracked an egg the same way every morning – three light taps, then pour it almost raw into her porcelain bowl .And there she was. She didn't know how to face Clara after what happened

What if Lucien– Good God... She didn't want to think about. it.

All that Michaela wanted that morning was to get away from there, into the street to be by herself, to refresh her throbbing head. All she would have liked at that moment was to be able to go out on her own to see Paris, walk through the streets and find all those famous historical places she had dreamed of visiting... She would die of embarrassment at seeing Lucien again... If all of that had actually happened... It might have all been just a dream... Well.

But Clara dissuaded her as soon as she arrived for breakfast.

"Go by yourself, Michaela, in this weather? It's not safe to go out alone in this fog; you can get lost in the parks, or be robbed... Paris is a large city with many traps! Blind alleys, hooligans, drunken people, killers..."

Lucien appeared, laughing at what he had just heard.

"Good morning, ladies!" he greeted them, smiling as he kissed Clara on the cheek. "*Maman*! Let me take a look at you... My, how you've changed... How lovely you are!" Backing away to see her better, he looked at Michaela, who felt as if her chest was about to explode.

"Lucien, dear, when did you get here? I wasn't expecting to see you!" exclaimed the baroness, her voice muffled by her son's affectionate embrace.

"I came last night," he answered, smiling. "I got in late, on that wretched train from Brussels. Uncle Ferdinand told me you'd be arriving about now, but he wasn't sure of the date... I thought I could surprise you and moved up my trip. I wanted to put the house in order, but you got here first! All I was able to do was procure some sweets for your arrival, those sugared almonds from Ladurée, that you love.

Well," and he looked at Michaela with a mischievous smile, "I met Miss Varsano yesterday... What a coincidence, I thought. She was—"

Michaela interrupted him.

"It was a scare, Clara," she tried to explain. "I heard the sound of a door shutting and footsteps in the gallery. He came in, and I was in a robe, looking for a book to read. I almost died of embarrassment!"

Clara looked at her son and spread her arms to hug him again. She embraced him tightly and closed her beautiful blue eyes when she kissed his cheeks. And clinched in his mother's arms, he winked at Michaela...

At that moment, Michaela began to know Lucien Hirsch.
The man of her dreams...

෨

Those were happy days for Clara, who spend most of the time
close to her son. Entire afternoons closeted in the library, catching up
on conversation or strolling in the garden, arm in arm with the young
man, or else beside the fireplace, until late hours. She admired the new
trophies, coins, and documents he had acquired in recent years,
augmenting his precious collection. When she was with her son the
baroness was a different person. She would laugh and chat,
unburdened by ceremonies and worries. She was unconcerned with
schedules and slept till later. Lunch and dinner could wait; in those days
there was no timetable for anything. It was Lucien who determined the
time. And she would say:
"This house is his, Micha, he is the one who guides us here in
Paris."

Michaela remembered her times in Taormina, Clara at
Mongibello for Shabbat, and how her mother had done everything
possible to prepare for such an illustrious visitor that evening. And
now, sharing her life, Michaela was better able to understand her. Clara
was an unpretentious woman with simple tastes and, above all, a
mother like all mothers, concerned with loving and being loved by her
son. With her son Lucien she felt happy, and he in turn found no more
time for Michaela.

In addition to following her from a distance with his long gazes, Lucien wrote her a few lines, kisses and embraces were exchanged secretly one night at the stairs and in the balcony. He sent her notes setting a meeting outside, but the two never had a real opportunity.

Clara monopolized his every second.

After the Baron arrived, everything changed. Lucien and Michaela hardly spoke in the days that Maurice dominated the conversation at dinner. His expression became once again that of the old portrait. Sad and taciturn, he didn't wait for dessert or the liqueur and excused himself. Maurice tried to lighten the atmosphere by telling anecdotes or inviting his son to a dinner at the Café Anglais, the place where aristocratic young men and single European women met.

"We must go there one of those nights Lucien! It is just time to put aside for a bit those coins and books and see other wonders. The world is more than just the library at Rue de l'Élysée! I would have liked for you to accompany us yesterday, when we had dinner with your uncle Ferdinand. I met a fantastic girl for you and I wanted you to see her, son. She is your type, English, as had to be. A lady, petite, elegant and independent. And best of all, she has good ideas!"

Lucien closed his eyes, irritating his father, who continued telling of the encounter. "Listening to Margot Tennant's ideas at the table I said to myself: this is the daughter-in-law I would love to have! Don´t you agree, Clara?"

"Which ideas are you referring to... that Lady Tennant mentioned to you?" asked Clara, gauging her son's expression.

"Idea..ideas about marriage! What else could I want to know from a young lady? We talked about it a lot; she's single and attractive and in no hurry to find a husband. She wouldn't marry for money even if tempted. And to be frank, I tempted her with my ideas, but she was emphatic and even became nervous when we discussed the idea of marrying for money. We talked about London society. I said people there were more drawn to money than anywhere else. And that a rich Englishman finds it easy to get the wife he wants and that, faced with money, there's no such thing as a difficult woman."

Lucien nodded his head, puzzled by what he was hearing.

"She turned red with anger and confronted me, *la mignonne!*" the baron concluded.

"And what did she... Lady Tennant, reply to your rudeness, Maurice?" asked Clara, shaking her head in disapproval.

"She replied, 'Sir, I doubt it! English girls do not marry for money.' Imagine... English girls don't marry for money!"

And he burst into sarcastic laughter. "Then I answered," the baron continued, laughing heartily,

"You speak for yourself, my dear Lady Tennant, but I think you'll never be disappointed in the future, because I don't believe it's your dream to become the wife of a poor man, is it?... And to live at the edge of town. Think what your life would be like if you couldn't do what gives you pleasure: go hunting and ride your horses, always well dressed, or have those wonderful Worth dresses such as you now wear and have just stained with this marvellous Champagne...'"

"But father!" exclaimed Lucien. "And you still want me to meet her? I would die of shame after what you told Lady Tennant... Do you honestly believe in the ideas of that lady?"

Maurice de Hirsch took a long swallow from his wineglass and carefully placed it on the immaculately white tablecloth. He ran his fingers over the glass and looked at Lucien seriously.

"To be totally honest with you, my son, I believed her when she denied to the end that she would ever marry out of interest and failed to show the slightest curiosity about meeting you.. And that's why I want you to meet her."

✍

# XVII

## BERKELEY SQUARE

London, spring 1885.

Living in Berkeley Square implied getting to know and greeting one's neighbors, a totally different experience from the friendships, Michaela had had in Taormina or in Planegg. There, while her responsibilities were great, she wasn't looked upon as the Sicilian savage or scolded like a schoolgirl by Helga, the housekeeper who had stayed behind in Bavaria.

Now she was Miss Varsano, Michaela Varsano, assistant of the Alliance Israélite Universelle, who coordinated funds for the schools, studied of German and Greek, took part in meetings, and, according to her neighbour

Hannah Rosebery, had amassed a legion of suitors. But Michaela didn't have eyes for anyone.

There was a music teacher in Munich madly in love, and they exchanged letters after she left Planegg. But with time, she lost interest in continuing the correspondence. Clara thought she had found a beau or a great passion…

After this first encounter with Lucien in March, Michaela received a letter he sent from Paris, as if he had known her for a long time. He knew everything about her, he said, spoke of his jealousy when Clara in her letters mentioned the Sicilian girl affectionately. He apologized for the tense moments generated in the presence of the baron.

*"Someday you'll understand the reason,"* he wrote. *"I admire my father, I love him, but there's a secret in his life that for some years has made my mother suffer. You, who live with them, must have realized it by now. His presence and his absence, it all affects my life. He wants me to think, act, and love like him. He's the Baron. I chose not to be like him; I will never marry only to later repent."*

At first Michaela couldn't understand Lucien's harsh words against his father. A father who was concerned with him, who gave him everything, an admired man of character who loved Clara and treated everyone in the best way possible. What did he mean about marrying and later repenting?

But Lucien also seemed to be repentant. Not another word about those dreams, about the encounter in Vienna that night .

One day he wrote saying that he had one dream in life: to see once more the girl he had glimpsed at a ball. He loved her. He dreamed about her every night, but when he approached, she fled from his hands. And then his father would interrupt his dream, introducing him to some princess or countess.

One day he met her, finding her in his library, sleeping in an armchair, shivering from cold, wrapped in a robe, clutching his photo to her breast and, as if in a fairy tale, he awoke her with a kiss.

He whispered in her ear, his heart racing, that he had found her, that she was the woman of his dreams and would someday be his forever…

❦

In Taormina, Anna Varsano read aloud to Raffaele Michaela's letter, speaking of her friendship with Lucien and their almost secretive exchange of correspondence. Fearful that the baron would eventually open one of his letters, all of the correspondence coming from Paris, from Rue de l'Élysée, was addressed to Miss Varsano of Berkeley Square but with a different number, that of Hannah's house, care of Lady Rosebery. A mature woman who had shown great friendship to Michaela, Hannah Rosebery would keep the secret. She knew the two young people were in love and regretted that Clara couldn't be part of the secret. The mere thought of it made Michaela blush in embarrassment.

In Mongibello, Raffaele reread Michaela's letter. To him it was more than just a friendship, for there are no friendships between men and women. There's attraction, interest, love. To him what Michaela was feeling was love.

"Poor Michaela… *Poverina mia*," he murmured. Only he really understood his granddaughter, and he foresaw the reaction of the Hirsches.

Clara Bischoffsheim is a straightforward and wonderful person, he thought, but in all certainty it wasn't his Michaela who would be a candidate for her son's wife. And then there was the baron, who was constantly arranging suitable matches for the young man.

"What if they found out about the friendship?" asked Anna, concerned. Micha would find herself in a tight spot. She would lose the credibility and affection of that family and might even be called a user or a gold digger!

"And besides everything else," Raffaele commented, "do you remember what you told me about those women at the hotel, trying on your clothes. That the baron has a mistress…"

"Poor thing!" sighed Anna. "Could there be another woman in the baron's life? Could that be why his son feels such resentment toward his father and made that remark to Michaela about repentance in marriage? There must be something going on!"

Raffaele laughed at Anna's naïveté.

"What rich men in Taormina does not have mistresses, two or three houses and illegitimate children? And it wouldn't happen in other places, with other respectable men just because they have titles of nobility? And you, *signora* Varsano, earn your living sewing for whom? Isn't it you who dresses most of the mistresses of those nobles who come to Taormina while their poor rich wives, covered with jewels and living in castles and palaces, are merely governesses for their children? How ingenuous my daughter is!"

Anna was thinking of Alberto, whether he would one day summon the courage to act like those men, find a lover and set up another house and family, or had already done so! She was angry. For months, Alberto had disappeared with a Moroccan, someone called Daud, and perhaps they were living in a harem with sultanas and odalisques… Like in *The Thousand and One Nights*. With him paying the Sultans with his creams and perfumes, and that Daud fellow opening doors to some Ottoman Empire palace for him. No one had news of Alberto Varsano. Not even his brother David, nor even Michaela, who in her latest letter related events of the trip to Constantinople and Büyükdere. And nothing else. Since then she had learned he had left his lodging in Marika's house in Salonica, and no one knew his whereabouts. Alberto's last letter to Michaela had been sent to Planegg, and Micha was no longer there. It had been in Paris that one April evening the baron had handed her the yellowed envelope bearing stamps of the Ottoman Empire.

"Count Frederick sent it to me from Planegg," he told her. "It came in the pouch from the Bank of Paris. News for you, *signorina*!"

The long-awaited letter arrived just as dinner was served. Michaela left the envelope beside the crystal glass in order not to appear discourteous to those at the table. Lucien signalled her not to read it in front of the others. Clara touched her leg and whispered,

"Leave it to read later, dear…"

But her desire was to dash to her room and read her father's letter. She had often dreamed about him during those months. She had sought news in the reports of the Alliance Israélite Universelle arriving from Salonica, pictures of groups of men who maintained or ran the institutions there. But her father had surely not yet become an important man, a rich merchant; he must still be living off his brother. Or, now that David and Katherina were married, he had simply vanished from the city with that man Daud. What a strange friendship theirs was!

"Micha is *distrracted* and *harrdly* touched her dish," the baron remarked, smiling at seeing the girl blush. "Let's go to the library, son, and have a cognac; that way the women can be free to talk about the news," he said, rising and tossing his napkin on the table. As the two walked away, Michaela, remained seated, awaiting the moment when she could open the letter.

"What torture!" Clara commented. "You must be in agony. Open it and read it at once!"

The letter, written on common brown paper, had a map on its other side.

Clara calmly finished eating her profiteroles and kept her gaze on the Sicilian's face. Her large and expressive eyes, shining in the candlelight, attentively followed each line. Gradually her forehead knitted and her eyebrows rose.

She accompanied the young woman reading in a silence broken only by Michaela's sighs. She knew the latest news from the *Dottore*, still in Constantinople, worried his daughter. It told of his plans to bring the Moroccan Daud to live with him in Salonica and to undertake a new business venture. But *Dottore* Varsano had a head full of plans and empty pockets. He had bought a piece of land distant from the city, using the last of the savings he had managed to accumulate in twenty years of working in Galliani's pharmacy.

The *Dottore*, full of hope, said that at the foot of Kortiarthis mountain, well above the Vardar district and near the Jewish cemetery, was a good strip of land for planting, with its own source of water. According to his friend Daud, who was knowledgeable about that type of plantation, they had managed to bring many seedlings of Damascus roses, the so-called *Kazanlik*, from Isparta. Seedlings that made the journey from port on his friend Levy's wagon.

He happily related that the roses were of a species so rare that there was nothing like them elsewhere, and that they would be specifically for the manufacture of essences and the perfumes he dreamed of.

And that later, after the rose plantation was producing, he and the Moroccan would set up a distillery of essences. Then they would construct a shed and maybe afterward, who knows, a small house to receive Anna and Michaela.

She read and reread the letter, then turned it over to see the map.

There were scribbles, arrows, and drawings. He described the city, the port, the Promenade, various houses, a tower, and with arrows indicated the land and the cemetery. A circle marked the spot.

In larger letters, Alberto wrote:

*Here, my daughter, will be constructed the first "factory" of Rose Water in the Ottoman Empire, he wrote below the arrow pointing to the site. The perfume that I plan to dedicate to you, my dear, will be made from the attar, with the essence of those roses and nuances of jasmine and sandalwood...*

*The "Rose du Soir" will be in your honour.*

"May God assist him," muttered Michaela, sighing and slowly folding the letter. Tears were streaming down her cheeks. The baroness, caressing her hands, asked in a soft voice, "What's distressing you, Micha? Can you tell me, dear?"

"O Lord! Don't let him go wrong this time, make everything turn out right..." she murmured.

Michaela handed her the letter, and Clara felt awkward, not knowing if she should read it. "Please read it, Clara, and see if what my father is dreaming of can someday come true. I don't know Salonica.

How can I judge whether the piece of land he bought is worth his life savings?"

Bringing the candelabra closer, the baroness accompanied each line with a nod of her head. She turned the page, and a questioning wrinkle appeared on her brow. Then, placing the letter on the table, she said:

"I don't know what to tell you, my dear. I was in Salonica for just one day. I don't remember it well... Maybe Maurice can help you. If you want, we can show the map to him."

They didn't even have to leave the dining room. The baron returned from the library with his customary cigar and a glass of cognac in his hand.

We were just speaking of you, Maurice, and about our trip to Salonica. Maybe you can help Michaela. Show him the map, dear... Perhaps he knows where it is," said Clara.

"Do you know this place?" asked Michaela, showing him the map. "It is a piece of land my father bought in Salonica."

The baron calmly set down his glass, removed the monocle from his pocket, and took a puff of his cigar. He sat down in Michaela's chair and pulled the candelabra nearer his eyes. "Let's see," he said. "Close to the *cemeterry*... Hmm. Between Vardar and... I don't understand. Even if I were an *experrt carrtographer*, I couldn't say exactly what the *arrea* is like... But now I'm *currious;* why do you want to know?"

"Nothing important. Just curiosity," Michaela replied in a faint voice, embarrassed.

"You *rreally* are *currious*, my little one," he said, stretching the map over the linen tablecloth. "But we'll soon find out."
He again perused the map, turning it in various directions.

"Hmm... the sea, the port, the Promenade, hmm, now I know... Clara! Don't you remember that we visited that area during the eight hours we were in Salonica?"

Clara went back to the map, her head almost touching the baron's. She squinted as if making a powerful effort to recall every detail.

"Maurice, is that by any chance the area you bought near the cemetery?" she said, pointing to a spot very close to the *Dottore's*.

"It may be, dear, but perhaps this drawing isn't all that precise."

"Near the cemetery?" asked Michaela, startled. "My father expects to live with my mother near a cemetery?"

The couple burst out laughing at Michaela's uneasiness.

"Near is a figure of speech," explained Clara. "It's just a reference point."

"Give it to me," said the baron, laughing. "Women don't understand maps. If you'll allow, Micha, tomorrow I can ask the Porte cartographers to conduct a survey of that area. They can even take photographs! In a short time you'll satisfy that Sicilian curiosity and– *voilà!*–hold Salonica in your hands, my little one."

That night, in the Hirsches' bedroom, Clara was unable to sleep. She left the bed and got the map from the baron's desk.
She reread the letter. Then, on stationery with her letterhead, she wrote to Maurice:

> *Maurice,*
>
> *Read this letter carefully.*
>
> *I had no idea of the Varsanos' situation. Now I have.*
> *We cannot allow our Dottore Varsano to suffer a new disappointment.*
> *He cannot and must not wait for the roses to blossom with his pockets empty, and I am also sure that his Venetian pride will not accept collaboration on our part.*
> *Why don't we buy that land and incorporate the rose plantation as a garden in our project? There we can build our new Hirsch villa and a large hospital...*
> *And we can send there, many families that we are rescuing from the hands of the Czar.*
> *Think about an urgent solution.*
>
> *May you have a good day, my beloved.*
> *Clara*

# XVIII

## HANNAH DE ROSEBERRY

London, summer 1886.

The Hirsches arrived in London in the summer.

The townhouse, number 12, Berkeley Square, was lit, its windows opened after many years, and Hannah was the first neighbour to knock at the door in welcome. Michaela was there, lost in the dark dusty house. It all belonged to Clara, part of the patrimony from her family's bank and was a strange and poorly kept place. There was no sign that anyone had lived there for years. Other than a small number of pieces of furniture, an immense table with a few chairs, along with trays and china for tea, there was nothing else.

Nor was there anything in the kitchen besides old teakettles. A soot-covered stove betrayed how long it had gone unused. Seen from the street, the house had an elegant facade and blended in with the other identical dwellings across the square. But from what she had heard from Clara before departing, the townhouse was a place to discuss business, where meetings were held to settle accounts as well as sporadic encounters with her brothers.

The Baron refused to stay there a single day. His pride would not permit it. After all, he was the new lord of Bath House in Piccadilly, and even though every argument was used to persuade him, his answer was always:

" I have my principles... I'm not going to live on the Bischoffsheims' property!"

He strongly resisted sending his belongings to that address, and only after Clara, hurt, stopped speaking to him for days, he phlegmatically nodded at her, as was his custom, and accepted that all would be as she desired."It will only be for a short time," she repeated.

"Just long enough for the work in Piccadilly to be completed."

The Hirsches' new address, Bath House, must be worthy of princes and kings, nobles like Edward, Prince of Wales. It would be the most palatial pied-à-terre in London .He was in a hurry, but anything less than a year would be unreasonable. So for now Berkeley would do. It would be necessary to designate someone to take charge of the move and the small-scale remodelling of the house until it was habitable. Clara's health wasn't up to visiting a dusty house to choose everything, and in any case there were architects and firms for such things.

Clara and the Maurice would go to Vienna in August and then spend some time in Beauregard. November was the month for London and the palace balls, and they would be with Lucien on Rue de l'Élysée in Paris.

The Baroness appointed Michaela to put everything in order. Impossible, thought Michaela. Who am I to assume all of this?

She didn't know the place, had no experience, and there was the language question, her Italian accent always getting in the way, plus mixing German in all her utterances... But there was no way to refuse; Clara gave her total power and freedom to do whatever she wanted, to hire the finest in London, in personnel and materials, to make it the most enticing, most elegant townhouse in the city.

"Now it's a matter of honour," repeated the baron softly to Michaela when they left the dinner table. It's a kind of competition, thought Michaela. The baron, with his mansion in Piccadilly and an arsenal of builders, and Clara, passing the baton to her. The account at the Bischoffsheim Bank was at Michaela's disposal, along with its director, a Belgian, two servants who barely understood her orders, and a coachman contracted by the hour. The remainder of the people who wandered about the house were workers hired to deal with the roof and the chimneys, cabinetmakers, and painters.

She must not fail. In her task she was the representative of Clara's self-esteem, wishing for the first time to demonstrate independence and will to her husband. After a certain age, people begin to see everything from a different perspective. It's like going from the orchestra section in a theatre to a box seat when attending an opera, she remarked one day. One can't fail to notice any small slip there on stage, as if everything had become more transparent."Like a sparkling glass where we see our own image reflected in one light and that of others in a different light. Do you understand me, Michaela?"

She had long been in the baron's shadow, but now something had changed.

Michaela knew Clara as two different people. One, a fragile and delicate figure, with an ever benevolent gaze, the baroness of the frozen mornings in Planegg, crossing to the hunting hall, at night tending to the elderly religious refugees fleeing persecution, the blankets, Mirla's soup, and Yosef's shoes—everything that she took care of personally.

The baroness, ensconced in her chamber from early morning, calculating funds, the thousands of pounds intended for new works of hospitals and schools, visits to the sick, comforting the poor, going from one institution to another, never discriminating if they were Jews or gentiles. She was a different Clara when she was alone with Lucien. A loving mother, laughter, hugs, a woman inspired, cheerful and voluble, with shining eyes and the rosy skin of happiness. Maurice de Hirsch made of her a solicitous wife, his faithful secretary and, probably, his wisest adviser.

Michaela felt ill at ease with such thoughts, as if her stomach were frozen. A sensation of wanting everything and knowing nothing. She needed someone! She imagined herself there with Gisela. What would she advise?

Or Helga, with her sarcastic smile and wishing her good luck as she departed for her new life in the city where the sun never shone...
She looked at the picture frames, lined up to be cleaned, the canvases leaning against the walls and the mirrors covered with thick layers of wool, trying to imagine everything in place and herself in the library amid gleaming crystal. At the baron's desk she saw Lucien, saw him approaching, so near that she could feel his breath and the heat of his lips against her cheek.

A tremor ran through her body, as when he had embraced her.

She breathed deeply, her eyes half-closed, leaning against the library door. And there she remained, until surprised by an unknown and unexpected visitor.

∼♉

Hannah Rosebery appeared from nowhere, entering the vestibule with a plate of cookies in one hand while with the other hand she held a small blond boy who stared at Michaela with curious eyes.

It was raining heavily that day, and no one had heard the neighbour knocking at the front door. They came in with their shoes soaked and stained by the rain.

She sat on the steps of the staircase, apologizing to Michaela, and removed the boy's shoes.

Michaela, still startled and not knowing what to do to help the lady, placed the dish on the mantel of the fireplace and dashed to fetch a towel.

The neighbour thanked her, drying her face and her son's head, and remained sitting there, displaying a friendly smile and observing the still bare house. She looked around, then with utmost simplicity addressed Michaela:

"It's just like mine, but seeing it this way, still empty, it seems much larger! Oh, forgive me, I haven't introduced myself. I'm Hannah de Rosebery, your neighbour to the right."

"A great pleasure Madame," said Michaela, curtsying. "I'm Michaela Varsano, I'm– I'm– well, a friend of the Hirsches, I mean, I live with them…" She smiled, not knowing how to explain succinctly what she was, what she wasn't, and what she was doing there.

After all, it was difficult to explain in English, even more so to a stranger!

Hannah got up from the stairs with difficulty, and Michaela observed that the lady with the fine and delicate features had a body disproportional to her face.

"Well, I'll leave you with my wishes for happiness, Miss Varsano, both in this house and in this city, which must be new to you."

The boy, seeing Michaela looking at him and smiling, hid behind his mother.

"This is my son Harry, the most curious of all four and also the most outgoing. Since the masons and painters began their work here, Harry and Neil, when they saw the movers arriving, couldn't resist, wanting to know how many children would be living in this house. I think the workers, to get rid of them, must have told them that a prince would live in the blue room, and in the pink room, a beautiful princess! You know," she went on, "Neil couldn't come with us to take cookies to the princess because he's got a high fever. But he's anxious to meet her."

" Who, to what princess are you referring?" asked Michaela with an expression of curiosity.

"*Thaat… princesss…* you know who… Miss," the neighbour answered, making a signal for her to not say anything further in the presence of the boy.

"Ah yes, Mrs. Rosebery. Now I understand about the princess… She hasn't arrived yet but will get here one of these days, and then she'll meet Harry and Neil," Michaela said, winking.

"You know," said Mrs. Rosebery slowly, "Neil is very ill today, but he'll be very happy to know he will one day have a 'princess' as neighbour and friend, and even more so to learn that you also tell wonderful stories…"

Little Harry ascended two steps and pulled on his mother's arm to whisper something in her ear.

"But of course, Harry, as soon as the lady finishes her work she can come have dinner with us! Do you accept, Miss Varsano?"

Thus was born the great friendship between Hannah de Rosebery and Michaela Varsano.

The Sicilian spent the winter months without the presence of Clara and Maurice, only sending telegrams and letters through the bank's mail pouch. Clara answered Michaela's questions monosyllabically. She must be enjoying herself so much in Beauregard or the south of France that she didn't care about the color of the dining room chairs. Or where this or that picture would be hung.

She merely wrote: "Micha, do as you like, I have confidence in your good taste, and in any case we won't be there very long!"

The move would be temporary, for the large *"maison* de Piccadilly" should be remodelled and decorated by the following summer.

But with the help of Hannah, a woman with experience and refinement, the Berkeley Square house was turned into an exceptional dwelling.

As Michaela had no obligations, she spent hours thinking of what to do, and Hannah, at the end of the afternoon, after freeing herself from social tasks and leaving the children with the nannies, would come to plan the details with her and how to execute each step.

They visited galleries and the leading furniture dealers in the city in search of chairs and chaises, lamps and chandeliers from Paris, crystal and mirrors–an immense number of objects that would replace those left behind in Planegg, but with an air of newness, less heavy, more comfortable and elegant: after all, the house was only a house and not a palace!

∽

Lucien's room remained as it had always been in Bavaria. That was Clara's sole request. After becoming acquainted with the real Lucien and not the spoiled young man that Helga described, Michaela understood Clara's request.

Lucien, she thought, would come to London one day and find there everything he had left behind in Planegg; his memory and his childhood would be there, awaiting him. His stamp albums kept in the drawers of the dresser, his childish sketches painted on yellowed cards, his games and riddles, and his travel notebooks that recorded everything, with drawings and descriptions.

Michaela would go into that room every afternoon, caress the sheepskin blanket, straighten the voile of the curtains, and sigh…

The house in Berkeley Square had an aura, and Michaela felt as if it were her own home. The home of her dreams, the dreams that lately she experienced even when awake. A poor Sicilian woman and an enchanted prince, who lived there happily ever after.

But the house was the Baron's, or rather, Clara de Hirsch's, that house Michaela had found empty and little by little had transformed, like a fairy godmother with a magic wand, into an enchanted castle.

The reception area was lit by a large stained glass window and had a staircase of black marble, while the vestibule formed a rotunda with double doors leading into three rooms: the library, the music- and sitting room, and the dining room .The kitchen was located some steps below the dining room, next to the wall of the gardens that in the rear abutted that of Hannah's house. Two stoves had been placed in opposite corners, and in the middle was a stone table for preparing food. The worn porcelain sinks were refurbished and hot water came from a new coal-burning boiler.

Hannah de Rosebery helped Micha catalogue the Baron's books, as she had earlier done with the library of her husband, Lord Rosebery. Sybil, Margareth, and the twins Neil and Harry, Hannah's still young children, formed a line, passing from hand to hand the books from the boxes. To entertain them, Hannah designated a stack of books for each one to take care of. Harry and Neil handled Jewish, political, historical, and geographical themes. Sybil was in charge of books on philosophy, mathematics, law and science, and Margareth had the stack with literature. It was amusing, since none of them knew how to read yet. And when the task was complete, all the books belonging to the Baron's family were there.

Her eyes closed, Michaela caressed the books. The smell of the leather brought back memories of Lucien in the library at Rue de l'Élysée, with his precious ancient coins, the large chest full of small velvet-lined drawers in which he stored his treasures. The sight of Lucien at his work desk, the heat of his proximity. The covert stolen kisses… The fine blouse of pink organza, the lost buttons, the strong agile hands of that man, the first to embrace her, to kiss her. Embers crackling in the fireplace, hearts racing. Her cheeks were burning when she came back to reality and heard Hannah calling her.

The girls had put the picture frames and the nymph-clock on the mantel. They wanted to know whose pictures they were, and Hannah spoke of Lucien.

"I met him some years ago. Right after I married, they would come sporadically to London, and sometimes he would stay at this house. I remember him, very genteel, a young gentleman. He was talkative and happy. But in recent visits, whenever we chanced to meet, he had changed. He had become a handsome man, but a sad one. I don't know what could be missing in his life. Do you know him well, Michaela?" Michaela....? Hannah asked.

She shrugged, then blushed.

"I met him in Paris, when I went with Clara to visit him. He's a good son, affectionate with his mother, but near the baron he is transformed, and I don't understand why... You know, Hannah," she said, pensive, "I really feel sorry for Clara... She's always making plans, and at the last minute Lucien finds some excuse not to leave Paris. But when she goes there he's somewhere else. I don't know why he acts like that... and he's the only son she has in the world!"

Hannah sighed. She changed the subject and called the children:

"Let's go, little ones, today you worked like grownups. Your father will be so proud when he finds out you know how to organize a library!"

The children closed the doors and all four left arm in arm, skipping with joy. With Michaela now free from work, they could listen to more tales from her native land.

"Just where is your home, Miss Varsano?" asked Margareth, the most curious. "Show me on the globe again."

She pointed on the globe to the boot of Italy and there below, a place called Sicily, and to the side a small dot called Taormina, and inside that dot a place known as Mongibello.

"The loveliest place in the world!" she exclaimed.

"You know what my dream is, Michaela?" said Hannah. "To someday buy a house on the Bay of Naples, with an immense garden, and spend all the summer holidays there with the children. But, as you know, my husband is a politician, and Parliament doesn't leave any time for family life. So I don't even dare mention the subject; we go to Dalmeny, and that's all. Let's go home now, children; tell Miss Varsano good night."

In the dining room, the walls covered with lemon-colored silk brought the sun of Taormina into the room, matching the set of dishes with their lemons painted in the Bongiovannis' studio. Michaela opened the china cabinet, ran her hand along one of the plates. She missed her mother, her home, the happy times with just the four of them, in Mongibello. She traversed the silent and deserted house and went down to her bedroom, the smallest of all, in the rear of the house, which she had chosen as her refuge, fell onto the bed and, hugging the pillow, cried herself to sleep.

⁊

In the days that followed, Berkeley Square was overtaken by frenzy—carriages, people in the streets, and facades being cleaned. Window boxes, their contents desiccated by the long winter, were replanted or received green seedlings. For the first time, the Sicilian saw a ray of sunshine in the garden. And, almost without believing it, she saw the tiny buds of white narcissus sprout from the earth. At the start of spring, the Hirsches' house as organized as the hands of the nymph-clock, which didn't lose a single minute, and all of it thanks to Hannah's help. A new coachman at the disposal of the house took Michaela to shop every morning: Jeremy, an old sailor from the north, married to a Portuguese woman named Amelia. She took care of the kitchen and washed the household clothes, and her daughter Manuela was the pantry maid, all under the command of the butler, Sebastian. He had known Hannah de Rosebery since she was a child and had been her riding instructor at Mentmore, her father's properties in Buckinghamshire. It was he who accompanied Baron Meyer de Rothschild on his outings and the purchase of animals.

Hannah had learned much from her father. But with Sebastian Clair she learned to be brave, fearless, to leap over obstacles both in competition and in real life. Orphaned at an early age, losing first her mother then her father, it was Sebastian and his wife, Elizabeth, in whom Hannah confided. Raised, comforted, and loved by two simple people, she learned everything that a woman needed to know as human being, wife, and mother to have a worthy and happy life.

Elizabeth said that all the money in the world could not bring happiness or joy. But a sincere and unselfish love was the principal thing in life, health, children, a happy home and a stove always lit–these showed more joy of living than a mountain of pounds in the bank.

"The worst thing in life is being the custodian of a fortune," Elizabeth would say. "You have to live a normal life, Hannah, and you only live once! The size of the inheritance doesn't matter; what matters is that you can't let it weigh down your life, can't let it dominate your days and your future. You must choose your future and find your own happiness."

Sebastian rose from coachman to manager of the lands, and afterward to all of Mentmore, until in 1878, at the age of 27, Hannah Rothschild married Archibald Phillip Primrose Rosebery, a member of the House of Lords. Young, intelligent and attractive, the fifth earl of the Primrose dynasty, had inherited in 1868 the titles of Lord Dalmeny in Eton and the properties in Scotland and Epsom. He fell in love with Hannah because, unlike other heiresses, she was simple, human, and different.

The marriage was noted in the upper levels of Parliament: the orphaned daughter of Baron Meyer Rothschild, heiress to an immense fortune, beautiful, delicate, and an excellent horsewoman, joined her life to the most promising young politician of his time. All under the sponsorship of Lord Disraeli, who had introduced them.

When Sebastian Clair came from Mentmore as a widower, without his Elizabeth and ready to help Hannah in Berkeley Square, Lord Rosebery wished to sever his wife's ties to the past and bought a small house for Sebastian in Reeves Mews, almost six blocks from their residence. He knew everything about castles, was well mannered and sensible, and over the years had acquired refinement and good taste. Sebastian was a strong man and desired to go on working, and Hannah wished to find him employment with people who would recognize his qualities.

With Michaela and the Hirsches he would have more motivation to go on living, taking care of everything with attention and would be able to participate more closely in the life of Hannah and her children.

He was the butler Michaela dreamed of finding for Clara.

And it was with his great assistance that everything was made ready. He organized the clothing list, purchases, garden work, the service schedule, trained Manuela to take care of the pantry, and taught the tricks of a well-made bed: sheets and pillowcases ironed on the bed itself, sprinkled with lavender water. In the bathrooms, alongside basins of water, hot towels on which were placed a bouquet of dried flowers.

Sebastian Clair was so in love with his work that he trained the servants in every detail. He planned with them how they should serve, bought special silverware for each type of dish, and demonstrated how to conduct themselves in front of the master and his wife.

Only one problem occurred in the house. The butler chided the strong spices used by the cook, Amelia. But Michaela loved them. The house full of the smell of food prepared by the Portuguese woman recalled Mongibello, and with time, she thought, Sebastian would come to like it. English food was a horror, and she wrote to her mother in Taormina:

"Send me your recipe for lamb and eggplant, because here in London there's a market so large that I found even our lemons. There are gallons of green olive oil, and sometimes eggplants and tomatoes. And even bell peppers. All of it from the coast of Spain or other warm places. When Clara arrives I want to surprise her on Shabbat by repeating that dinner you offered them. Without, of course, our Indian figs and our Sicilian orange slices with almond paste."

Very early, the coachman Jeremy would go to the fish market, accompanied by Amelia and Michaela. The butler advised the Portuguese woman: "For a good stew, Amelia, one has to make good purchases. And both of you, buy with care and love. Each fish must be carefully chosen. Red gills, shining eyes. The perfume of the sea."

And Amelia complained to her husband in that thick accent of hers.

"Who does that 'lord' think he is? Some Portuguese count from the estate of don Alfonso?"

I'm going to show him what our cooking is like. Just wait till the master gets here. He'll love it. With our seasoning, with olive oil and onion..."

" Heaven give me the patience to deal with these English!"

The smell of the seaweed in the noisy Fish Market brought back distant memories to both woman, recalling the sea, the sun, the wind and the perfumed breeze, and they would spend hours there, going from basket to basket in search of one fish here, another there, chatting with vendors and fishermen, exchanging ideas about recipes and seasonings. Amelia introduced into the cuisine of the house dried salted fish with its terrible smell. Codfish, which the English sold for pennies because it was something only sailors ate, was for Amelia an incomparable delicacy. And what a recipe...To disguise the strong odour, she would place the pieces on the top shelf in the scullery, in clay bowls, and change the water several times a day for three days. After soaking, the fish would swell up, and the meat was seasoned with dry herbs, olive oil and garlic and put onto the large wood-burning stove to cook for hours and hours in a covered pot.

The dish became famous in the dinners the Hirsches gave after their return from Beauregard. The earthenware dishes went directly to the table, in a lemon-colored dining room with Sicilian plates and copper pans with rice or mashed potatoes. Everything was accompanied by small sauce containers, with peppers from the northern coast of Africa.

Michaela wrote to Anna Varsano telling bout her new house, for she felt she was part of it, of the remodelling, the decoration she had done, of Amelia's recipes, of Sebastian, her friend Hannah de Rosebery, née Rothschild, and her children. She wrote about the arrival of Clara and Maurice as well, their surprise and joy at seeing how the old townhouse had been transformed, and what the baroness had told her after a few days living there:

*"Micha, I'm so happy here that I cannot think of living in Piccadilly. For what? More servants, more work and bother... To host kings and princes? Only in Maurice's mind... He doesn't even have time to live, to have a private life, he is always tied up with one thing or another,"* she continued.

*"This house has a different aura from all the others where I've lived. It seems filled with happiness, it has light and colours that transport me to a warm and sunny place. It has much of you and of Mongibello.*

*You made it the way it is... And I want to tell you that it's the best present I've ever received in my life! The greatest demonstration of affection I've ever had. Arriving here, a place that was so sad and abandoned, and seeing it transformed like magic into a house full of aromas, a stove that's always burning, the table set and everything in its proper place..."*

Clara hugged Michaela and kissed her forehead.

"You know, my dear," she said, laughing, "you can even get married now! And to a good match! With this experience and refinement, you can easily run a house with ability and taste. But before that, let us begin looking for a match, shall we, dear?"

"Match?" asked Michaela, distracted.

"Micha, do you find it normal for a grown woman, young and beautiful like you, to spend all her time inside this house? Staying here taking care of everything and in addition the bills and funds of the Alliance, the things that Maurice pushes onto you to handle, with no social life, without friends! After all, Hannah Rosebery is older than you, a married woman with children, and you know what her husband is like, a bit jealous of her free time. We are going to find new friends for you, so you can get out of this house and see the world outside!"

Now Clara was speaking the way Maurice customarily spoke to Lucien. She had pretended not to notice that for Micha everything had changed since that trip to Paris. Clara no longer spoke of Lucien as before: "You would love to meet my Lucien."

Nor had she mentioned whether he had appeared at Beauregard. It was as if the subject of Lucien Hirsch had ceased to be of interest to her. Or was now beyond her reach .Even after the compliments from visitors and friends who had seen what Micha had done to please the Hirsches, Clara never again spoke of the friendship between her son and the Sicilian. It seemed unimportant or something better forgotten.

And Michaela, ever since she had met Lucien, couldn't get him out of her mind. She waited anxiously for Hannah to deliver, through the garden wall, the brown envelope from Paris that she had received weekly dating from her time at Rue de l'Élysée. And when she went up to his room, lay on his bed and kissed his letters, the scarf with his scent recalled every minute spent at Rue de l'Élysée.

Lucien wrote her constantly, and since she had confided the secret to Hannah, the letters were sent to the neighbour's address.

Hannah, older and more experienced, advised:

"Tell Clara everything, my dear; she'll understand and help you two. She is a woman and a mother, and she likes you, Micha. Clara recognizes your worth; every mother wants her son to be happy, and you will make Lucien happy!"

But Michaela knew it wouldn't be that simple, because the baron had big dreams for his son. To see him married to an English or French woman who frequented high society and parties like Lady Tennant, who was independent and wore dresses and shoes by Worth.

How could Clara persuade the Baron to welcome into the family as daughter-in-law a poor Sicilian woman, daughter of a pharmacist without a pharmacy, with no title, no home, and no dowry? He would never accept her. She also knew that Lucien had attempted to speak to his father about his feelings for her. At dinners between father and son, in Paris, over wine and cognac, Lucien had tried to talk about Michaela. But Maurice ignored the matter, as if she were merely a trophy won by the Hirsches, or a little sister that Clara had found to take the place of the real daughter prematurely deceased.

"Marry Micha? How did such an idea come into your head? You have candidates on your own station, son! She's beautiful, healthy, and desirable and should be excellent for bearing children, like all the Italian Sephardim. On the other hand, to marry, there has to be a lineage, understand? Bed is one thing, marriage another! Don't forget, everything I have will one day be yours. However, grandchildren need the right blood to continue our line!"

After each meeting between father and son, another letter would come from Lucien, who was devastated. The Baron treated Michaela as always, genteel and interested. He told her he had visited Lucien and that he was happy, for he had fallen in love with so-and-so and it was requited.

One day it was a Frenchwoman, another day it was an Austrian, still another an Englishwoman, one Lady Katie Lambton or Lady Mary Archer, who now lived in Paris, from British high society.

Clara was curious to know who was her son's passion, and Maurice smiled.

"Dear, that is a matter for men. He has his flings everywhere. Men are men... Don't be surprised that your son is like all the others and frequents every type of society and meets every type of woman! Good in bed and good to marry, and with breeding and nobility! We have time, Lucien should make the most of it; he is a man, and there is no shortage of women!"

Clara silently understood the venom launched by her husband, who ingenuously looked probingly toward Michaela.

"And our Micha... Clara, have you found a good match for her? " He asked as if caring.


Maurice de Hirsch continued to treat Michaela as he always had and made , Clara aware of his concern about the girl, for whom they should soon find a marriage partner.
He did not understand that Lucien could love a woman; his son was detached from everything, from business, from social life, and would marry only when his father approved of his choice.

And when the Baron spoke, it was an order!

❧

# XIX

# THE GREEK THEATRE

Taormina, January 13, 1886

*My dear Alberto,*
Three months ago my poor father, Raffaele Cohen, was buried
here, near Mongibello, but I lack the courage to visit him.
I never imagined that would become crazy with yearning, as
I am today, now, these days and months. I look at his bed, chair, and
see Pappá there, with his tiny smiling eyes, or nodding his head as
always, censuring me...

"Don't deceive me, Anna," he would say, laughing at my excuses when I immersed myself in my sewing, for time to pass more quickly, or to hide my sorrow. "You do not make any time for yourself... *Per chè* ? Day and night you are thinking about patterns, embroidery, and life is going by... I see wrinkles in your eyes, my daughter. Leave here, go and be with your husband... Time flies, I cannot do anything else, my land is here, but you– You must go, and right away, Anna... Go, get your things and..."

Only today I see, my beloved Alberto, that we have been apart for three years, and far from our daughter... That we are like strangers. What will become of us?

Today I found a letter my father wrote you but never sent. It spoke of our future, of Michaela, as if saying goodbye to all of us, always with affection, about Mongibello, the Greek Theatre, the view of the sea, the jewellery shop, his dreams, talking about my mother, my grandmother. He said.. he missed them. Poor Pappá...

He never complained of pain; he wanted to walk to the Theatre, always wearing his beret. He pretended to eat everything on his plate, and the food would disappear. He kissed me on the forehead each morning, looked me in the eye and thanked me after I served his meals.

"Everything was delicious, daughter, thank you," he would say, closing his eyes and waiting for me to caress him.

He pretended he was still strong, but he could only walk as far as the chicken coop... And finally , he would sit there for hours, until twilight, thinking, sometimes talking to himself.

Often, hearing a distant chant, I even thought he was praying.

From the window of the new kitchen I tried to understand what he was saying. Then he would turn, his chest puffed out, as if he had just run around all the columns in the Greek Theatre and climbed all the steps in the amphitheatre.

"What a lovely afternoon," he would say, taking me out of my bad thoughts. "Anna, get out of that room, go outside for a while and breathe the sea air. Come see all the people going up to the Greek Theatre, come see life here outside!"

In the evening, he would sit beside me while I sewed or pretend to entertain himself with the catalogs. He would stay in the shadows, watching what I was doing. To break the silence he might sigh, or cough, asking permission to tell me something.

"Can you listen to a story now, Anna?"

I would raise my eyes, sometimes impatiently, may God forgive me for being impatient with him, and barely respond, nodding and thinking he was going to talk again about our religion, about the family of Baruch Isaac Cohen... About their origin in Toledo around 1500, which he always heard from his grandfather... Three and a half centuries have gone by, and I have to listen once again to the story of the Inquisition, the flight to Portugal, changing the family name, forced baptism, the persecutions, and tortures they suffered, the family scattered, the teachings handed down from fathers to sons...

In those days, my beloved Alberto, I was trying to meet my orders, with so much work still to be done... Poor Pappá, I did not have a single moment to give him attention, to show him affection. How I repent...

However in the final evenings, it seemed to me that my father's memory had become clearer. He managed to talk for hours on end, sitting at the table, and with his trembling hands made a map, using buttons, spools, and pins, and I did not understand what he meant to do. He asked for my attention.

"Look here, Anna... There was Sefarad, the kingdom of Ferdinand and Isabella, and to its left was Portugal, the Kingdom of Don Manuel. To its right, this is Sicily. Going upward, we have Venice and the Austro-Hungarian Empire. To the right of Sicily is the Aegean Sea, and down below is your husband, in Salonica, in the Ottoman Empire."

" Why does the world have to be divided into empires and kingdoms?" he asked as he changed the position of the pins. "Why do empires and kingdoms judge us, human beings, as if kings were ordained by God? Why do we have to love our God and not 'the God,' who is the same for us all? Can it be that those men who think themselves so important, who control our life and our death, haven't yet discovered that to love God we do not need intermediaries, books, or what they claim to be His word, priests, and theologians, kings and queens, sultans, saints, prophets...

It would be so much simpler if they freed God from that chain that binds His name to churches, kingdoms, to imaginary accounts of revelations and miracles...

We could live free, like birds, if none of that existed, my daughter," he said, in tears. "It would have been so good... Without books dictating intolerance, hatred, untruthful writings, accusations in the name of God and all the Scriptures... The ones that speak of his Son and his Mother...

"There would have been no persecutions, Inquisitions, autos- da- fé, massacres, such barbarism and bloodshed, all in His name. The fallacy that only those who call themselves His followers are worthy of seeing Him, of hearing Him, of proclaiming at the top of their lungs what God told them, and that only those who obey and blindly follow those heralds deserve paradise.

I have tried my entire life to be honest and good, Anna, to help our neighbors, the beggars, always dividing with the poor whatever extra I received, as did Alberto, who worked for years in the old kitchen, making medicines for so many who could not afford them in Galliani's pharmacy

" What did he gain, daughter? Neither our God nor theirs, recognized him, or helped, no one came to his aid, no one did justice! Do you know why dear Anna?

Because God is not with us to recognize our acts or to help us; but we, humans, who must have Him with us. He is not going to appear to me or speak to me, just as He never spoke to anyone. It is we who speak to Him, who discover Him in everything; in our thoughts, in our attitudes, even in flowers, stones, trees. In all we see and feel, because He is in everything we love."

" *He is Love*," he said, brushing aside the map and piling everything in the middle of the table. "We have no need of intermediaries, my daughter... All of us need tolerance and kindness. And it is with these things, that humanity should nourish itself..."

I think about his words every night and keep them in my memory like the Shabbat prayers my grandmother taught me. I am thankful because today I understand, because I am able to love. My ties to my father are much stronger now. I am proud of who he was and admire his thoughts. I feel his presence beside me at every moment, helping me to learn, to understand what we do and our role in this theatre that is our life.

His old scarf, beret, and cane are on the chair opposite me. It is as if he were still going to pick them up and go out for his walk, to breathe the sea air he loved so much."

"Today I listen to the waves beating against the rocks, and they are my only voices... I look at the columns of the theatre, my dear Alberto, and remember my childhood amid those ruins, my stage, the whirling sky, and you so young and full of illusions, coming up to Mongibello for the first time. The young Dottore with the basket, and I can still see when you left, your bags piled on old Giovanni's wagon. I see when we said goodbye to Michaela the day she left for Bavaria...

Then my beloved father went away. He rose slowly, using his cane, his breathing laboured. Disguising his weariness, looking at the sky and scratching at the ground with the end of his cane, finally making his way to the centre of the theatre to smooth the stones, to warm himself in the rays of the setting sun. And there, in the centre of the amphitheatre, lying down with his eyes fixed on the blue sky, he left us.

His body descended in the direction of the Giardino, in a pinewood coffin. But his soul, I am certain, remained there.

At first, when Giovanni arrived at our door with the wagon and the empty coffin and found me with Giovanna, preparing and cleaning the body, he understood that he could not call the priest from San Nicolò. There were no prayers for him; the neighbour women did not want to come in ,without the priest.

There were no flowers, or anyone to comfort me. I was alone, and I am still alone.

My father took with him only his prayer shawl, but I kept a piece of that cloth with its worn-out fringe.

I stood at the left side of his body, as he had taught me when my grandmother was buried. He died where he wanted to be, in his land, the land that wasn't really his, died in Taormina, died hidden from everyone, without even a candle, a lament, a prayer, a homage, a friend, a Kaddish. He went away, without his body being washed and prepared in the manner his ancestors taught, to meet the Eternal.

That is the price we pay for being here, like birds of passage.

I only remember Giovanni tossing earth over his body, the sound of the shovels in the ground above the coffin, and him with his head covered by the shawl that was my grandmother's, reminding me of his lifeless expression in the middle of the theatre.

Poor Pappá… There facing Etna, with the cypresses around him, and me.

In silence, we offered a final tribute to the last Jewish man in this city. To the guardian of the theatre, of the memories of his people, of the art of gilded chains learned from his ancestors.

And as if in the final act in a theatre, I am going to write on his gravestone:

*Here rests in peace*
*The great man*
*Beloved father, father-in-law and grandfather,*
*The jeweller*
*Raffaele Cohen of Taormina*
*1819–1885*
*In fond remembrance*
*Anna*

*Post-script:*

The entire city surely knew of the death of Raffaele Cohen, but no one came to speak to me except Giovanni and Altanario. I cannot wait for the day when we three are together again. I miss you both so much. I am arranging everything to leave on the next steamship, as soon as I have news from you and from Michaela.

Please, Alberto, tell David to get word to Michaela. I couldn't send a telegram because she would be very shocked by the news. Write me soon, I'm desperate with no news from you for such a long time.

*Ti amo,*
Anna

In Taormina Anna Varsano dressed in mourning, like all the widows and orphans in the city. Sitting at her dining table, which was covered with cloths and pins, she went through the pockets of her coat looking for an envelope.

She had received a letter from her daughter at the end of December, sent from Paris. And the letter was read and reread every day and night. She couldn't really understand what was happening on the other side of the world. As a mother, Anna tried to fathom her daughter's feelings and the world she lived in. Deep down, she knew, Michaela was unhappy and unprotected, confused and alone.

And she, so far away in Mongibello, with the wind howling with the fury of winter, her eyes fixed on the flames crackling in the old fireplace and the envelope in her hands.

Anna daydreamed about her Michaela. She thought about that happy girl with the green eyes, her skylark voice, her delicate and skilful hands. She had grown up and must not be the same, the Bongiovannis' brilliant student who would come into the house like a ray of sunlight. Now, Anna thought, my little girl is a woman, suffering from love.

Yes, she had really grown up, in a way none of her classmates could even dream of. But, at that moment, she felt that where she now lived, whether Paris or London, was not and would not be her place in the future. The people there, for all their upbringing, culture, and money, were no happier than the four of them had been in that small house in Taormina.

She had thought many times of returning to Sicily, but to do what? It would no longer be her place. Who had she become, she asked herself. Go where, do what, live how? I'm a foreigner there and here as well. Michaela now was neither noble nor rich, but also she was not the poor Sicilian in a gray alpaca skirt and mended shoes who had arrived in Planegg. She did not want, indeed could not have, ambitions; she could plan nothing.

She had fallen in love, deeply in love, with Lucien de Hirsch and was loved by him but saw no perspectives for the future. Everything was becoming so complicated that she no longer knew how to explain her feelings.

❧

Hannah de Rosebery, her friend, and counsellor, said that everything was transitory and that, after all, she had had the tremendous good fortune of having Clara de Hirsch as her guardian.

"Just imagine," she told Michaela, "what if you had never painted the lemons on those dishes? Take advantage of Clara's intelligence, her understanding of the world, her upright character; everything about her serves as an example. She is special and is the only woman among us who has the internal strength to overcome adversity of any type. She is the *barronesa*," Lady Rosebery joked, imitating the baron's accent. "She decides the outcome of things... You still have not understood, Micha?"

In Michaela's eyes, Clara had accomplished her mission and lately was apathetic and sad.

Also there, was so much work to be done that anything relating to the Sicilian was of lesser importance, she thought. Talk about personal matters with her, in those horrible times when the world was upside down?

So many unfortunate people in the world. Entire families in poverty, out in the cold, without health, with no money, wandering about looking for work, for a piece of bread.

There are persecuted, stripped of their belongings, Jews murdered daily by the czar's forces, pogroms, ghettoes, the political cynicism of the French, the anti-Semitic paranoia of the Germans, the game of the great powers, the hateful caricatures of Jews and accusations of Edouard Drumont in *La Libre Parole*–

It was all happening daily, and wherever she was Clara de Hirsch received every morning folders with newspaper clippings, requests, papers demanding hours of her time, late nights sitting hunched over in her library, analyzing, making notes, dispatching documents, funds, and reports to organizations, families, or individuals. She was not afraid of anything, guided by a sharp perception of what was yet to happen.

The worst is still to come, she told herself, quite sceptically, when she read about the Jews in charge of the finances in all of Europe. And Clara was among the targets of so-called "investigative" journalism, were attacked day after day in the newspaper *La Libre Parole*.

In those times false news sprang up like bubbles, and the organizers of those movements loaded special trains with mobs to fight the satanic trio of Jews, Protestants, and Masons. Mendacious pamphlets were hurled from the doors of Catholic churches and burgeoned in the France of Liberty, Equality, and Fraternity almost a hundred years after the Revolution, full of hate and envy of all who were not exactly the same.

"A new Inquisition is about to explode from one day to the next," Clara wrote from Paris to Maurice, who was in Moravia.

In the following weeks, *La Croix* again cast blame on the trio of supposed conspirators. The "triumvirate of hate," as they were called, must be "re-Christianized."

And thus history repeats itself, wrote Clara. "It is urgent for us to solve the Russian situation. Here in France the state of affairs is a powder keg that can explode at any moment, and elsewhere as well. Lucien has put aside his personal projects and is studying day and night the possibilities of definitively setting up our colonies in Argentina, through the project entrusted to Dr. Wilhelm Loewenthal. The research on land, conditions and possibilities that you had ordered was completed tonight. We did not even go to sleep. Lucien wrote and reread everything, to send it to you.

"And as you foresaw, my dear Maurice, the research, after all these years, shows that the Russian émigrés who went there are protected and utilized by the large landowners; they have become excellent farm workers. Despite the work conditions being the worst possible, Dr. Loewenthal explained to us, that he was enthusiastic about the tenacity and will power of those Russians, and added that within a short time, after we negotiate with the government of the province of Santa Fe, the lands will be ready for installing the colonies.

"With Dr. Loewenthal came the English engineer C. N. Cullen and the Belgian specialist Col. Vanvickeroy, who studied the soil and the viability of the project.

"All of them agreed with your conviction that those hundreds, perhaps thousands, of people who will be settled on those lands can in the future become excellent ranchers. Sustaining themselves from the land, they will in a short time form an agricultural and industrial nucleus on Argentine soil.

" And they will be free, self-supporting men, their own masters, integrated into society, raising their children and progressing in a part of the world where intolerance and persecution does not yet exist.

"Congratulations, Maurice. You were right, Lucien are very proud of that work and of your struggle to ease the suffering of the poor and persecuted."

Michaela was living in Paris at that time, at 2 Rue de l'Élysée.

In a word, she wrote Anna, that it was another world. It was Paris, the center of the world, of culture, finance, elegance… It was like living in a golden nimbus. She saw people walking elegantly down Faubourg Saint-Honoré during the day, gathering in soirees, in restaurants and cafes at night, and heard here, and there comments about one or another occurrence in the neighborhood.

In those months, a dark aura enveloped the blocks of the Champs-Élysées. The coveted heirs of many families lived intensely, between seduction and tuberculosis.

The women, many come from the other bank of the Seine, parading in the vicinity of the *Faubourg* in carriages drawn by plumed horses, visiting or shopping, could see large mansions, private palaces, with their windows shut. Sadness hovered over those ornate black gates. There, imprisoned by Koch's bacillus, young heirs stifled their cough using cambric handkerchiefs embroidered with their monogram and soaked with blood. Young men and women, in the prime of life, panted in the half-shadow of their bedrooms, amid lace canopies and works of art, dark spaces redolent of ether and infusions of exotic herbs. In those months, heirs lived between casual affairs and the terror of death.

Sarah Bernhardt was applauded tearfully for her *Camille*.

The name of the disease was taboo.

Everything was spoken of at dinners and receptions, except the reality. The ladies commented on the dalliances of Uncle Louis-Raphael Bischoffsheim and his lovers, the model Nana, *the Petit- Bisches*, the salons and cabarets he kept, the prejudices of a rich and awkward man. He spent those final years giving women apartments on Avenue de Friedland. It was said that his new protégé was Laure Hyman, Marcel Proust's inspiration for the character Odette de Crécy, after having been– "Poor Uncle Raphael, betrayed by Rachelle, the famous *Madame* Tartuffe, who abandoned him for a certain friend..."

Everything and everyone was talked about in those tumultuous days in Paris, from Drumont's scurrilous articles and his newspaper to salves and cures for bronchitis.

Oh yes! wrote to Anna Varsano in her letter: also about milk-based diets. Creams were mentioned as recipes to keep the skin young. Hygienic strolls in the morning were prescribed by doctors, and horse stables were meeting places for young heirs wishing to demonstrate health. They must promote the idea that they were healthy and nothing could affect them, must look rosy and well fed. There were smiles, games, and charm among them, but all of it superficial.

The terror of contagion from someone carrying the bacillus led to rejecting invitations. Fear was symbolized by absence. And what was felt most of all was the absence of real love.

In those months in Paris, at 2, Rue de l'Élysée, the Hirsches' address, and at 11, Place des États -Unis, the famous residence of Clara's beloved brother Ferdinand de Bischoffsheim, Michaela came to understand the world that Lucien so disdained.

∽

Lucien de Hirsch, the young bachelor almost thirty years old, was the next successor in the lineage. He bore the expectations of his uncle Ferdinand and the rest of the family. The future marriage of his nephew, the only first-born male, should have been the Hirsch-Bischoffsheim tie to a family with important links to noble, political, and social circles in France. This would impose silence on many of the intolerant and on Drumont as well. It would destroy one of the malignancies in his two-volume *La France Juive*: "French noble blood would never mix with that of the Jews..." It would be Ferdinand's small revenge if Lucien could achieve this dream for him.

So Ferdinand Bischoffsheim went looking for a candidate, a demoiselle of noble caste but, like the majority, from a family in serious financial straits. It would be about easy task because there were many young marchionesses, countesses, and even princesses desperately seeking a husband, preferably a financier.

The great banker searched the elegant salons of Paris for a *petite contesse* for Lucien Hirsch as if for his own son.

Lucien hated hearing anything to do with the subject. His expression would darken and he would impatiently twist his moustache, trying to act as respectfully as possible at those interminable dinners. Afterward, he would argue with Clara all the way back from the Trianon, up to the gate of the garden at Avenue Gabriel. They were often seen in the garden arguing in low tones for hours on end, to avoid being overheard in the house. Lucien always encountered an argument *en famille*.

To him, no man was an example. Ferdinand de Bischoffsheim could not serve as such, as he had married a New York woman named Mary Paine, for love. He had become a widower some years earlier and then, with the death of his first-born, Jonathan, lived a melancholy life, unable to overcome the losses.

But in recent months, with so many important issues to be resolved, the elderly banker did not revisit the subject of the hunt for a *petite contesse* and the family's succession. To his surprise, it was Ferdinand who encouraged young Lucien. After meeting *mademoiselle* Varsano, soon after her arrival in the city in late 1886, he summoned his nephew.

"Is that beautiful girl the Sicilian? The one your father talks about so much? And he thinks she's not the one for you?

As for me, I'd even give up a throne to keep from losing her," he said, winking. "

Lucien blushed like an adolescent and felt his mouth go dry.

That same night, in Michaela's room, his heart racing like a little boy engaged in great mischief, he spoke of the good impression she had made on Uncle Ferdinand.

Lucien, sitting on Michaela's bed, placed her on his knees like a child. He stroked her long hair and kissed her forehead;her cheeks flushed with desire, and her supple neck scented with jasmine.

He was truly happy, and with his uncle's approval he felt free, free of the burdens on his conscience. Now he whispered to his loved one that he was certain he would not fail, wouldn't disappoint his parents and uncles, or hinder the family's plans, diminish its name or its pride.

Why must he be responsible for the happiness, the progress, and the future of the family? he thought. A family whose name was found, since 1880, in the *Dictionnaire Universelle des Contemporains* as patrons of the arts, of science, as donors to the Scientific Library in France, astronomic observatories, and schools. Donors of hospitals, roads, ports. Through organizations incalculable amounts of money went to the four corners of the earth in their name. Every month, thousands of francs were donated in Paris, which seemed to feed the envy and cynicism of those who had done nothing for France but write slanders and calumnies about the Bischoffsheims and the Hirsches.

✥

Lucien Jacques Maurice de Hirsch seemed like a happy young man that January night in 1887.

Michaela, her hair down, in the moonlight that penetrated the large windows of Rue de l'Élysée, resembled one of the ancient bronze sculptures in his the library.

He caressed her, kissing every part of her warm, golden body, and they made love until dawn. Exhausted, they slept and only awoke, startled, to the cornet of the milk deliveryman. Tiptoeing, Lucien dressed and said goodbye in silence, with a kiss and a whispered promise.

In April, they would be together forever.

That morning, Lucien would leave for Brussels and Michaela would return to Berkeley Square in London.

And the new year, was greeted with sunshine.

∿

For Michaela and Lucien that was not the right time to speak of marriage. Nor the right time to worry the baroness, or for her to discuss with her husband such insignificant matters as the desires of two young people in love. It would be absurd to divert the attention and energy that Clara and Maurice dedicated every hour of every day to a noble and urgent cause, one to which only they and few others could devote themselves. Time was short, and for them the moment was one of great commitment.

It was time to save lives, to settle thousands of individuals—persecuted, threatened, starving, homeless, with no hope of surviving. They could not be sidetracked by two young people in love.

In the first days of 1887 a great deal of correspondence came to the Hirsches, numerous proposals from various Jewish societies, and an assortment of projects for helping the emigration of refugees from the Russian pogroms.

In the time she spent in Paris, Michaela worked in the library every morning, separating the documents for the Alliance Israélite Universelle, clipping newspapers, reading the correspondence and preparing folders for Clara and Maurice.

The questions everyone asked the baron were countless, and they all boiled down to one issue: Where to send the Russian Jews? What to do with the persecuted? When will we have a nation? This is what they all wanted to know.

Clara and Maurice had sufficient arguments to debate the ideas for colonization of Palestine, widely discussed in recent years in Jewish cultural and philanthropic centers in Europe. Both had primarily in mind the Russians: getting them out of there was an emergency. Afterward, emptying the refugee camps on the Austrian border and, to immediately free them from oppression, send them to the Western Hemisphere. That would be their salvation. For a decade the Baron had devoted his every effort, his money, and his time to negotiating the relocation of Jews persecuted in various countries. For years now, he is removing them to safety, making sure to provide them with conditions for an honorable life, studies, an upbringing more fitting to those times, and training for the productive occupation of the land donated to the colonies.

Since 1881, shocked by the pogroms and the absurd laws imposed by the czar's right-hand man Ignatyev, he had spent tens of millions of francs to remove Jews from Russia to beyond the Austrian border. Since then, his ideas about support and aid had begun to change. They could not be maintained as refugees, for now, the emergency comprised thousands concentrated on the borders who must be dispersed with the help of entities throughout the world. They must go where they could have a productive life of dignity.


Certain groups wanted to send them to Palestine, led by the pioneer of an idea called Zionism.

Yes, it would be lovely—even Maurice de Hirsch had daydreamed about that powerful legend called Palestine. He would be foolish or insensitive if he did not at least imagine a Jewish nation flourishing in the cradle of its roots, next to Jerusalem, which had been built by the Jews. Built beside the temple, with date trees and green fields in the middle of the desert, where milk and honey would feed thousands and thousands of refugees.

But he would awake from his dreams to reality. Palestine was not the ideal place for them. The Baron was a sensible, practical man. There were no lands to plant, the climate was inhospitable, and the surrounding areas barbarous.

"Do what in Palestine?" Maurice asked. "Pile them up without structure, without water, without conditions?"

Those families should go to a place with no history of persecution. A place where they could live on the land, from their labour, and raise children who would have the same chance as everyone else, to be part of society. Over generations, excel through their efforts, become citizens. Integrated, they would never again be a "Jewish problem," the Baron preached at Alliance meetings.

"I am not a visionary or a philosopher, like that well-intentioned young man Theodor Herzl. But I have often wondered: how to send Russian, Ukrainians Romanian ,Polish Jews and all the multitude of old people, children, the young and the infirm to become colonists without at the very least, having surveyed the lands in Palestine?

"Without a plan of selection and purchase of those lands, without the assurance that there really exists the possibility of negotiating for those lands with the local government? The government of the Sublime Porte? And just a samll question… assuming that such land concessions can exist, what would be that area, and consequently, the importance of its soil?"

"How to send thousands of people, without the least infrastructure, to colonize a locale, without support, and cultivate the soil, plant and wait for the first harvests? What would they live on till then? And what will be their safeguard after having built, sown, and planted? Will they garner the benefits or will they be cheated by the sellers and neighbors of those lands?

What guarantee will they have, once everything is ready, planted, constructed, that their neighbors will not reclaim the land, expelling or exterminating them? Who can say?

None of us is blind, and we can easily verify that agriculture does not thrive on the soil of the Ottoman Empire. The reasons are well known as well.

"I admire the pioneering spirit of the 'bilus,' the young 'Zionists,' admire also the motives of our religious among us in dreaming of return to the Holy Land, to our Promised Land, the land of our ancestors, the land of Solomon's Temple. And I will assist whenever I can, but we are not creating beggars, and it is a matter of not help, but of strategy!" the Baron answered when others tried to convince him.

"Do you need an additional argument, gentlemen? Leaving aside the lack of infrastructure, soil, and water, think about politics! About the physical proximity of Palestine to Russia, the possibility, anything but slight, of falling into the hands of the Russians. The Promised Land in the hands of the archenemies of the Jews!

It is in all the newspapers, between the lines: if Constantinople falls into the hands of the Russians... The British Empire do not do anything by accident," said the baron. "And they have been prepared for some time now. They have chosen their secure territory in the Middle East in case that happens. Also, we must consider the reason that the British troops are in Egypt. Are they, just because they like the climate there?

"In the possibility of bankruptcy or the fall of the Ottoman Empire, and even if it doesn't happen in the next twenty years: how can we negotiate with them, buy the rights to the land, pay them the agreed-upon price, and after everything is settled, by some act or other the government of Abdül Hamid–as is always his right, and often happens–underhandedly changes policy, taking back what belongs to his empire by law?

Who of you gentlemen, has ever negotiated with the Sublime Porte? Who of you has had a Sultan change his mind in the middle of negotiations?"

None better than Maurice de Hirsch, the "Türkenhirsch," as he was nicknamed in international financial circles, to feel in his flesh the scars caused by contracts and negotiations with the Ottoman Empire. In 1887 they had been the lords of the lands of Palestine for over five hundred years...

"Today the Ottomans, are the best actors to represent the Greek Theatre."

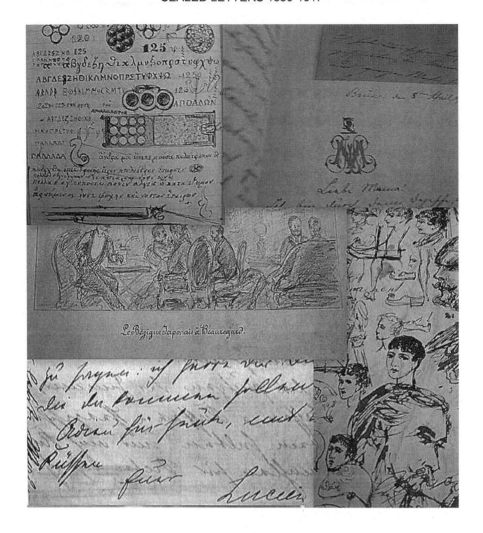

# XX

# LUCIEN DE HIRSCH

End of January, 1887.

An extremely cold and gloomy morning. At 12, Berkeley Square, the world seemed to turn slowly. Wood burned in every fireplace. In the London fog a single dim light illuminated the window of one room of the Hirsch residence.

Michaela had returned from Paris and was concentrating on accounts at that early morning hour; a pile of documents awaited her. She found it strange when a carriage stopped at the door. No one was expected, and she could not imagine a visit at that hour.

Perhaps it was a caller at Hannah's house. With that cursed weather, she thought, who would dare set foot outside? She could not stand the humidity and practically lived in her old pink shawl, with lots of wood in the fireplace, avoiding going out into the cold.

"Till when?" she complained to Sebastian. "It will soon be springtime, Mr. Clair, but the weather will not get any better in this wretched land that you British are so proud of."

He laughed at the feelings of the Sicilian, always good-humoured, who raised her eyebrows and blinked her large green eyes at him with a wide smile.

∽

The previous afternoon, Michaela had gone to Oxford Street, to the Neuhmans' shop, which belonged to a family that she visited periodically of late. They had been in the ready-to-wear clothing and millinery lines for some time, carried good clothes at prices accessible to all pocketbooks, often altering a coat or exchanging a piece for a new one. It was hard for Clara to imagine Michaela buying from a place like that, a dark, badly laid-out shop where notions, fabrics, and second-hand clothing were thrown together on shelves.

Michaela liked the Neuhmans. She had met Esther Neuhman at a meeting of the Alliance school, and she had seemed like an affable and good person. A red-headed woman with curly hair, smiling, with a face full of freckles and very lively, brilliant eyes. She had an air of a woman who knows all there is to know, always ready to advise or help everyone at the Alliance meetings. They were Ashkenazi Jews; their grandparents had been born in Poland, as she recounted one afternoon. They had arrived without a penny and worked hard until they could open their first small shop on Rotten Row.

DORA OPENHEIM

From then on, everyone pitched in, sons and grandchildren, as
well as those who came later. It was the first time Michaela visited a
Jewish family, with parents and grandparents, children–all with
different customs from the Jews of Sicily.

The Neuhmans' home was in the back of the shop. A dark,
windowless room separated by a faded velvet curtain, with a large table
for meals and a dresser piled high with books and various objects.

That family had become for Michaela the counterpoint
between the dream of counts and barons and reality–humble, hard-
working, and with a generous soul. Esther's mother, a corpulent lady
with delicate pink skin, received her with suspicion upon her first visit.
Michaela was someone so strange in those quarters that, to them, it was
impossible to believe she was Jewish, as Mrs. Neuhman declared.

"Are you sure, Esther? A dark-skinned girl with green eyes and
straight hair, who has an accent and doesn't understand Yiddish...?

Where is she from, the moon ?" she asked in that dialect that
struck the Sicilian as German spoken backwards.

Esther replied, embarrassed, "And if she is not ... just like us,
what difference would it make now?"

Mrs. Neuhman shook her head, dried her hands on her apron,
a and returned to the kitchen. The house was redolent of onions and
goose fat. Gradually, suspicion gave way to liking. The father, Jacob,
was an older man with delicate features, quite thin, white temples, and
never without his *yarmulke*.

He attended the customers for needles and thread, advised on
the colours of yarn for crocheting, and at night, to the light of oil
lamps, sewed with the assistance of his daughter, mending threadbare
coats and trousers. A cordial, well mannered person, when he wasn't
working he would read, sitting on an old wooden bench by the kitchen
door. They stopped working only on Shabbat.

On Fridays, after three in the afternoon, when the door to the
shop remained ajar for some customer emergency or to allow the
residents to pass through to the rear of the house.


Esther had fallen in love with a gentile. And perhaps that was
what had led the two women to become friends. Michaela sympathized
with the girl's situation. She would never be able to tell them of that
love without causing panic in the family.

The young man was a tailor who came to make deliveries and arrange alterations for good customers. The clientele for coats ranged from intellectuals, writers, and poets, or small businessmen in the area, to the poor and drunken of Camden Road who asked for mending and swaps.

Michaela had given the Neuhmans and Esther clothes she no longer wore, and they had turned everything into gold, as the aged grandfather said.

"Donate all your trash, and I will transform it into gold...!"

Mrs. Neuhman would remove lace and linen from old trousseaus and nightgowns and adorn the pieces with beautiful and precious items like frills and jabots. Micha had bought more than a dozen of those pieces, and also new lace corselets dyed in tea and petticoats worthy of a queen. Everything she bought from the Neuhmans she kept as part of her trousseau.

⊷

Without knowing why, she thought about Esther and her family that morning. She saw the grandfather, old and toothless, in the backyard opening bags of old clothes, separating them by quality, and tossing them into kettles of boiling water.

"Gold, Esther... Here everything turns to gold," the old man said, happily. His granddaughter blushed the first time Michaela, from the kitchen window, observed the scene and tried to distract her by offering her a piece of *challah* bread.

"Try this specialty of my mother's. I think in your country Shabbat bread is different, isn't it?"

Everything of theirs was different, thought Michaela, not only food but customs, relationships. They spoke with their eyes, in a silence intercut with long, painful sighs. Everything was heavy and sad, full of rules and furtive glances. It was like that book by George Eliot, she thought. The story of Daniel Deronda.

Maybe that young man, the Florentine tailor, could be a new Deronda. A gentile in love with a Jewish woman, who after reading Josephus had since early youth, been interested in Jews, their religion and customs. Perhaps, she thought, Jacob Neuhman, the elderly tailor with the *yarmulke*, always in the rear of shop on the Oxford Street, sitting and reading his books, could one day be a Mordechai, the learned man who guided Deronda, designating him as the restorer of a political existence for the Jewish people and as the one who would give them a nation.

Hopefully, the Neuhman family, proud of its new son-in-law, would one day accept him with open arms.


*Rrromantic drreams*, she said, laughing, remembering Baron Hirsch's criticism of George Eliot, holding the novel *Daniel Deronda* in his hands.

"This was written for dreamers like you, Micha," he said, laughing as he watched her discussing with Clara the hero's intention in the chapters of the *feuilleton*.

This had taken place at a significant dinner at the home of the Roseberys. Michaela was at the table, flanked by important political personalities, ministers and financiers, and the subject of Deronda came up.

Asked about the novel, whether he had read Eliot's work, the great minister  Benjamin Disraeli, who had been the best man at the wedding of Hannah and Lord Rosebery, answered disdainfully, "When I want to read a novel, my friends, I write it myself…"

George Eliot, was one of the topics in Jewish circles, debated at many gatherings of European aristocracy. But "she" would surely never be read by the poor Neuhman family. And they would never understand how a gentile could come to be part of them, and even become a hero and save them. Why would he do that?

Esther believed in it and longed for something to happen. She wanted to be free from those sighs, from that sad house, the imposing rules, the ancient customs, wanted to leave, to find the sun, she said.

"To be like you, Michaela. To smile, to laugh. I've never been able to do that!"

She would meet Andrea, the young man, in secret.

One afternoon, Michaela witnessed one of those meetings; he had an open smile, was very thin, and taller than Esther. He wasn't English. Also an immigrant, he came from Florence, son of a tailor, but he strove, had neither the accent nor the mannerisms that would give him away as a foreigner in London.

"He's like you, Micha, the sun shines in him, like the Mediterranean!" Esther said.

⚘

Lucien also had his moments of internal sunshine, thought Micha, but only when they were alone. Then he became another Lucien, his eyes glowing with happiness and desire looking into her eyes. His beautiful smile, his warm embrace, his voice into her ears, telling her softly promises of love. She couldn't stop thinking about him, not for a single day. She dreamed about him, felt his embrace, his body, his lips hot with passion.

They had not seen each other, since that unforgettable night of the full moon, the ninth of January.

When the Baroness learned of Maurice's impending arrival in Paris, she looked for an excuse to send Michaela back to London. Under no circumstances did she want her to witness an argument between father and son. She wanted time to resolve everything in her own way, as was Clara's custom. She would air an idea to the baron and he, taking it as his own, would fight to achieve it.

Ferdinand de Bischoffsheim, her brother, laughed at his brother-in-law, Baron Hirsch, who was continually leaving for Paris in search of a good match for his son, while in that family, comprising Hirsch, Bischoffsheim, Goldschmidt, Caen d'Anvers, Montefiore, Avigdor, and all the rest, the heirs of those powerful men, were disappearing.

Ferdinand had lost his first-born son, despondent, saw in his nephew Lucien a beam of light. He had changed his mind and now was eager for the marriage to happen. By having Lucien marry, they could engender a new lineage of young heirs, who would later run the banks and manage the family fortune. Uncle Ferdinand still couldn't understand the reason behind Maurice's scheming against Michaela Varsano.

What could be so terrible about his nephew marrying a vivacious girl, a beautiful and healthy Sicilian, when the entire city gossiped about the extramarital romances of the Bischoffsheims and of the baron himself?

It was with such arguments that Uncle Ferdinand approached the subject of Lucien's marriage. After hours of discussion, between cognac and cigar, in one of the most desirable dining rooms of Paris, witnessed by marble worthy of Versailles, rococo panelling, and canvases of Mantegna, Rubens, Rembrandt, and Delacroix, the Bischoffsheims won the argument. Clara, her brother Ferdinand, and her sister Regina convinced Maurice.

When Clara conveniently left to retouch her makeup, the two men reached a gentlemen's agreement.

Lucien could swear later, when informed by his mother of that conversation, that his uncle had a very important letter in his vest pocket to persuade his father. Perhaps a secret, one he had long suspected but of which he was never sure, one involving a certain Madame Deforest and her two sons.

The carriage stopped at the door at Berkeley Square with a special delivery for Michaela Varsano.

In a pouch from the bank, labelled "important and confidential," was a package, a box from a jeweller in Place Vendome. A beautiful engagement ring with diamonds mounted in gold. A card with a promise of love from Lucien Hirsch and a brief goodbye.

Michaela opened the box with trembling hands and could not believe what she was reading.

*Paris, January 24, 1887*

*To my beloved Michaela,*

*I desire to tell you again and again, now and forever that, I love you and will always love you.*

*Michaela mia, I must leave tomorrow for Sicily, your homeland, and seek the completion of this dream of ours. The coin that I have dreamed of finding for so many years, the    tetra drachma about which I told you, has finally been discovered near Messina .I am going there to fetch it and will return very soon.*

*The two most important dreams of my life I will see realized. Later there will surely be many more, our children and our entire life together.*

*In Sicily, I will go to your home, to Mongibello. I greatly wish to know where you came from, your family, and everything else that you and my mother tell me about that paradise.*

*I am going to ask Signora Varsano and your grandfather, Signor Cohen, permission for our marriage. I would like to bring them back with me, as I know that would be the greatest gift for you.*

*I love you, immensely Michaela.*

*Receive this ring, as a promise that in April we two will be together eternally.*


*Yours, Lucien*


That was when she began to plan her marriage.

Her heart seemed about to burst from so much joy. Hannah de Rosebery, as soon as she found out, placed herself at Michaela's disposal to help her. But Hannah gave Michaela some stern advice.

There were rules, and she must await the initial signal from Clara, her future mother-in-law. How and where the nuptials would be, everything should come from her, who would orchestrate it all in her own way and would manage everything… As was her wont. And Michaela went on waiting for a sign from Clara Bischoffsheim de Hirsch.


Weeks passed very slowly. Spring offered the first narcissus in the windows of Berkeley Square. Every day, she would wait by the post box, and nothing came from the Rue de l'Élysée or Sicily. Not from her mother, not a telegram or postcard from Lucien. Nothing also from Salonica. David had sent no news since the birth of his daughter, Sophie Karakassos Varsano.

And her father ? He had disappeared with Daud, that gardener, and the last news came in a letter written at Rosh Hashanah, the Jewish new year. He had sent a letter with a map drawn on the back talking of a piece of land he had acquired near an old cemetery, where Daud and he would plant the rose seedlings to extract the essence for making perfumes in the future.

When she received the letter she had become concerned.

Alberto Varsano was not the kind of person to buy and sell anything. He was a man attuned to the suffering of others, to alleviating pain and illnesses; he was a student of medicine, of botany, of pharmacy, and of the essences he prepared, like the cologne from Sicilian lemon.

Poor Pappá, if he were here, or in Paris, he could work in a large pharmacy. He might have had the chance to become a great scientist or, who knows, save the sick from that cursed bacillus. She so wanted for him to one day to be respected–and what had they done to him?

The things that greed and envy do... What makes human beings destroy a lifetime of work and dedication?

Michaela wrote: "Now, after living these years with people of higher social position, extremely rich people, nobles, people with culture, educated, so different from the people of Taormina, I have come to the conclusion that envy and greed exist everywhere and among all social classes."

She thought about Mongibello, her mother, her sewing. What was her new work like and from where did she summon that strength and creativity?

What would Lucien think of her?

She imagined Lucien knocking at the door of the small white house, in that gentlemanly way of his, removing his hat to recover from the long uphill climb. She imagined old Raffaele peeking out from behind the shutters to see who the foreigner was. And her mother coming from the kitchen, taking off her apron and tying back her hair.

Michaela pictured her surprised expression, her wide snowy white teeth in a broad smile, her gestures, straightening things here and there. The oak table in the living room being set for lunch, and the *spadone* that the fisherman Altanario always brought would be in the oven. A bottle of wine, warm bread, and tomatoes with basil. She saw her grandfather putting more olive oil on the plate of the illustrious visitor, serving him wine and winking at Anna.

Afterward, she could see Lucien trying to express himself in the best of his Italian and telling them of his intention. "I want to marry Michaela and am here to ask your consent."

Anna would surely sigh deeply the way she always did when taken by surprise, holding her breath. And her eyebrows would rise, displaying a pair of bright eyes and a wonderful smile.

And in that instant, beyond a doubt, Lucien would see how much alike the two women were. They shared the same expressions, the same gestures, the untamed manner, the fury of Etna and the strength of Persephone. He would become acquainted with that place, its roots, its perfumes and its savours, the colours of the land and the sea, the sound and music of the wind—everything that she had tried to convey to him through letters or words.

How she would like to be there at that moment. And be the Michaela of old, concerned only with her lemon plates.

✍

The news of Raffaele Cohen's death arrived in London in a letter written by David Varsano and posted from the Grassi office in Salonica. Reading it, Michaela forgot her own problems, her future marriage, and the silence of Clara and Lucien.

She had spent recent weeks crying secretly, but her swollen eyes had no more tears to weep at the death of her dear grandfather. She couldn't imagine what might have led Clara to maintain her silence. Neither the baroness nor Lucien had written a single line. Nothing.

Some of the newspapers arriving from Paris for Lord Rosebery mentioned in the society columns the most recent appearances of the Hirsches.

Hannah read aloud the newspaper reports:

"Clara de Hirsch attended the wedding of Constance Schneider the evening of March 14, and Le Gaulois of the 17th describes the presence of the baron and Baroness Hirsch the night before, among the one thousand and five hundred persons invited to the soiree of Baron Alphonse de Rothschild."

In those last few weeks, the names of Clara and Maurice de Hirsch appeared constantly in the social columns of Le Gaulois, and those accounts came to take the place of the letters that Clara no longer wrote. Definitely, she was very busy at the beginning of that year.

Hannah, her dear friend, would bring Lord Rosebery's newspapers to show how busy Clara was, with so many obligations to take care of. Logically, she would not have had time to think about Michaela.

She opened the box holding the ring, which she had never worn, and with each passing day its brilliance reflected Michaela's unhappiness. Deep down, she thought about the baron and Clara. Something was happening... He still had not accepted. She was not the choice for his son. Michaela was certain of it. And Lucien had given up; he was frivolous and would soon forget the romance.

Travel is a saintly cure, the Sicilians would say...
And Lucien, on his journey, without sending a single word, a telegram, may have changed his mind or, who knows, fallen in love with another woman.

Why hadn't Clara written? She hadn't sent orders to the servants, or a trunk, nothing. Clara, who had never failed to meet her obligations and had never gone so long without sending word. Now... Deep down, Michaela thought, anguished, perhaps the baroness also had not accepted that union and wished to postpone the preparations... She no longer knew what to make of that silence, which now had lasted almost two months.

Sebastian, without knowing what was occurring, watched the Sicilian grow thinner day by day, and not even Amelia could convince her to eat.

When Michaela read the letter from her uncle David, she felt a bit relieved. She wanted to be taken away from that house, to be given reasons to cry openly, to bring her back to reality. How childish she had been to have such grandiose dreams! How irresponsible to give herself to that man, to yield her heart, her virginity, everything she had of value.

Her love... poor little Sicilian girl, poor romantic!

∽

The envelope with the seal of Master Grassi's office contained everything necessary to get Michaela safely to Sicily and arrange for her and Anna Varsano to travel to Salonica. David had made arrangements for Michaela to take the train to Naples and from there a steamship to Messina.

"Today you're a grown and independent woman who speaks many languages, able to easily make the crossing with Anna. Your mother, in Taormina, needs your company and assistance now more than ever."

In David's letter were also news of her father and a train ticket, a map of the route, and the promise that there would be money available from his account and the Grassi account at the Bischoffsheim & Goldschmidt Bank in London.

Michaela sighed in relief. She was ready to leave. It was her family that was rescuing Michaela from despair and humiliation. Her mother, her roots were calling to her, and it was to them she should now devote herself. It's all over, she thought. The Hirsches and everything else were just a dream, one that in time she would forget. Or else a terrible nightmare that would stay with her for the rest of her days.

That afternoon, she began packing her bags. From minute to minute she went to the window to look out at the street. She had the feeling that at any moment someone would knock at the door with a telegram, a letter, but nothing broke the routine in that house.

She locked herself in her room and opened the armoire, saw her blue dress, her pink blouse, the robe she wore that first night with Lucien, her petticoats from the Neuhmans' shop, the blouses knitted in Planegg, the citrine necklace, poor granddad, she thought, her eyes swimming with tears.

She didn't hear when Amelia knocked at the door, once, twice, three times. She called Sebastian when she heard no movement from Michaela.

Sebastian forced the lock. The room soon smelled of ether. Michaela was found lying near her travel trunk, fainted, with the green citrine necklace in her hands. Pale, she came to when she felt Hannah caressing her hair.

"Don't be afraid, my dear, it will pass, it will all pass," she whispered.

Sebastian had called a doctor, Hannah's doctor.

Dr. Lang used the stethoscope and applied balm of mint to her nostrils while Amelia changed her vomit-stained nightgown. He put a number of questions to the patient, who answered in a murmur. After he left, Hannah returned, with a worried expression, and asked Amelia to leave the room. She closed the door and sat beside Michaela.

"Stay calm, Michaela," she told her, gripping the girl's hands.

"The doctor told me there is nothing seriously wrong with you. May I just ask one question? How long since you had your last period?"

Michaela was shocked and felt her heart racing. In the anguish of the last two months, she had even forgotten that every 27 days she would bleed and suffer cramps and be unwell. Her head spun. Then she remembered:

"Since the third week in December... Lucien arrived from Brussels." The eighteenth of December, now she was sure. She was at Rue de l'Élysée and had shut herself in her room, looking at the garden, for three days, with terrible cramps. Later it had passed and her color had returned to normal. That had been her worry those days, that Lucien might see her in that condition, pale.

"Dear," Hannah told her, smiling, "now I understand... You're not sick, your sudden illness, your vomiting, your lack of appetite– there's a name for it: pregnancy... Micha, you're going to be a *maman*!"

The day had dawned with a ray of sunlight in the midst of dark clouds. Michaela Varsano took a final look at her room and on a sheet of paper hastily wrote her last words to Baroness Clara de Hirsch. As if nothing had happened, and only the loss of her grandfather was taking her away from there, she left on the table, impeccably organized, the baron's correspondence and accounting folders.

She also left the baroness's pearl earrings, a bracelet, and a ring lent her to wear at receptions in Paris. Clara nonchalantly had told her to keep them, as there would be many more parties and they looked so good on her... But they were the baroness's and must be returned.

And to Lucien… The untouched ring in the box from Place Vendôme remained in the dresser drawer in the blue bedroom that was his. There, on top of his albums of childhood drawings, she deposited the small box with the engagement ring. She wouldn't need it, for there had not been, and would not be, any engagement.

He had undoubtedly been dissuaded by the baron.

If he truly loved her he would know where to find her, she thought, closing the bedroom door.

With grieving heart she went into the baron's library, where the sight of the nymph-clock shook her from her reverie.

It was seven o'clock, and she should be heading to the train station. It would be a long day until she crossed by boat to France.

Hannah de Rosebery was waiting at the foot of the stairs. She went with Michaela to the carriage. Sebastian put her bags inside and took his place next to the coachman, and Amelia smoothed a blanket over the young woman's legs.

"Take care with the cold, my dear," the Portuguese woman told her. "May God go with you and the Virgin Mary watch over you."

The carriage circled Berkeley Square and headed toward Waterloo Station. Sebastian observed the young woman through the small glass window and saw her green eyes, buried deep under dark circles, flood with tears. Miss Varsano, the sun that illuminated the town house and the entire neighborhood, seemed at that moment to shine no more. In addition, it began to rain copiously that London morning of April first, 1887.

Almost instinctively, Michaela clutched her belly at each jolt of the carriage. She watched the landscape through the dull panes and saw the surroundings, the streets, the people hurrying along the sidewalks of Oxford Street. She said farewell to Mayfair, the Neuhmans, Hyde Park, Piccadilly, and all of London.

She knew it was a farewell forever, that she would never return.

And everything remained between four walls. Neither Hannah, Sebastian, nor Amelia would mention, for anything in the world, what they had heard.

Never, without Michaela's permission, would they tell the secret:

That Michaela was going to be a mother.

The postman delivered the day's correspondence and the French newspaper *Le Gaulois* arrived to the home of Lord Rosebery.

Hannah, waiting at the front gate, watched as Michaela's carriage disappeared from Berkeley Square. She opened the newspaper, dated March 28.

On the social page was a odd news that Baroness Clara de Hirsch: She had cancelled the philanthropy tea with a piano concert in Rue de L'Élysée was giving the following Wednesday, because of an illness of her son Lucien.

Hannah closed the paper and sighed.

"The child's father," she said to Amelia. "Something unexpected with Lucien Hirsch is going on in Paris... Poor Michaela..."

Sebastian went that afternoon inside Michaela's room to close all the windows . Her perfume of lemon was still on the air.

Her beautiful citrine necklace was laying on the floor. He close it with the things to give it back to the Baroness.

She´ll know what to do with all of it.

∾

Taormina, the fifth of April,1887

Atop the hill, Mongibello was more beautiful than ever. The whitewashed house shone in the sun, contrasting with the cypresses and the plane trees casting their shadows on the path.

Michaela descended from the wagon. Her legs trembled with fatigue and her head was spinning. She had not eaten since Naples. A piece of bread and some coffee were all she had ingested on the dock, prior to the ship's departure.

She had been nauseated ever since, and all night the wind had contributed to the rocking of her cot. Michaela had not dozed for a single moment, and throughout the night her thoughts were on the child she carried inside her.

On the other hand, she was back home, to her roots... finally.

# XXI

## BLACK BORDERS

Taormina, spring 1887.

The months passed slowly in Mongibello, and all of Sicily was resplendent with the flowers of spring. Tourists came for the festivities, jamming both the Hotel Timeo and the agenda of the dressmaker Anna Varsano.

Since the day she had returned to her native land, Michaela had shut herself away, her life circumscribed by the whitewashed walls of her late grandfather's house. The magnificent days of blue skies, perfumed by the flowers of almond trees, beckoned people to stroll, to sit at the edge of the precipice and breathe the sea breeze, to gather bouquets of chamomile, but those days were no more.

Michaela had become a prisoner, and that place was her prison for expiation of her sins. And to think she had heard similar stories of love and sin, of vows, just like the story of pitiful Sister Antonina, the poor woman. Now, she could understand her, the woman who had been condemned to silence for the rest of her life.

The openings in the shutters now constituted her entire world, and she looked at life outside, straining to see the ruins of the Greek Theater, illuminated by the rising sun, and tried to glimpse the sea down below, golden in the dying rays of sunset.
And counted the days...

Looking at herself in the mirror, unable to recognize the Michaela she saw: unkempt, badly dressed, dragging herself about the house in an old nightgown. She didn't put on weight; rather, she became thinner. There was only a large belly that grew, sadness and shame. She would not have had the courage to go outside and face the truth, exposing it to the city. So she lived there in Mongibello, hidden.

Only Giovanna, the oldest seamstress and virtually a sister to Anna, knew of Michaela's return to Taormina. With Anna's husband far away and the death of her father, she had invited Giovanna to live in the house with her. Not even Antonio, the postman, who passed by there weekly, or the fisherman Altanario, as well as the neighbors who knocked at the door, would ever imagine that Michaela was back. It would be a disgrace...

" Raffaele Cohen's granddaughter came back pregnant and single !"

"*Dottore* Varsano's daughter is going to be an unwed mother…"
Such thoughts tormented her day and night.

There had been times in school when she herself had spoken of female friends who had fallen into disgrace. How she regretted it now … She had heard stories with unhappy endings, like Francesca Cossimo's father disowning his daughter, or that cousin of Maria Galadoro, Nedda, beaten by her brothers until she miscarried and then thrown onto a cart and imprisoned in the Carmelites Convent, never again to see the light of day.

She shuddered thinking how through a thoughtless action, she had compromised her father's name and the efforts of her mother, who so quickly had become the premiere dressmaker in the city. She feared that her schoolmates, the neighbors down below, the gossips who spent their time talking about the shortcomings of others, would learn of her condition. Surely they would make the sign of the cross when they encountered her in the street, to exorcise the demon she carried in her belly.

Her mother would lose her job at the Hotel Timeo and the blessings of Father Battistini, who visited Mongibello at least once each season to seek help for his asylum and his small church. He alone in the city had extended a hand to Anna and thanked the pharmacist for his help with medicines and for the clothes and utensils donated by Anna following the public humiliation of the notary Tiopanni's farcical edict.

Still, nothing could compare to the suffering and humiliation that Anna felt now. Nothing in her entire life had been as painful as seeing her daughter in that desperate condition, hiding in her room like an animal in a cage, peeking at life through slits in the shutters.
Anna could not understand how that could be happening to her.
It no longer mattered what she had achieved entirely on her own, working day and night to maintain the house and the display window of Raffaele Cohen's shop in the best location in the city, next to the Clock Tower, as a reference point of honourable, hard-working people who had nothing to be ashamed of…

And now her Michaela came with her leather bags full of clothing smelling of expensive perfume, cashmere, rustling silks, and lacy petticoats.

"For what?" asked Anna, her lips trembling as she watched Michaela unpack. "What was it all for, my daughter, if shame is growing in your belly? A child with no father, the child of a loose and irresponsible woman who thought that one day she could become a baroness or who knows what! How could you have believed the son of a baron would marry you? How could you have been so ungrateful to Clara de Hirsch and have all those thoughts of grandeur ? Who are you, Michaela Varsano?" she said in a faltering voice, while tears flowed from her sad, swollen eyes. "How can we tell your father?      He'll never forgive you. Neither would your grandfather if he were alive. They had such faith in you. They imagined so many good things for you: a fine marriage, a small business. Your grandfather even thought about   a   ceramics   studio   with   your   wonderful   dishes!

"What did you learn there with them? Nothing useful for your real life, nothing that can provide for us in Salonica. And that child, may God forgive me, comes at the wrong time for us. How can we go to Salonica with a baby ? Did you think of that? Neither of us has any way to conceal it, and your name will be ruined forever. Think about it, my daughter, whether it will be worthwhile to raise a bastard, whose existence his own father knows nothing about, to be one more wretched soul... Think: what will become of us when we arrive in Salonica with him in your arms to be greeted by your father? And to think I had dreamed so often of the joy of that day..."

Michaela tried to explain what she felt for Lucien, how what had happened between them had been for love. There had not been a single second, Michaela said, when considered using that love to her advantage. She had never thought how it would be in the future, it would be– it would be– As it had always been, in Munich, in London, in Paris... How could she explain to someone who had never left Sicily what she had experienced in those places?

There she lived differently, luxury was completely normal, from the first day she had gotten into that carriage at the station in Munich to go to her new home, a castle in Planegg. There she had learned refinement: not to turn to look at people going by in the street or in restaurants, how to sit at the table, proper posture, flower arranging in crystal vases, how not to guffaw like a Sicilian, to dance the waltz, play the piano...

There she had learned to take the reins of an immense house, compose letters, learned the difference between charity and philanthropy, about bank accounts, politics, literature, how to live among nobility, to receive diplomats, how to dress, behave, and even how to think like one of them. There she made every effort to be useful, had learned to be the way the Hirsches taught her, but had never thought of a position in society. That had been Clara's first lesson...

But she could not explain to her mother what had been Lucien's reason, after asking her to marry him, to change his mind and vanish like smoke, without a word, a letter, or even an excuse. Never again, she thought, her eyes swimming with tears, I'll never see him again...

She relived in memory the two letters, the last ones he had written from London. When she received the postal pouch from the bank, containing the ring and the promise of marriage, she had felt they had nothing more to hide.

She wanted Lucien to know everything her soul was hiding. She spoke of her plans, her desires, and her dreams. How much she loved and wanted him, how much she missed him. And how happy she was now, knowing that April was so close, and that afterward nothing would separate them.

❧

That day when she learned that Michaela had a child in her womb, Hannah Rosebery accompanied the doctor to the door. She returned to the bedroom carrying a tray, with drops of an elixir, a glass of water, a sheet of paper, and the silver inkwell.

"Write him, Michaela," Hannah implored, as she gave her the medicine. "Tell Lucien you're expecting his child. Ask him, if he hasn't already left for Sicily, to come to London to get you, because the months pass quickly and your belly will start to show soon. Don't be afraid or ashamed, dear. Clara will surely understand and protect you. That will give the baron time to accept you as the mother of his future grandchild. For him to think about it and not be taken by surprise."

Hannah took Michaela's hands, affectionately looking deep into her eyes.

"Remember, my child, that the baron must know about everything and take part in Clara's decisions, in order not to think himself the victim of a conspiracy. The baron will try to forget his dream of marrying his son to some aristocratic name in Europe. And he will come to love you; in fact, I'm sure he admires and loves you already, Micha. But you must let Lucien know right now, so Clara can prepare the way as soon as possible for your marriage. You have to tell him now, my dear…"

Michaela wrote a few lines as Hannah watched. But tears clouded her eyes, and she was shaking. She didn't know how to express all that she was feeling. She was nauseated and afraid, tasted the bitterness of shame. She saw before her that haughty man staring with disdain and asking, Who are you, *signorina* Varsano, to bring the dishonoured, a bastard in arms to this house? Who are you, Sicilian, to steal from us the future of our son? Our only son… our Lucien de Hirsch!

In her mind, one thought persisted: it had been he, the baron, who had made his son give up the idea of marriage. He would never accept a poor Sicilian woman as his daughter-in-law.

∽

At the Hotel Timeo, Anna Varsano had for some time kept the room number 8 for her customers' fitting. All of them were tourists staying in villas or in the hotel itself. They arrived with enormous trunks full of the most expensive and up-to-date clothes, fashioned from famous names. But none of that was sufficient, and they always wanted more… She had been summoned several times by Angelo Paternò, the concierge, and introduced to Madam So-and-So or Countless Such-and-Such.

Now, every afternoon, at the time Anna said goodbye to Anjù, as he was affectionately known at the reception desk, Anna would leaf through the register for a sign of someone named Hirsch.

"He was never at this hotel," Anjù told her. "Just a baroness by that name who stayed here years ago," he recalled in his refined manner.

Lately, *signora* Varsano asked everyone in service at the hotel for the newspapers brought by the tourists. The order was given to the chambermaids, and the papers went to Anjù's desk, to be placed in Anna's bag when she left for home.

In recent months she had bought many spools of wool yarn and new knitting needles. In the intervals between fittings, she would knit small booties and little jackets. The foreign clients, intrigued by those delicate pieces, curiously inquired for whom they were intended. Whose baby was it?

Anna, expressionless, replied it was for the baby of one of her seamstresses, Giovanna. And the subject ended there.

One afternoon, a maid, a relative of Giovanna's, overheard that reply. And soon almost the entire city knew that the seamstress, who was past thirty, had finally gotten pregnant .It was Anjù himself who congratulated Anna on the good news as she was leaving the hotel.

"You didn't even tell me that Giovanna had a child in her belly! Finally our friend Angelo is going to have an heir!"

Anna's throat went dry and a wave of heat swept across her cheeks, a sensation of shame she hadn't felt since childhood, the only time she had ever lied to her father.

"*Acqua in bocca*, Anjù, why should I talk about it? To attract bad luck? First let the child be born healthy, and may it all go well for her!"

Anna hurriedly left the hotel. She took the shortcut in the rear crossing the Greco-Roman amphitheatre, empty and silent at that late-afternoon hour, shrouded in long black shadows without a single soul to hear her distressed and terrified heart.

How had she come to that point? she thought. Lying like that, involving her best seamstress in the farce?

When she got to Mongibello, Giovanna was waiting for her. Her daughter was there, lying down, feeling pain, and the seamstress, pallid from concern, was heating a kettle of water.

"I think the time has come," Giovanna told her, waiting at the kitchen door. "It won't go beyond tonight."

Anna dashed to the bedroom and found Michaela panting. "It hurts so bad, Mamma," she said, gasping, sweat running down her cheeks. "It hurts too much…"

Anna counted the time between contractions, then ran to Alberto's old laboratory, looking for something for cutting, alcohol, and towels.

The child came into the world crying lustily. First its tiny head, with a few golden hairs, then its little body, its perfect arms and legs. It was a girl! Crying with all the power of her lungs. It was late on the night of October 6, 1887. Dawn was breaking and yellow sunlight was entering Anna's bedroom.
Sitting exhausted in a chair, she admired her daughter and granddaughter as they slept in her wedding bed.

A beautiful little girl. Her granddaughter!

But the farce had begun. Giovanna was now the mother of a lovely baby, and Anjù was responsible for spreading the news. "Our poor friend Angelo," he said, "so far away… In Naples, at the Church of Santa Lucia, working on that roof, and his wife giving birth here alone!"
The priest was quickly charged with sending a telegram with the good news to the Santa Lucia parish. "The priests are going to let the new pappá know," Giovanna told visitors, feigning weariness.
Michaela nursed the baby, who cooed at the breast and in the arms of her true mother, who at the slightest sign from the seamstress would hide in the bedroom when visitors appeared. The infant had two names: she was called Lucienne by Michaela when she and Anna were alone. But to Giovanna she was Lukia, as she pronounced it. "I'm going to call her Lukia, like the saint."

Michaela couldn't take her eyes off the baby. The finely shaped mouth, the brilliant blue eyes, the golden hair, and above the left eye was a small dark spot. A spot whose shape was so familiar that she could describe with her eyes closed.
Almost a fleur-de-lis, as Lucien would jest when he shook his head and combed his hair with his hands to hide it. "It's a special lucky flower," he would always say, closing his eyes.
A spot identical to that of Lucien Hirsch. In the same place, equally dark, but much smaller. The baby is a faithful copy of her father, Michaela thought.

It was now the end of November, and the weather had changed in Taormina.

The olive harvest had called the majority of the neighbors to the fields, and Mongibello was the only house in the vicinity that kept its stove lit. A strong wind rattled the windows, the days dawned cloudy, and the house grew cold as evening fell.

Anna had provided much wood, and in those days it cost a fortune. The men were in the olive fields, which meant there were no mules available to haul a basket of wood to Mongibello. It seemed the entire city had gone mad with the desire to make money working in the cold wind and the heavy rain. When they returned, it was like an epidemic, the pharmacies packed with sick people, and they would spend everything they had on medicine for coughs, high fever, and chills. And that meant more profit for the Gallianis, who still controlled the pharmacies in all the surrounding area.

Giovanna was very excited. While Anna attended to matters at the hotel, she did her sewing and prepared Michaela's food. She didn't want to tire the girl, who was breast-feeding, and thus lose the milk for "her" daughter.

That morning, Michaela was eating a bowl of bean soup, wrapped in an old robe, when she heard the shout of Antonio, the postman:

"Giò, ò Giovanna... A letter for *signora* Varsano. And it can't be anything good," he said, changing his timbre. "Some bad news on its way," he said at the door, in a low voice.

Giovanna looked at Michaela, who stopped eating and ran to hide in the bedroom. The seamstress opened the door and saw the postman, red in the face and out of breath as always. She looked at the envelope, which bore a black border, and her legs buckled.

She didn't know how to read very well, but she understood there was bad news in the envelope.

When the door closed and Antonio had descended the hill, Michaela came back out.

"What is it?" she asked, stammering. When she recognized the handwriting of her uncle David from Salonica, her heart raced, and she screamed: "Pappá... Something's happened. It was my father, Giovanna! The letter's from my uncle."

With trembling hands she opened the letter, unable to understand what was written there.

Salonica, Ottoman Empire, 28 of September 1887

*Carissima Anna,*

*It is my duty to inform you and Michaela of the passing of Lucien Jacques Maurice de Hirsch, only son of Baron Maurice and Baroness Clara Bischoffsheim de Hirsch.*

*The tragic event occurred because of a strange and powerful influenza contracted last February en route to Sicily, where the illustrious collector went to seek one of the most important coins of his collection, the Messina tetradrachma. Lucien also fell ill with pneumonia.*

*Unfortunately, on his return trip to Agrigento, with a high fever, he had three very powerful pulmonary haemorrhages, suffering greatly until he arrived home in Paris.*

*Many medical specialists were called to help young Hirsch, but there was no way to save him, as the cursed bacillus had already taken hold in his lungs.*

*He passed away in Paris, at the family home on Rue de l'Élysée, surrounded by his inconsolable parents, aunts, and cousins, the morning of April 6, 1887.*

*The funeral was held on April 7, at the Montmartre Cemetery.*

*I also want to tell you that a letter from Baroness Clara de Hirsch was sent to Michaela in May, to the address of our office in Salonica.*

*As I expect your arrival very shortly, I was afraid to send it along with this letter, though I believe it will contain a communication similar to what I send you now.*

*The baron and baroness departed in mourning to the castle in Moravia, the address of which I do not know.*

*I hope to see you both soon and have word of the date of your arrival in   Salonica.*

*Respectfully,*

*David Varsano*

*Postscript:*

*I haven't seen my brother Alberto for a long time. In just the last few days I learned that, in the land where he established himself to plant that rose farm, there and on the nearby area, the possibility is being discussed of building a   large hospital and a village to receive Jews fleeing the Russian pogroms*

*Everything is being negotiated by a European benefactor. As a result, the Alliance Israélite Universelle and its directors are trying to find Alberto.*

*They came to our office looking for him, with documents and a large deposit on a French bank.*

*I hope that, this time good luck has knocked at his door and that he has rid himself*
*of his impossible dreams...*
*As I was in Constantinople for several months, I left Salem, my assistant,*
*in charge of tracking the steps of my brother and his friend Daud.*
*I hope to locate him in the next few days, on top of the mountain where he*
*is still hiding from the world.*

Tears streamed down Michaela's cheeks and she stared into space, seeing nothing, the letter clutched to her breast and her mouth half open as she shivered from cold. And she remained there, sitting in the same position in the same chair all day and all night.

Her head was spinning, full of confused thoughts. She was trying to understand, to imagine Lucien still alive, Lucien sick, and later dead. She imagined the cemetery at Montmartre, an enormous line of men dressed in black. A cortege... The Hirsch, Bischoffsheims, the Montefiore Levy, the Goldschmidt, Bambergers and Camondos all taking part in that painful moment. A gravestone, a piece of cold marble, amid plane trees and chestnuts.

Now her Lucien would lie there, forever.

When the morning light illuminated the room in Mongibello, Michaela, still immobile, sighed in relief. She felt the heat of sunlight on her back like warm hands caressing her neck. She would be alone no more, and suddenly she felt a strange lightness, an immense tranquillity, as if her body were floating about the room. She felt as weightless as a spirit, a spirit that had found another spirit. They had loved for the last time, saying farewell with a promise.

"One day, my love, we will meet again," she said to herself. "Every day, when I see the sun shining in my eyes, I will see you," she said softly. "When I hear the morning songbirds, I will hear you, my beloved Lucien."
And, murmuring as if in prayer, she repeated:

"Forgive me for having doubted your love... Forgive me my love..."

∾

On the afternoon of January 25, 1888, the wind shook the windows at Mongibello, whispering melancholy songs of farewell.

The Varsanos' chimney would never again announce life in that house. Nor would the hens flee to the amphitheatre or the goat lent by Anjù to feed little Lukia, his "friend's daughter," graze there.

The neighbors would no longer pry into the Varsanos' reserved life; Antonio, red-faced and huffing, would no longer climb the hillside, shouting the news to Anna; and Altanario would never again come by there offering his fish.

The house would remain boarded up. Bars were placed on the doors, the shutters were closed, and weeds would soon take over everything. The Varsano-Cohens would bring to an end the final chapter of their story there.

Anna Varsano looked around her for the last time while Michaela and Giovanna climbed into the wagon. The infant, nestled to the breast of her true mother, warm and content, slept quietly. Anna climbed onto the footboard, clutching a bundle of cuttings from her lemon trees. Small and leafless, they were nevertheless certain to take root in the new land that was to receive them. And would surely one day provide shade and fruit in the home Anna would build to house her granddaughter, the blessed fruit of her Michaela's love for a worthy and honourable man named Lucien Hirsch.

Someday, to be sure, Anna would clarify everything to her husband, the great *Dottore* Varsano, but not now. For now, no one would understand. They would forge ahead, preparing the path, and the future. And it was with these thoughts that she locked the gate and looked at Mongibello for the last time.

A dark cloud and a haze covered the ruins of the Greco-Roman Theatre. No ray of sun brightened that morning. She quickened her pace and resolutely climbed into the wagon. She looked at Michaela, took her daughter's hands, and kissed the brow of the sleeping infant. She whispered in her ear:

"We will be returning soon and take you with us… We're just lending our little Lucienne for a few months. She'll be older and stronger and can face the journey better, and the two of us will calmly tell Alberto the story…"

Giovanna, seated in front with the driver, smiled with satisfaction and commented proudly:

"They're taking the steamship in Naples to the land of the infidels... And the two of us, *mia bambina* and me, we are going to Naples, to the Church of Saint Lucia, to find Angelo Catanzaro. And my husband is finally going to meet the *figlia* I gave birth to!"

Michaela and Anna Varsano said goodbye to Giovanna and little Lukia at the Piazza della Charitá. She didn't want them to accompany her to the church; she wished to personally explain the situation to her husband and the Varsano women's charade. She would say she was merely shielding an unwed mother, and the girl was only a loan for a few months.

That was the agreement, and Michaela made Giovanna swear to honour it. Giovanna would make the sign of the cross every time she was questioned by Anna.

"You're not going to forget to tell Angelo all the details, are you Giò ?" asked Anna, looking directly into Giovanna's small protruding eyes. "You're not going to give him false hopes, are you? Or let him think you're going to raise the child?"

Giovanna kept all the Varsanos' pots and bed linens, and before departing Anna placed in her hands a small bag of coins, pounds sterling, and two heavy gold chains.

"This is our payment, for now. Find a good place to live and don't skimp on anything for the child. In the bag is the address of my brother-in-law in Salonica; please don't lose it. As soon as you have an address here in Naples, ask Angelo to please send us word of our little girl."

"And thank you for everything, Giovanna. We'll be back soon," Michaela said, her eyes brimming with tears at the separation from her child. "I think that by August or September we'll return to fetch her."

Michaela took the baby in her arms again and kissed her forehead. The little Lucienne smiled at her for the first time.

Her heart pounding, in tears, she watched Giovanna get into a wagon, carrying her daughter. The wagon rounded the Piazza della Charitá, on the way to the port, disappearing into the dry mist of morning.

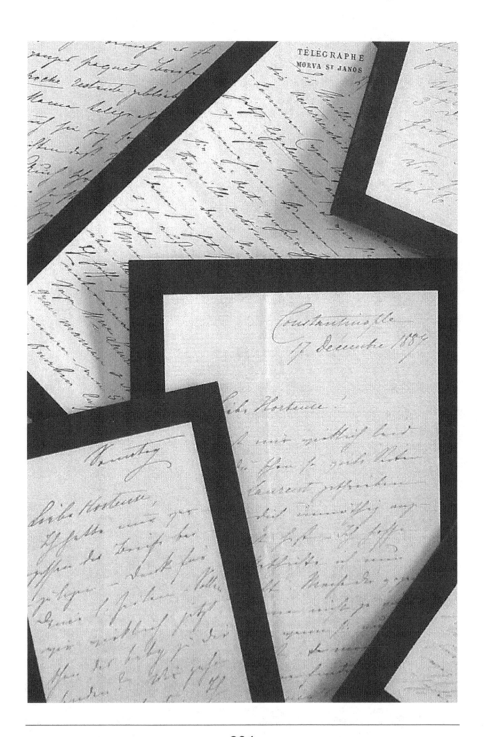

# Part III

# XXII

# THE ROSE OF NIGHT

Salonica, Ottoman Empire, 1887.

The last letter Alberto had received from Taormina arrived on the eve of the celebration of the Jewish New Year of 5647.

At the end of September 1886 he came down from the mountains, after having spent more than a year planting roses and hearing news of the city once per month. Only when Daud, would descend and come back with supplies and old Europeans newspapers, that the Moroccan received from the famous Hotel Splendid in exchange for pruning and cleaning the interior garden.

287

Every month, Daud had a secret job to do in the city. He would stay there for over four days and always returned with an excuse for the delay. He always would come back happy and talkative, balancing a heavy box of provisions containing cereals, sugar and salt, eggs packed in straw, along with gallons of olive oil, wheat, semolina, and sometimes dried fruit.

Daud was always given jars of sweets, cherries, apples, or other fruit in season, or small tubs of the preserves  from the merchants in the Aun Kapan market bestowed upon the Moroccan, calling him into the interior of their shops:

"*Éla kirie Duuud*. Come in, Mr. Daud," they would say happily, greeting him with sweeping gestures in their accented speech. "*Éla méssa Kirie*. Come in, come in, sir."

And from there, the market where he was known and loved, he would cross the Vardar district and climb to the shed housing the materials of the railroad workshop. From that point on, the path was steep and slippery; sweating profusely, famished, he sat down on some rocks and used an old spigot to cool off. There was no longer a track, only the path he and Alberto used to arrive at their shack. No wagons made their way up there, and only rarely did shepherds pass by. There was no sign of human life, just the harsh wind that blew in the winter months, the incessant hum of cicadas in the summer, and the buzzing of bees hovering over the wildflowers growing among the rocks.

The black man in a turban ascended the mountain, carrying a crate on his head, whistling the latest tunes of a group of tambourine players, which he had memorized like a schoolboy. And when he made it to the top and entered the shack, he took a deep breath as he unpacked everything, placing the "gifts" on a shelf improvised from crates. He related what he had seen, who was there, and the novelties in the city and the market. What most impressed Alberto, was how many people the Moroccan knew.

After his secret work, he would wander through the markets, and in late afternoon went to 23, *Longeant le Quai*, the home of Marika Karakassos. He sat in that magical kitchen like a member of the family and joked with little Sophie, relating news of *Dottore* Alberto. He would sit there and talk without stopping, until his voice grew hoarse and his accent stronger, speaking with his hands while Cassandra and Marika prepared the evening meal for the young couple David and Katherina Varsano.

As for the absence of David, Daud understood that he was working at that time in Constantinople, and Katherina was out of the house giving piano lessons. She now worked for the children of the city's wealthy.

One afternoon, the lawyer Emmanuel Salem learned that Daud was in the city and kept watch over the home of Marika Karakassos awaiting the Moroccan's return. He handed him a letter from Anna Varsano, sent from Taormina, along with a notice from the office addressed to *Dottore* Alberto Varsano.

With his habitual elegance the lawyer asked about the *Dottore* and evinced interest in the rose plantation, demonstrating satisfaction when the gardener calculated how many kilos of petals they would soon harvest., Diplomatically, the lawyer conducted the Moroccan to a café in the *Quartier Consulaire* and there, in a setting replete with dress-coated men, he besieged him with more questions.

Daud told him that for months the *Dottore* had not had a penny but didn't want his brother David to know of his pitiful situation. He was ashamed to appear that way. He wore his old rags from sunrise to sunset, he was as sunburned as a Moor, and now he was even cutting back on lamp oil, giving up reading his pharmacy compendiums at night. Daud further related that his greatest worry was the arrival of his wife Anna from Taormina. Where would she live?

But the *Dottore* wanted no help or charity. Daud asked the lawyer to swear he would never repeat what he had heard, for in his pride his master would never forgive him.

The lawyer smiled broadly, offered his guest another mint tea, and patted him on the back.

"Daud, do you believe in miracles?"

The black man's eyes widened and he wrinkled his forehead, not understanding the question.

"A miracle, Daud… Didn't Muhammad speak of miracles?" asked the lawyer, laughing. "For example, a good person receives a miracle and is cured, a benevolent but poor person receives a miracle and becomes the owner of a large inheritance… A miracle, Daud, understand?"

"Yes, but… What miracle has happened?"

"It hasn't happened yet, but this document I'm holding will be a miracle for your master. If he stops being stubborn and a dreamer, he'll be the recipient of a miracle. All he has to do is sign a paper and he'll become one of the richest men in this city... But don't say anything about it to him, because he'll be suspicious. You must convince him to come to our office. First take him to the large *hamam*, bathe him Turkish style, cut his hair, trim his beard, and dress him like a gentleman. Soon we'll have the Grand Celebrations begin, and he must come before then, before the buyers change their mind," said Salem firmly.

"Buyers for what?"

"For now, I can't say anything further, Daud. I merely represent a company. But he must come as soon as possible. Make up any excuse you like, that Mrs. Karakassos is ill, that Cassandra is dying and wants to see him, but say nothing about David or the office."

The lawyer checked his pocket watch and paid the bill; he said goodbye and proceeded with long strides toward Sabri Pasha Street.

Marika had already prepared the food parcel to Daud to take to the *Dottore*. She put everything into the box. She uncovered one of the pots and the aroma of her eggplant *alla Turca* flooded the kitchen.

"*Kiryê Dauudd...*" She called the gardener, showing him the food in the pot. "*Imam Bayldí...* Stuffed eggplant... Care to try it?"

"Hmm." He breathed deeply, as if intoxicated by the aroma, and smiled with his ivory-white teeth. "*Parakaló, madam.*" Please, madam, bowing to her.

Marika, standing on tiptoe to reach the bottom of the pot, prepared a plate and offered it to the Moroccan. She toasted over the coals some day-old bread, pouring olive oil onto it. She rubbed a bit of dried oregano between her hands and spread it over the hot bread.

Daud relished everything, and without leaving a single crumb behind, rayed his eyes to the ceiling as if giving thanks to Allah. Then Cassandra came with a jar of curds that she kept under the stairs, the coolest place in the house at that time of year. Marika ceremoniously opened her cupboards and served him a generous spoonful of peach compote.

Afterward, she heard Katherina arriving from her piano lessons. She entered exhausted, overheated, carrying a pile of scores; she came into the kitchen already making a din: "Aunt Marika... I need to tell you what I heard today!"

She was startled to see the gardener. "Daud, what a surprise! It's been so long since we saw each other!"

"*Mademoiselle* Katherina... Madame Varsano," he said, confused. "How beautiful you are as a *maman*! You seem even more– even more like an open rose," he said, gazing proudly at her.

Daud adored Katherina. When he first arrived in Büyükdere, coming from Astrakhan, transported by Nico in his three-master to work in Alexandros Karakassos's house, Katherina was still a girl in pigtails. Later she had gone to study music in Paris, and it was during that period that he created the secret garden for her. When she returned, at Easter, she was a beautiful woman, and as soon as she met David her heart had been stolen away. Now she stood before him, married and with Sophie.

"*Mabrucks... mille mabrucks*," he said, greeting Katherina. "Congratulations, a thousand congratulations and good fortune to you and your beautiful little girl Sophie."

"*Merci*, Daud, could you tell me, how is *Dottore* Alberto? Did he come with you?"

"No, Mademoiselle– excuse me, I mean, Madame, he's there with his roses. He has become a better gardener than the teacher. So fanatical that he doesn't let a single bee get close to the buds," he said, laughing. She remained serious and took a deep breath.

"Daud, tell me something, because you understand it well... How long do you think growing and harvesting roses, and then making perfume, will take to become a reality? I don't know what to think, because my husband David believes it's all craziness, and how will he, the *Dottore*, live until he realizes his dream?"

"Oh, madam!" he said calmly, to soothe her. "It will take the time that nature wishes. Before then, it won't happen, and if it comes about that the buds open at the right time, all at once, they say it's a miracle! If that doesn't happen, and they don't open, Allah teaches that we must be patient and go on tending the rose bushes, for one day you arrive at your destination..."

And with these words the Moroccan bade goodbye to everyone. It was late, and the path was long and steep. He would arrive by dawn, with the crate on his head and without the sun at its zenith.

When Daud said that possibly before the celebrations they would probably descend the mountain together, Katherina told him that it was time for the *Dottore* to meet his niece, little Sophie, and that there was a spare room in the house, where her brother-in-law would always be welcome.

Before he left, Cassandra stuck everything she could, taken from Marika's pantry, into Daud's parcel.

"It's all for the *Dottore*," she said. "Take it to the *Dottore*..."

Nothing could persuade Alberto Varsano to leave the mountaintop. He always had some excuse and knew that Daud could be counted on to bring everything they needed. But with what money? That was another mystery .He wouldn't descend from there because his clothes were threadbare. Because his hands were calloused and sunburned. Because he was ashamed of his empty pockets and didn't want anyone to feel sorry or perhaps try to help him. That would be demeaning.

Furthermore, he was dirty with soil, his hair was long, tied back like the shepherds. He had kept only one set of clothes and his boots for when they might really be necessary. Perhaps, who knows, for when he went to fetch Anna at the station or at the dock.

Fetch Anna and take her where? Pay for lodging with what money?

It was with such thoughts, gnawing at his soul and giving him no peace, that he, absorbed, remained there all morning, in the middle of the Sibi market square, sitting on crates, waiting for Daud to return from some "business" that he had to take care of.

In his pocket, the last letter from Anna delivered by the gardener, rolled up, crumpled, read and reread.

It was September now, and Salonica was enveloped in sweltering heat.

The sun lashed like fire on the tents of the carpet merchants stationed at the entrance to the Aun Kapan market. Alberto waited there impatiently, motionless, sitting on the crates Daud had arranged. He wanted to return to his lands immediately and see how his buds were opening, wanted to unpack those crates containing the precious goods of his future. Bottles, copper boilers and cookers, pieces of tubing and marble pestles, white cloths and mallets.

Under him, as he sat there, was the raw material of his future, everything he had dreamed about for the last several years. Equipment to make the attar, the golden essence of Kazänlik roses, and manufacture a wonderful perfume. And the Rose of Night was very close to becoming a reality.

Alberto was dying to climb the mountain to harvest the flowers.

His right hand in his pocket, he grasped Anna's letter. She had written at length and said that she would soon be with him again. He needed to think what to do! She had said that Michaela had returned to Taormina and had become a beautiful, intelligent, refined woman; she looks like a grand lady, Anna had written. It was now only a matter of Anna finishing the orders promised for the Grand Ball of the Teatro Regina Margherita at year's end. "This year a great part of the nobility will come from Piedmont, Bavaria, and France," she wrote, "and Michaela is going to help me. After that, the three of us will be together forever…"

She related that both she and Michaela had accumulated some savings, which would suffice to purchase a small house in Salonica where they all could live. With the help of Michaela, who had come back with a French mentality, Anna continued, they could sew and embroider lovely clothing for the richest women there. Anna also asked Alberto" how much a house in Salonica would cost".

Reading the letter, he had never felt so tense, so nervous, so alone and unprotected. And at the same time so confident and happy to see his dreams on the verge of coming true. First he would harvest the roses, distilling their attar, and then think about a house.

ॐ

Lost in thought, he didn't notice the crowd gathered around him in the shadow of the plane tree. Beside him, a group of musicians were beginning their small spectacle. Three young women, dressed in multicoloured silk *sayo* and *bustikó*, played tambourines, accompanied by an older violinist. The melody sung in Judeo-Spanish animated all who entered the market. Vendors of figs and pistachio nuts laid their trays on the ground and clapped in rhythm with the tambourines.

Unconsciously, Alberto began rhythmically drumming his fingers on the crate but couldn't sing because he didn't understand the song. Someone came up to him and, in rudimentary Italian, started to translate the Ladino lyrics. Alberto turned, surprised. It was Moise Covo, the fat man who, seeing the *Dottore* across from his shop, had approached to welcome him to the market.

"*Señor* Varsano," he said in his accented speech, "I'm happy to see you and I wish you a special New Year. May all of *sus sueños* come true in this our Mother of Israel!"

Alberto was perplexed by Covo's gesture, for they had seen each other only once following Victor's disappearance. He and David had sought out Covo for information about Victor's death and to ask to settle the deceased's debt with him. Covo was shocked by what he had been told, by the encounter with the Moroccan and his burial.

"Don't worry about the money," the fat man said after listening attentively. "After all, risks are risks, and business is business. We no longer have with us that *aventuroso* young man. That is *lo peor*... We no longer have our Victor Varsano... If you go to the Yashan synagogue, the Castelaña, our Synagogue for the celebrations, *señor*, look for me and we'll go to my house for the Yom Kippur dinner. It will be a blessing to receive you, *señor* Varsano."

When Daud returned to the marketplace in the square, his arms loaded with rolls of cloth and coils of rope, displaying a smile as white as his turban, the *hamalitos* and vendors made way for him. The musicians under the great tree bowed, shaking their instruments, and the girls smiled. Covo greeted Daud, who addressed him like an old friend.

Alberto, still seated on the crates, was astonished. How had a poor black man won the respect and friendship of so many people?

It was true that he was a figure who stood out in the city. Son of a Somali father and a Berber mother, of ebony color, with his height and physique as elegant and supple as a leopard and the manners of an aristocrat–that was Daud. He was unique. He looked like a Venetian Moor stationed behind Alberto.

Alberto looked at Daud and shook his head.

"We've finished everything, haven't we? We can head up the hill and be there by nightfall."

Daud couldn't believe the *Dottore*'s stubbornness.

"But, what about the celebrations? I met Mr. Covo and he told me he wanted to invite you and– not to say that.. Cassandra is very ill. Please, *Dottore*, she needs to see you before she dies!"

"Daud," he whispered in his ear. "Take a good look at me. I've already been humiliated by old Covo recognizing me in this condition. Do you want me to visit Mrs. Karakassos and meet my brother and my new sister-in-law the way I am? Let's head home, Daud," he said, quickening his pace, while the *hamalitos* loaded the boxes of materials onto their backs.

"I have just one more request, *Dottore*," said Daud formally, showing his discontent. "I have to go to the Grand *hamam* before we set out on the road."

⚜

The Turkish baths known as *hamam*, or *turkika loutrá* by the Greeks, were normally found in every district of Salonica. But this Grand *hamam*, called Yaudi Hamam, located next to the Quartier Frank, was the largest and most luxurious. It was frequented by financiers and industrialists, lawyers, doctors–in a word, the highest aristocratic caste in the city. There everyone would greet one another with a nod of the head and then silently enter the marble chambers with gigantic vaults. And silently depart.

This bath house also received the Pashas, such as high governors of the Ottoman Empire, who visited the city. It was a place where the water and the steam transformed visitors, where everything possessed an aura of peace. The perfumed oils, the echo of olive branches that, beaten in cadence like the hands of some gigantic clock, and the copper tankards of warm water splashed over bodies relaxing on heated marble slabs provided the only sound to accompany the thoughts of the bathers.

In a gallery were small curtained cubicles where the men removed their used clothing and an attendant provided fresh clothes. This was taken to a laundry, where the *sideróstrias*, or ironers, using coal-heated irons, would hand the attendants the still-hot garments on a hanger. The visitor, with a white cloth called a burnoose wrapped around his naked body, wearing only cloth slippers, would proceed to the first chamber. There, he would spend over an hour, lying on heated stones amid light steam emanating from golden spouts between cascades of running water. Diffuse sunlight came through small openings in the vaulted ceiling, forming a rainbow of colours on the marble.

How could he be there, Alberto asked himself. And with what money did Daud plan to pay for all that? What had the crafty gardener done to gain admittance to that luxurious place?

Too late, he thought, unable to concentrate anymore. The heat relaxed his body and inebriated his mind, opened his pores; a sensation of well-being overcame him and he felt benumbed by it all. An attendant came to rouse him from his torpor.

Alberto was like someone waking from a dream. "Effendi," the youth said softly, bowing and handing him two more clean dry burnooses. "Effendi," he repeated, pointing to another door, "the bath, it's your turn."

Slowly, Alberto rose from his marble slab and followed the man.

Alberto was the only one who had remained there. He had fallen asleep, and Daud was no longer with him.

 The other bath chamber was majestic, full of cascades that gushed water into basins that formed fountains, large marble tables in its center, and two bathers being massaged by experienced Turks. Each of them had a *tapsí*, a copper basin, and numerous cloths that appeared to be cotton gauze. The masseurs placed them in a bucket of soapy water and the cloths swelled as if by magic, turning into a large white ball that was used to massage from the nape of the neck to the toes.

Then came the tubs of water–for the hair, the neck, and on down. And last, in the third chamber, where the tables were lined with other cloths, came the oils, heated in small blue vials. There mint tea was served, on *chaises- longues*, for the visitor to relax.

After this ritual, the attendant who had received him would ask if he wanted his hair cut and his beard trimmed.

At that moment, Daud entered from another door, his face glowing with happiness. "*Merci*," the Moroccan thanked the youth.

"But Effendi Varsano is going to shave and cut his hair in the private compartment. Please take his clothes there," said the gardener, modulating his voice.

Alberto stared at Daud, incredulous.

"Have you gone crazy, Daud? What is this habit of wanting to play my servant, Effendi here, Effendi there, to demonstrate wealth that doesn't exist? We don't have a single lira to pay this place! You told me you were just going to prune the *hamam*'s garden as you had promised Effendi Aziz, the proprietor. The work of an hour. And you said he had invited your master to wait for you in here. Resting from the heat of the street. But not using his services! You put me in this compartment here, and I thought it was compulsory to remove one's shoes, then the clothes. All right, I even thought it might be the custom to lie down on their divan, but sending me to the baths crossed the line!"

Without answering, Daud took from his *entari* a small pair of silver scissors.

"Hold still, *Dottore*," he said, grasping Alberto's head. "Stay calm, sit there, and you'll see you feel better. Every day I ask myself whether you, a respectable man, aren't ashamed of going around like that, of hiding in the mountains, of not sending word to those who are looking for you. Why do you want to suffer? What did you do so serious that you have to hide away like that? Now that you're clean and bathed, I'm going to cut your hair and trim your beard, and you must have a bit of patience, *Dottore* Varsano, my Effendi!"

Daud looked at Alberto, who contemplated himself in the mirror for the first time in many months. The Moroccan was right. He appeared old, as dark as a Moor, scruffy. His beard was like a hermit's, his expression sad and weary. He was ashamed of what he saw.

And he allowed his friend to take charge of him. Little by little those agile gardener's hands, armed with scissors, worked a miracle. Next came the ceremony of dressing.

First he handed him the underclothing, then the white shirt, the vest, the trousers, straightened his plastron, inserted the crescent-moon cufflinks, then kneeled to attach the gaiters. On the way out, he had Alberto slip on the dress coat, the *stambuline*, and before they arrived at the street, the door a servant brought him a velvet wine-colored fez.

"Effendi," the young man said, "it's for you, with the good wishes for happiness and peace from Effendi Aziz!"

There was a wagon at the door of the Great *hamam*.
Alberto frowned, asking where they were going, and Daud sat beside his master and instructed the driver: "To the Quartier Consulaire, *parakaló*. Please," he told the driver, in Greek with a French accent. The driver turned the wagon around in Konak Square and entered Sabri Pasha Street.
How the city had changed... Stores, display windows, advertisements and well dressed people walking along paved streets. Alberto had never been on that elegant portion of Sabri Pasha. Fabric shops, furriers, display windows with jewels, silver chandeliers and candelabras, a new arched gallery called Passage Lombardo, the Imperial Ottoman Bank, the Mallah et Frères store advertising new *montres Omega, or argente et metal*, the Molho bookstore, cafes, theatres and new hotels—and none of what he was now seeing did Alberto know existed in the city.

"It's another world!" he exclaimed. What he knew was a different Sabri Pasha, the part near Vardar, next to the Talmud Torah synagogue, full of observant Jews; the region near the Aun Kapan market, teeming with vendors of lemons, cucumbers, and melons; the noises and cries of shepherds selling their sheep, farmers bringing to market bushels of lentils and rice, Albanians selling their yogurt; and Muslim butchers who hung lambs' heads, considered a delicacy of Ottoman cookery, at the door of their tents.

"Effendi, do you know what I thought?" said Daud, rousing Alberto from his reverie. "That for you to make your perfume, first we need customers. Where do you plan to sell it, and in what vials? Shall we go to the French Pharmacy, which is so famous here, and see what they sell?"

The gardener descended first and, with a bow, helped the pharmacist place his feet on the footboard. His gaiters shone in the late afternoon light.

Alberto looked like one more financier visiting the city. His carriage was once again that of *Dottore* Alberto Varsano from Venice. When he saw the Moroccan bow, he burst out in laughter. All of it was like a theatrical performance, something from the puppet opera in Taormina. Daud saw Alberto laughing, and for the first time the two had an attack of laughter that left them gasping. He, costumed as a lord, as Count De Brazza, or some such. With that dress coat of expensive cloth, with that clothing that only God knew from where and from whom Daud had gotten it. On his head, a brand-new fez of brilliant velvet.

"*Un cadeau* from Effendi Aziz for the *Dottore!*" said Alberto, imitating the French of the *hamam* attendant.

They walked down Sabri Pasha to the Café Crystal, laughing, chatting, and attracting the attention of passersby, who turned to watch them. On that side of the street, Emmanuel Salem was waiting for them. He found Alberto Varsano's happy expression unusual. Laughing and gesticulating, one speaking Italian and the other replying in French, they seemed like two students after school, talking incessantly. From the little time he had spent with the pharmacist, Salem expected to see him almost mute and ill-humoured, with that pride so characteristic of Venetians who grew up under the laws of the Austro-Hungarian empire. Alberto was one of them.

His motto was:" what he could not have, he did not want. Everything must come from the sweat of his brow"... To buy a house with money from Michaela and Anna would be the greatest shame, and the fact of his being dressed this way, in borrowed or donated clothes, even though he was clean and redolent of jasmine and pine, did not prevent him from feeling humiliated.

෯

*Every caution must be taken*, thought Salem. *I can't make a faux pas.* The lawyer adjusted his steps and, at precisely the moment he passed in front of Alberto, brushed against his arm. He pretended not to recognize him and pardoned himself even before looking to see whom he had touched.

It was Alberto, then, who recognized him.

"Hello, Salem. How are you?"

"*Dottore*, what a pleasure to see you in the city! How is business?" And, turning to Daud in surprise, he greeted him heartily.

"Hello, Daud, a long time, eh? I thought you were with the Karakassos family in Constantinople," he said seriously and surprised, looking at both of them. "So, are you two together in this enterprise?" Simultaneously, both nodded affirmatively.

"I just left an important meeting and was going for coffee," the lawyer told them.. "Care to join me?"

"We were going to the French Pharmacy to see what stock they carry. And the perfume vials," replied Alberto, trying to avoid going for coffee. "Now that we're going to prepare the perfumes, I need to see the vials."

"And the competition too!" said Daud, winking. "If you'd like to join us, come along. We're not going to take long."

The three men went into the pharmacy. Alberto wanted to smell the aromas and the mixtures of those perfumes and analyze, vial by vial, what was sold there. The majority came from a place in France called Grasse. They were light mixtures of lavender and a woody scent, or jasmine with spices. Nothing with roses, just rose oil or rose water for sweets and syrup. He breathed a sigh of relief.

The vessels were indeed beautiful. Crystal in the shape of flowers and small atomizers overlaid with strands of colored silk; hues of rose, plum, and deep green gave him ideas for his Rose of Night. It would be terrible to have wonderful contents and not offer the proper packaging, thought Alberto.

Salem closely noted Alberto's observations. "Lovely, those atomizers, so delicate for preserving a rare fragrance, such as must be the one that the *Dottore* is planning. This Lalique, for example, is marvellous," he commented, holding it against the light from the street. Alberto was impressed by Salem's observation. An elegant man, intelligent, with good taste, and he spoke of crystal and Lalique...

"*Dottore*," Daud said, "I have an idea! Why don't we put the Rose of Night in an atomizer like these and offer it that way?"

"Yes, Daud, you always come forward with excellent ideas, but you forgot the main thing–Turkish liras. How much will we need to buy those vials? Have you done the calculation? No, because while you're excellent for some things, you don't know how to do accounts. Money has never entered your thoughts," said the pharmacist, laughing.

The black man gestured with his hands as if yielding to the argument, then fell silent.

Clearing his throat, Salem entered the conversation between the two.

"*Dottore* Varsano, I think I may have a solution," the lawyer said tentatively, measuring his words.

"What solution, Salem? Do you know some glassmaker or someone who sells Lalique at a good price?" he asked, curious.

"Neither one nor the other, because your perfume in a Lalique will be a true perfume; without it, it will be just an ordinary perfume facing the competition of all the others. And every Lalique has its price, the price suggested by its maker. Just as your perfume will bear your signature. Let's go have some coffee and I'll tell you what occurred to me."

The three men sat at a table in the Café Crystal, teeming with people at that late afternoon hour. Ladies wearing large hats, nannies who took care of children and offered them sweets made with milk and rice, a specialty of the house. Businessmen, poets and intellectuals smoking cigars or hookahs, and a piano that played melodies, according to Salem, by a Pole named Chopin. He explained:

"Listen, Alberto, what the pianist is playing now is a type of composition its creator calls a *nocturne*."

Salem ordered ouzo. Daud asked for mint tea and an almond sweet, called *kurabié* by the Turks, and Alberto ordered coffee.

Also brought to the table were small plates with dates and dried figs, sunflower seeds, and toasted almonds that Daud devoured little by little; watching intently as he waited for Salem to get to the principal subject.

They spoke in banalities. Salem told about David, Katherina and her piano classes, and little Sophie. He said that Marika and Cassandra missed him and were always asking for news. But he made a point of not getting to that other matter until Alberto, curious, raised the question.

When the moment was right, Alberto asked:

"About the glass, Salem, what was it you were going to tell me, do you remember?

"Oh, yes," answered the lawyer, pretending to have forgotten.

"It wasn't actually about glass but about an opportunity that has arisen for you. An interesting proposal, or rather, from my point of view as an attorney, *highly* interesting. And with your agreement–that is, arriving at an understanding with the interested party–you will not only be able to buy all the Laliques you choose, but also set up your perfume factory, a pharmacy, buy a house, and still have enough money to live like a wealthy man should you elect not to work…"

"What's this, Salem? Are you playing with me? Is it an inheritance or a miracle?"

"Neither one," said the lawyer calmly. "Just a business dealing, all a matter of luck. And luck seems to be knocking at your door."

Alberto looked suspiciously at the lawyer and asked, "And what do I have to do for this to happen, kill somebody?"

Salem laughed and gained some time by ordering more ouzo.

"Another coffee, *Dottore?*"

He waited for the boy to serve the coffee and, when he withdrew, calmly relit his cigar and took a puff, as if he had a lifetime to tell the story. He sensed that Alberto was tense and nervous, but he wanted to gain time and increase the impact of the proposal.

"Well, *Dottore*," he began, modulating his voice as a good lawyer does, "first I want to ask you a question: the lands you bought from that Turk, that Effendi Ali, the owner, did you get from him and from the Porte the property documents?"

Alberto paled and stopped to think.

"No," he answered, almost stammering. "When I learned the land was for sale, I closed the deal directly with him. I met him in the Egyptian Market and paid him with my savings. And he wrote, in Turkish, to the guard of the railroad gate, saying that I was the new owner of that piece of land and to let me through whenever I wished."

"And you believed in that document, and it is all you have?"

"Is there some problem, and is that why you sent me that letter to go to your office?"

"More or less, *Dottore*," said Salem calmly. "More or less. A client of our firm, a great benefactor of this city, is interested in buying all the nearby land and donating it to Salonica. He wants to build a hospital and a villa of houses for refugees from the pogroms in Russia. At this point you're in the middle of everything. Effendi Ali sealed the deal with him, through our intercession, and we have on our side the authorities of the Sultan. Our law firm specializes in properties and concessions, don't forget. And you made a terrible deal on your own.

"He can simply claim he never sold you any property at all, just the usufruct, the right to plant on his property. Those lands are not and never will be yours."

Sweat was running down Alberto's face.

Salem could sense Alberto's tremor as he asked the attendant for a glass of water. Alberto sighed deeply and, placing his hands on his knees, jerked his head nervously.

"You mean I was cheated... robbed... by that... *ladro*," he said in a halting voice.

Salem clapped him on the shoulder and asked him to stay calm.

"Listen, *Dottore*, we have just one way out, and that's lucky for you: the interested party doesn't want to harm anyone, just the opposite; he wants to hand you a fortune.

He'll buy everything from the Turk, ownership and property with the *tugra*, the calligraphic seal, of the Sultan and the Pasha.

He's going to pay more than its value to have an extension of eight and a half acres. The sum asked by the effendi was 3,700 Turkish liras.

But, believing in you and your work of having planted your rose farm there, he bargained with the seller and will pay only 1,700 liras, with the remaining two thousand liras going to you. Everything will come to a total of ten thousand liras, which he deposited in the name of our firm, for the construction of the houses.

He wants it to be clear that the product of the rose farm is yours, and that after the harvest it will be enclosed by cypresses, forming a *gülbahcer*, that is, a public garden that will be part of the parcel of land."

Still not understanding fully, Alberto asked, "What if I do not agree to sell?"

"*Dottore*," replied the lawyer, "I don't believe you understand. You're not selling anything, because the land isn't yours. You're winning, and it's unfathomable whether it's luck or a miracle, but it happens once in a lifetime! I'm waiting for your signature for you to have your bank deposit. Good luck with all that money, but be careful not to be swindled again. They say that luck never knocks twice at the same door ..."

Alberto became pensive. "May I ask you something, Salem? Who is this benefactor?"

"Unfortunately, *Dottore*, he prefers to remain anonymous, but in time, when the hospital and the *quartier* are completed, everything will bear the name of that great philanthropist. We expect that one day you will know."

" *Mabruck*...Good luck!"

# XXIII

## SINIORA MODIANO

Salonica, 1888.

At the beginning of May, Michaela Varsano was introduced to Jacobo Montefiore.
Salonica was celebrating the beginning of spring, and the colours of the city had changed since the arrival of the two women into the pharmacist's life.

Anna Varsano now had a large streak of white in her dark hair, but her slim and supple body hadn't aged. Just the opposite: the years had not passed for the Sicilian, for she continued with her powerful gaze, her thick and expressive eyebrows, her sensual walk, and her affectionate gestures. And a smile that enchanted everyone.

Her daughter had become a beautiful and intelligent woman.

Physically, she was a copy of her mother, but with large green eyes, a veiled gaze like that of a cat, and the expression of an aristocrat. But since her arrival at the home of Marika Karakassos, she had yet to smile. She had arrived from the journey to Salonica tired, a bit too thin, and with an air of sadness.

She told her father that the boat pitched a lot and that she had almost been unable to eat. No one understood why the two had come by steamer and not by train; by taking advantage of the new interconnected lines of Baron Hirsch's company, they would arrive easily in Salonica.

Anna convinced Alberto that the two women wanted to travel together, and that she, who had never been out of Taormina, had been especially enthralled by Naples, walking down *Via Foria* and looking at the facades of palaces. She had seen the towers of the Sanfelices, the walls and coats of arms of the *Dorias*, the *Cassamassimas*, the *Siciliani di Rendes*–ultimately, they visited all the churches, the botanical garden, the seaside *villa* and the wonderful Belvedere.

Michaela recounted that many English people, in the time she lived in London, spoke often of Naples. They considered the city one of the most beautiful rivieras they had seen on their trips, through the kingdom of the Bourbons. She said that the city and its vicinity had so many palaces, that its walls must shelter at least a third of the riches of Unified Italy.

Whichever dynasty had reigned, whether related to the Bourbons or the Savoys, nothing had changed for the nobles and aristocrats. So many revolutions and wars had swept through those streets, Redshirts, blue uniforms, and the rich were still rich, the less rich grew richer after the departure of the kings of the two Sicilies, and the poor were still poor.

In Salonica as well, the rich increased their wealth day by day, with just one difference: they had arrived there without a lira to their name, with nothing but the desire to work. With rare exceptions, there were no families who had inherited anything. All those who dominated the city market, whether Jews or Greeks, not been left a single lira, explained David. In Naples that never happened, seeing a noble working. Everything was family inheritance and titles or dowries. The institution of the dowry and the uniting of families transformed the city, more and more each day, into a fortress.

The subject of dowries engrossed those in Marika Karakassos's dining room that evening.

"In Italy, no one marries without a dowry," said Anna. "Pity the young woman whose father doesn't have a substantial dowry. I heard incredible stories!"

And Marika Karakassos threw more wood on the fire:

"And who says that here, in our time, there's such a thing as marriage for love? It's rare. The only one I've seen lately was my daughter Katherina and your brother-in-law David. They truly married for love! My brother Alexandros even today wants to give her the dowry to buy their house, but David refuses, he doesn't want a penny from his father-in-law or participation in the profits from the winery."

"*Crissó pedi... Iné o kyrios David,*" said Cassandra, clearing the rest of the dishes from the table.

"What did she say, Mrs. Marika?" asked Michaela.

"That Mr. David is golden... and he really is! Just for putting up that he is Jewish, living with four women in this house, and living happily and smiling! He has me all day, the landlady and aunt... a fanatical Greek Christian, as if I were a mother-in-law; Cassandra, who never stops talking and singing her Byzantine prayers; there's our little Sophie, who grumbles when she gets hungry; and Katherina, who sometimes shows her *anatholikó* side, her bad humour like the Anatolians... Isn't that right, Katherina?"

"*Éla tia mou...* Stop it, aunt Marika, don't talk about those things. They are our business, and it is not always. Sometimes I do lose patience..."

"Didn't I say? She is just like my brother Alexandros: she is nice, sensible, but gets nervous in a flash and then forgets why."

Anna was interested in learning more about the city's ways of life. About the customs of so many races and religions living together. Marika Karakassos explained, between cups of coffee, that there was a different custom for each race and religion.

Michaela could see where that deceptively light conversation was leading. It would be a pretext for bringing up the subject of her suitor Jacobo Montefiore, Yako.

※

Since April, when she had first been in the home of *siniora* Fakima, one of the most respected women in the city, and mother of the well known Modianos, all topics revolved around marriage, at breakfast, at dinner, and even at bedtime.

Her mother came into her room to speak with her. And the two spoke softly, with Anna whispering so her husband wouldn't hear in the neighbouring bedroom. There were two empty bedrooms in Marika's house, one of them occupied by Alberto since the start of the year ,when he had received that huge amount of money from the bank. He had to come live in the city and had abandoned his shack in the mountains. He had insisted on paying room and board, but David, who was now the breadwinner, had not accepted and would never accept. Alberto, his older brother, would be the Karakassos' guest–in the manner of the Turks a *misafir*, an honored visitor.

The other bedroom would be for Michaela when she arrived with her mother.

Alberto's room was the same one he shared with David when he first arrived in the city. But it had been redecorated by Katherina. In place of the old divan there was now an iron double bed, a desk with books, a tall chest of drawers, a copper oil lamp, and to the side a washstand with the Venetian mirror. And, facing the bed, the watercolour of Venice by Turner.

Michaela's room was the smallest of all and now accommodated the divan, covered in new fabric, Katherina's idea, and cushions embroidered with flowers, on which Cassandra and Marika had worked incessantly during the last two months of winter. There was also an old oak dresser with mother-of-pearl filigree that had belonged to Marika's grandmother.

The hosts, in their haste to receive the two women, had arranged a new coal-burning *sobah*, for the cold of January was one of the fiercest in the region, with snowfall and icy winds.

The night that Katherina was to appear at the Modianos' to give a recital, accompanied by a lyric soprano from Paris, the house at 23 Longeant le Quai was turned upside down in preparation. Everyone had been getting ready for the big night since March.

David had commissioned a tailor-made suit, and Alberto was persuaded to do the same. Katherina, who would be one of the highlights of the concert, spent a great deal of time in search of a dress for the party. She went up and down Sabri Pasha Street dozens of afternoons looking for a lilac dress to wear with her bouquet of velvet violets. And *Dottore* Varsano, Anna, and her daughter Michaela also were on the guest list. It was Michaela's first time going anywhere in the city, and she would likely be introduced to many people.

Anna, more worried than she, began rummaging through the trunks.

"You can wear your green dress," she said, "with that necklace of citrines. It will be beautiful, daughter, setting off your eyes."
Michaela didn't answer. She spent hours looking outside, her eyes fixed on the horizon, neither speaking nor hearing.

"Michaela, I'm talking to you! Answer me. Do you want to wear your green dress?"

She raised her eyes, expressionless.

"Mother, do you really think I should go to that party? Are you going to force me to go? I don't want to see people, or to dress up. For what? Only you know how I feel! I miss her so much. I'm so worried, mother. I smell my *bambina*, the smell of my milk when I go to sleep, feel her, warm, at my side, breathing contentedly, feel her tiny hands squeezing my breasts, and I still haven't received a letter from Naples. Why doesn't Giovanna send word of my *bambina*? *Dio mio.* She's still mine, momma, not hers," said Michaela, staring at the sea outside as if absent from that room. "From here I can see the steamships passing and I want to go with them, I want to look for my little girl. Sometimes, like last night at dinner, I feel like facing all of you at the table and telling everything! Help me, Mamma; I'm afraid, I have a knot in my throat that won't go away, that won't let me breathe. What have I done?" she said, tears flooding her eyes. "What have I done? Why did we leave her there?"

Anna Varsano sighed and tried to change the subject.

Her heart was racing, she felt like crying, the desire to hug her daughter and ask her forgiveness for her fear, for her selfish thoughts, for the farce that she had invented. Now she searched for a solution day and night, but nothing came to mind. She imagined Alberto's reaction. It could kill him from grief and shame. He had always been so correct; he didn't deserve to have a fallen daughter and a grandchild without a father.

And who would believe now that Lucien de Hirsch was really the father of little Lucienne? He no longer existed. And then, how to face the baron? He would never accept a child born after the death of his son and call her his granddaughter. And the baroness, poor Clara, would be poisoned by his thoughts, that Michaela had done it all in order to become an heir, that she was nothing but another of those women in search of riches and a good life, like those who flocked around Lucien. Like the woman, that singer Michaela had spoken of so often, whom Lucien had met in Vienna, who had pursued him incessantly, claiming everywhere in Paris that she was the lover of the baron's son.

In recent months such thoughts had tormented Anna's nights.

She would leave her room while Alberto slept soundly, to sit at Marika's kitchen table. And there, in the silence of night, she would think, write, and weep.

She was to blame for her daughter's suffering. Of that she was certain.

The Modianos were one of the most important families in Salonica. And *siniora* Fakima was its nucleus.

Everything she said, everything she did was revered, imitated, and obeyed. She treated her children and grandchildren like vassals, and nothing could make her change her rules. She had built a synagogue in honour of her beloved late husband Saul, spending a fortune on marble and velvet and procuring a Torah written by celebrated rabbis in Jerusalem.

The synagogue had become a philanthropic point of reference in the city. With or without money on hand, her order to Saul Modiano and her sons was to give the small fortune of one hundred sovereigns on the twentieth of every month to the Alliance and other institutions to pay for the meals and schooling of poor children.

On the night of May 25, 1888, she commemorated another anniversary of the coming of the Modiano family to the Ottoman Empire, and like every year her house, one of the most luxurious villas in the elegant Hamidie neighborhood, would host the cream of local society. The garden would receive personages ranging from the supreme authority representing the Sultan and his advisers to doctors, entrepreneurs and industrialists, lawyers and bankers, teachers and artists, and almost all the diplomatic representatives from other countries. On that occasion, the consulates of the Quartier Consulaire would receive the coveted invitation with its red seal, bearing the name Modiano. And the party would be a mixture of diverse races, languages, and religions; of Jewish converts to Islam, Jews from everywhere, as well as Greeks and Turks.

It was always that same evening, every year, that *siniora* Fakima prepared her team of servants and took from her china cabinet the dishes with the family monogram to serve exotic delicacies. The main room was set for the recital, with hundreds of small chairs arranged like a theatre. The large crystal chandeliers glittered, and finally the massive and luxurious grand piano Steinway, was uncovered, the only one of its kind in the city.

Katherina Varsano rehearsed on it every afternoon that last week in April, always taking with her the unhappy Michaela. Neither she nor David could understand the sadness in the eyes of that beautiful young woman, her melancholy, her gaze always clouded with emotion, and her fragile voice. She seldom spoke when at the table, and at times the others sensed she was far away, her thoughts immured in some other place or time.

∽

One evening, at dinner, when the subject was marriage and dowries, she became tense when Katherina told her about the wedding of her best friend Revveca Lagaridis.

"Revveca had a marriage arranged by her father, her stepmother, and the groom's family. She's not pretty, but she's elegant, always been intelligent, and very well educated. She reads book after book. We studied together in Constantinople, then her father came to Salonica, lost his wife, and remarried.

The stepmother, seeing the daughter an old maid at 22, introduced Mr. Lagaridis to the family of his cousin Baruch Alcalá for the preliminary understandings .Isaac Confino and his wife Diamantá, who own the fishing boats at the pier, received the couples for the introductions. He, the would-be groom, came from a very religious family whose men are known as translators and writers on Hebrew themes.

"The young man had studied a lot and in rabbinical circles was considered a promising writer. She, Revveca, was the only child of a widower, a wealthy tobacco merchant. The girl was well travelled and had even lived in Paris for a time. Her uncle, brother of her late mother, would write her from America, sending postcards, books, and invitations for her to come live with him and his wife, who were childless. The father of the fiancée spoke with the suitor and his father. The young man had never seen the girl, and she had never dreamed she'd have an arranged marriage. The news caught her by surprise. First, because she dreamed about a teacher at the French Lycée where she taught French and he History. Second, because he paid no attention to her because he was in love with Stella, a Greek girl whose father owned a store in Vardar.

"When I married David, Revveca was one of the witnesses to that secret wedding, along with Salem, and kept it secret from everyone. And she confided her feelings to me. Suddenly, Revveca stopped visiting me, and I, having to take care of little Sophie, had no news of her. When I started leaving the house, I left Sophie with Aunt Marika and went to the home of the Lagaridis family.

"It was her stepmother who received me coldly.

"'Revveca doesn't live here anymore...' she told me, scrutinizing me from head to toe. 'She got married.'

"Surprised, I said, 'Married? To whom?' I immediately thought of the teacher, and his name was about to escape my lips when Mrs. Lagaridis spoke first

"'Didn't you know? All of Salonica knows my Revveca married the most intelligent man in the city. The Talmudic scholar, the writer Baruch Alcalá, my second cousin! It was last week,' she said haughtily, her face flushed, cooling herself with a silk fan. 'And today we're preparing for the consummation of the marriage!'

"Days later, at the end of the afternoon, I was putting Sophia to sleep and Marika came into the room, rather frightened, and said that Revveca Lagaridis was waiting for me in the kitchen crying her eyes out.

"And that was when I learned the whole story.

"Revveca told me that when she found out, the marriage was already scheduled.

"The parents signed a contract called *ketubah*. In it, following custom, there was an agreement between the parents, as well as the groom's marriage proposal. It described item by item the contents of the bride's dowry, all the pieces she would take to the new house donated by her father, and the list of everything like furniture, clothes, trousseau, and even underwear. And lastly the gift from the father of the bride to the groom. A fortune in Turkish liras.

"She had never seen the groom. She told me she had cried, pleaded, begged her father not to do that to her. She couldn't marry someone she had never seen.

Such a nightmare couldn't be happening to her... And when her father was almost yielding to her supplications, certain he would lose a large sum for breaking the contract, the stepmother intervened, speaking of Jewish rules, saying that a woman and her husband do not need to know each other beforehand and that love and respect always come after marriage. And that she would never again arrange a suitor.

"She would be marked and bring bad luck for her own daughters who were also of marriageable age."Just imagine! The daughters of the widow Medina, wife of the well known Lagaridis, with so many chances for a good marriage, would be stigmatized because of Revveca!' she shouted. 'If she refuses the *kiddushim*, this marriage contract, I'm going to ask for a separation, do you hear, Lagaridis!' she told her husband, sobbing.

"Neither he nor his daughter had any way out.

"So she agreed to sign her death certificate, as she called the commitment.

"'I'm going to marry, but I'm also going to die, to you and everyone else.'

"Revveca's marriage was controlled by the groom's family and consecrated according to the most demanding rites the bride had ever heard of.

When the groom's father chooses a bride for his son,' Revveca told me, 'his priority is virginity. After that he's interested in her assets as a good housewife and her social position in the community. And a promising suitor with so much study also merits a good present from the bride's family, duly assured in the contract.

"The marriage is consummated only after a series of rites," she explained.

On the Wednesday before the date, women from the families of the bride and the groom accompany her to the baths known as *mikvah*, the baths of purification. After the rituals, once the bride is dressed, they all look toward the door. If in the street they see a boy, they proclaim the woman's good fortune, as she will be fertile and produce male children, but if they see a dog or other animal, the bathing rituals are repeated.

"Revveca didn't know about these old customs and felt insulted when her future sister-in-law said she had to disrobe again for a second bath. On Friday morning they dressed her in a hat and a kerchief with gilded beads, a blue dress and new shoes. She was taken by the groom's family to the garden of the Synagogue of the Castellans. At the entrance were a little boy singing verses and violinists hired by her future mother-in-law. Then a group of young men appeared and formed a circle, and in it Revveca glimpsed her fiancé. She identified him by his clothes and hat.

"Her heart raced and she was overwhelmed by a feeling of fear and disgust. The following night she would have to give herself to him after vowing fidelity and respect. Revveca trembled and perspired.

"She remembered her History teacher, tall with straight hair, a well-groomed moustache, and an enchanting smile. And she glanced sidelong at her future husband. A short man with a thick curly beard and a hook nose. Small expressionless, tired-looking eyes, much older than she. He was a stranger who in a matter of hours would touch her, deflower her, and imprison her life and her heart forever.

"When the groom heard the boys singing '*Yale, yale, yale Hatan Larosh,*' Come, bridegroom, come forward, and Baruch Alcalá smiled at her with yellow, rotted teeth, Revveca looked to her father to implore him to yet perform a miracle. Lagaridis her father, with his eyes closed and his lips compressed, gestured that nothing more could be done. The stepmother stood before her, smiling and fanning herself, and said with satisfaction, 'Look how lovely the bride is!'

"Following the ceremony, the couple returned separately to their home, but the bride was forbidden to sleep in her room. She had to sleep with her stepmother. Revveca tried in vain to find a way to escape from there. She asked to be allowed to speak to her father, but the request was denied.

"Afterward came the morning of Shabbat. The groom went to the synagogue escorted by nine men to read the Torah, and the bride's family escorted Revveca to the place set aside for the bride in the synagogue. The groom, seated beside the Holy Ark, and the bride, behind a screen, attended the prayers. Revveca cried, her eyes swollen from sadness and fear.

"The time went by quickly, and she had to think of some way to free herself from the nightmare. In a few hours she would have to show her mother-in-law the proof of her virginity. The sheet or her underclothes, stained with the blood of her hymen, would be shown to her mother-in-law and then to the others present as witnesses. That was the ritual of consummation. And in this way would the contract be duly observed.

"Poor Revveca wept as she told the story. The night of the celebration, she still had not heard the sound of the groom's voice. He was surrounded by men and she by women.

"Suddenly, her stepmother came and took her from the circle and said in a malicious tone, 'Come, my dear, the time is now; your husband awaits you.'

"On the way to the bedroom, when she tried to break free of her stepmother's grasp, she leaned against an armoire, pretending to be afraid, and stole a bottle of ouzo and hid it under her shawl.

"Revveca smiled at her stepmother and asked her for glasses and a pitcher of water. One of the sisters-in-law brought what she had requested. Gathering up her courage, Revveca went into the bedroom and arranged everything on the dressing table. She removed her *kofia* from her head and let down her hair, damp with sweat, as if she were alone in that space.
"The man approached slowly, in order not to frighten her. He smiled and said, 'I'm Baruch, your husband. Do not be afraid of me.'
"Revveca didn't turn her head toward him. She poured a good dose of ouzo in the glass, topping it with cold water, and handed it to him.
"Drink, my husband,' she said, 'It will do you good and take away your fatigue.'

"He took the glass and drank, killing his thirst in a single gulp, clicking his tongue. Then she asked him to take off his coat and hat. He sat on the edge of the bed. She removed his shoes. She offered him another drink, stronger this time.

"Drink, it will kill your thirst and refresh you.' Then she asked him to remove his shirt, arranged the covers, and went back to the dressing table, watching him in the mirror. She poured him another glass and toasted his happiness once more .He drank. She removed her dress behind a screen and put on her wedding clothes. And she slowly approached the bed, while he lacked the courage to face her. She took with her another glass containing more ouzo and a drop of water; in her own glass, just water perfumed with a drop of anise.

"In my family, we always toast the most important moments and occasions of life. It was the habit of the family of my departed mother,' Revveca said, without facing him. 'They say that that way we can sire healthy children.' And she got in bed, pulling the covers over her.

"The man was sweating and drinking, and his breath reeked of anise. Revveca saw that his eyes were half glazed and that he was no longer able to stay seated without steadying himself with his hands. He smiled and kept his eyes shut, his head hanging like a weight.
She looked at the rest of the bottle and thought: now or never. Carefully she set him leaning against that mountain of pillows and offered him the final toast, completely draining the bottle.

"And this one will be for our future son that we will make now, my husband.'

"He laughed, guffawed, and, his speech already slurred, said 'And we're gooona make 'im nooow...' And he closed his eyes and dozed off. He soon fell into a deep sleep, snoring.

"The celebration continued outside, and many were still waiting for the consummation.
"In the bedroom, Revveca inspected herself in the mirror, mussed her hair, moistened her wedding dress, her underwear, and poured water onto part of the bed sheet. She disarranged the bed entirely, tossing pillows on the floor. She threw the bottle out the window, where it rolled under a poplar.
"And Baruch went on snoring.
"When it was late at night, she shook his arm and woke him from his stupor. He sat up in bed bewildered, not really knowing what had happened. Sheepishly, she handed him a bundle with a wet sheet. He looked at her, puzzled, and she nodded. She stood there, looking at him with a painful expression and said:

"'It hurt a lot, my husband, but it passed quickly. This is for my mother-in-law; you must take it to your mother right now.'

"He got out of bed, still groggy, looking for his shoes. He put on his shirt without being able to button it, and, dragging his feet, opened the door. Revveca remained in the bed until her mother-in-law came to look for her.

"That was the tradition…The bride dressed slowly while the women looked for the stain on the sheet and the underclothes. There were wet stains, but nothing that soiled the white. The mother-in-law went back into the bedroom and with her daughters and the stepmother looked for some sign of red or even pink. And found nothing.

"They stared at the bride, who came from behind the screen unkempt and sweaty."None of them wanted to touch her to help tie her corset strings."The impure woman must be taken back to sleep with her stepmother, but first they wanted to discover the proof.

"And scandal invaded the Alcalá household. Baruch swore he had consummated the union, while the girl, mute and looking traumatized, refused to raise her head.

"The father-in-law appeared and asked where was the proof of her purity. She didn't answer. And began to cry. She cried copiously, and overflowed with happiness at seeing all those women desperate to find proof. Old Alcalá, not knowing what to say or how to act, ran out to consult the Rabbi, his neighbour.

"The old man, considered a sage, asked permission to enter the room." Examined the bed, stroked his beard, and asked them to open the underclothes."He looked at the dishevelled, crying girl and resumed his search for a sign of something wrong…'

"Afterward he gathered the men and opened a book. He spoke seated at the dining table, where there were the remnants of the sweets and fruits and candles in the candelabras were melting onto the silverware. Even with night clothes beneath his black overcoat, the old man retained his authority.

'He read a passage from the book: Before we suspect or accuse the bride, we must know there have been cases of jurisprudence written here in which a virgin woman left no stains or traces because her hymen had a different makeup, from birth. 'Different how?' asked the mother of the groom boldly. 'All of us present here, married, left our mark on the sheets. We were pure, virgins, worthy. Why is she any different, if she's a woman?'

"And all the others laughed in derision, accompanied by the men present. There was a murmur in the room.

"The old man asked for silence.

"Revveca Lagaridis gathered up her clothes and the sheet, and headed for the street. Her father went after her. 'Come back, Revveca, you can't leave your in-laws' house like that… You have to defend yourself. I'll help you.'

"She looked at her father, crying, begging: 'Father, believe in me, no one ever touched me before, I never lied to you, and you always trusted me. I had never seen *that* before. That, that thing, you know, that a man has! I don't know if what he has is normal. I'm embarrassed to talk to you about it, but I don't have a mother to talk to, it's just that he didn't–Understand? I don't think he even has that, understand? Or if he does– I don't know… But it can't be like what other men have. Why don't you ask the other men in there, whether all of them managed to deflower a woman? Whether there aren't men with problems too, who are less virile or, as they say, potent?'

"And shame invaded the house of cousin Alcalá. The women were removed from the room, and the subject was discussed in various places and circles in the city. There were meetings of Rabbis, there was a Council, and finally the *ketubah* was rescinded. The girl was not branded impure, nor the man defective or incompetent. But neither of them, to be sure, would have a future in that city. Would the girl, and this would forever be in doubt, be a virgin to marry again?

"And so Revveca Lagaridis was sent to live with her aunt and uncle in America."I received a postcard from her. Revveca was there, and very happy."

Michaela smiled sarcastically when Katherina finished telling the story of the customs and traditions of religious Jews in that part of the world and the case of Revveca Lagaridis. Anna felt she was about to ask something and tugged on her skirt under the table, forestalling the danger.

"*Acqua in bocca, figlia*, it's no business of ours," she whispered, gritting her teeth. But Michaela raised an eyebrow and, challenging her mother, asked everyone:

"And what if she were a deflowered woman, a woman who had even had a child with another man, what would it matter if she came to be in the future a good or bad wife? Why judge a woman by a piece of membrane? People should be judged by their actions, their good or evil thoughts, their attitudes, without dredging up their past."

David, trying to temporize, said: "Michaela is right, people aren't horses, to be sold based on their teeth. That's very depressing and antiquated. Fortunately, Michaela, not all men think like that, and today there are people much more liberal, who don't seek proofs. It's not your case, you can choose anyone you like, you're free and a maiden. You can have a first-class marriage, without concern or fear."

Michaela blushed and her throat became dry. Anna came to her rescue.

"My daughter, after so long living abroad and spending time with so many intellectuals and aristocrats, so-called moderns, you've come to argue like them. I myself, there in the Hotel Timeo in Taormina, used to listen to lots of conversations of that kind," said Anna, rising from the table, "but tomorrow I have to get up early to sew our pianist's lilac dress. Come along, you need to rest because in a few days your *carnet de dance* will be full. I hope our David will introduce you to some gentleman like those he described, more liberal– isn't that how it's put nowadays?"

At Katherina's rehearsals, Michaela sat in one of the last rows, her thoughts far away, observing the room that brought back memories of other soirees. Such as the one she had attended with Lucien at her side, in the home of Ferdinand Bischoffsheim, when her loved one did not let go of her hand the entire evening, stroking her back under the stole rising and falling over her breasts. And he would brush his legs against hers in a frenzy, with a heat as great as the fire growing in her, which would only be quenched upon their return home, when the two of them, after kissing throughout the journey in the rented coach, went up to her room.

Katherina's music was like a conductor for the images and sensations flooding her mind.

She could stay there eternally, listening to the sound of the piano, waltzes and nocturnes, looking at the crystal chandeliers reflecting the sunlight from the garden. She could stay there, stroking the velvet of the chair and being transported to be with Lucien.

She smelled his vetivér scent, felt Lucien behind her, watching her, caressing her, and her head nodded and took wing to the bedroom. She could feel her underclothing, damp from arousal and pleasure. She closed her eyes for a moment, there in *siniora* Modiano's house, and was transported to distant Paris. Katherina's grand piano had fallen silent, but Michaela continued to sit there, still, waiting for another piece. She was startled by the sound of applause.

"Brava, Katherina! Brava!"

She turned to see the source of the acclaim. Behind her was David, accompanied by a tall, dark man who smiled and exclaimed, "Brilliant, our pianist. Brava!"

*Siniora* Fakima Modiano, trailed by her entourage of servants, entered the room and pointed here and there to chairs and stains on the white marble floor. Michaela rose to greet her, but her shawl was caught in the chair. The man who accompanied David immediately came to help her. He freed the shawl entangled in the leg of the chair and placed it on Michaela's back.

"*Voilà, mademoiselle,*" he said, smiling. And at that instant Michaela smelled the scent of *vetivér*. The aroma that had penetrated her nostrils that entire afternoon came from him. He must have been sitting behind her for a long time. So the sensation of being observed came from him. It wasn't a dream but a person of flesh and blood.

David came forward and stood beside Michaela.

"This is my niece Michaela, and this is my good friend and colleague Jacobo Montefiore."

He bowed and kissed her hand. "A great pleasure, *signorina*. I have heard so much about you, as your uncle has a special admiration and friendship for you. I know you from the unusual encounter the two of you had at the Hirsches' home in Planegg. He told me of your shock and your reaction."

David laughed, and Michaela, remembering the incident, opened her wonderful smile.

"That was some time ago, wasn't it, uncle? And it's still a good story. How ridiculous, the two of us down on our knees, drying hot tea from the carpet…"

# XXIV

# THE PERFUME VIAL

Salonica, 1888.

Alberto Varsano was a happy man.

He had realized a dream— more than that, a miracle. The first Rose of Night, his essence of jasmine, *Kazänlik* roses and sandalwood, was ready, as were the black vials, lined up on the white marble of his new laboratory.

It had been a wonderful year, 1888, the year in which everything in his life had gone well. Anna and Michaela had come to Salonica to stay. They had bought a two-story house with a garden on the side facing the White Tower. It couldn't be better, thought Anna. In the rear was a room for Daud, a pergola and a terrace, and in a tower a room for her to sew without being interrupted by Alberto's new employees. He had taken over the living room and the kitchen, which was immense, and there set up his laboratory. Searching through his books late at night, noting down recipes and weighing essences, he was once again the old Alberto.

It was Alexandros Karakassos who on a visit from Constantinople convinced him to relinquish the obsession of personally doing the planting and making the attar of roses. He brought him a vial with the essence of the famous Kazänlik roses.

"That thing of wanting to plant and harvest doesn't exist anymore, Mr. Varsano. Nowadays, everything can be purchased! I was in Isparta and Bürdur. There I was shocked to see kilometres of roses in bloom, a pink ocean. Hundreds of women work in those rose plantations, from every village in the vicinity. All of it is picked before the sun is fully up and transported in sacks to the foothills, the coolest place for them to be preserved and aired.

It's hard work," he said. "The old men, carefully using their shovels, continually sift the petals so they won't stick together; afterward, another group places them in the *imbik*, the retort, for the oil to be distilled.

That's what I brought you. The attar, the *itir*, as the Turks call it. Ready to be used in your mixtures to make the perfume you've dreamed of for so long."

The oval vial bore a red lacquer seal engraved *Gül Yagi*.

"They're making use of a way of sealing in the essence, because now they're sending bottles to Grasse, in France,"

Helena Karakassos told him. "I have heard people in Bürdur talking with essence buyers. They said the best perfume makers are in love with roses, but I thought to myself: No one has ever succeeded in reproducing the perfect mixture of the perfume in our garden!"

Daud's garden had finally taken off. It was now called the Rose of Night.

David, recalling the Murano glassworks where he had worked as a student, offered an idea: a black Murano vial would be more mysterious than a Lalique. The designs were done, and the first samples arrived from Venice via the Orient Express at the beginning of December, an elegant vial of black Murano glass for the Rose of Night. That evening the dinner commemorated two events: the opening of the Varsano Perfumery on Sabri Pasha Street and the future marriage of Michaela Varsano and Jacobo Montefiore.

It was the beginning of winter, December 21, 1888.

Michaela had fled from Yako every time he tried to get close to her. She would isolate herself in the garden, and when she sensed the man and his smell of *vetivér* approaching, she would leave to retouch her makeup in the nearest powder room. And there she would remain for the longest time possible, peeking out the door to see if he had given up and was chatting with other people. For the last three months at all the parties she was forced to attend, she felt it would be his opportunity to ask for her hand in marriage. And her legs trembled

Not that Yako was unattractive. He was a good-looking man, as Anna said. Well-bred, charming, with a lovely smile, he had something that attracted women, and Michaela liked his broad shoulders, his dark hair always tousled like a horseman riding in the wind. He was Lucien, she thought, with a different countenance.

David grew impatient with Michaela's reaction to his friend Jacobo Montefiore. He had kept the man in Salonica, always postponing his return to London, for he was sure the two were attracted to each other. He swore Yako was right for her. Both were cosmopolitan, a difficult thing to find in those parts of the Ottoman Empire, as he told Anna.

"I don't know what the Michaela hopes for from life, but here in Salonica it will be difficult to find someone more open-minded than Yako. He's the best catch in the city. If she hesitates, there are dozens of women of marriageable age, even some with fantastic dowries, to choose from. He's a gentleman."

Anna smiled and said nothing. She knew where her daughter's head was and the effort she had made in these last months to escape Yako and anyone else. Michaela would never marry. Her head was in Naples, thinking about her daughter. And when David spoke to her about the Murano glass, she didn't hesitate even a second to volunteer to make the trip to Venice. It was she who designed the black glass in Murano.

Everyone asked whether it was a good idea for her to go to Venice alone to deal with a matter that was more a man's affair. And to accompany the first pieces at the glassworks, the molten glass and the shaping. She smiled. "You're forgetting that I worked in a ceramics studio. And handled bills and participated in institutions in the name of the Hirsches and travelled everywhere with no one at my side, and still came back in one piece…"

She packed her bags. This would be her opportunity to bring back little Lucienne. She would go to the ends of the earth to find her. And if Yako truly loved her as he had said, he would accept her child; after all, wasn't he the modern, liberal man?

When Anna learned of her daughter's plans, she decided that the best pretext for going with her and helping her would be to claim she had received a letter from Taormina that a buyer had been found for Mongibello. She would go and settle the problem of the shuttered house and visit Giovanna and her *bambina* while Michaela stayed in Venice waiting for the glass moulds.

David was concerned about Anna, who would go by herself to Sicily. She smiled that sly smile of hers and raised her eyebrows in indignation:

"My dear brother-in-law, you have nothing to worry about… In Italy we speak Italian. Even if I have a Sicilian accent, I'm not going to get lost on the trains. Rest assured: I'll be back soon."

After that, nothing could stand in the way of the departure of the two women.

It was the beginning of September, when their bags were packed. Michaela had written two letters in her mother's name, looking for Angelo and Giovanna Catanzaro, one addressed to the Church of Santa Lucia in Naples, and another to Father Battistini, in Taormina. In them, she asked for news of Giovanna, Angelo, and the *bambina* called Lukia.

It was the priest who answered months later, in a long letter to Anna. It arrived on the eve of the women's departure for Italy.

*Taurina, August 5, 1888*

*Egrégia Segura Anna Varsano.*

*Forgive me for the delay in this letter, but with so many events since Easter and the San Giovanni festivities, I was busy almost every day gathering support for our church, with no time to catch up with my correspondence.*

*Now the tourists are going back to their homes and the city is returning to normal.*

*I was reread your letter, signora Anna, and sensed your anxiety to know of Giovanna, Angelo, and the poor bambina.*

*I sought Father Agostino, that new young man in our parish who was transferred to Naples. It was he who gave me the following news:*

*Angelo no longer works there in the Church of Santa Lucia.*

*The priests said that since the first of the year, when Giovanna arrived from Taormina with the little girl, the two quarrelled and he started drinking heavily. He even went around with a bottle of Chianti under his arm and would balance himself on the scaffolding of the church, shouting curse words.*

*One day, one of the priests had to climb up there and bring him down. And they tried to help him. But to no avail, and he disappeared.*

*As for Giovanna, we know that she works in one of those villas near Belvedere, but no one is sure of the address.*

*Of the poor little girl, and this is a mystery, no one knows for certain how she came to her end. Some of the pious church women said that in a fit of rage Angelo Catanzaro threw the baby to the floor, taking the life of the poverina, then set fire to the house. Others say the little girl died in the fire, asleep.*

*What is known is that Giovanna's house caught fire while she was away, working. And that inside were Angelo, totally drunk, and the little girl. When Giovanna arrived and saw the tragedy, she began to scream and was ministered to by neighbors. She screamed and called out to the baby, but the charred body of the blessed infant was mixed with the rubble and never found. Only that of Angelo, was buried. And since that time no one has seen Giovanna.*

*Knowing that you were friends of long standing, and how helpful you were to the poverina and her small child, I greatly regret having to inform you of this unhappy news.*

*I have seen Antonio, the postman, who misses all of you.*

*Altanario is now the grandfather of a little boy and is thinking of setting out to sea fewer days in the week.*

*The shop that was your father's belongs to the son of signora Paternò, who turned it into a store selling torrone and orange sweets.*

*I have never again gone up to Mongibello. But when I meet Anjù he always speaks of all of you and becomes emotional. He says he passes by there on Sundays and that your house, which was always so well kept, is painful to look at, given its state of abandonment.*

*You are greatly missed in Taormina, my dear Signora Anna.*

*We will always remember you, Dottore Alberto, your daughter Michaela, and your honored father, signor Cohen, and the help he gave us with our poor children.*

*May God bless you all and may you and your family always find love and peace.*

*Father Andrea Battistini*

&

Since that afternoon, when Michaela had come in holding the letter in trembling hands, mother and daughter had barely spoken...

Daud found strange the sadness in the women's eyes, the conversations in low voices, Anna's lack of appetite and the abandonment of her studio. Michaela didn't change her housedress, her hair was poorly braided, and she shuffled about in her slippers; nothing could make her smile.

Mother and daughter never again broached the subject.
Nor did they travel.

Anna claimed a sudden illness and Michaela, closeting herself in her room, would not come down even to eat. Only the *Dottore*, whose head was in his work, would descend for lunch, inquire about them, and return to Sabri Pasha Street to finalize the works for his perfumery.

Two months of anguish.

Since the end of July, David and Yako had been in Constantinople to help Baron Hirsch effect another agreement for the concessions of his new railways. Baron Hirsch, under pressure for several years, saw his funds, sunk in a twenty-year investment, being lost through the simpleminded despotism of the Sultan and his collaborators.

What had been previously agreed upon and contracted no longer mattered, and what did matter was an incalculable fortune that the Sublime Porte was demanding from Maurice de Hirsch.

Jacobo Montefiore was part of the negotiations team.

He was practically a diplomat, with his demeanour and abilities and a head trained for numbers. Behind the scenes he was a counsellor in the confrontations and had the ear of Oscar S. Straus, the American ambassador charged with mediating the case.

Jacobo had written several letters to Michaela. In one of them he told her she had been the center of conversation at a dinner at the residence of Ambassador Straus and his wife Sara, in Constantinople.

At the table was Clara de Hirsch, dressed in mourning, sitting beside David.

Clara had asked about Michaela, Anna, and the *Dottore*. She told David that she missed her immensely and was still awaiting an answer to the letter she had written in Paris, days after the death of her beloved son Lucien.

A letter she had sent to Salonica in care of David. Upon hearing the baroness's words, he had gone pale, Yako said.

Remembering what had happened to the letter, David had apologized.

"I received that letter. I even wrote Anna about it. But, for fear of losing it, I put it in the office safe, planning to deliver it to Michaela as soon as she arrived in Salonica. But with all my travels here and there, it slipped my mind."

The baroness smiled, relieved. She wanted to know more about Michaela and her life in that distant city. Whether she had fallen in love with anyone; after all, she was a fine young woman and deserved to be happy.

David looked at Yako and smiled. And ventured a particular comment sitting close to Clara:

"I am of the same opinion, baroness. We have here beside us a genuine suitor for Michaela. This young man before you, Jacobo Montefiore, has serious intentions, but you know the temperament of my niece better than I myself. She seems unhappy all the time, and there is some great mystery in her life. We have never been able to understand, my wife and I, whether Michaela is really attracted to him.

She always has some evasive reply to our questions and continues to avoid everyone. I have the impression that she loves, or loved, someone all those years that she lived with you, and that for some reason it was unrequited. Perhaps you, knowing her better than I, can help me and provide arguments to persuade her to give my friend Montefiore a chance. He has been awaiting an answer from her for months."

At the conclusion of the dinner, Clara de Hirsch whispered a few words to the baron. He looked at her and nodded. Later, over the liqueur, he approached Jacobo and they went to the garden door, where they talked for hours.

Clara, using the ambassador's stationery, ensconced herself in the library and wrote a long letter to Michaela. At the end of the evening, she handed the envelope to David.

"Please, Mr. Varsano, give this letter to Michaela, instead of the one you have in your safe. The earlier one is no longer valid, as it deals with a matter already past. Please, if you can, burn it for me, and I'll feel relieved. Do that, please..."

And, grasping David's hands, she said goodbye.

David and Sara Straus watched as the baroness crossed the Straus garden and got into a carriage. The baroness, always strong and proud, was now dressed in black, her body bowed from the weight of grief. David remembered the Clara receiving him at Planegg, in the blue
bedroom belonging to her son. He reflected on the coincidences and jokes that life thrusts upon us. Unfortunately lost her only son, her sole interest in life...

Poor baroness… So rich and so unhappy, he thought.

It was a simple and lovely ceremony. Anna sewed the wedding dress in the style of wealthy Taorminans, with tea-dyed lace and appliqués of small flowers. She didn't carry a bouquet like Sicilian brides because synagogues do not allow flowers. Her face had to remain behind a veil almost throughout the ceremony.

Michaela looked magnificent when she entered the Great Synagogue on the arm of her father, who stood proud in his new dress coat. Present were friends of the Varsanos, Master Grassi, Emmanuel Salem, and the entire group from the office. The Karakassoses from Constantinople, the Levys, the Herreras, the Covos, the De Buttons, the Matarassos, the Allatinis, and the family of *siniora* Modiano. Among the Turks, some ten represented the authorities, and Effendi Ali, Daud's friend and owner of the baths, was also there.

Gathered around the nuptial tent, which was decorated with date palm leaves and candles, the guests witnessed the ceremony. They admired Michaela's beauty and applauded when Jacobo smashed the wine glass underfoot.

That night, everything cooperated for the realization of Anna's plans. The Varsanos' house and the tent in the garden, adorned with camellias picked by Daud and candleholders with white tapers, welcomed the guests for dinner. In the bride's room were the gifts.

From London came sets of silverware and dishes from the Montefiores and a silver box sent by Hannah and Lord Rosebery; inside, a pearl necklace with a medallion for portraits, with bas-relief of blue sapphires and an affectionate letter from Hannah; in another envelope was a ring. It was Lucien's engagement ring and a letter from Sebastian Clair.

He was returning to Michaela the ring she had left in Lucien Hirsch's room, in that drawer in Berkeley Square. And the ghosts, the letter said, would disappear, giving way to a lasting happiness.

"Wear it, for it's yours, and you are deserving of all the happiness in the world."

Clara de Hirsch was the first to send a wedding gift. From Paris arrived an immense canvas, almost as tall as Michaela.

On it was painted a young woman looking outside to the gardens of Rue de l'Élysée. Standing surrounded by champagne-colored roses, the girl was wearing a green taffeta dress and a necklace of citrines.

It was the portrait of Michaela. It was she, at dusk in December 1885, with braided hair pulled back, looking to the window, ready for the Bischoffsheims' dinner. The canvas was signed by a painter named John Singer Sargent, based on drawings by Lucien de Hirsch.

There she was, Michaela portrayed forever. Her serene moment had been captured in that canvas.

Along with it, a card from Clara: *"Be happy, my little girl..."*

Among the presents, wrapped by Anna and sent to the couple's new address in London, were also some vials of Rose of Night.

And so Michaela boarded the Orient Express at the Vardar station in the company of her husband, Jacobo Montefiore, on the way to a new life.

# XXV

# *PICCADILLY*

London, 1889–1896.

Anna Varsano, in her atelier in Salonica, received her first letter from the new Mrs. Montefiore, or rather, from her daughter Michaela Varsano Montefiore ,of number 106, Piccadilly, London. The letter, dated January 8, 1889, recounted everything about her arrival at the home of her husband's family and how everyone there was waiting to greet her. Michaela described her new home, her new life, and the family to which she now belonged.

The Montefiore home was a mansion, an old house on a corner, with one of the facades facing the mews and the other looking out on Piccadilly.

Abramo Montefiore, Yako's father, was a tall and elderly Florentine, slim and elegant, with slender hands and long arms, delicate manners, and a heavy accent when he spoke partly in English and partly in his native dialect. He counted in Italian whenever he did accounts, and in the house was an office where he received clients for loans.

Yako's mother, Mrs. Tilda, never entered that part of the house. She would use the mews door when returning from shopping and knew everyone and everything that went on in the neighborhood.

One wing of the house had been set aside for their first-born son and his wife.

The entrance hall in black and white marble, with a statue of Venus, marked the boundary of the commercial entrance of the Montefiore lending firm.

A side door had been opened next to the rotunda that provided access to the great hall, the dining room, and the stairs to the upper floor with its many rooms. Two of them had been transformed into a sitting room and library for the young couple, a bathroom and a bedroom. But the kitchen on the ground floor continued as before; thus Michaela had no space for her own. If she wished to cook, it would be for everyone in the house. But since coming to London she had never even dared to boil a pot of water.

Mrs. Montefiore, Yako's mother, was determined to please her new daughter-in-law. She had had an unhappy experience with her daughter Lina, who when she married a French banker was also obliged to take in the mother-in-law. And what a mother-in-law! A jealous Frenchwoman with a personality so acerbic that within a few years she had been the cause of her daughter-in-law's sickness. Lina was in a clinic for the mentally ill, and her thirteen-year-old son Edgard was in the preparatory course at Eton.

As the elder Montefiore said, "Our grandson carries our blood, despite having his father's name. He's going to follow the career that Yako pursued when he was that age. He's at Eton to learn to be a clever and well-mannered gentleman."

In actuality, Michaela hoped to live in a house with only her and her husband, but that was utopian as the two old people, with a thirteen-year-old boy to educate, needed Yako nearby.

Tilda, the nickname of Matilda Montefiore, was also born in Florence and had known her husband from the age of twelve. There was much in that house that was very familiar to Michaela. Certain foods, the dining room table always set, and the frequent coming and going of business people, their guests.

Yako would leave after breakfast, giving Michaela a big kiss, promising to be back for dinner. He worked as a financial adviser to banks. There were nights when Michaela waited for Yako without dining and would fall asleep in one of the armchairs.

At breakfast the elder Mrs. Montefiore would reproach her son in Italian, forgetting it was the language of her daughter-in-law. Yako hugged his mother and kissed his wife. "A good thing she likes you, Michaela. My mother defends you every morning, when I come home late from those endless meetings at the bank."

Good-humoured, affectionate, Yako got on well with everyone. With Michaela he was an insatiable lover. He would sometimes return in mid-afternoon, pretending to be looking for some document, and she knew what would happen…

He said that those visits were for her to repay with interest the desire he had experienced, for months, waiting for her decision. They didn't even seem like husband and wife but rather two lovers meeting in the middle of the afternoon. Sometimes he wouldn't go back to the bank because he felt exhausted and slept until dinnertime. After bathing, he would dress in elegant clothes, promising her a festive night in London. They would ride through Hyde Park in a carriage, and he, his arms around her, would kiss her bosom, her neck, and lips, until their return to Piccadilly. And everything would begin anew.

The days passed, and every week Michaela wrote to Salonica. After having put everything in its proper place and having nothing to do during the day, Michaela decided the time had come to walk to Berkeley Square. She had worked up her courage to return to her past.

Since she had left Clara de Hirsch's house, carrying a child in her belly, almost two years had passed. It was as if time had stopped. Nothing had changed. The trees, the houses, and even the postman crossing the street–everything was familiar.

When she approached the square in the direction of Hannah's sidewalk, she could hear her heart pounding. She rang the Roseberys' bell. A servant came to attend her.

Then she heard the noise of the children running to the street door and glimpsed one of the twins. Then Sybil and Peggy. They were tall and looked like two young ladies. She hugged them emotionally. Little Neil, thin and lanky, no longer remembered her.

Michaela was led by the hand to the sitting room.

Hannah was there, reclining on a large velvet chaise longue, gazing pensively at the garden in the rear. She was partially covered by a blanket. Hearing footsteps, she turned toward the door. Her eyes met the visitor's.

Aged and deformed, she didn't seem like the same person. With difficulty, she sat up and raised her arms to embrace Michaela.

It was a tremendous effort. Hannah's hands trembled; her skin, which had always been wonderfully rosy, had turned greenish-yellow. Michaela, startled by what she saw, didn't know what to do to hide her emotion.

Hannah apologized for her appearance. For months her kidneys had been failing. No diet had helped. Nor any doctor whom she had consulted, she whispered. She said she was waiting now for a professor from Austria who specialized in kidneys. "He's my last hope," said Hannah.

The diagnosis was Bright's disease. Her kidneys were poisoning her body, and day by day her strength was dissipating.

Three afternoons a week Michaela returned to Berkeley Square to visit her dear friend. She gave her lots of liquid to drink, her medicines, read pages from novels, chatted, and talked about her life. But nothing about what had happened after she left Berkeley Square with the baby in her womb and her return to Sicily. Nothing that had happened in Taormina was mentioned during all those months.

Hannah sometimes tried to ask her, but Michaela pretended not to understand.

One afternoon, Michaela could no longer hide her emotion and wept copiously.

She said she was pregnant by Yako. And all her fear and shame came to the surface. She was afraid he would discover that she had given birth to another child and the entire story would come to light. She related the tragic end of her little girl at the hands of an unbalanced man named Angelo Catanzaro, who in a drunken fury set fire to his own house, killing both himself and her tiny daughter.

Hannah lacked the strength to argue with Michaela. Tears ran down her pale cheeks. Each day, her system was being poisoned by toxins from her kidneys. And there was no palliative.

Sebastian Clair was with her every day, like a friendly and protective shadow– nurse, friend, and mother. It was he, day in and day out, who offered her hope and faith.

To give her strength, he inverted the roles.

"We're not going to leave our Michaela on her own, are we, Hannah? Now that she's having a baby she's going to need us; so she wants you to get well soon, to help her!" he said, winking at Michaela.

Hannah smiled and closed her swollen eyes, nodding her head. And it seemed that little by little, Hannah's crisis abated, and there were days when the two women stood in front of a mirror and Michaela performed her transformations. She would comb Hannah's hair, pinning it back with clips of silk flowers, and apply a fine coating of face powder and rouge for color.

When Lord Archibald would arrive from Parliament, Michaela saw the man who had always struck her as haughty and often dislikeable kneel beside the chair where his beloved wife rested and kiss her hands, offering vows of love.

It was rumoured in high circles in London that Lord Rosebery was a resolute and ambitious man who thought only of achieving three things—marrying the richest woman in England, winning the Epson Derby, and becoming prime minister. The first had been realized, having Hannah for his wife, and demonstrated that it was not ambition but an impassioned heart that made that marriage one of love and respect. After all, Hannah was happy.


It was Sebastian Clair who showed Michaela the letter from France.

Soon after Lucien's death in Paris, the house in Berkeley Square had been closed by order of Baron Hirsch.

Sebastian had remained behind to close the house, pick up any correspondence, and handle payment of the servants. No one ever set foot in the Hirsches' house again.

And it was Sebastian Clair who handed over Michaela's correspondence. He came into Hannah's living room with a brown bundle tied with string. He explained that the correspondence had been kept all those years, waiting for her. The letters that arrived after Michaela's departure were there, sealed, and as a precaution had been stored in Hannah's safe.

Michaela's hands trembled as she untied the bundle. She saw the date. The letter written by Clara, soon after the death of Lucien, was addressed to Michaela Varsano. She opened the black-bordered envelope.

Clara's unmistakable handwriting, the stationery with the Hirsch coat of arms, and the smell of leather from the library at Rue de l'Élysée seemed to evoke the voice of the baroness:

*Paris, April 8, 1887.*

*My dear Michaela,*
*Yesterday we lost the man we loved most.*
*We lost our Lucien.*

*His life was snuffed out like a candle and my son breathed no more. I stayed at his side, unable to do anything, unable to help him in his desperation suffocated by the haemorrhage and in his struggle to breathe and survive. It was the cursed bacillus that took him.*

*Everything was done to cure him, we called in the best specialists and he, my poor son, had thoughts only for you. Every minute that he had left, he murmured for me to call you... In his delirium, in the midst of his fever, he called out only for you, Michaela.*

*He loved you deeply.*

*Today, what I feel in this emptiness, returning from the cemetery at Montmartre, is that we wasted time, and you were not there, and we did not even consider calling you.*

*Forgive me for not doing so. As a mother, I never wanted to believe I would lose my son to death.*

*I was certain that it was all nothing but a slight illness, a strong case of influenza, a scare, just a nightmare, and that nothing more serious would happen to my son. Surely Lucien would recover and you two would meet again and be together forever. How ingenuous I was!*

*Before Lucien departed for Sicily in February, he left with me the preparations for your wedding. Because I was worried about events and had all those requests and legal actions to analyze and resolve, I continued absorbed in my day-to-day. Maurice had to determine the lives of hundreds of thousands of people who had miraculously escaped the clutches of the Czar. And I felt obliged to first solve the problem they posed.*

*I failed to realize the problem inside my own house when my son returned from Sicily on March 16, moaning with fever. That night, when we came back from the soiree at the home of Alphonse de Rothschild, we found Lucien in the library, wet with sweat and with a cough impossible to assuage. The next morning, we called in two specialists.*

*That day, a Grand Soiree and recital were scheduled to take place at Rue de l'Élysée. With the house packed with people and applause, I left my son in the care of Madame Lory upstairs, so his coughing wouldn't interfere with the music. How petty and irresponsible of me.*

*Nothing serious that rest wouldn't cure. You two had all the time in the world to be happy, and I had no wish to worry you. You were young and healthy, you would have a future together. I should take care of the less fortunate and the wretched.*

*But in a few days the gravity of the situation became apparent.*

*It was too late, the doctors said. Nothing could be done...*

*Doctors from the medical school in Germany came. The influenza had become pneumonia, with an aggravating factor that could have its origin in tuberculosis. They listened to his chest and discovered a perforation in his lung, in contact with his bronchi.*

*His chest, consumed by pain, and his dyspnoea worsened day by day, despite the efforts of the doctors, who never left his side.*

*My poor son, on the night of April 5 to April 6, had a few moments of peace, managing to whisper his last request.*

*His thoughts were of you... and at eight o'clock in the morning, just as the first rays of sunlight entered through the window to brighten his room, his soul left us forever.*

*I don't know why I am telling you all these terrible details. But in those days I experienced the worst nightmare of my life, and I feel as if I were going to wake up at any moment and find our Lucien smiling in his library, his eyes clear and shining with love, his hands separating his coins, his large safe open with his treasures, to smell his cologne and hear his voice. "Bonjour, maman...!"*

*Today I discovered these letters. Letters written to Maurice, letters addressed to you, and various gifts and writings kept in the drawer of his nightstand. Do you remember the sketches he did in Beauregard and Rue de l'Élysée ? Drawing you, while you read in the garden. Everything he had set aside for your wedding, and his plans to reside together in Berkeley Square.*

*My dear, I want to say to you, with all my heart, that everything that was Lucien's, I want to be yours.*

*Everything... His properties, his collections, his memories and his love. Everything belongs to you. I know this is what he would have wanted.*

*To me, you two were already husband and wife. I never needed a document or witness, and you made him a happy person, someone at peace.*

*He has gone away, loving you and feeling loved, to his final dwelling. I promised him on his deathbed that I would take care of you, and here I am, waiting for you.*

*I know I cannot tie your life to mine forever, for I know you may feel resentment in relation to us, but believe me, Michaela, I love you like my own daughter and ask you not to harbour any resentment toward Maurice because he failed to understand and accept the love between you.*

*He has aged these days in a way he had never aged in years, and he has already suffered enough.*

*I do not want to lose you, Michaela, and I cannot. If you can, stay with us; if you can, please forgive me. And if you forgive, answer this letter, telling me whether you have done so. I will wait however long it takes. Think about it, my dear.*

*With all my love,*

*Clara*

༄

Along with the letter, Michaela also was given a brown envelope by Sebastian Clair, addressed in the baroness's handwriting. Inside were dozens of letters wrapped in tissue paper.

Michaela opened the envelope. They were her letters, her secrets send to Lucien. They were sealed, had never been read. She pressed the letters against her tear-stained face. Caressed them, and without opening them, replaced them in the envelope.

Shaking, she looked at Hannah.

"I can't... I mustn't... It's over, Hannah..." She returned the bundle to Sebastian.

Hannah nodded, and Sebastian left with the bundle of letters. Michaela didn't want to read them. She had a new life now and would never take those letters to the Montefiores' home. She had a good husband and couldn't hurt him. He didn't deserve it.

"I can't read them now, maybe someday, when I'm over this suffering…"

Nothing would bring back Lucien and their daughter; almost two years had passed. There was nothing for which to forgive Clara nor anything to receive from her.

So she would not reply.

"Nothing would bring Lucien back," she told Hannah, her eyes swimming. And now she was carrying Yako Montefiore's child.

She feared he would someday discover everything and hate her for having hidden the truth. Yako didn't deserve to suffer.

Lord Rosebery wanted to do something to make his wife happy. He negotiated the acquisition of the new home in Piccadilly, but when Baron Hirsch closed the Berkeley Square residence he thought seriously of quitting the purchase, offering Baroness Hirsch a good price for 12, Berkeley Square, and consolidating the two houses into a mansion.

"But," he commented with Michaela, "a lot of work and a bother: where to take Hannah, the children, and all the objects and furniture without setting up a battle camp? Making Hannah even more ill? It's better to close the Piccadilly agreement right away." And that was what he did.

Archibald Primrose Rosebery, with the help of Michaela and Sebastian, put everything in the most perfect order. Every afternoon, even with her advanced pregnancy, as she had done earlier at 12 ,Berkeley Square, Michaela brought a bit of Taormina and its sun to the new home of Hannah de Rothschild.

Thus, Lord Rosebery, a husband much in love, would surprise Hannah. He would do anything to see her happy and healthy.

Piccadilly was a dream. Hannah would finally have her view of the park, a house with large windows where the sun would bathe her golden hair and clear away the illness that, day by day, consumed her strength.

At 40, Piccadilly, Hannah Rosebery would be reborn, with new strength, to contemplate her sunny halls, her garden, her immense solarium with Lalique glass, where the diffuse light on winter afternoons would recall her childhood in Mentmore.

∽

One afternoon at summer's end, when people at Piccadilly strolled protected from the sun by colourful silk parasols, Michaela arrived at the door of the Roseberys' new residence and her eyes suddenly met the gaze of Baron Hirsch.

She felt her heart race and her hands tremble.

He came toward her smiling, dragging two boys who were arguing.

"You're still beautiful, my little Micha," the baron told her, smiling and kissing her hands. "How long it's been since I saw you, and how Clara and I have missed you!"

He was accompanied by two boys: the taller one, about ten years old, was called Maurice Arnold, and the other one, small and restless, Raymond.

"These are my two boys," he said, introducing them. "Maurice Arnold and Raymond Deforest Bischoffsheim. Clara adopted them, you know," he said in a low voice. "After we lost our Lucien, everything changed in our life," he added, without looking directly at Michaela.

She nodded, not uttering a word.

"How I've wanted to see you again... We've always thought about you... I don't know what you know," the baron continued, "but our life lost practically all meaning. Our Lucien is gone, but we gained three children."

"Three?" she exclaimed in a tenuous voice.

"Yes, it was a surprise... We received a little granddaughter, a small girl named Lucienne... A beautiful girl who was presented to us as soon as Lucien left us. It was all that remained of our son."

Michaela was so shaken and nauseated that she thought she would faint. The blood rushed from her cheeks.

*A granddaughter?* she thought. How had he found out about little Lucienne?

Are you all right, Michaela?" the baron asked, startled by the girl's pallor. "Come," he said, offering his arm. "We were heading to the park. Let's catch up on things, and you can rest while the children play."

They went to Green Park and found a bench on which to rest.

Michaela's mouth was dry and her lips seemed incapable of speaking a single word. Her heart was pounding so hard that she was afraid Maurice de Hirsch could hear the arrhythmic beats.

"Now then, my *dearr*.. What were we talking about just now?" he said, adjusting his coat as he sat down. "Ah, yes... I remember... About little Lucienne! Little Lily! Did you know we have a granddaughter? A beautiful little girl..."

Michaela trembled. *We have?* she thought. How? My Lucienne is gone... She died without me even being there to protect her.

She shook her head without replying, her eyes watering. And a terrified shudder ran through her body. *He knew everything.* A whirlwind of memories swirled in her head. He was the man who knew everything, who was informed of everything.

"I know," said the baron, "that we should have told you this before, but Clara wrote to Salonica also, right after the death of our son. I don't know how to tell you now without hurting your feelings and your memories of our son," sighed the baron, visibly abashed and disheartened.

He gazed at the ground, his hands unconsciously hugging his stomach. He was white as a sheet and didn't proffer a single word...

"I didn't want to hurt you, my dear Micha," the baron said, staring at her. "I myself didn't want to believe what was happening; after all, you two seemed to be so much in love, and my son wanted to marry you, he talked about it so much... Right after his burial, I discovered that he had a lover, who had given him a daughter. An actress, a woman with a dubious life. And I swear to you, Micha, that at first I refused to believe the woman! She appeared at Rue de l'Élysée the day after the funeral, with a child in her arms, and Clara and I refused to see her.

"A week later, she returned with a birth certificate that said: 'Lucienne, born October 16, 1885, *père et mere non déclarés'*–Just imagine... father and mother undeclared–claiming that the little girl was my son's daughter!

"I swear I tried not to believe it. I sought out witnesses everywhere, people who could tell me if they had an affair or lived together. It was all a huge secret, no one had ever see the two together. She said she had met Lucien on one of his trips to Vienna and that she had come from there with him, that he paid her bills, that they hid the affair because we would never have accepted that romance...

"Months later, a reply came from London.

"It was from that woman who worked with you, that Portuguese from Berkeley Square, that the testimony came: Lucien must be the child's father. She didn't know the sex of the child, but she did know the mother, a woman who was pregnant by him, and had sworn to the woman not to say anything to anyone about the pregnancy.

"She told Madame Lory that she knew the pregnant woman and that the woman saw Lucien periodically in London and Paris, and that they concealed the affair precisely because Baron Hirsch would never have approved of the relationship."

"Madame Lory," whispered Michaela, raising her eyebrows.

"Yes, Madame Clemence Lory." Michaela had forgotten Lucien's *dame de charge*, who answered to the baron.

How often they had had to escape from Clemence Lory, from her gaze, never allowing any sign of involvement to appear in her presence.

Amelia, she thought. The poor simpleton had been used for that testimony.


Michaela's head seemed about to explode. So Amelia, the poor woman, had told Madame Lory, who had then understood– Oh, my God!

Who is that girl, that Lucienne? she wondered.

"Tell me, Michaela," said the baron. "Now that everything is past, my dear, and we have lost Lucien forever, did you ever hear of any romance of my son's before you and he fell in love? Did you ever hear the name Irene Premelic?"

"No, sir," Michaela answered, tightening her lips and shaking her head.

"As for me, my dear, I have yet to convince myself… I think of it every day. On the little girl's birth certificate was the date of birth as October 6, 1885, and it stated that she was born at midnight at 24 Rue d'Anjou. I think to myself, even today, wondering how my son could have left the house to visit that woman two blocks away without being seen by some neighbour. After all, Rue d'Anjou is a small street, and around here we all know one another. I also wonder when you and Lucien fell in love. I was never sure when it was, and I wanted to know whether you were ever in the house on Rue d'Anjou," said the baron, placing a hand affectionately on the young woman's head.

Michaela shuddered. She lowered her eyes and was unable to answer.


She stood up and took a few steps, fixing her gaze on the children in the distance who were throwing stones into a fountain. Her eyes were so filled with tears that the baron seemed to be a shape behind fogged glass.

"Rue d'Anjou," Michaela said, sighing. "Now I remember, that was the street where I used to take the baroness's dresses to be sewn. It's just two blocks away from Rue de l'Élysée !"

"Yes, now I remember, on the corner, wasn't it? And wasn't there someone else living with her?" he asked in distress.

"I only met Madame Bertrand," she replied. "She was the dressmaker who fixed the baroness's dresses and sewed mine when I was in Paris. I always counted on her services, and it was Madame Lory who recommended her. Maybe she also knows a niece of Madame Bertrand's about whom she spoke so often. '

"Did you hear her speak of anyone else?" the baron asked. "Number 24 had a lot of residents, as best I recall, but I never heard anything about that Irene Premelic woman."

She said nothing more; her legs were heavy, and she felt a lack of air. Michaela wanted to get out of there, to leave Green Park as quickly as possible.

When said adieu to Maurice de Hirsch, he called his two boys to bow to *signora* Varsano Montefiore. Poor little boys, she thought. They're going to become Hirsch soldiers, like Lucien… She patted the boys on the head, gave a polite smile, and asked to be remembered to Clara.

Micha left, walking almost aimlessly down Piccadilly, her head throbbing. Lucienne Premelic de Hirsch, Irene Premelic. Who could those two be... who stole her Lucien?

And when Michaela recounted that unexpected encounter with the baron in her letter to Anna Varsano in Salonica, she cried so much, in a mixture of hate and commiseration, that her unsteady handwriting and her tears rendered the letter almost illegible.

But Anna, with a heavy heart, replied in a telegram.

*Happy for you, now that you're happy.*
*Forget Rue d'Anjou and everything forever.*
*Think about your beautiful son Victor who just came into the world.*
*With love,*
*Your mother,*
*Anna Varsano*

That was the last time Michaela ever saw Maurice de Hirsch.

This despite the baron's name being constantly in the newspapers and having word of him through Yako, who worked in a bank with various firms connected with or belonging to the Orient Express Company.

Maurice de Hirsch occupied a significant space in *The London Times*, the *Westminster Gazette*, *Le Gaulois* of Paris, or the *Neues Wiener Tageblatt*, as well as other papers that weekly publicized his every move. News items that described his intimate friendship with the future king Edward VII, Prince of Wales, or the baron's funds in New York for the integration of immigrants in America, the colonies of the Jewish Association that he was founding in South America, his hunting trips with King Ferdinand of Bulgaria or Rudolph of Austria, his horse La Fleche winning the Derby–in sum, Maurice de Hirsch was spoken of more than the Queen of England herself.

He was detested by Queen Victoria, who had a thousand reasons for considering the baron, the Jewish banker, a terrible influence on her son, the heir to the throne, paying his gambling debts, buying horses for the Derby, and stables in Newmarket, and even "lending" hunting lodges for his romantic encounters, as in the well known case of Grafton House. However, the worst ill for the British Empire was that the tug of war between Maurice de Hirsch and the Czar of Russia, combating the problem of the persecution and killing of Jews, had spilled over onto the English court.

Thus Queen Victoria, heeding the criticisms of her relatives Wilhelm II, the young emperor of Germany, and Nicholas II, the future Czar of Russia, had in resounding tones declared the baron *persona non grata*.

But the baron had in his favour countless good actions.

Among the English nobility, the rumours that circulated about the two adopted children had several versions. One was that they were the children of the future king of England and a married lover. The Prince of Wales having his close friends adopt his illegitimate offspring would be a common thing.

In another version, certain in-laws of Clara de Hirsch's family, the Bischoffsheims, who would be the natural heirs after her death, jealous and feeling injured by that double adoption, made known to her a different story: a secret betrayal by Maurice.

Immediately following the adoption, they told Clara that the children to whom through charity she had given her name might be the illegitimate progeny of her husband by his mistress, Madame Deforest. Michaela kept up with progress in Maurice de Hirsch's efforts to implement a method for extracting persecuted Russian Jews and sending them to safety. The colonies that he was trying to establish in Argentina were criticized by certain groups opposed to that type of colonization, who wanted the resources to be channelled to the Palestine cause.

The Holy Land was the place they should go—or return to—as the Rabbis argued.

To the baron the Promised Land was the Americas, and not a tract of desert belonging to the Ottoman Empire. In the midst of that polemic, the baron still found time to invest in his horses in the Derby, host illustrious guests at his hunts, manage his fortune, maintain interests in four corners of the globe, and accommodate Clara de Hirsch.

Maurice de Hirsch was truly unique, she thought.

∽ઠ

On the morning of April 22, 1896, newspapers in Paris, London, and Munich announced the death of Baron Maurice de Hirsch. *The Times* of London and the French *Le Gaulois* dedicated lengthy obituaries to that special man.

"*Friend and patron of the arts, founder of schools, benefactor and philanthropist, entrepreneur and sportsman, he died on the morning of 21 April 1896, at his hunting lodge in O'Gyalla in the Austro-Hungarian Empire; his body is to be transported on the 25th to his Paris residence, Rue de l'Élysée.*
"*The rabbinate of Paris and its directorate, with Rabbi Zadok Khan, will conduct the services as the body lies in state and final homage will be paid to the great man before interment in Montmartre cemetery.*"
*Members of the high European diplomatic corps, bankers, rulers, friends and politicians would be on hand to pay their last homage to Baron Maurice de Hirsch auf Gereut.*

Michaela sighed deeply and closed the newspaper.
She thought about Clara, imagined Rue de l'Élysée. Maurice's casket in front of the monumental staircase, the mirrors covered, and Clara in mourning dress, bent by pain, inconsolable once more by another loss, receiving all those dignitaries with condolences.

Despite everything, she had never ceased to admire and love him. Clara, who had always been the alter ego of a great man, his most trusted counsel, his secretary and best friend, would be there, gathering all her strength and seeing that everything was worthy of her husband.

Michaela looked around her. Her world was there. She kissed her sons, first caressing the dark hair of the *Mégas* Victor.

"The great Victor," as her father, *Dottore* Alberto, called him. She looked at her daughter, who came dragging her nightgown to embrace her... Sweet little Adele. She poured her a cup of milk and closed the garden door to cut off the inclement wind of morning.
She looked out at Piccadilly. Spring would arrive soon. The day was cloudy and melancholy, but before long it would turn colourful again with strolling ladies carrying their silk parasols.

# He Had Been the Chosen Friend and Associate of Kings and Princes,

## His Was Marked in Fields Ra Horse Racing to the F Colonies, and His Phila as as Unlimited as His W

VIENNA, April 21.—Ba de Hirsch, the great financier a pist, died last night on his esta sburg, Hungary, from a stroke of apo y.

Considering that the Baron Maurice de Hirsch de Gereuth s one of the richest men in Europe, t years his colossal gifts to charitie ort have excited the world's w has been the chosen frier Kings and Princes in s, that his

*DEATH OF BARON HIRSCH*

# XXVI

## NAPOLI POSILLIPO

*Posillipo vuol dire "fine del dolore"*

*Possilipo means the end of the pain...*

Napoli, Summer 1898

In 1898, Lord Rosebery carried out the last wish of his beloved Hannah de Rosebery. They had finally bought a home on the Bay of Naples, but Hannah no longer existed. Eight years earlier, she had departed the new house in Piccadilly in a black casket, taken away in a carriage and accompanied by hundreds of people. Flowers, dozens of wreaths, women in black, and men in dress coats and top hats, forming a cortege from Piccadilly to Regent Street.

But few who accompanied that slow procession had known the real Hannah. Since her death on that rainy day of November 19, 1890, interred in her parents' vault in the Jewish cemetery at Willesden, from that day on, Archibald de Rosebery could no longer sleep. Suffering from insomnia, he read, wrote poems and political speeches during the night, and all those years, despite the efforts of friends, never showed any interest in remarrying.

The children had grown up. Harry and Neil, the twins, were already fifteen, studying at Eton like the majority of young men who would one day inherit titles of nobility or political positions in Parliament. Yako Montefiore's nephew was also at that school, where Arnold Deforest Bischoffsheim, Clara's adopted son, had studied for a time.

All the young people of Piccadilly had a predestined course. In the home of Yako and Michaela Montefiore it was no different, for their efforts were bent toward assuring that their son Victor would be admitted to Mr. Carter's preparatory school in Farmborough, Hampshire, and follow that same path.

In reality, Michaela did not want to be separated from him. She said she did not have the blood of the English or the arrogance and prepotency to see a son in Parliament or as owner of a bank.

"Why Eton College?" she argued with Yako. "Victor likes to have fun, to play the piano for Adele, to tell stories, and he draws very well. He's going to be an artist, he is sensible, but he'll never be a lawyer or accountant."

Yako disagreed. His son must be better than he, have great opportunities in life, speak several languages and associate with colleagues of a more noble caste, who would open doors for him in the future.

Michaela raised her eyebrows in despair.

In that spring of 1898, Lord Rosebery sent Michaela an invitation: the house on the Bay of Naples was ready to receive her.

Posillipo means the end of a pain...

*Naples... Posillipo.* That poetic name given by the Greeks, who lived there before any of the Romans and founded the new city they called Neapolis, who carved their script on gravestones; proof and witness to their myths and customs, and the achievement of a people, of their philosophy, that had lasted all those centuries in the shadow of Vesuvius.

The poetry of that place, surrounded by serpentine roads, abysses covered with plane trees and cypresses, long shadows and deep blue beams of light from the sea, was intoxicating.

To Michaela, going there would be her return to paradise. Like arriving at the Garden of the Hesperides, to the hiding place of Persephone, a spot where the soul undergoes catharsis and renews itself, and where pain ends at last.

She and her children disembarked from the steamer, surrounded by tourists, and waited for the two coaches from the Rosebery villa. The dock was thronged with people, and Michaela almost gave up hope of spotting anyone who had come to fetch them.

Then she heard her name being called.

Lord Rosebery was there, accompanied by friends. Among them she recognized the lawyer Emile Vanières, who had always assisted the baron in Paris and who at that moment was saying goodbye to two ladies behind him.

One of them approached, her back to the sun, and for a moment Michaela was unable to identify the lady clad in black who was walking slowly toward her.

Michaela felt her heart race when she recognized Clara de Hirsch. She had also arrived in Naples that morning and was accompanied by her secretary, Madame Clemence Lory. Fatigued and very thin, dressed in heavy mourning, she appeared more stooped, and her bearing wasn't the same. As she embraced Michaela emotionally, her body seemed fragile, small and trembling, as if it were about to break. She looked at the children, who were leaning sleepily against their mother's skirt, and smiled at them.

"They're beautiful children, Micha, how happy I am to see you again and meet your little ones."

Lord Rosebery excused himself from Vanières and came over to embrace Michaela.

"How good that we're all together," he said happily. "I was thinking about not letting the baroness slip away from us to the hotel. With so much time gone by, I have a great idea. What if we hold a reunion here in Naples, of our neighbouring houses, numbers 12 and 14 Berkeley Square, and spend a delightful summer here at the villa?"

The baroness was confounded, trying to find a way to decline the invitation, for she was there "on business," and claimed she had obligations in the city. But Lord Rosebery gave her no opportunity and placed a coachman at her disposal for her to come down to Naples as often as necessary. There was no way for Clara to refuse, and the wagons left packed with luggage.

"After all," Lord Rosebery said, appearing relieved, "it was to keep a promise I made to my Hannah that I bought this villa. And if she were here now, she would do the same thing, and be glad to have you and show you Posillipo, which means *fine del dolore*. And it is just that, ladies… The end of our pains and sorrows…"

Clara de Hirsch, Lord Rosebery, and Michaela followed in one coach, and the children, the nannies, and Madame Lory in another.

As the coach followed the seaside road to enter a peninsula, Michaela observed the sight of Naples and Vesuvius in the distance.

She could feel Clara's eyes on her. The three passengers fell silent, all seemingly lost in their own thoughts.

Vesuvius lay before Michaela, exactly fifteen years since she was there with the baroness. And it had been in Naples that she had abandoned her little Lucienne, and in that city her baby, her poor daughter, had burned to death, victim of Angelo Catanzaro's insanity.

"So much happened during those years, my dear Micha," murmured Clara, breaking the silence. "And everything here remains the same… The city down there goes on living, with the same stones, the same history. Only stones and history survive time… What do we have left of life?" She sighed deeply. "When we age, what we keep are the good memories of what we experience…

"It is they that make us smile, even when the sorrow and despair of being totally alone disheartens us. One day the good remembrances and the good moments creep up on us, calming our anima like a sweet treacle down our throat when we have a cough. It warms us, soothes us, nourishes us…

"Now, Michaela, I live on those memories. And Naples is part of the treacle that sustains me..."

Michaela took Clara's trembling hands. They looked at each other as in earlier times and embraced.

Lord Rosebery was seated facing the women, his attention turned to the magnificent sight of the Belvedere.

He was still a man of striking features, with the same clear gaze and beautiful hair, now quite gray. His famous bouts of insomnia were his greatest problem... And loneliness without Hannah.

The road to Napoli Posillipo was breathtakingly beautiful. The immense trees shading that steep and dangerous route, flanked by deep abysses, with date palms, cypresses, and ancient pines, formed a dense forest where only the sound of horses' hooves and waterfalls broke the silence.

The coach slowly climbed the road that wound through the villas.

The children got out, amazed.

Lord Rosebery's four children, perfect hosts, were lined up at the entrance to Palatine, well dressed and combed, to receive the guests. With them were servants waiting for the baggage, as well as a little girl some ten years of age, who hid behind a column.

"She's the daughter of one of the servants," explained Lord Rosebery. "She's lived in the villa since she was born. I bought the property and inherited from the previous owners both her and her mother." The little girl was introduced to Adele. Her name is Lukia.

The hot, sunny days went by slowly in that dazzling garden. Everything there was perfect: the perfume of flowers, the song of cicadas, and the sunset turning the sea below golden.

Victor and Adele ran through the gardens, hiding from the nannies and quickly involved the young Neapolitan in their play. Only language separated them. Victor and Adele speaking English and the little one, irritated, shouting, "*Non capisco niente!*" I don't understand anything! The poor girl!

Adele set up her doll house in the solarium, where the baroness and Michaela spent the first weeks of summer in conversation. They had so much to talk about that Clara had possibly forgotten her business trip.

Madame Lory had gone down to Naples, where she remained for two or three days, and returned with a sheaf of papers and a reserved demeanour. Michaela saw Clara sit next to the *dame de chambre*, and begin to examine the papers, shaking her head in indignation. Finally, she sighed and said to Clemence Lory:

"Advise her that this is the last time I'll pay her debts. I won't come back to Naples, and our agreement ended with the death of my husband."

"She's still the same unscrupulous woman. Marchioness Siciliano di Rende... a swindler, that's what she is..." murmured Madame Lory.

The children gathered around Adele's doll house. Everything was a novelty to them. There was a living room, kitchen, and the doll's bedroom. Victor brought plants and flowers to make a garden, and Adele was the doll's mother. The little Italian girl, with her heavy accent, cried in a corner, disconsolate. She hadn't joined the play. She couldn't make herself understood, and Michaela ran to help her.

"What's the matter, pretty girl?" she said in her dialect. "Don't cry, I'm going to help you, and you're going to play with Adele's doll house too."

Drying her tears, she sat beside Michaela, sniffing, her legs swinging in that high armchair.

"Where's your mother?" she asked. "Have you had your milk yet?"She nodded, her eyes shining happily as Michaela smoothed her hair. The Roseberys' nanny said that her mother was ill, and it was the cook who took care of her.

"But if she is bothering you, Missus Montefiore, just say so and the girl will go back to the kitchen!" she added, with a formal bow.

Michaela smiled and hugged the girl.

"Leave her, Liza, I'll take care of her. After all, we speak the same language, don't we, *piccolina?*"

Lukia accompanied Michaela every minute of the day like a shadow. From early morning she was waiting for her; she would stay in the corridor leading to the bedrooms, sitting at the head of the stairs, smiling at her and afterwards, holding her hand, spend the day beside her.

Clara admired Michaela's patience in dealing with the children.

For the first time the baroness spoke of her granddaughter Lucienne. She told her the little girl had appeared at the gate of Rue de l'Élysée the morning after the burial of Lucien, in the arms of an unknown woman. It was her granddaughter. Her name was Lucienne, the woman told her, she was two, and the daughter of Clara's son.

Clara spoke of her initial shock. She felt betrayed by her son. Maurice, cooler, hadn't believed it and demanded a document or other proof from the woman.

The girl had a birth certificate, on which appeared only her name, Lucienne Marie, born to undeclared father and mother at midnight on the sixth of October 1887 at 24 Rue d'Anjou. And after a few weeks Clara and Maurice, without ever truly having concrete proof, had adopted the girl as granddaughter and heir under Austrian law.

She was called Lily.

In reality, the baroness had never had her granddaughter with her for even a week. As soon as the girl arrived at Rue de l'Élysée, Clara and the baron had been obliged to spend a lengthy period in Constantinople solving serious railway-related disputes with the government of the Ottoman Empire.

She thought of leaving the little girl with her family, the Bischoffsheims, in her mother's home in Brussels. But her mother refused, so Clara's sister Hortense, who was never able to have children, asked to take care of the girl.

"You've heard a lot about Hortense," Clara told Michaela. "You know about her temper, her not being able to walk and living trapped in a wheelchair, and now with the passing of time her problems have increased. She never returned the girl to me. We even tried legal means to get her back, but my brother-in-law, poor Georges, was always writing me and trying to appease and help my sister…

"He asked Maurice to be patient, because Hortense, given her inability to walk and her depressions, couldn't stand to lose her.

"I tried in vain to at least have her come to Paris or Beauregard for a vacation, for us to spend some time together, but my sister would never dream of allowing her out of Rond-Chêne. When I would write, asking to visit her, she would reply evasively about the bad weather, or that the girl had an upcoming piano recital and couldn't take the time away from practicing, and that I might be a hindrance.

"And so the time went by.

"After Maurice found out that Lucienne was studying catechism and getting ready for first communion and was strongly influenced by the bishop in that city, he wrote indignantly saying that she should be returned. That was not the kind of upbringing he wanted her to have. Nor would his son, were he alive, approve of it for his daughter.

"But no one could dissuade Hortense from belief in her new faith. She was always attracted to superstition and, motivated by her mental weakness, was exploited by quacks and charlatans, and now they control her life. Poor Hortense! She's surrounded by stories of miracles and mysticism, believes she's paraplegic because she was a sinner in another life, and that she doesn't deserve the happiness or money she has. It's the bishop of Esneux who rules her. She does nothing without his permission, my brother-in-law Georges told me. Everything is a sin, and he extracts from her whatever he wishes for issuing indulgences.

"Poor Hortense... And all at the expense of poor Georges!" she said, sighing deeply. "Did you know that Georges has the same surname as your husband, Michaela? He too is a Montefiore, Montefiore Levy."

Michaela smiled.

"Georges is a wonderful man," Clara told her. "And very affectionate with Lucienne; he calls her Lily."

Clara opened her purse and showed a photo in a small silver frame.

Little Lily and Georges in an embrace. She kissing his cheek.

Michaela took the picture into her hands, her heart leaping. The girl had no feature that recalled Lucien, nothing that resembled her father.

Michaela sighed heavily and returned the photo to Clara, who was awaiting her reaction.

"What do you think?" Clara asked, with an ambiguous expression.

"A pretty little girl. Maybe she looks like her mother."

"Yes, maybe like her mother, a lively woman, but unfortunately vulgar. The little girl doesn't have a trace of my son. Nothing... that proves... nothing that resembles–That's why I can't bring myself to believe it, Michaela! Now Madame Lory and I are here because of the girl's mother, Irene Premelic, an empty-headed woman. I've come to Naples to pay the bills she owes. A fortune! Wherever she buys, she gives the Hirsch name as guarantee. It never ends," she said almost inaudibly.

"Maurice paid a fortune to have that woman stay away from the girl, and we even introduced her to a suitor, financing her marriage to a marquis named Raffaele Siciliano di Rende, from a totally ruined Neapolitan family. My husband also paid for her new home, with luxurious décor, and deposited a very generous dowry for Marquis Di Rende and his aged mother. But Irene never lived within her means, and she continues with her extortion. She'll never change... I'm afraid that someday she'll try to exploit my sister Hortense and harm the little girl."

Michaela sighed and looked at the little Italian girl, who was kneeling in the chair and listening without understanding, entertained by the photo of Lily: "Who is it?"

Michaela replied gently, explaining: "It's Lily, the lady's granddaughter. The baroness is *la nonna della bambina* in the photo."

Lukia hugged Clara, looking at her with aqua-marine eyes, and said, "I don't have a *Nonna*. Are you *mia Nonna* too?"

Michaela smiled, and Clara commented in a soft voice:

"She looks more like Lucien than Lily does. If Lily were like that, I would have no doubts... Did you see that she has the color of my son's eyes? Her look and her hair are just like his when he was small. She could even be my granddaughter!"

Michaela shuddered and felt her face go red, remembering her little daughter dead in that fire. But Clara had never known about her Lucienne, and now it was too late to tell her.

The next morning, the day was overcast, and a fine rain fell on the Villa Rosebery garden. That two women had breakfast without the presence of Lord Rosebery, who was waiting for the rain to stop and readying the coach to descend to Naples, when little Lukia entered.

The women affectionately greeted the child, who walked from one side to the other, showing her dress, when they heard a guttural voice coming from the pantry. "Lukia, *vieni qui!* Come, Lukia, don't bother the ladies!"

The girl answered her mother, who was behind the dining room door.

"Come out here, Mamma, come see *mia nonna*. She said she can be mia *nonna* too. Come see my *nonna*, mamma!" insisted Lukia.

Michaela had her back to the door when the girl, pulling on her mother's apron, introduced her to Clara. And when the woman's eyes met Michaela's, it was as if she had seen the devil. She backed away, brusquely dragging the child, and they dashed toward the garden. Michaela ran after them, and through the windows Clara saw Micha shouting:

"Giò! Giovanna, wait, for God's sake!"

Clara rushed to the garden as quickly as she could and only managed to see Michaela running behind a cart rapidly descending the ramp. Then Clara understood and, heart racing, for the first time in her life asked God for a favour. Endless minutes of anguish and fear. A crowd gathering at the first curve in the garden. They shouted for Lord Rosebery, the gardener, the coachman. The women servants returned from there crying, their hands covering their faces, after witnessing a terrible scene.

They wept and shouted:

"She is dead … *la poverina è morta… Dio mio!*"

Minutes seemed like hours, when Michaela, helping to carry the blood-soaked child, arrived back in the shadow of the mansion.
They laid the girl down on the one of the marble benches of the Pallatina, and around her everything was stained with red. Michaela ripped her dress to make a bandage and desperately wound it around the girl's bleeding head.

Clara, trembling, approached the unconscious Lukia. She ran her hand over the pallid face and, drawing closer to clean the bleeding forehead, saw the tiny fleur-de-lis birthmark over her left eye.

A waiting wagon took the still-breathing girl to the hospital. Lord Rosebery, without understanding what had happened, followed Michaela's wagon, with Madame Lory.

Clara de Hirsch, for the first time in her life, without knowing what she was doing, entered the chapel on the property and, in unison with the women servants of Villa Rosebery, prayed with them an Ave Maria as she asked for the life of her granddaughter.

# XXVII

## ADIEU    MADAME

Paris, April 1, 1899.

The Montefiore house in Piccadilly had been lit up since early morning of March 30, 1899.

Michaela prepared her bags. She was going to Paris, taking Victor and Adele with her. Both were on Easter vacation and had long dreamed of this trip. Nothing she had explained to the children could convince them to stay in London with their grandmother Tilda and the nanny.

She had spoken of the gravity of the moment, the baroness's illness and the problems she would face in Paris to help Clara and find a place for little Lily, or Lukia, the orphan of Napoli Posillipo. Otherwise the girl would be alone, without her *nonna*, when death came for the baroness.

Adele, her eyes shining, asked Michaela:

"But, momma, why can't my friend live here in my room? She was so happy when I gave her my doll house! She could live here in our house... I have so many toys that I can share with her. Poor little girl, she doesn't have a mother, she doesn't have a father, and now her *nonna* is sick..."

Victor, still in bed, sat up with a start. An expression of hatred on his face, he screamed at his sister:

"What for? I don't want another girl brat in the house. Adele is enough, she messes up my things and gets my piano out of tune... I don't want to, momma... If she comes, I'm leaving!"

"Calm down, Victor. Your sister is right. She's a girl with a good heart, and that's how we should act. Just imagine, my dear, if one day I die and pappá too! Who would offer to raise an orphan boy?"

"My grandfather Abramo, naturally! He's the father of my father. And my grandmother Tilda... What a question, momma!" replied Victor, with an air of superiority.

Michaela nodded her head, displaying fatigue, and looked at Adele, who was chewing her nails. But she continued to explain:

"But suppose they can't... You know, Victor, grandpa Abramo and grandma Tilda are old, and besides that they have your cousin Edgard, who's already a handful for them. Eton costs your grandparents a lot of money."

The boy, still unconvinced, continued to challenge Michaela.

"Well, then would we have to call grandma Anna and grandpa Alberto from Salonica to come live in our house?"

"Look, my dear, it's not that simple. Your grandparents live in Salonica, which is a long way from here. They have their home, grandpa has his manufacture of perfumes, and grandma sews clothes for her customers, and because of that they couldn't move here... And there's Daud, who lives with them... It would all be very complicated!" said Michaela calmly, smoothing Victor's black hair.

"Then," said the boy, with a frightened expression, "if you both died... we would have to go live in Salonica?"

Michaela nodded, biting her lip.

"Yes, dear, I believe that would be the only solution. You two would go live with them."

"Is there a piano in Grandma Anna's house? Is there?" Adele asked.

"Well, in Grandma Anna's house... I don't think there's a piano, because no one plays, but you have an aunt named Katherina who's a piano teacher with a degree from Paris. Surely she and Grandma Anna will provide a piano for Victor. Then he can play in the salons of *signora* Fakima Modiano. She's very rich and has a Steinway grand piano," answered Michaela, smiling.

"Wow!" said Victor. "Then I want to go to Salonica!"

To Michaela, that trip to Paris would be the most important of her life. She wanted to be alone with Clara, wanted to see her daughter, her Lily, dreamed of hugging her. And there was so much to discuss and resolve!

Just she and the baroness, behind closed doors... Talks and memories, like before. She wanted to stroke her hands, tell her how important she was in her life.

Michaela was assailed by a terrible premonition. She had already waited two weeks for Yako to return from an important business trip to Vienna and Budapest, and since his arrival the day before, she had left Madame Lory's telegram on the dinner table. She had hoped that upon reading the telegram he would respect her anguish to depart immediately. But her husband had always been a calm, optimistic person who gave the impression that everything around him could wait, except his work...

He knew his Sicilian wife was eager for a heated argument. So he kissed her on the forehead and, apologizing because he was late for some commitment, asked to finish the conversation later...

Later she would forget, and that way he avoided the outbursts and the impetuosity of the creature he considered the wildest but also the most beautiful and sensual woman in London.

Michaela looked at him, her green eyes flashing.

"I can't wait anymore, Yako, not a day longer! From the news in the telegram, I believe the baroness's days are numbered... I can't fail to go and see her! Look at today's paper, Yako! The situation is critical..."

Yako sighed, did not answer, turned and left the room.

Michaela finished braiding Adele's hair and thought about Clara and Lily, her beloved daughter, alone and unprotected in Paris, when she lost her *nonna*...

The Baroness had written her last letter twenty days earlier. It was her farewell, replete with implied meanings; she knew she wouldn't last much longer and asked Michaela to come as quickly as possible to Rue de l'Élysée, for many important measures must be taken before her death.

She spoke of her death now in a cold, almost ironic way, as if she were going out for a walk. She had no more hope, the cancer was eating away at her from inside, and the pain didn't allow even a minute of relief. In the letter Clara de Hirsch wrote that this was the moment to leave everything ready, not to neglect any detail while alive, while her hands could still sign any change in her will.

For months, fraudulent miracle workers came and went through the front door, some called by Clemence Lory, the faithful nanny; one sent by the corner baker who had heard stories of cures; another sent by the notary Dietz, a caring and selfless man who was always at her side in case she needed another codicil, or a change in her final wishes. Clara de Hirsch drank exotic herbal teas, followed diets, and did everything prescribed to her. Until, one morning, she saw that none of it had solved anything. Just as it had not solved anything in those terrible days when she had been told of her beloved son's illness.

Twelve years had gone by without her Lucien.

Haggard and exhausted, she lacked the strength to ascend or descend the monumental staircase that Maurice had ordered built as the pride of his palace.

She hated it and always had. It was overly pretentious, and living with it had become her via dolorosa.

She didn't want to stay locked up in her room in the upstairs of that immense palace, lying down and staring at the Bellini canvas, the virgin with children and cherries... she didn't want to drag herself through the corridors anymore and look at the Breughel paintings, the scenes of allegories and abundance... None of that any longer said anything to her, she wanted to get well, to gain time, a few days, a few weeks... Just a little time, nothing more.

And the days went by, without her having a clear awareness of what was happening, her vision cloudy, forced to view her emaciation in the mirrors, but still she had the will to make entries in her notebook of daily expenses and monitor those who came and went in her house on Rue de l'Élysée.

She ensconced herself in the entrance gallery, in the room that had once been her son's hideaway. In that place where she breathed his presence, where she could still smell his *vetiver* aroma, read his notebooks and commentary, and caress his collections. That would be her world until death took her away!

Lucien's library, with its bookcases full of rare volumes, pieces from the tombs of pharaohs, small Greek sculptures, delicate profiles of women who had once inhabited the lands of gods and prophetesses. The room housing Lucien's dreams... With its large white safe, its marble drawers that meticulously held his coins, his remembrances, his sorrows and his secrets.

She looked at the coin safe... It was there, just as her son had left it. She often thought of opening it and touching that treasure. The safe hidden in that room had heavy doors bearing the Hirsch coat of arms.

Now there was no more time. She would like to have Michaela open those drawers and choose one of the coins for Lily. She wanted the little girl to have something of her father's on a golden chain. A remembrance, a relic of her father. Perhaps that wonderful gold coin of Cleopatra, or the first of the entire collection, of Alexander the Great, or the last one he had acquired: the Taranto tetradrachma, which had been found in one of his pockets, damp with sweat from his fatal fever.

But Michaela was delaying, and soon there would not be time.

Clara looked around her and knew she should say farewell to all that, to put an end to everything. She would donate that room to a museum. To the kingdom of Belgium, to the Bibliothèque Royale...

"Yes, that would be the right thing, the most just," she had commented one afternoon to Gustav Held and Paul Barillet. After all, Lucien was Belgian like her, and his early education had been in Brussels; that library had afforded her son the beginning of knowledge. The donation was stipulated by her, with one proviso: Lucien's collection would be housed in a special room, in a safe, separate from other collections. And it would be opened only for those who had true interest in and admiration for rare coins. It would be the continuation of her son's thought.

From now on, Lucien would not be remembered merely as the son of Maurice de Hirsch, the sole heir who had died prematurely; now his memory would have a story to tell. A legacy bearing his name, an important collection to which he, with his great knowledge of history and archeology, had dedicated the largest part of his life. Seeking and locating all that material, and with talent and effort, bringing together its history and cataloguing it. Work and dedication that in Maurice's eyes was always a waste of time and the cause of arguments.

Because of this work, her son had always been humiliated, viewed as a parasite in that house. Now it was time for Clara de Hirsch to change that story.

Lucien was not the son that Maurice had planned on. Just the opposite. He lacked the charisma for large-scale business, for important friendships and fantastic ideas like his father.

But he had exerted every effort to please him. Even after graduating *cum laude* as a lawyer in Berlin, the son had not succeeded in satisfying his father. Nothing was enough to convince the baron that his son was working. It was one argument after another...

Lately, before Lucien's death, they were so estranged that they communicated only by letter. He wanted to flee from the disapproving gaze of Maurice. He wanted to leave Paris, reside in London, open an antique shop, and live his own life. He wanted to marry the woman he loved; after all, he was thirty and told Clara:

"I don't want confrontations with my father; I love him and admire him; but I don't want to confront him... Ever again!"

From that room, its windows open to the Avenue Gabriel garden, its camellias already dried by winter, Clara watched the days pass, waiting for the arrival of spring...

She went through moments of concealed pain, others with her eyes flooded, or smiling alone with her memories. But each day she waited for death.

Abruptly, Clara de Hirsch exited her thoughts and pushed aside the cup with an infusion that Madame Clemence Lory brought her.

"Enough, Clemence. I don't want any more of that, please..."

She had lost her patience that March morning, lacking the strength to argue about anything. She didn't want the presence of that director of the Alliance, who lately would spend hours asking for more money for the care of the children, or the visit of other *schnorrers* who came trying to nibble away something from her fortune for a cultural foundation to benefit themselves. Or the fake healers who were infesting her home.

"No one else is coming in here!" the baroness said with a sigh. "Please, Clemence, understand... We don't have any more time... Close the doors to this house. I only want you to call Michaela! I sent her a letter at the start of the month, but I think her husband opposed her coming. Send an urgent telegram... Bring her to London, please... Say that if she has problems she can bring the children with her, have Victor and Adele come so I can see them... Together we'll decide on the future of our Lily... I want Paul Barillet and Gustav Held here every day so we can speed up the details and all the documentation, which must be taken care of as quickly as possible. I don't want any more medicines, Clemence, no more doctors, potions, I want peace... and for everything to be in order when I'm gone..."

Day and night, Clara remained seated in that room, looking at the garden, which was still dry and gloomy, waiting for spring to come.

She knew that spring would be her liberation, that she would suffer no more and would be laid to rest beside her beloved son Lucien, and Maurice, in the tomb she had ordered built in Montmartre.

The tomb... There, amid cypresses and silent *allées*, where two stained glass windows captured the sunrise and sunset, a confessional with bronze doors and marble walls, where she had wept hundreds of times.

That would be her final dwelling.

From there, 2 Rue de l'Élysée, surrounded by works of art, by Baccarat dishes and crystal, books, candelabras, silks, and tapestries; from there, with its many rooms, so full of people, where every Wednesday flutes, violins, and her grand piano entertained hundreds with wonderful music; from there, from that same immense vestibule, with Venetian mirrors covered with black cloth she would be taken away silently. She would be accompanied by carriages, without flowers, buried without eulogies, in the heights of Paris. She wanted nothing, no speeches, no homage.

Now her only worry was that her will, with the latest changes, made since her return from Napoli Posillipo the previous September, would finally be honored.

Six months of doubts and questioning.

And it was thus that Clara Bischoffsheim de Hirsch lived out her final days. Revising everything that she wanted to take care of and everything she wanted to erase, without leaving a trace of her private memories. She ordered Gustav Held, her loyal amanuensis, that everything left should be burned–her correspondence, intimate things, her letters and those of Maurice. Everything must disappear.

"Everything must be burned... I've taken measures so that no paper will fall into the hands of strangers. Only the will and the contents of these two boxes should be distributed."

She rewrote her life in those last six months.

∽

On September 23, 1898, the last day of summer, as soon as she returned from Naples, Baroness Clara de Hirsch had called her executors and dictated codicils to her will.

There were also still some people who must be helped. She had to think of a way to benefit them, but without changing the guiding principle of her will. That was already written and determined in Maurice's will, and she could not further modify it.

That her son's blood ran in the veins of a beautiful little girl with eyes the color of sky, born in Taormina on October 6, 1887, six months after Lucien's death.

She could no longer allow others to believe that Michaela Varsano, the Sicilian who had been her protégée, that girl with the bearing of a princess and a wild spirit, had hidden the truth for so long.

But no one would believe Clara de Hirsch. Not this time!

After all, she had been mistaken, years before, by agreeing to adopt a granddaughter when an unknown woman had brought that child to her door. She had never believed the woman's statements or the investigation by Maurice's lawyers, who with the best of intentions did everything to promulgate a new fairy tale of poor tearful damsels and the story told by Irene Premelic.

For Clara, as mother, knew her son better than anyone and was sure that Lucien, even if he had been weak, would only be with some woman for whom he felt passion and admiration–not that woman, who was so unlike him!

She had a deep understanding of her son and knew he would never hide an affair or a passion from her. His eyes would give him away, as would his smile. Even far away, he would write and had never hidden anything...

Clara knew that Lucien loved Michaela in secret ever since their first encounter. She knew of his fears, of the criticisms and sarcasm of Maurice, and was witness to their plans to marry.

She knew all this, but she had gone along, lacking the strength to confront her husband. She should have told Maurice everything right away... That very same day. She should have shouted the truth to the baron the morning that vulgar woman showed up at the door with her triumphant smile, carrying that child, a two-year-old girl, an innocent used only to be sold for some thousands of francs in exchange for a good life and a noble marriage.

When Maurice, suspicious of the story told by a singer and would-be actress, in a mixture of commiseration and amour-propre, had asked for a thorough investigation to find out the truth about the secret relationship between Irene Premelic and their deceased son, she had erred again.

Clara should have told him that Lucien could never have deceived them like that... But she had tolerated the reproachful look of the baron, who felt betrayed, not only by his son but also by her, Clara had always been his confidante and closest friend.

Once again Baron Hirsch won, with his verdict: Lucien was a weakling! And after that Maurice spent days and nights sitting in the library, repeating to Clara:

"My son... My dear son! He never had enough confidence in me so I could make him a man with a great story..."

It was the fault of Clara, who had protected him.

It was to Hortense, her younger sister, that Clara vented in a letter about everything that had happened.

When Hortense replied that for some time she had known of the existence of the child and that on a visit to Esneux Lucien had confessed that, if someday he was gone, the child should be baptized in the church in Esneux, Clara's world collapsed.

It couldn't be true; it could only be her poor sister's invention. She clearly understood the intentions of Hortense Bischoffsheim Montefiore Levy in that letter written weeks after the little girl's adoption. Poor Hortense... It was always like that when she wanted something... And Clara was familiar with her tricks since childhood, but what to do? She was her dear sister...

Georges Montefiore Levy, her brother-in-law, never accepted the idea of adopting just any child. But a child of Lucien? Of his favourite nephew, dedicated, sensitive, and intelligent? Why not have that child with them, who besides everything else came with a destiny, a huge fortune and a title of nobility?

It was a sign... Yes. Clara understood the intentions of her sister.

Poor Hortense... she had even dreamed about baptism... Poor sister... who stopped being Jewish and became transformed into a plaything, easy prey with her limited intelligence, dominated by the bishop of Esneux with her fears and mysticism, with her newfound belief in miracles, her thousands of francs coming from the bank, from her inheritance, to pay the Church for indulgences...

Hortense had never had children.

Clara was to blame for that too. She had been the cause of her sister's unhappiness, her paralysis, her life trapped in a wheelchair, the fall she had suffered in the children's bedroom in that large, cold, dark old house in Brussels. To blame for having hidden behind Hortense's cradle when the little girl, already purple, writhed on the floor. They had never spoken about it. Never... But it was her burden, her guilt. And Hortense, now more than ever, wanted a child, wanted to raise that little girl, and this would be her only chance.

And Clara, assuaging part of her guilt, delivered the girl to her sister a few weeks after adopting her. This was Hortense's ultimate triumph. She handed over the girl almost with a sense of relief, claiming it would be for a short time, just for a few months while she was away on a long trip to Constantinople. And it had all happened in the months following Lucien's death. They didn't even wait for the wound to heal. The baron and baroness departed for the Ottoman Empire and scarcely remembered their adopted granddaughter.

Later she erred again, despite having been warned, despite the slanders against her husband. Horrible tales were told that afternoon in the Trianon, 11 Place des États-Unis.

Surrounded by her brothers-in-law, his brother Ferdinand and her sister Regine, she erred when, in Maurice's name, she announced the future adoption of two young orphans, Arnold and Raymond Deforest. It was horrible, she recalled, a chill running up her spine. Many things were said during that family meeting.

They tried to convince her that she couldn't adopt the two children, and why would they carry the name Bischoffsheim? Clara would be used merely to provide the family name. Those children were the result of a liaison of her husband's—they were certain of it and could furnish proof—or was it a highly secret affair that implicated the son of Queen Victoria, always shielded by the baron?

What was certain was that Clara was forever wounded by the adoption. Secrets of her husband's infidelity arose from all sides. Her relatives recounted stories, and newspapers gossiped about the life of the future king of England. One more instance of the secret loves and bastard offspring of the heir to the throne, said the columnists.

The heir to Queen Victoria's throne had numerous romances outside the palace, and many illegitimate children raised by close friends, Maurice de Hirsch among them. A loyal friend who paid his bills and gambling debts. Everyone knew that. And that the queen hated him.

But Clara, outraged at her brothers, had once again sided with Maurice, demonstrating a wife's loyalty and understanding. On her conscience was the weight of Hortense and the Premelic girl, who came to serve merely as consolation.

After some months, upon giving her name to two unknown boys who also became her sons and heirs, she tried to compensate Maurice for the slanders. To her, it was only a question of philanthropy, of helping one's fellow man, doing a mitzvah, and never afterward, until that moment of her life, did she succeed in unravelling the real motive of the adoption.

She had never had the courage to ask for the truth when Maurice was alive, and now it was too late.

She regretted that those boys, despite all she had done and all the love she had shown them, did not return her fondness. Raymond was good, affectionate but very sickly and mentally unbalanced. Arnold, the older of the two, was already twenty and thought only of himself and material things. He demanded everything and in exchange–

Sometimes Clara wondered where they came from… what they had been promised or told for them to act that way…

Now that she had her true granddaughter with her, Lucien's blood forced her to hide her from the world! And that was quickly killing her.

"It's too late," she told Gustav Held.

They, all of her own family, the Bischoffsheims, the Goldschmidts, the Montefiore-Levy, the Avigdors, the Hirsch brothers-in-law, her nephews–all of them might still allege she was insane, the executors advised. A fact that had now become much easier to prove…

"One denunciation and a doctor is all it takes! Everything you swore to conserve and benefit, all your work of philanthropy, your organizations, the schools and colonies–everything would go to collateral relatives," the notary Dietz explained.

Now it was too late for the world to know the truth, to meet little Lucienne Varsano de Hirsch. To see she was really the living picture of her father.

Sweet, loving, smiling… To meet that thin little girl who slept beside her, curled up, keeping her company like a faithful puppy, stretched out on the carpets in the library, opening books of drawings and trying to write what Mademoiselle Romana, her instructor, had taught during the week. The small Sicilian called Lukia, Lily, Lucienne, or simply *mademoiselle* by the servants, was in those days the breath of life in Clara's world. She would embrace her lovingly and ask:

"Are you better, *Nonna*? Are you feeling any pain, *Nonna*?"

But other than her faithful amanuensis Gustav Held, the notary Dietz, and Madame Lory, no one knew the truth.

To know the truth, to tell the truth to the people circulating in or visiting the house would be very dangerous, both for her and for Michaela's marriage. If Micha had hidden the truth when she married Jacobo Montefiore and spent years deceived by the farce of the fire and the death of her daughter, nothing could be done other than hope that one day Yako would agree to adopt an orphan. And she knew that would be difficult.

She could not make her sisters Regine and Hortense, or Ferdinand, her dear brother, or even her brothers-in-law Leopold Goldschmidt and Georges Montefiore Levy accept the story of the true granddaughter and help to raise the child, even seeing in her every sign of Lucien.

Clara had already suffered too much with her two adopted sons, with Arnold's jealousy, with Raymond's horrific disease, locked in a padded room in Beauregard with two male nurses to attend him in his crises.

She had given her name and her love to those two boys who were not of her blood, and it was they and the golden-haired girl who had come from 24 Rue d'Anjou who would carry on her lineage. It was Lucienne de Premelic, Irene's daughter, who bore her name, her title, and her heritage. It was too late, wrote Clara, venting her feeling to Anna Varsano:

*I am here, my dear Anna, in my last nights, sitting in the library at Rue de l'Élysée, watching our granddaughter as she sleeps. She dreams of her doll and smiles. She shows me affection and combs my hair in the morning. She plays every day with the doll house that Adele gave her. She asks about her and about Victor. She is learning to write some words in French. She's a good, beautiful little girl and has Lucien's features and complexion, even the same birthmark, a small fleur-de-lis over the left eye... But the glow and happiness she has comes from your daughter Michaela.*

*I hope that one day you too will be called Nonna and receive her affection.*

*But Michaela has to decide what to do! Once, you wrote from Mongibello and spoke of your fears, your problems and your distresses. Now it is I who ask for your assistance, my dear Anna.*

*Help Michaela to find a way to be able to raise Lily. Perhaps the time I have left will not be sufficient to wait for your reply. I am too tired to go on writing...*

*With affection and eternal gratitude,*
*Clara*
*Paris, March 21, 1899.*

She closed the envelope, addressed to Anna Varsano, in care of David Varsano, at the office of the esteemed lawyer Master Grassi in Salonica.

Thus Clara de Hirsch spent her final days. She painstakingly separated her son's letters and drawings. Lucien's life was told in drawings; and in every corner of his notebooks were passages of his life: the house in Beauregard, the terrace with guests playing *bezique japonais*, the dances, the military uniforms, the Greek columns and the profiles of the women with whom he fell in love. He had drawn life in Constantinople, his trips, it was all there. Lucien kept everything; even a leaf from a plane tree at the Acropolis in Athens had been later pinned and wrapped in tissue paper. That was one of his memories in that box that should be preserved.

Little Lily, sitting on the carpet in the library, asked, "Who drew this, *nonna*?"

"It was your father, my dear, your father, Lucien de Hirsch, the man in this photo, who had your eyes and your smile."

"Where is he, *nonna*, why doesn't he come to see me?"

"Why? Well, he went away to heaven… And no one ever returns from there, my dear…"

Some of the documents were going to Georges and Hortense.

"Poor Georges," she thought out loud. He had a genuine passion for Lucienne Premelic. He couldn't manage to get the girl away from Hortense; it was as if she were part of her wheelchair. It was Hortense, and her craziness, who indoctrinated and educated her. And to think that she would be her successor, her heir… Clara separated the memories into envelopes…

To Lucienne Premelic de Hirsch, she would leave some remembrances of a man who was supposedly her father. But she also wanted to be able to remind her that everything that would one day be hers, everything she would inherit, her name and title and all the responsibilities, had been made by a Jewish family. It had all been done over decades, through hard work, persistence, and solidarity with the neediest. Such actions were known in Judaism as a Mitzvah.

Clara de Hirsch then wrote her last letter intended for the future heir to her title: the young baroness De Hirsch, in care of her brother-in-law, Georges Montefiore Levy.

She wanted her to never forget that the Hirsches were still Jews. For in that house in Esneux, with Hortense surrounded by doctrines and mysteries and even taken to be baptized, she, the little girl from Rue d'Anjou, the future baroness Lucienne Premelic de Hirsch, was being led to blindness. She would never possess the knowledge and greatness of spirit to see for herself the world as it was and human misery.

She should know that part of what one receives must be set aside for the poor, the sick, the oppressed and persecuted. To live with dignity and love. That was the motto of her family.

There, in the library, the other Lily, played and hummed happily. The little girl, still without a name, was her granddaughter from Taormina, found in Napoli Posillipo.

The girl with her son's eyes was her true Lily and should be adopted by someone Michaela trusted.

Someone, Clara thought while she finished to sew a small doll, to her granddaughter... To whom she would leave a small fortune to raise and support her. "The girl should have a name, should be the real baroness, a Bischoffsheim de Hirsch auf Gereut," she told her confidant Gustav Held. But who would do that without revealing Michaela's secret? Who would give the child a name? Lord Rosebery had mentioned the possibility of raising her along with his sons immediately after the accident. He had always been a doting father and would do anything for Hannah's memory.

But scandal at court and in Parliament, any step out of the ordinary, would serve to start an investigation into the truth about the girl. English newspapers gave no quarter in dealing with the personal lives of politicians.

She thought again about Lord Rosebery. He would be good... Living a few blocks from Michaela. Perhaps one day, little by little Yako would warm to the girl. And she could be adopted. But only Michaela could resolve all that... and she would arriving at any moment!

Clara finished to dress the doll ,and went to her save...Back she said to the girl." Lily , pay attention... this is very important for you to know.. This is my gift to you. This  small doll is a magical doll..

It  will be  for you...like your sister..You can talk with her if you will be alone and sad..You will sleep with her, care her all your life...Never let her go from your side..Understand..never ? Is very significant..It is so important as this coin from your father, that one you have around your neck...Do you promise ?

Lily gave a smile and kissed her Grandmother's front..

Clara continued to write splitting all, into two  named boxes...

Ah! I forgot... she thought here is Michaela´s green necklace...Maybe she wants to give it to Lily one day ..Better to keep it inside Lily´s box...She will keep it .

෮

When Michaela returned from Napoli Possilipo in September, she told her husband about the accident of a female servant of Lord Rosebery's and how taken she was with the young Neapolitan girl called Lukia. Yako laughed, hugged his wife, but laconically dismissed the idea to taking in an orphan to be raised in their home.

And nothing further was said about it. He wouldn't even let her broach the subject. The nannies, when they returned to Piccadilly from Lord Rosebery's villa, commented on how loving the mistress was and her dedication to the girl's recovery after she lost her mother in the accident and was hospitalized for over a month. Yako thought that Michaela was exaggerating, and when he caught his wife with tears in her eyes, always hidden in some corner, he joked with her:

"Still thinking about your *poverina*?" he asked, with a half-mocking smile, trying to soften his wife's incomprehensible suffering.

Michaela had changed; she was downcast, sad, avoided sitting at the dinner table, and retired very early. Now she said she was worried about the illness of Clara de Hirsch, and nothing could change her mind. She had to go to Paris as quickly as possible and would take Victor and Adele.

That morning, as she prepared for the journey, Yako came again into her dressing room, closed the door behind him, and confronted his wife.

"I understand your urgency, dear, because you owe a lot to Clara de Hirsch, but taking the children with you, on a trip of farewell, at such a sad moment, is madness," he said, worried. "Leave the children with my mother and the nannies, they'll be fine without you, and you can travel calmly."

Michaela sighed deeply, relieved, but said nothing and went on closing her bags. Minutes later, Yako returned with a small valise, smiling, spreading his arms to Michaela.

"I just had a great idea! May I spend my Easter holiday with you, dear? How about it? We'll go to Guernsey tomorrow and then take another boat to Le Havre and catch the train for Paris. I'll show the children around while you visit the baroness. But at night we'll all be together… The children will love it!"

Michaela smiled for the first time in months. Yako picked up his wife's bag and left the room.

"If we hurry now, we can catch a ferry by noon!"

Victor and Adele put on their overcoats and continued to chase each other, singing happily.

"We're going to Paris! And Pappá too!"

They took a carriage to Waterloo Station. There were two special cars added for the boat transfer. Both were full.

Nevertheless, they were lucky. The two companies that handled transport across the channel had begun a competition for Easter week. They opted for taking the London & South Western Railway, which also operated a channel crossing, from Southampton. The two competing boats departed at the same time and arrived on the same schedule. The vessel chosen by Yako was the elegant and new *SS Stella*, which still had a few places available. It would be interesting, commented Yako, for this was the first daylight crossing of the year.

The steamship left some ten minutes late. But the captain announced that they would be anchoring at Guernsey without fail by five-thirty that afternoon.

Yako laid out the plans: a hotel and a dinner of fresh fish, and the following morning they would cross and catch the train to Paris. Adele and Victor, leaping with happiness, left the area and wandered about the quarterdeck. After two hours the sun warming that chilly but glorious day gave way to a dense fog.

Michaela told the children not to leave her sight, but they went on deck to look at the heavy fog and came back with a fearful expression on their faces.

The ship was proceeding at full speed, which was quite dangerous, a passenger sitting beside the Montefiores commented.

Someone said the *SS Stella* was steaming at over eighteen knots, inadvisable in a fog.

Suddenly, the ship diminished its speed and slowly penetrated that dark cloud. This lasted for more than an hour, and both the visibility and the velocity returned to normal.

After some time, they again encountered a fogbank, but by now the children had lost their fear and pursued new adventures, seeking to discover the most secret places on the spacious *SS Stella*.

Yako, in the passenger area, was concentrating on his reading, and Michaela was crocheting but keeping an eye on the children. Adele whispered something in her mother's ear; she asked to go to the toilet.

Michaela went with her. Instants later, the boat was steaming onward under full power.

From the corridor, waiting for her daughter, Michaela looked at the weather outside. The night was cloaked in dark fog. No trace of light was visible in the sky, nor any reflection on the water. They should be arriving, as it was already past five.

Suddenly, she lost her balance. A horrible rolling and a loud muffled sound. The rolling swung in the opposite direction with a whirlwind of noises and the ship tilted to one side. Shouts of terror could be heard. Trying to keep her balance, Michaela was unable to open the bathroom door where Adele was.

The girl was crying in the dark, startled and afraid.

"Stay where you are, I'm going to call Pappá, hold on to something... I think there are bars on your side... Don't get up," her mother shouted, desperate.

Michaela tried to run to the passenger area to ask for Yako's help, but a horde of frightened passengers were pushing against the door from inside. The captain, coming down from the bridge with a megaphone, was giving orders to his sailors, shouting, "To the boats, women and children, to the lifeboats. Quickly!"

A sailor handed her a life vest. With it in her hands, she dashed back to the bathroom, trying to maintain her balance by holding onto the rails when her feet no longer touched the floor. The boat was foundering...

Her heart racing, with all her strength she kicked the jammed door of the bathroom, praying to God it would work. The door opened and Michaela lost her footing, hitting her head against the jamb and twisting her left ankle.

The little girl came out, sobbing.

"Momma, mommy," screamed Adele, trying to help her mother up.

"Put this on, Adele," she shouted in desperation. "Run back there, your father must be waiting for you with Victor. Get into a lifeboat, tell them I can't walk. Ask someone to come help me here in the toilet... Go quickly, for the love of God!"

The girl left with the life vest, running as she supported herself on the corridor handrails.

In a matter of minutes the steamship, the famous and secure *SS Stella*, pride of Channel Island Services, capsized completely and began to sink to the bottom of the sea.

There had never been a shipwreck so rapid and so widely reported.

*The Times* of London told the following morning, the 31st of March, 1899, of the great tragedy of the *SS Stella*.

There was no list of passengers. According to the agents of St. Peters Port, in the heavy fog the ship had struck submerged granite in the Casquets reef.

There were not enough lifeboats for everyone.

Worse yet, many had no life vest. One estimate said that more than ninety passengers and twenty crew members died trapped inside the ship, which sank in less than eight minutes. Some survivors were found in the frigid waters twenty miles from St. Peters Port.

But the London & Western Railway still did not have all the names on the list, and many were considered disappeared, sought by relatives and friends.

# WRECKED WHILE RESCUING

## Steamer Searching for the Stella's Victims Runs Aground.

## ENGLISH CHANNEL DISASTERS

### A Collier Goes Down with Several on Board—Campania Delayed by a Storm.

SOUTHAMPTON, April 1.—The London and Southwestern Railway Company's steamer Southwestern, which was sent to search for bodies of victims of the wreck of the same company's steamer Stella, sank after running on the Casquet Thursday afternoon, went ashore

the disaster to the Southwest ... rived in a dispatch from the Si ... at Cape la Hague, on the coas... opposite Aurigny Island in t... as the Casquet Rocks. The ... that the vessel was ashore wit... stove in. The crew remained on

On the first of April, 1899, another report in *The Times* told of two children, brother and sister, who were miraculously found far from the site of the accident.

They were clinging to a lifeboat capsized by heavy waves and almost dead from hypothermia.

They were saved by the *SS Vera*, a steamship on its way to Jersey.

The children who survived through a miracle, according to the newspaper, were named Victor V. Montefiore and Adele V. Montefiore, from Piccadilly, London.

There was no news yet of their parents.

On April 2, all the newspapers published the loss of a great woman.

It spoke of Baroness Clara de Hirsch, who had passed away on the first of April in her residence in Paris on Rue de l'Élysée.

A model of philanthropy. She left all her goods to charitable organizations and foundations, a total of millions of pounds sterling, wrote *The Times* in a front-page article:

*'The greatest female philanthropist of the century left most of her immense fortune to be distributed among her social works throughout Europe and the Ottoman Empire. Using part of her bequest, the Society for Agricultural Colonization founded by her husband will maintain in America, Canada, Argentina, and Brazil the Russian colonists who emigrated there and support the schooling of their descendants. The will further stipulates that a large bequest will aid for more than one hundred years new foundations maintaining schools, crèches, and hospitals created by Clara de Hirsch.*

*As heirs, in addition to her brothers and sisters, the greatest beneficiaries would be three minors. A granddaughter, adopted after the premature death of her only son Lucien de Hirsch; Miss Lucienne Premelic de Hirsch, who lived in Belgium; and two adopted sons, Arnold and Raymond Deforest Bischoffsheim.*

*The three young people will divide all the furniture and real estate and a large fortune coming also from the will of Baron Maurice de Hirsch, deceased in 1896. A great financier, among many activities, he had been majority stockholder in the Banque de Paris et Pays-Bas and builder of the Orient Express railways.*

*The body of Clara de Hirsch was accompanied yesterday, April 1, 1899, by hundreds of carriages with ministers and politicians. Part of European nobility was present. The coffin was taken from Rue de l'Élysée to the cemetery at Montmartre, where she was interred in the family tomb. As specified in her will, the burial was to be simple, without flowers."*

There were no speeches or eulogies for the Grand Dame of philanthropy.

# BARONESS DE HIRSCH DEAD

## Was Said to be the Greatest Woman Philanthropist of Her Time.

## SPENT MILLIONS ON CHARITY

Completed the Work for Persecuted Jews Begun by Her Husband—Gave $1,000,000 for New York Hebrews.

PARIS, April 1.—The Baroness de Hirsch, widow of Baron Maurice de Hirsch, is dead.

She leaves several million pounds sterling, most of which is said to be bequeathed to charities.

The Baroness de Hirsch continued the highest and best work of her husband. With him philanthropy was part of his varied life; with her it was everything. After the death of her husband, in 1896, she devoted herself to carrying out to their fullest reach the enterprises undertaken by the Baron for the benefit of his race, and to discovering new avenues for the pouring out of the vast treasure he had stored up in a life of tremendous energy and marvelous success.

She was the daughter of a banker, and it was said that she had almost as good a head for business as the Baron himself. Her father was the late Senator Bischofheim of Brussels, and under his care the daughter learned the value of money, how to in-

# XXVIII

## VICTOR AND ADELE

Salonica, October 5, 1899.

Anna Varsano did not dress in mourning. She declined any ceremony in the synagogues of Salonica, received no neighbors or friends, did not cover her mirrors as a sign of misfortune and sadness.

She, Anna of Taormina, could not weaken and show what she was feeling. It was a greater pain, coming from inside her battered soul. She felt that life no longer had any value, any direction, as she wrote in her diary. Now reality beat at her door, and it would do no good to cry further. She should put on a *bautta* mask from the Teatro Regina Margherita and socialize with them. Only Anna Varsano and God knew how terrible it was to lose Michaela in that tragic accident.

She thought about her grandchildren, who had survived through a miracle, her two little ones, lost in a dark and frigid sea. The nightmare tormented her days, but had now passed—or must pass.

She ordered the house whitewashed, sewed new awnings for the terrace, and made poor Daud's life unbearable. She wanted everything to bloom quickly, to welcome her grandchildren.

Since the last of April, after the news came and she had received David, as pale as a sheet of paper, with clippings from English newspapers in his trembling hands, she had thought about the children, the poor children, who had already suffered enough for the rest of their lives and who deserved a new life in Salonica, filled with happiness and love.

Anna took an unhurried bath that hot morning toward the end of September. She looked at herself at length in the mirror and suddenly saw the form of a woman dressed in white. She turned around, startled, but the form had disappeared, and the room was invaded by the familiar strong perfume, the essence of lemon that Michaela had worn since she was a girl. She smiled at the mirror, and that afternoon lit the Shabbat candles again after a long period of no observance.

She went to see David in his office in the *Quartier Consulaire*, in the days before Yom Kippur.

She had gone to Sabri Pasha Street hesitantly. She paused at several display windows and for brief moments saw her reflection in the glass. It was that of an old woman, bent under the weight of a lie and great regret. She wondered whether, when she asked for David Varsano, she would have the courage to tell everything, to take from her purse the envelopes that tormented her.

Her heart accelerated. David came to attend to her.

He was surprised and felt flattered by his sister-in-law's first visit to his place of work. He brought her a comfortable chair, sent the office boy for a tray of Turkish coffee to serve her, and waited patiently for *signora* Varsano to begin. He didn't understand the reason for that unexpected visit.

"So, Anna?" asked David ceremoniously. "To what do I owe this visit?"

Anna opened her purse and handed him an envelope.

"Before reading this, David, I'd like you to swear an oath on the memory of my daughter, your niece Michaela."

He took the envelope, nodding in agreement, and stared into her eyes, then turned the envelope over to see the name of its sender.

It was a well known envelope, one with the Hirsch monogram from Rue de l'Élysée. It was from Gustav Held, addressed to Anna Varsano.

"The letter is in French, but written in a very difficult way, and I didn't understand it all that well..." said Anna. "But first I want to show you the reason why I'm here by myself, without your brother."

Opening her purse again, with quivering hands she took out another letter.

"Read this one first, please, and you'll understand better," Anna said.

Without understanding, David left the first envelope on his desk and put on his glasses.

"This is the last letter from Clara de Hirsch, which you brought to me as soon as we learned of all the misfortune, remember?"

David unfolded the letter.

Anna carefully watched her brother-in-law's expression as he read. She could hear her heart beating, and a hot wave swept over her face.

David gulped, and he did not blink. Those minutes were interminable. He read and reread the two pages and then laid the sheets on the desk, scrutinized Clara's signature, and his eyes filled with water.

He took off his glasses, cleaned the lenses with his handkerchief and sighed, as if unwilling to believe what he had read.

"I never told the secret to anyone, none of it, so as not to kill Alberto from shame," she said in a fragile voice. "But my God, how I repent! How thoughtless I was..."

David remained silent. He held his forehead in both hands, while Anna, her voice choked, told him about Michaela's pregnancy, her return to Taormina, her shame upon learning of it, the lie she had invented involving the seamstress Giovanna; afterward, no longer able to hold back the tears, she spoke of the letter that David had sent from Salonica announcing the death of Lucien...

"You sent the letter with news of Lucien's death... But it was already too late. Too late for Michaela to reveal that the child existed... to my neighbors, to all of you, to the baron and baroness, who would never believe it and might judge Michaela a tramp, trying to take advantage! She had to hide, I had to lie, for Alberto, for you, who introduced her to Yako, for the sake of her marriage, and later we found out the child was alive. Oh God! Michaela is gone, Clara is gone, and I don't know what to do!"

David sighed, rose and picked up the second letter, which had been sent months after Clara's death, written by Gustav Held, Baroness Hirsch's amanuensis and executor.

He went to the window, his back to Anna, and stood there with the letter in his hands. Seconds, minutes, or hours... There was no measure of the time and the anguish of that encounter. He folded the letter, replacing it in its envelope, and looked at Anna, breathing heavily.

"How are we going to explain this to Alberto? And how are we going to bring the girl?" she asked, distressed.

David sighed again and cleared his throat.

"I'll take care of everything, Anna, don't worry anymore, please. Now we must prepare for the arrival of Victor and Adele and for Alberto's reaction; immediately afterward I'll go to Paris to look for the girl. She too, who until now has had neither mother nor father, deserves to have a future, a family, affection, even if she has to live with Katherina and me and keep company with our Sophie. Go home in peace, Anna," he continued, calmer now. "I know what we can do, but first I have to tell the executor what he wants to know about you. Where is the girl? With whom did she stay in Paris after the baroness was buried?"

"What? Where is the girl?" replied Anna, startled. "What a question! That's what I ask you!" she exclaimed, desperate, her voice rising. "Where is Lucienne? Until Clara's letter came from Paris, she was there, in that house, that palace where she should be living with her *Nonna*! The Baroness wrote saying that the girl had been with her since the accident at Napoli Posillipo. God! Read it again, David, it was written some days before the baroness died, and the girl was with her!"

David reread Clara's letter… and bit his lips. He became pensive and suddenly stood up to accompany Anna to the door.

"Leave the documents with me. Don't worry, I think it was just a misunderstanding on our part and by the baroness's executor. Maybe the girl, on the day of the funeral, stayed with some friend of the Hirsches, I don't know, but we'll find out… Everything may be just a misunderstanding!" He led Anna to the door. "Don't worry, I'll write the executor. I think he meant to ask something else, and we both understood it differently. Don't worry about it anymore…" he said.

The fall rainy season was about to begin. It was the same every year, and Anna had become accustomed to Salonica, its people, its history, its way of life. She loved the city and knew that from that day on she would have to make her grandchildren understand what Salonica represented and little by little forget all that had happened to them, and also forget Piccadilly. She knew it would be an arduous struggle, but she was prepared to fight for the happiness of the children.

The Orient Express train arrived at Vardar Station at nine a.m. on October 5, 1899, bringing Anna her two most precious treasures, Victor and Adele. The children descended from the train looking worn and tired, accompanied by a man of some years but physically strong and with impeccable bearing. A Scotsman named Sebastian Clair.

Accompanying him was a short, stout lady named Amelia, and a nanny who introduced herself as Miss Gordon.

Mr. Clair saw to the luggage, which was extensive: four large trunks and numerous bags. Amelia held Adele and the dolls, Victor descended with a heavy bag full of marbles, and Miss Gordon's hands were occupied with the basket of provisions and medicines.

Anna embraced the children at length, *Dottore* Alberto took Adele into his arms, and David left to help the very solicitous gentleman who had quickly organized everything.

Two carriages were waiting at the entrance to the station, bustling at that hour of day, and the two little ones, still dizzy from the noise and the whistles of manoeuvring locomotives, began to smile. They found a point of attraction: the *hamalitos*, old men who looked like elves and carried huge loads, a spectacle not to be missed by anyone coming to the city.

The Varsanos' home, which had always seemed so large to the couple, that day became small. Daud was waiting for the children at the gate, and as soon as the carriages rounded the corner of the White Tower, came in his *entari* and white turban, dragging his slippers, to meet them.

"*Habibi! Habibi!*" he shouted and waved, celebrating the children's arrival with his broad smile, and they, to everyone's surprise, remembered old Daud! To them the gardener was a different type of person both in color and dress, remembered for the exotic songs he had taught them during the summer holidays they spent in Salonica.

Wonderful holidays... The children, guided by Daud, went on peregrinations through the markets, along the ancient walls of the city, or to the Promenade to visit Mrs. Karakassos and help to take her famous *tiropitas*, delicious cheese puff pastry, from the oven.

Days passed slowly during those summer holidays, and later Yako would come, arriving from his trip always weary from the many numbers and contracts he had completed in London. Alberto would close the perfume store for a few days, and son-in-law and father-in-law would head out to the beaches north of the city. Often they would rent Nico's kaïk and the entire family would journey to the border with Hagios Oros. Those times spent with everyone together, smiling and having breakfast under the white tents of Daud's rose garden, laughing, with the children running around and Michaela still sleepy lying on the divan in her long nightgown.

Mr. Clair, who communicated with Anna in a mixture of sign language and a few words, took the baggage inside. David had to stay as interpreter, for neither she nor Alberto understood English well. Anna had no notion of who were those people accompanying the children and the nanny. "Who are Mr. Clair and that lady called Amelia?" she asked David.

All the things were taken to their places, and Alberto returned with David and the Scotsman to the veranda. Anna arranged the bedroom beside the atelier for Mrs. –? She hadn't even understood her name! And the small bedroom in the tower, next to the atelier would be for Mr. Clair.

The children went with the nanny to the room that had been Michaela's, and by lunchtime everything was organized.

Anna heard part of the conversation on the veranda when it was already well under way, but David, who served as intermediary and translated for the *Dottore*, omitted part of the information.

"Yes," explained David, "Mr. Clair accompanied the children, for he was always very close friends with Michaela... ever since she lived with the Hirsches in the London home. He wouldn't allow such a long and dangerous journey merely under the protection of a nanny. Unfortunately, the grandfather, Mr. Montefiore, after all that had happened, had neither the health nor the conditions to accompany the children to Salonica. His wife, Tilda, suffered a stroke upon hearing of the shipwreck and is still bedridden, paralyzed."

"So," continued Mr. Clair, explaining for David to translate, "Lord Rosebery, who was my late mistress's husband, and who was very fond of Michaela, suffered greatly because of the tragedy. He organized everything, bought the tickets and also sent Amelia with us, as she has been cooking for the Montefiores lately. That way the children wouldn't feel they were in the hands of strangers, or that they had been abandoned."

The Varsanos changed their habits beginning that day. The *Dottore* had almost no time for research in his laboratory, because the children's lessons in the Lycée were complicated. They had rudiments of French, but their accent was terrible; in addition, in that polyglot city everyone spoke everything, and schoolchildren would argue in Ladino, Greek, Turkish, French, or Italian. Everything depended on the district, the market, or the street where they lived. Daud was also one of those who used terms and expressions in Arabic. He was constantly saying *Mabruk... Mabruk...! Habibi, Habibi...* And all of it was beginning to get confused in their little heads!

The foods had strange names, and Adele, when she wanted something, would tug on Anna's skirt, cry with Miss Gordon, who tried to impose an English diet on the children in a Mediterranean climate. It was she who disliked the spicy food in the Varsano home and said that Adele would never eat this or that. And just what *was* that?... *Bammies...*Okra? What an awful slimy thing. Or that mound of nearly unrecognizable greens and legumes that they ate in that house, and *garbanzos*, white beans and a flower called *anguinares*.

"Ridiculous!" exclaimed the Englishwoman.

Amelia gradually came out of her silence and ventured to speak. First she understood that in English the mistress of the house didn't dare answer.

"*Parla italiano,*" Anna would say. "*Parla portoghese, Amelia... Parla tedesco, ma inglese... Niente, no!*"

She discovered that the neighbors spoke a language that was familiar to her, a mixture of Spanish, Portuguese, many things, a language that was old Judeo-Spanish, known as Ladino, with archaic words that recalled her grandmother in Portugal, using similar expressions and grumbling when fishing was bad, or lighting candles and praying for the protection of her grandfather, who must be far off at sea in the middle of a storm. A language that, despite the accent, she could understand if she paid attention and mentally cancelled out that singsong, interrogative cadence of the women of Salonica.

And, unexpectedly, she found herself involved in a circle of chatty ladies who knitted as they sat in chairs on the sidewalks, under large plane trees or near the chestnut roasters.

Amelia demonstrated her talents in the months she spent with the Varsanos. This was a little piece of her land! Even better, she were with her family, her dear daughter. And she thought about her Jeremy and his coach, poor thing, in that London cold.

Mr. Clair, when he would leave with the *Dottore*, wearing his top hat and cashmere coat, could stroll through the Quartier Consulaire like a banker or ranking representative of some wealthy country.

He was greeted with deference by merchants in the markets, and when accompanied by Daud was introduced as an important emissary of Queen Victoria's government. Complimentary fruit, candied almonds, and coffee were offered by the merchants. The two of them established a code, and the black man in a white turban again used the stratagem of the *hamam*.

The sober and proud Sebastian Clair also became a habitué of Marika Karakassos's home, where he would wait for David's return from the office to learn the latest happenings from newspapers arriving from London.

In late afternoon, when the streetlamps lit the Quay, they would head to the Pallas, a den of intellectuals open only to men, for coffee or anise, with hot pistachios and a stimulating conversation about the Turks and the sultan's politics.

A conversation so exotic for an Englishman raised in the stables of Mentmore that he listened to David's stories with full attention, as if wishing to engrave them in memory, in order to later repeat in Piccadilly his new knowledge and experiences, and show Lord Rosebery, the man who knew everything, his political and historical erudition about the Ottoman Empire.

That would doubtless give him more credit and importance, and perhaps, when Sybil married, he would be accepted in the family like Daud and not die alone in a small house at Rives Mews. It would be sad to return there and have nothing to do.

He would also have to talk about the Muslim gardener's rose garden, the essences, the perfumes, the *Dottore*, and marvellous Anna.

She was a woman out of the ordinary, with an alabaster smile, shining eyes, and an elegant gait–a majesty wrapped in her shawl, with the white streak in her dark hair contrasting with her olive skin.

There was something about her that energized her conversation. She would stay for hours after dinner, discussing with *Dottore* Alberto items from the newspapers, commenting on this or that, chatting and sewing the model of a dress for a customer, under the dim light of an oil lamp. Often she would place Adele on her lap and continue memorizing a French parable with Victor in her strong Sicilian accent.

Alberto would bring home several vials of essence and line them up on the table after dinner, to be analyzed. Daud would take a dry leaf and, removing it from the vial, fan it in the air to evaluate the dispersed perfume, opening his nostrils and breathing deeply, his eyes half shut.

"*Très fort!*" he said mischievously, grading it. Or he would attempt to recognize the mixture. "*Cinnamon, musk, uh... lavender and vetiver!*" he would shout in his hoarse voice.

The *Dottore*, with an exasperated look, would open another mixture, and they would spend hours discussing roses, lemon, lavender, cedar... And Mr. Clair watched, learning.

It was as if nothing had happened, and life in that house next to the White Tower were magical and all the sadness were swept from there, never again to disturb the harmony and the sleep of the hosts.

But Sebastian knew that when she retired to her bedroom, Anna removed the mask of peace and harmony and entered her private hell. From his room in the tower he could see Anna every night huddled over her table by the window, writing and weeping. Lit by a flickering flame, she was not the same woman. Worn and aged, she would remain there hour after hour, her hands on her head in a gesture of despair, her hair dishevelled, trying to find words to put into those pages on which she wrote.

Sebastian remembered Michaela's desperation when she had felt rejected by Lucien, the affection she had shown Hannah in the face of her terrible disease, the secret letters, the last ones from Lucien, which he had kept for so many years. And he longed, in those moments as he observed her, to be able to go into her room and stroke the hair of that desperate woman and speak to her, to tell her part of the life of her daughter of which she must be unaware... The envelopes and a small box of jewels, which had been kept all those years in the safe of Hannah and Lord Rosebery and which he had brought with him in the bottom of his suitcase.

He didn't have the heart to give them to Mrs. Varsano, but he would have to find the right moment, for the months of his visit were coming to an end.

On his next-to-last night in Salonica, on the eve of Passover, when he was sure everyone was sleeping, looking from behind the curtains of his room, he saw her there, sitting in her room, writing.

He gathered his courage, descended from the tower, and entered the house.

He knocked softly at the lady's door. Anna was startled to see Mr. Clair.

"Madam, this is for you... It was from Michaela... Take it, please!" And he handed her a thick brown package.

She took the package, and without a sound, silently closed and bolted the door.

His mission was accomplished.

There lay a part of her story, of the life of her daughter, the death of Lucien, his promises of love and the agony of Clara de Hirsch at the loss of her son, everything that Michaela had never been aware of. And which he had kept for all those years.

Sebastian Clair returned to his room, and from the window in the tower saw Anna Varsano open the envelopes. He slowly closed the curtain and said farewell to Salonica.

Day was breaking. From the tower he beheld the sea and the Promenade, still illuminated by streetlamps.

From the top of the minaret, the muezzin called to prayer.

Street vendors began to proclaim their wares. "*Lavanta... lavanta, lavender, perfumed lavender, madam!*"

Sebastian Clair wrote a postcard addressed to Lord Rosebery, 40 Piccadilly, London.

*Salonica,*
*What a sad, poor, and fascinating city!*
*Where all the inhabitants speak different languages, like in the Tower of Babel, pray to a single God but don't accept the God of their neighbour.*
*A city of perfumes, flowers and spices.*
*Of the odour of sweat, work, and effort...*
*Of memories and stories engraved in the stones with blood from the heart of each one of its inhabitants.*
*A magical place, never to be forgotten...*

That morning, Sebastian Clair would return to London, and the postcard languished forgotten in a drawer in his room.

# Epilogue

Buenos Aires,1974

São Paulo, 1974

On a cold, misty morning typical of June in the city of São Paulo, I entered my grandparents' home with my  baby daughter Patricia in my arms.

They lived a few blocks from my apartment, in Bom Retiro, the district with the greatest Jewish concentration in the city.

The Winicks' small house was a duplex, a two story structure bought in the 1920s, when they arrived from Poland and which I was used to visiting from the time I was a little girl. I would always climb the stairs carrying purchases at least twice a week and was received with kisses and merriment.

The house, small and cosy, was redolent of my grandmother's cooking—barley soup, or chicken soup with dill. It was my oasis, and at any time of day or night the couple, already advanced in years but very happy and talkative, always had something tasty to serve and something amusing to relate.

They spoke heavily accented Portuguese mixed with Yiddish, and I loved hearing them comment on events in the newspapers and would laugh heartily at the expressions they used.

"*Nu?.. Bis shoin du?* You're already here?"

That morning, my grandmother was seated, wearing her glasses and reading the Jewish newspaper that my grandfather received weekly; thus entertained, she continued with her eyes on the paper, holding a cup of tea in her trembling hands.

"Ah, my beautiful *sheine meidalles*, you came in this cold, you maybe want some tea?" my grandfather offered.

Behind her newspaper, my grandmother started to laugh, catching his attention.

"Listen to this, Shloime: in Argentina there's a pianist named Victor Montefiore who still plays tangos in the theatre, and you know how old he is? Eighty-five! *Oy vey...* Is it even possible to play piano at the age of eighty-five?" she said, winking at me.

My grandfather, thinking the mention of age was a criticism of his shakiness, answered:

"Piano... *groisse mainze...* Big deal, Mirle ! I'd like to see this Victor character dance the samba! Piano— Everybody plays the piano!" And he left the room, grumbling, headed for the kitchen for another cup of tea.

I was intrigued by the name of the pianist. I picked up the newspaper, but the article was in Yiddish.

"*Baba*," I asked, "read it again for me to understand." And she read the entire news item, slowly, faltering on complicated or unfamiliar words.

"*The great pianist Victor Varsano Montefiore will perform at the Teatro Soleil, on Avenida Corrientes, the night of July first, 1974, at seven p.m. The concert will be a benefit for the works of the Asociación Mutual Israelita Argentina (AMIA). The artist has a rich background. Born in London in 1889, the son of a Sephardic father of Italian origin and a mother born in Taormina, he was orphaned at the age of 11 and was raised in Salonica, Greece, by his maternal grandparents, the Varsanos. He studied piano in Paris and Belgium and was considered a virtuoso by the age of 16. Still very young, in London in 1916, he composed music for several silent films like A Bunch of Violets, starring Chrissie White. He also composed A Grain of Sand and Drake's Love Story.*"

*"He always loved music and the ladies. He told our reporter, at the café of the Hotel Claridge, that he had come to Buenos Aires in 1919, after an unhappy love affair. He had decided to emigrate to the New World after the First World War, in which he had fought as a lieutenant in the English division in the Balkans, and arrived in Buenos Aires in search of adventure and new rhythms. Victor Varsano Montefiore has lived in Argentina all these years and has worked in various tango clubs giving shows. Tickets are on sale at AMIA headquarters, 63 Calle Pasteur. Article from the daily Yiddishe Zeitung of Buenos Aires, Data facsimile – June 1974."*

My grandmother had to reread it twice. Intrigued, she wanted to know what was the importance of the article. I almost leapt for joy.

"I think I've found him, *Baba*... I think it's him, it has to be, with that name!"

"But who *is* he?" they asked, not understanding.

"The brother of that woman in the hospice in Salonica. Remember, *Baba*? Remember when I told you about the letters and that woman?"

My grandmother's blue eyes widened as she sought to understand. She thought a bit and then exclaimed:

"Oh, the story about the box in your closet! And you promised you would look for the brother. That woman's brother that she never saw again," my grandmother said. "You're thinking the piano player is him? Oh my God..What a small word! If it really is him, you're going to hand over everything in that box, aren't you? *Oy vey*," she said, shaking her head. "*Oy vey Naches*. Good luck. I wish someone could find my sister *Frimale*..." and went on talking to herself.

Upon arriving at Ezeiza airport in Buenos Aires on the first of July, I sensed unusual movement; something serious was going on. People were gathering around transistor radios and listening to the news, and some of the women were crying. I took a taxi. As we ascended Avenida Corrientes, huge groups of people came walking slowly toward the Obelisk. Merchants closed their doors, and not knowing what was really happening, I asked the cab driver.

"*Señora*," he said, sighing, "it's sad... We have lost our president, Juan Domingo Perón. He's gone. A fatal heart attack!"

What a terrible time I chose to come to Buenos Aires, I thought, especially to attend a piano concert.

At the hotel, I tried to understand the news on television, but it was nothing but hysteria and lamentations. People were shouting in the streets: "Perón... Perón...!"

At the hotel door I took a taxi to Calle Pasteur to buy a ticket to the concert. At the AMIA I was informed that the theatre was closed in mourning and the concert postponed with no date set for its rescheduling.

I insisted in my Portuguese-ridden Spanish that I needed to get in touch with the pianist and explained that I had come from Brazil to write a story about Victor Montefiore and that it was very important. I asked the woman at the ticket counter whether it would be possible, in the name of the AMIA, to telephone me and set up an appointment with the concert artist, as I only had two days in the city. After much argument, the secretary very reluctantly took out a file and called the pianist, nodded, and wrote an address on a piece of paper.

"Lavalle–2093, second floor, corner of Junín, *mañana* at 11 o'clock. *Buena suerte, señora!*"

The next morning I was overcome by anxiety. I smoked, swallowed my coffee with a *media luna*, got the box with Anna Varsano's things, and headed to El Once.

In the taxi my heart raced. I didn't know how to begin the conversation. I essayed various approaches on the way.

I'm a journalist, señor Montefiore... or *Mister* Montefiore. I'm going to speak English. *I am writing a new book*... No... Not like that! I'm a writer... writing a new book... but about what?

I also thought: I love your music, love the tango... and then talk about music? Very dangerous, since I didn't know anything.

Mr. Varsano... I met your sister Adele in Salonica, she survived the Holocaust, but unfortunately she passed away this year and I have with me all the story of your family... No, that way I'd kill the man with a heart attack... It wouldn't work!

Oh God, I asked myself: how to approach him? What was I doing there?

Victor, what would he be like today? Little Victor, so loved by his grandmother Anna. Pages and pages in her diary were dedicated to him. At the end, she bitterly wept over his absence, blamed herself for having been the cause of his unhappiness, for having implored him, when he returned to Paris, to never again look for the woman in the photo, for having made him swear never to marry her.

"But why, *nonna*?" he asked.

"One day I'll have the courage to tell him," wrote Anna. "But today I cannot, my little Victor. I swore I'd never tell, and I can't break a promise, especially one made to someone who is no longer among us."

He'll have to read this, I thought. He must read everything I've read if he's to understand. He should be given the chance to read his grandmother's diary and all those letters.

The taxi stopped at 2093 Lavalle. There was a pharmacy on the corner. I paid the driver, picked up the box, and found myself in front of a door with an iron grille. I looked through the glass. A small vestibule was lit by a lamp with threadbare tassels. I took a deep breath and looked for a doorbell.

An elderly lady approached, curious, leaning on her cane.

"Who are you looking for?" she asked in a Spanish with heavy *r*'s like a Frenchwoman.

The old lady seemed like a caricature. She was wearing a dark-green coat with worn fur around the neck and had very blue eyes, painted with heavy lilac shadow. Her lips outlined with carmine gave her an expression of sadness. Her poorly applied face powder and rouge could not hide the ravages of time upon that very white skin. She must have been a beautiful woman once, I thought.

I explained that I was looking for Victor Varsano Montefiore, on the second floor. She got the key ring and opened the door of the small entrance hall without a word; she examined me from head to toe, waiting for me to enter the building. She came in after me, closing the door with her cane.

"*Señorita*," she said, "it does no good to ring. Go on up and go in without knocking; he never answers the door, which is always unlocked."

Upstairs, out of courtesy, I rang the bell. The sound of a piano flooded the hall. A tango. I waited for the music to end and gripped the doorknob.

I was trembling and could hear my heart beating.

There was  Victor, or the Mégas, as his grandfather *Dottore* Alberto called him in Salonica.

It was as if I knew his entire life without ever having seen him. An old man behind a piano at the rear of the living room; he didn't raise his eyes but went on with his music.

The room was almost dark at that time of morning, the tattered curtains were closed, and only two lamps lit the high-ceilinged room. In the foreground, a sofa with numerous disarranged blankets, a china cabinet, a table, and two chairs. In the rear, a grand piano occupied almost all the remaining space.

I entered slowly, hugging the box, afraid of interrupting or startling the pianist. I still had not seen him full-face, only in profile. I tried to step with my high heels as softly as possible, until I bumped against a low footstool, which skidded nosily across the floor until it collided with a radio-turntable console in the corner.

I was alarmed, and the music stopped instantly. Victor turned to see what had happened.

At that moment our eyes met and I saw a man with broad shoulders, in a dark coat, and a silk foulard around his neck, his sparse whitish hair tied in back like an artist. He stood up to greet me.

"So," he said in a firm gravelly voice in Spanish with a slight Italian accent, "you're the reporter from *Brasile*? What can I do for you?"

"Please don't get up, maestro," I told him. "Go on playing, Mr. Montefiore," I said in English. "Your music is wonderful. I was listening just now in the hallway."

I set the box down on the sofa and moved close to the piano.

The light from the lamp fell on him. A gentlemanly carriage, strong features, and a silvery beard, as yet unshaven. His eyes were deep green and his skin olive-colored. He had traces of Mediterranean men, and his long hands were poised over the yellowed ivory keys. He looked at me and nodded his head as if seeing a child wishing to do something naughty.

He coughed and cleared his throat. Then he calmly took a sip of wine from a glass at his side. He struck a match and slowly lit a cigarette, looked at me and smiled, blowing out smoke with an air of challenge.

Eighty-five years old, I thought, he must smoke and drink to excess, but he has the pose and vitality of a young artist, the type of leading man you only see in films.

I needed to gain time, as I didn't know how to begin the conversation.

"Do you know this song?" he asked, fingering the keyboard firmly, a cigarette clenched between his lips, his eyes half-closed.

*Adiós Nonino*, I thought... I recognized the hit by Astor Piazzolla, who used to play on the late afternoon programs on Radio Eldorado. But he played the song with a new introduction, as if recomposing the melody, his fingers flying over the keys.

Marvellous, I said to myself. My arms had goose bumps and I felt cold. He left the burning cigarette in the ashtray and continued. I became more relaxed and slowly approached and leaned on the side of the piano, where, on a velvet cloth on the closed lid I saw the photos.

I shivered...

There was Lily, the same as in the photo in Anna Varsano's album. It was the picture of that young woman with her necklace and her lace dressing, looking at the two of us!

In another picture frame, a collage of photos of Salonica, overlapping hand-painted postcards, a sepia photo of the Eiffel Tower, and a large portrait of Victor with Carlos Gardel, wearing a bowtie, tuxedo and a silk foulard around his shoulders. He was smiling, his teeth shining, his glowing eyes framed by long lashes, his hair slicked down and combed back.

"That's me," he said, when he caught me looking at the photos. "It was so long ago! Many years ago... with Gardel. That photo is from when I played at the Teatro Colón... and those are souvenirs of the city where I grew up, called Salonica."

"And that woman. Who is she?"

"My first girlfriend," he replied, without attributing any importance to it.

"I suppose you never heard of Salonica, young lady... Probably no one in Brazil has heard of or studied the history of Greece or the Ottoman Empire. You people there must not have that many books..." he said in a provocative tone.

I smiled and said I knew Greece and by coincidence had been in Thessaloniki twice.

He stopped playing, closed the piano, took another puff of his almost finished cigarette, his eyes on me as if wishing to test me.

"Not only have I been to Salonica twice, Maestro Montefiore, but I also brought from there some things that I imagine belong to you,"

I said quickly, my heart leaping as if wanting to immediately free me from that responsibility. I thought to myself: now I've said it, there's no turning back!

He came out from behind the piano toward me.

"What kind of joke is this?" he asked, verging on nervousness. "What from there can possibly belong to me–a piece of pita? A slice of *fetta* cheese maybe? Are you aware that I left Salonica almost sixty years ago, young lady?"

"Sir," I said, frightened, not knowing how to conduct the conversation, "what happened to me was a coincidence, a trick of fate, you know? I don't even know how to explain it to you; it's a long story. I brought this box with me, and when you open it you'll understand what I'm trying to say."

I pointed to the box on the sofa. He sat down, and I pulled up the stool that had skidded into the console.

He opened the box. First he took out the fragile yellowed newspaper clippings that I had left on top in order not to further damage them.

Victor Montefiore looked at the first pages as if he had seen a ghost. His hands shook.

He read the headline from the 1917 newspaper, about the great fire in Salonica, picked up the bundles of letters, opened a few envelopes, looked at the return addresses.

The silence was such that I could hear only the motor of the water tank on the roof of the building.

"Letters from my mother to my grandmother. My God! Where did you get these, young lady?"

I couldn't answer right away. My mouth was dry and my lips were glued together.

He went on looking through the box until he came to the volumes of his grandmother's diary; he leafed through one of them and opened another.

He forgot I was there. He read passages, muttering to himself, and his body began to curve. With an effort, he moved closer to the lamp to see better. His expression was one of pain, tears welled in his eyes. Suddenly, as if in a fury, he started putting everything back in the box, talking to himself:

"It's too late now… I don't want to know… I don't want to, *nonna*," and closed the box. "Adele, you know Adele? She was the one who gave you this, wasn't she? For the love of God, where did you get all this?"

I spent some hours telling him. He didn't look at me.

My dry throat ached. I asked for some water; with a gesture of his head he indicated the door to the kitchen. I found a glass among a dozen dirty glasses and plates in the sink. I opened the faucet and filled the glass. I was so thirsty that I drank it all in a few gulps. I looked around.

There were dingy shirts and panamas, dried and hung on a line, pans on the stove, a disconnected heater, an old Frigidaire refrigerator with peeling finish–everything was old, dirty, and neglected.

Poor Victor, here all by himself, with no one to take care of him.

When I returned to the living room he was bent over, with his head in his hands resting on his knees. He was crying… I felt like stroking his sparse white hair, comforting him, and finally found the courage to do so.

He burst into convulsive sobs that lasted for some time. He took my hands , his eyes very red, told me:

"Thank you, young lady, but I can't read all that. I waited for an answer for many years of my life, I wanted someone to explain to me the why of certain things, but the answer never came. Now I think it's too late, and there are things I don't want to know and cannot know anymore. Now it's too late, I can't read everything that's here…"

The door opened, and the old woman who had opened the gate to the building came in carrying a tray covered by a napkin.

"It's time to eat, Victor," she said in French.

She moved close to him, looking at him, finding it odd to see him bent over, his head in his hands, hiding his face.

"What's the matter with him?" she asked me. "What did you do to him? Victor, is she from Burzaco?" she asked, very close to his face. "Did she come from Burzaco to take us away from here?"

He shook his head, his face still covered.

"Go down to your apartment, Lily," he said in a voice nearly hoarse. "I'll have the soup later. And you, young lady," he said, speaking to me, "take this things out of here and go back where you came from. Don't ever come back here… please!"

I left slowly, frightened by his reaction, taking with me only my purse. I was undecided whether to go back to get the box. I waited in the hallway to see if anything would happen. I descended the stairs, and the light coming through the windowpane obscured my vision. It was as if I had spent hours inside a movie theatre, with no air to breathe.

Out on the street, I lit a cigarette.

My chest ached. I wanted to go back there but lacked the courage.

I rehearsed my words... I wanted to apologize for having caused him so much pain, for having reopened a great wound. I wanted to take that box that so disturbed him and remove those memories from there before he actually read the diary.

I walked to the corner, shivering from the cold.

It was already past three in the afternoon. Around me, fog was whitening everything.

My stomach was aching. I spotted an *armazém*, a mixture of café and grocery store. I entered almost without glancing around, looking for a table in a corner. I sat down. Almost all the tables were occupied by older men or women chatting in Yiddish. A very fat woman in an apron approached to serve me.

"At this time of day, *señorita*," she said, reciting the menu in a thick accent, "we only have... *würst sandwich, pastrami with cucumber in brine or sauerkraut*... With *pletzalaj* and black bread... *non ay más varenikes, ni strudel.*"

"Thank you. I'd just like coffee with *pletzalaj* and a bottle of mineral water without ice."

She left, dragging her slippers in a sign of fatigue.

I looked around. The place was divided like an old-time *armazém*. Barrels of preserves, herring, dried fish, vats of pickles, green tomatoes in brine, and hanging salamis with garlic.

Loaves of rye bread fresh from the oven were stacked up; there were cans and jars of cherry compote on the old shelves. Everywhere, barrels and baskets of dried fruit, scales, and large sacks occupied the limited space.

Exactly the same, I thought, identical to the store run by Dona Bela and Mr. Jaime on Rua Newton Prado in my neighborhood in São Paulo. Even the smell of the place was just like it.

To the side, where once there must have been an entrance to the garden, was a corridor full of small tables.

I looked around and observed the people there with me.

At the table in front, very near the door, I glimpsed the old woman whom Victor called Lily. She was having coffee with a sweet of some kind. She looked around, and sometimes raised her hands to her head like a young woman before a mirror, arranging her white hair in a bun.

At the table next to mine, three women were speaking in Yiddish. One of them, who appeared the youngest, asked who that woman at the front table was.

The other replied, surprised:

"You don't know the *madama*? She is an old and authentic bordello madam. She's called the baroness. The famous baroness Lily or baroness Hirsch. *Eine alte mainse!*" she said in a mocking tone. "An old story. She came with Migdal, in the twenties, I think. You know, the men who lured Jewish women in Europe… Later she became the most famous procuress in Buenos Aires. Just imagine, she claimed to be the real granddaughter of Baron Hirsch, the man, God rest his soul, who founded our colonies!"

"Just imagine," said the third woman, laughing. "A *corve* like that, a woman from a brothel, trying to pass herself off as the granddaughter of a baron, a saint like Maurice de Hirsch! She ought to have been in Burzaco a long time ago, instead of wandering the streets painted like a clown!" she concluded, chewing her sandwich.

"But she's protected by the pianist," said the oldest of the three. "They say they were even lovers for a long time. I think most of our old men around here, playing dominoes because they can't function anymore, were customers of hers. And today they barely say hello to her, pretending they don't know her."

I wanted to hear more, but the cafe owner came with my order, sat wearily down at my table, and started a conversation.

"Where are you from? Are you Jewish?"

"Yes… From São Paulo, in Brazil."

"Oh, are you here to buy clothes cheap in El Once? Lots of foreigners come here looking for our leather and wool clothing."

I asked her what Burzaco meant.

"Why do you want to know, girl?… No one wants to be sent there! It's like being condemned to death!" she answered, her voice rising. "Don't you have old people in your country? What do they do with them when they start bothering the young people? Burzaco is an old folks asylum where they send us to die… *Señorita.*"

I asked for the check and looked at my watch. It was past three-thirty. My flight to Brazil would leave at seven that night, and I would have to pick up my luggage from the hotel.

I paid and left some pesos for the woman. I exited along the side corridor.

When I passed Lily's table she turned to look at me. I felt her eyes staring at me. It was as if she were shouting: "Talk to me, please!"

Her tiny blue eyes, smeared with lilac shadow; her mouth, where the carmine had disappeared into the deep wrinkles of her small, delicate lips; her eyebrows painted brown–could not conceal the sign of a minute fleur-de-lis.

I felt like hugging her tightly, like kissing her goodbye.

The radio was playing a tango, *Mi Buenos Aires querido…*

I passed by her, my heart leaping. I heard her voice. "*Mademoiselle, s'il vous plait?*" Please….

I turned and unwittingly replied, "*Oui, Madame …*"

"Do you remember the doll house you gave me?" she said in a tiny voice.

I trembled, my heart raced. I pretended I remembered. I could not understand…

"*Oui,*" I replied.

She gestured that she wanted to whisper a secret in my ear.

I bent down, crouching beside her chair.

She held my shoulders with her long and dirty nails.

"Listen, *mademoiselle*. I kept the doll house with me, brought it from Naples... Do you remember Naples? My mother and my *nonna* are there... Only Madame Lory stayed in Paris. My real mother is named Michaela, but don't ever tell anyone that, it's a secret, you know? My *nonna* Clara asked me never to tell anyone. You must never tell... never!" she repeated. "My father was named Lucien de Hirsch, he died before Lily was born. He was a *Barón...My petit doll...*she gave me and this coin around my neck is from him. My *nonna* gave it to me, and I've never taken it from my body." She showed me an old coin attached to a chain.

"Don't mention anything about this to Victor," she continued softly, almost in a whisper. "Don't tell anyone ever! I know you can keep a secret because you're just like my friend, the one who gave me the doll house. Her name was Adele... You're not going to take me to Burzaco, are you? Don't tell Victor about it... he doesn't like Lily anymore... he just likes the other Lily... the Lily in the photograph on the piano... and I like him so much!"

I was out of breath and for a few seconds I didn't know what to do. I gave her a hug and kissed her cheek.

"You swear...?"

"*Oui, Madame Baronne de Hirsch,*" I said. "I swear to keep your secret."

"You're a good girl..."

The owner of the café came to intervene, waving a napkin and shouting in Yiddish, "Leave my customer alone, Lily, she doesn't need to hear your *mainses*, your stories!"

"*Adieu, Madame,*" I said, rising.

"*A tout à l'heure, mademoiselle,*" the old woman replied, looking at me with a toothless smile. "Never forget what I told you..."

I caught a taxi two blocks away. I was already running late.

The taxi circled the block and turned onto Lavalle. It stopped to wait for an opening in traffic.

At that moment I saw Victor coming out of his building with Anna Varsano's box in his hands.

He slowly deposited it on top of piles of trash and rags from the nearby tailor shops. I watched Victor's movements through the rear windshield of the car.

He cleaned his hands, brushing one against the other as if freeing himself of a dusty load, looked at the trash, and calmly went back in the building, closing the door behind him.

# Afterword

# The Key

After that encounter in Buenos Aires in 1974, I gave up on my promise made to Adele in the sanatorium in Salonica. I hadn't read the complete contents of that box of memories, the secrets, not understanding that they represented any obligation. I was too young to understand.

Thank God my instinct led me back to Lavalle at the corner of Junín after asking the driver to turn around five blocks later. I recovered the box and returned silently to São Paulo, storing everything in a closet. Sometimes, I would open the box and try to read a few pages.

It would be an enormous job to translate and understand the diaries and letters; my children were little, I worked outside the home; after all, I was just starting out in life.

Little by little, my curiosity began to grow.

And my pilgrimage in search of history and places began. For three decades I searched through tombs, addresses, and archives. On every trip, I found another passage, a new trail, and new friends willing to help me. But a strange event in the year 2000 was what really made me take all of it seriously and subsequently find an answer to my questions and doubts.

I was never religious, much less mystical. I think I've always been somewhat of a skeptic.

That October, on Yom Kippur, the Day of Atonement, when Jews fast and pray, I was in Paris

. It was Sunday, and I was there for the fashion fairs.

Accompanied by a friend, Aissa Basile, I didn't feel comfortable far from my family and not having gone to a Synagogue to at least hear the sounding of the shoffar, the only tradition I had retained from my grandparents and parents. Hearing the final blessing and sound of the horn blown by a rabbi would comfort me for a new year that ought to begin with health and peace. In a foreign land, however, I didn't venture to look for a Synagogue. So I decided to fast.

We spent the day walking around, from Saint Germain to Avenue Foch, talking, window shopping, and sitting on garden benches...

At the end of the afternoon we were on Faubourg Saint Honoré. In those days, walking through there, near the Palace des Champs-Élysées, was safe, and just one guard occupied the sentry post, and we enjoyed the fashions in display windows, and my friend photographed some models for her consulting work.

My empty stomach was growling. Aissa asked when I planned to end the fast. I looked at the sky, which had turned dark blue, and told her I would do so when the first star appeared. I looked for the star but couldn't locate it.

Strangely, the street had become silent and dark—no cars, no noise, no one walking. We could hear our footsteps echoing on the sidewalk.

Then a man with a beard appeared, dressed in an overcoat and black hat, and came toward me. He asked where the Gare du Nord was. I was confused and tried to orient myself; when I managed to answer, I explained I was a foreigner and it would be better to ask at the sentry box.

At that moment, seeing the man was an observant Jew, I thought: the fast is over, Yom Kippur has ended, and we can have dinner! As he was moving away, returning by the same path he had come, a small narrow side street called Rue d'Anjou appeared, and, feeling sorry for the lost old man, I said:

"Shana Tovah!"

He turned to me and asked, "Did you hear the *shoffar*?"

Embarrassed, I replied that I hadn't, because I was from somewhere else and didn't know where there was a synagogue. An infantile excuse!

He looked me in the eyes and asked if I would like to hear the shoffar. At that instant I thought, Poor man, he's crazy; where will we find a ram's horn here in the street? Beside the display window that Aissa was admiring was the entrance to a building. The man gestured for me to go with him. A weak light illuminated that tiny passageway.

Like magic, he took out a *talit*, a cloth prayer shawl, and with it came the horn, the *shoffar*. He covered his head and, wrapping himself in the shawl, began to blow.

I gazed at the old man, lit in that unique hallway light, and thought how strange he looked. He wasn't old, his skin was very white, almost transparent, in that lighting his beard had turned the color of fire and his eyes were so blue they seemed like marbles. He radiated kindness, affection–I don't know how to explain it. The shoffar sounded...

When he finished, I thanked him, very moved. I felt like crying. He brought his index finger to his lips, indicating that I should say nothing more, and in an instant he stored everything somewhere that I didn't see. He left in a flash, returning to that dark and narrow street from which he came.

My friend, her camera in hand, ran after him, saying, "Nobody will believe it... I'm going to photograph that little man!"

We turned the corner but, to our surprise, he had vanished. No car was parked, no door open, neither there or anywhere else. We walked to the end of the first block with long, huffing strides. Looked left and right. Nothing. Something had swallowed him up and he had disappeared like smoke. It was as if the world on Faubourg Saint Honoré had stopped for those strange and magical minutes.

We went back to the hotel and I called Brazil, told my father what had happened, and he, also baffled, said, "Either he's crazy or you've been having hallucinations, daughter!"


Those moments stayed in my head, and I always thought: Good thing I wasn't alone, or nobody would believe the story and I'd look like a crazy woman or liar.

After some months I mentioned the fact to an old college friend erudite in the study of Judaism. He put me in contact with a Rabbi from the United States who specialized in the studies of apparitions. On an international conference call, I spoke with the Rabbi. My friend, from his office, translated certain words and references from Hebrew, and I answered the Rabbi's questions, thinking deep down that he wasn't taking my responses very seriously, as he considered the whole experience surreal.

Weeks later I received a fax in English. The scholar from Philadelphia explained that, from all the writings he had found, the apparition that had manifested itself to me was a prophet. From the characteristics described in other apparitions, which are rare, the prophet Elijah had, at that date and hour, brought blessings and a mission.

One of the requests was *non confrontation*. I thought a great deal about the meaning of the word and tried to understand.

Another request from the apparition: to free and rescue the memory of someone who was never recognized. Free... Rescue...

In Paris? In São Paulo? Where and who? What memory?

I thought about everything, and nothing made sense. So I set the story aside.

In summer 2002, returning from Istanbul with my daughter and my grandson Felipe, we had a connecting flight in Paris to Brazil and many hours to wait till our departure. We decided to leave the airport and sightsee in the city. Walking down Faubourg Saint Honoré, we passed the corner and the doorway where the apparition of the rabbi had occurred. I pointed out the location to my daughter.

In April 2003, I was back in Paris for the fashion fairs and, taking advantage of the opportunity to continue my research about the references in Anna Varsano's letters, I found in the Grasset bookstore the biography by Laurence Benaïm of the countess of Noailles. She was the great-granddaughter of Ferdinand Bischoffsheim, brother of Baroness Clara de Hirsch.

I needed more information about that family. I was leafing through the book and found the address of Lucien de Hirsch's home in Paris.

In my imagination I had already described the Hirsches' home but had never seen it and didn't even know if it still existed. My daughter prodded me.

"Let's go together, mother, because tomorrow we return to Brazil and you're going to chew your fingernails for another year!"

I gave the address to the cab driver and Patricia went with me.

The taxi went down Rue Bonaparte, crossed the river, and took Saint Honoré. It went two blocks and stopped.

"Here we are, *Madame*," said the driver. "We have arrived: Rue de l'Élysée."

Confused, I saw we were still on Faubourg Saint Honoré.

I told the driver I wanted that other street. He answered that the street was right there, and was closed. It belonged to the government, and he pointed to a black gate manned by guards and with barricades. My daughter looked to her right, and nudged me.

"Look where the cab stopped, mother! At the door of the rabbi with the *shoffar!*"

I got out of the car, holding Benaïm's biography, and asked one of the guards for permission to go inside. Finally, we entered the street and searched for the house numbered 2.

Today it is the Ministry of Foreign Relations. The palace, or *hôtel*, as the French call it, was as I had described it: the garden, the windows,, the entrance door, and the gallery. It was as if I had already been there. I was a bit dazed. I wanted to see the inside. I had the floor plan in my head.

I wasn't allowed even as far as the reception desk.

I tried to take a photo from the corner of Avenue Gabriel, but a handful of guards surrounded us, grabbed my camera, and deleted the pictures!

"Gendarmerie!" No further argument. I think I must look like a terrorist.

At the end of 2004, I found an archive in Brussels—or rather, an angel who did an inventory of the Archives Générales du Royaume of Belgium.

It was everything I had dreamed of in order to understand the whole story. A treasure abandoned and boxed there since 1914.

The administrator of the inventory, Thijs Lambrecht, opened all the files, and afterwards we spent weeks analyzing the documents in person and later via the Internet.

The documents that Clara de Hirsch had separated before her death were there, those of Lucienne Premelic de Hirsch, the adopted girl, as well as those that would be kept for her true granddaughter, Lily, Lukia, the daughter of Michaela Varsano.

Someone had taken possession of it; someone had kidnapped and hidden little Lily.

We spent months searching, file by file, folder by folder.

Archive 305 was there, which listed the goods and documents found in the home of Edouard Balser, married to Lucienne Premelic de Hirsch, and the son of Charles Balser, a Belgian banker and industrialist, who in the First World War had been considered an enemy of Belgium.

For having furnished the enemy, the German army, with supplies of steel, arms, and raw materials from his factories, his goods in all of Belgium were seized at the beginning of 1914, as were those of Lucienne Premelic de Hirsch, who had a partnership with her father-in-law and her husband.

They fled to Germany, leaving behind the real estate, the furniture, and the memories also found in the home of Hortense and Georges Montefiore.

After much searching for answers, a miracle occurred. In one of the hundreds of folders, in a small book of prayers published by the Église Notre Dame du Sablon , was a small sheet of paper with the letter head of an orphanage, The Orphanage of Saint Vincent de Paul in Liége.. It was the listing of a female orphan, father and mother unknown, born in Taormina on October 6, 1887.

The name shown was Lily Napolitano. The signature was that of the chief superior nun, followed by the name of the benefactor, Charles Balser, and his son Edouard Balser, who through an annual contribution of 150 francs would maintain the girl housed in that institution.

The date was June 9, 1899.

The yellowed receipt, folded into a book that I was leafing through, fell to the floor, which was how it caught my attention.

Also inside the book were scribbles and drawings, with hearts and the names Baronne Lucienne de Hirsch and Edouard Balser, etc.

Folder 393, in the Royal Archives of Belgium, brought the final answer to my quest.

In that box were the birth certificate procured by Irene Premelic after Lucien's death, proof that she had staged the farce of introducing a two-year-old girl named Lucienne as the legitimate heir of the Hirsches. The certificate stated that the child Lucienne, father and mother undeclared, had been born at midnight on the sixth of October, 1885, at 24 Rue d'Anjou.

It had been that certificate that led to her adoption.

Years later, the circle of coincidences was finally closing.

Taking the copy of Lucienne Premelic's false birth certificate from the Belgian archives and the addresses I was seeking, I had travelled thousands of kilometres determined to untangle and understand the puzzle. I realized some time later that everything I was searching for, was within a few blocks and that the Yom Kippur apparition, even if I resisted belief, was part of it.

By studying a map of Paris, I became aware that everything had taken place inside a triangle connecting the Hirsches' home on Rue de l'Élysée to Irene Premelic's house on Rue d'Anjou, and finally, closing the triangle, I located the door of the apparition of the mysterious rabbi on Faubourg Saint Honoré.

In the same archive in Brussels we also found the last letter written by Lucien de Hirsch to his father. In it, the son said he loved, respected and admired him greatly but never wanted to confront him again. Lucien said he wanted to be free to pursue his life, he had reached 30 years of age and was ready to marry the woman he loved and live far from Paris.

And he ended the letter written shortly before his death. "Non confrontation…" Lucien wrote. "I never again want to confront you, my father, because I love you so much."

Comparing the contents of the letter to the fax I had received from the Philadelphia, I saw the similarity of phrases. The fax said that the coming of the apparition had a double mission: "no confrontation," and to rescue the memory of someone who had gone unrecognized.

And I, who had questioned what I had witnessed, thought I would never have an answer. With the passage of time, I had almost forgotten the promise made in Salonica, but that night, when I traced the triangle on the map, everything became clear.

Today, there is only one place in Paris that I make a point of visiting. Just a door, where I stop and remember and ask myself whether it was a dream or reality. The house on Rue de l'Élysée numbered 2 and 4 today is the French Ministry of Foreign Relations, which I recognize, that I will never be allowed to enter.

If I spent all those years, immersed in a story that was not my own, and if the promise I made to Adele in the sanatorium in Salonica was to be kept, I succeeded.

'Today, as I finish writing, I am comfortable at having related what I discovered, beginning with a box of correspondence and diaries of Anna Varsano hidden in an attic along with the yellow Star of David armbands worn by Jewish families marked for death in the Second World War.

I thank fate, which led me to find the letters, and am thankful for having had them all–the families Varsanos, the Hirsch, , Karakassos and my dear gardener Daud–as companions for such a long time.

And I thank whoever it may be, either here or up there, who entrusted me with this mission, and to all the good that happened to me, inside my life, in all those years inside a sewing box, offering me this adventure that is writing.

To all of them, inside those letters… my eternal tribute.

# Postscript:

Lucienne Premelic de Hirsch, the *baronne* who inherited the major part of a fortune estimated in millions of pounds sterling, was described in 1889 in *The New York Times*, when the will of Clara and Maurice de Hirsch was read, as the greatest heiress of the century. In 1904 she married Edouard Balser and had four male children.

Everything in their residences was confiscated in 1914 by the Belgian government.

The fortune of a Jewish family that distinguished itself as the greatest philanthropists of the nineteenth century took a different path from that so ardently desired by Maurice and Clara.

Everything that Lucienne Premelic received from the Hirsches was sent to Germany and with that fortune she and the Balsers became majority stockholders of the Deutsche Bank.

Decades later it would serve as a major source of funds for the rise of Nazism

.

As for Clara's adopted sons, Arnold Deforest Bischoffsheim, used his inheritance to become Count Bendern. He traded a Rubens canvas, *Lot and His Daughters*, from Rue de l'Élysée, for a title of nobility in Liechtenstein.

Arnold Deforest always concealed the source of his wealth and the name of his adoptive parents. He was accused of collaborating with the Germans in World War II. In order to avoid prosecution, and to remove his name from a dossier, he ceded the property at Beauregard to the local municipality. Raymond, the younger adopted brother, died at 31 and was interred in the Hirsch tomb. His assets were inherited by his brother Arnold. Thanks to the immense fortune from his adoptive parents his descendants to this very day live well.

The philanthropic work of Maurice and Clara de Hirsch, delivering from death or persecution vast numbers of Jews, led to the rebirth in the Americas of new generations who became citizens in the land that took them in free of persecution.

The institutions founded by Maurice de Hirsch in New York and many towns, educated children, orphans, youths, manual labourers, scholars, and liberal professionals in many parts of the world. A large portion of the wills of Maurice and Clara was allotted to these foundations throughout Europe, America, and the Mideast.

But of all this, today only the colonies founded in Rio Grande do Sul, Brazil, and in Argentina keep alive, with difficulty, the memory and the name of their founders.

All the others have disappeared.

There is no trace of the deeds of the Hirsches, nor even a plaque of gratitude, a square, or a monument, much less a vase of flowers or a stone on their tomb.

In September 2006, I visited the tomb of the Hirsch family in Montmartre cemetery, taken by my good friend and adviser Dominique Frischer, author of the biography of Maurice de Hirsch, *Le Moise des Amériques*.

I pushed open the gate of the sepulchre, jammed for a century, and found Clara's small velvet chair. There it was, threadbare, broken, the floor covered with dead leaves and the bronze door dark and peeling from time. Everything was abandoned.

There the couple lay with his son Lucien and with Raymond the adopted son, united, forgotten by time and by everyone.

I left to breathe the air outside, and a sudden sensation of freedom overpowered me.

Night was falling and it was threatening to rain; we hastened our pace and left in silence. From the cemetery gate I saw the illuminated plaque of the Moulin Rouge on the other side of the square.

Without knowing why, I remembered Victor at the piano with his silk foulard, his pose as a great musician; I remembered Lily, with her lilac eye shadow and the carmine lipstick on lips consumed by the ravages of time, at his side, taking care of Victor...

Poor Lily. She kept forever the secret of her secrets....

The Lily whom I met in *Sealed Letters* I still have with me, her supplicant gaze, her whispered words that were incomprehensible to me at the time.

I collected only pieces of her mysterious life after her disappearance the day of Clara de Hirsch's burial.

But, if I yet have a bit of life and health, I would like to pursue her story, to write and recount the life of that woman, the true Hirsch heiress who, through the mistakes and misfortune that life often brings us, carried in her trunk the lie of survival.

One day I still want to tell the life of the little girl Lukia, whom I met in Napoli Posillipo in 1898, of Michaela's Lucienne born in Taormina, of the Lily who was the true granddaughter of Baroness Clara de Hirsch, of the Lily Napolitano of the papers in the Belgian orphanage, and finally of the "Baroness of the Brothels."

Up to the day I found her in that *armazém* in Buenos Aires.

A day I will never forget.
At the time, I was just a young and inexperienced dreamer, and  it was impossible to understand all.

I was  too young to understand life…

Salonica, August 197        São Paulo, December 2005

# Acknowledgments

After all these decades, I would like to thank all those who contributed with enthusiasm and generosity their time and support to the research and for sending the materials for this work.

To my dear parents, my beloved father Abram Openheim, *In Memoriam,* and to my mother Berta, my love and recognition for everything they taught me.

My deepest gratitude to Stefanos, my dear husband and best friend ,for his affection, patience and support during this long journey.

To my beloved children   Patricia and Eudoxios,   for the encouragement and enthusiasm with which they always dealt with this work, at every stage of the research.

My recognition to my dear daughter in law Anna Lucia , for all her lessons  and efforts, teaching me how to use the computer in Word doing my first  archives.

My respect to Nicholaos Kouliumbas in reading this work for many times.

To: the editor Enrico Rastelli, *In Memoriam,* my Florentine good friend, for all the advices on the archaic Italian he gave me; for many years reading Anna Varsano´s letters and killing my curiosity.

To Dr. Theofanis Konstadinidis for all the memories of his family and about  the Greek Jews of Salonica;

To Marie Anastassiadis-*In Memoriam*, my dear mother-in-law, for all her love , telling me memories and giving the pictures and teaching recipes from Salonica and Constantinople from the nineteenth century.

My thanks to the team of my critical friends, Leni Lederman, Gleuza Lange, Carina Biaggi, Keila Matalon , Miriam Vassermann and Leila Navarro Lins, who kept on insisting that I take the original out of the drawer.


To the entities that very graciously cooperated in the task of procurement and research:

The Eton College in London, in the person of Penny Hartfield; Jean Derens, head conservator of the Historical Library in the city of Paris;

The congenial and genteel François de Callatay, professor of Economic Studies and Ancient Greek coins at the Sorbonne, curator of the Lucien de Hirsch coin collection at the Royal Library in Brussels, for giving to me the emotion to touch on that valuable collection, opening that save box and the entire library to see and understand better Lucien de Hirsch on my researches.

To the Archives de Paris, the archivists and researchers Fabian Camargue and Marie Tsakian.

To the writer Dominique Frischer, author of The Moses of America, for the debates of ideas about this work in Paris . To the team of the NY Times in Brazil, Mr. Romero, with his interest about this story writing about JCA ..

To the Archives of the Kingdom of Belgium for the permission to research the documents of Inventory 305 and for authorization to use images from the archive.

To my editors at the Grupo Record: Sergio Machado , Luciana Villas-Boas, Guiomar de Grammont, Bruno Zolotar, Magda Tebet, Livia Vianna, Ana Paula Costa, Renata Rodriguez and the entire editorial team, for without their kindness, attention, and competence this book would never have become a reality.

My special recognition to the Belgian Historian Professor Thijs Lambrecht, organizer of Inventory 305 in the General Archives of the Kingdom of Belgium, for his time and dedication, as we analyzed hundreds of documents in those holdings. Withouth him, I would not finish and discover all the end of this story.

To my constantly genteel friend: Anastassios Veryis ,who was on my side by letters during  many  years of this work.My  deepest appreciation  in always been supporting my questions, reading pages, and ever inspiring me, from the idea of the cover, up to  his beautiful descriptions of his harvesting time, colours and perfumes of Greece.

I am also grateful for the kindness of the Molho family, owners of the old Molho Bookstore in Salonica, for their countless clarifications and providing of materials about the city, its practices and customs from 1850 to 1917, as well as to the publishing house Cornucopia of Istanbul, for sending treasures about the History of the Ottoman Empire and the construction of the Orient Express railroad.

To the team of the NY Times in Brazil,  Mr. Romero, with his interest about this story writing about JCA ..

My thanks and special affection to the writer Flávio Braga, experienced critic and adviser, who supplied invaluable inputs into my originals.

My special  appreciation  to my English Translator, Professor Clifford E. Landers,for all his precious time, giving my voice to this book. To Vasda Landers, my love for all her care reading this work.
.       To Lina Sion, agent at Global Literary Agency, for all her advises.

To all my readers my gratitude, for their wondeful  letters, and affection.

And finally to my much adored grandsons Felipe and Stefanos, who grew up involved in this story, for all their good will in helping me, for the glasses of water and the sharpened pencils they offered me on those wonderful weekends we spent together working on the revision of this text.

To all, my love and sincere thanks.

# Glossary

**Ambelia** (Turkish) – place where wine is prepared and stored; wine cellar.

**Baksheesh** (Turkish) – tip, gratuity.

**Basturma** (Turkish, Armenian) – canned dried meat with spices and condiments of paprika and cumin, a favourite of travellers in the Ottoman Empire.

**Beÿler missafir** (Turkish) – guest of honour.

**Cabalist**: one who studies the Cabala, which in Hebrew means *tradition*. An ancient form of mystical and spiritual philosophy, it designates an age-old school of religious studies concerned with direct mystical relationship with the divine.

**Cabochon** (French) – the joining of two identical parts with a hook to form a closure.

**Caïque** – small Turkish vessel with a shallow bottom and raised prow, used on the Bosporus.

**Capolavoro** (Italian) – masterpiece.

**Carrozza** (Italian) – carriage, coach.

**Catiline, denunciation of** (Latin) – a series of four famous speeches by the Roman consul Marcus Tulius Cicero, delivered in the Roman Senate in 63 B.C.E. and studied in pre-law schools.

**Effendi** (Turkish) – an honorific meaning sir or mister.

**Entari** (Turkish) – garment worn by Muslims and Jews in Salonica; a long shirt overlapping the pants.

**Fez** (Turkish-Ottoman term) – see *tarbouch*.

**Hanukkah** (Hebrew) – the Jewish festival of lights.

**Hagios** (Greek) – holy.

**Halakhah** (Hebrew) – part of the Talmud directly related to practical questions of Jewish law.

**Hamals** (in Greek; in Turkish *hamalis*) – *hamalitos*, diminutive used in Ladino for the porters of cargo and baggage in seaports.

**Hamam** – steam bath; the public location for such baths.

**Imbïk** (Turkish) – cooker for distilling essences.

**Judeo-Spanish** – a language derived from archaic Spanish, and Portuguese-spoken by Jews since the Spanish Inquisition and used for centuries by Sephardic descendants. Also known as Ladino.

**Kaddish** (Hebrew) – Jewish prayer glorifying God, always recited at the ceremony for the dead.

**Kazani** (Greek) – boiler for heating bath water.

**Kyrie** (Greek) – sir, lord.

**Kotetsi** (Greek) – small place; expression; reference; a place as small as a matchbox.

**Kyria** (Greek) – lady.

**Ladino** – Judeo-Spanish.

**Mégas** (Greek) – the great, as in Alexander the Great.

**Missafir** (Turkish) – guest.

**Mordidita** (Ladino) – tip, fee.

**Muezzin** – Muslim cleric who proclaims the name of Allah from the minaret of the Mosque, calling the faithful at the hours of prayer.

**O`pra di Pupi** – Sicilian expression used in the nineteenth century for puppet theatre or marionettes.

**Oropes** – name given Jewish jewellers in Spain at the time of the Inquisition.

**Parakaló** (Greek) – please.

**Pasha** – high-ranking ruler in the Ottoman Empire

**Passover** – biblical Jewish holiday commemorating the end of Hebrew enslavement in ancient Egypt.

**Phyllo** – Leafy dough as fine as tissue paper, made from flour and water, shaped with wooden rolling pins and used for pastries or pita.

**Pita** (Greek) – a round, flat bread.

**Pogrom** (Russian, Yiddish) – anti-Semitic movement in Russia in the government of Czar Alexander II.

**Purim** – biblical Jewish holiday celebrated in memory of the triumph of Queen Esther, wife of Ahasuerus, the king of Persia, from whom she obtained pardon for the Jews.

**Saray** – palace.

**Sephardim** – Jews originating in Sepharad; from Spain and Portugal fleeing from the Spanish Inquisition; today the term is also applied to Jews of the Middle East and    Turkey.

**Shabbat** (Hebrew) – the Jewish day of rest, from Friday just before sunset to until nightfall on Saturday.

**Siniora** (Ladino) – same as *señora*, lady, missus.

**Skaffi** (Greek) – vat of hot water for washing clothes.

**Skiatro** (Greek) – scarecrow.

**Sobah** (Greek) – a coal-burning heater made of bronze for heating water for tea or soup.

**Spagnola** (Italian) – Spanish woman.

**Sublime Porte** – designation of the Ottoman government.

**Talmud** – sacred book of the Jews, a compilation of the rabbinical discussions pertaining to law, ethics, customs and history.

**Tarbush** (Arabic) – the conical hat or beret, always red or crimson, worn by citizens of the Ottoman Empire.

**Greco-Roman theatre** – archaeological site in Taormina; amphitheatre.

**Tiropitas** (Greek) – a cheese pastry made with phyllo.

**Vissino** (Greek) – a dessert made with sour cherries.

**Yali** (Turkish) – a house or mansion constructed on the Bosporus strait, with special architecture and always on the water. Used as a beach house, exclusively in summer, by the elite of Constantinople.

**Yashmak** (Turkish) – veil used following the rule of the Qur'an to safeguard women.

**Yiddish** – An Indo-European language of the Jews originating in central and eastern Europe, the Ashkenazim, whose writing uses Hebrew characters.

∾

# Bibliographic References

ALFREY, Anthony. *Edward VII and His Jewish Court*. London: Weidenfeld & Nicolson, 1991.

ANASTASSIADOU, Méropi. *Salonique, 1830–1912, Une Ville Ottomance à l'Age des Reformes*. Leiden: Brill Academic Publishers, 1998.

ANASTASSIADOU, Méropi. *The Ottoman Empire and Its Heritage: Politics, Society and Economy*. Leiden: Brill Academic Publishers, 1997.

ASQUITH, Margot. *My Autobiography*. London: Penguin Books, 1936.

BAHATÍIN ÖZTUNCAY. *Vassilaki Karagoupoulos. Photographer of His Majesty the Sultan*. Istanbul: Bös, 1945.

BONNER, Eugene. *Sicilian Roundabout*. Palermo: S.F. Flacco, 1961.

Catalogue. Tableaux Anciens, Galerie Georges Petit, Feu de Madame la Barrone. Paris, June 14, 1904.

GRUNDWALD, Max. *Samuel Oppenheimer und sein Kreis (ein Kapitel aus der Finanzgeschichte Österreichs)*. Vienna and Leipzig: W. Braunmüller, 1913.

GRUNWALD, Kurt. *Türkenhirsch; a Study of Baron Maurice de Hirsch, Entrepreneur and Philanthropist*. Jerusalem: Israel Program for Scientific Translations, 1966.

HILLAIRET, Jacques. *Connaissance du Vieux Paris*. Paris: Editions Gonthier, 1956.

JOHNSON, Paul. *A History of the Jews*. New York: Harper Perennial,1993.

LEVY, S. *Salonique à la fin du XIX Siècle*. Istambul: n.p., 2000.

MOLHO, Rena. *Oi Evraikoi tis Thessalonikis*, 1856–1919. Athens: n.p., 2001.

Newspapers of the period.

Le Gaulois Archives; The Times of London; The New York Times

PRŸS, Joseph. Die Familie von Hirsch auf Gereuth: *erste quellenmäßige Darstellungihrer Geschichte.* Munich: [The Author], 1931.

SAPORTA, L. *My Life in Retrospect.* Salonica: n.p., 1982.

STAVROULAKIS, Nicholas. *Cookbook of the Jews of Greece.* Port Jefferson, N.Y.: Cadmus Press, 1986.

STRAUSS, Oscar. *Baron Maurice de Hirsch.* New York: Jewish Encyclopaedia, 1913.

STRAUS, Sarah. *Clara von Hirsch.* New York: Jewish Encyclopaedia, 1913.

THIJS LAMBRECHT AND KRISTOF CARREIN – *Inventory 305,* Fonds des Archives des Séquestres – Algeheen Rijksarchief, Brussels, 2001.

TOMANAS, K. Croniko tis Thessalonikis, 1875–1920. Salonica: n.p., 1995.

VELAY, A. du. *Les Finances de la Turquie.* Paris: n.p., 1903.

VERGA, Giovanni. *Cenas da Vida Siciliana.* São Paulo: Berlindis & Vertecchia, 2001.

# SOME WORDS ABOUTH THE AUTHOR

DORA OPENHEIM is Brazilian living in São Paulo.

Mother and grandmother, Dora has a degree in Politic Sciences and Law by the University Mackenzie, a Master degree in Arts by the Armando Alvares Penteado Foundation- Is a professional trained by the Studio Berçot in Paris- working for many years as a fashion designer and development inside her family company .

In Arts, she is obsessed for old papers, Nanquin ink , writing calligraphies- seals, gold leaves over linen and bitumen , pastel and mix media.

During the researching time for this book, Dora was sharing thoughts once in her typewriter... in the computer... and.. as her family complains... "if she was not writing one night, she was inside her atelier painting words .

Painting words...?

She is recognized as a successful painter, with her canvases, inside many public and private collections in numerous countries.

Dora Openheim works for diverse charitable institutions, is founder by the side of their daughter and son, Patricia and Eudoxios Anastassiadis to The Anastassiadis Cultural Institute Foundation- ICA- providing support, classes in art, music and activities for retired seniors and underprivileged children in São Paulo.

"Cartas Lacradas" 1850-1917 in Portuguese became a best seller in Brazil
Published by the Grupo Editorial Record Rio de Janeiro-2013
In the second edition-2015

Sealed Letters 1850-1917 is her first work in fiction.
Translated from Portuguese by Clifford E. Landers
October -2016

In Non Fiction-
Debates de Arte - Published by Manuel Fairbanks Vieira Pub- SP- 1999
A moda como arte- Fundação Americana-SP- 1997
Caderno de cores - Grupo SENAI- Org.-1889
Old Jewish Recipes- from the Inquisition to Salonica-
to be published in June 2017

Fiction
To be Published:

Oblivion -1914-1974-  to be published in Dec 2016
Diamonds and Olives- to be published - Dec 2017

THE COVER;
 BY CHRIS POMAR

IN THE COVER:  DRAWS FROM LUCIEN DE HIRSCH- 1882-
THANKS TO  THE PERMISSION OF
 THE ARCHIVES ROYALES DE BELGIUM

PHOTOS AND DOCUMENTS-PRIVATE COLLECTION
LETTERS TO: THE AUTHOR

 OPENDOR@UOL.COM.BR

FOR THE BOOK TRAILLER-AND DOCUMENTS
 THE BACKSTAGE OF THE BOOK:

FACEBOOK/SEALED LETTERS/DORA OPENHEIM
FACEBOOK /CARTAS LACRADAS/DORA OPENHEIM


MUSICS:

THANK YOU-. DAVID BRUBECK

 ADIOR NONINO -ASTOR PIAZZOLA

Made in the USA
Middletown, DE
21 October 2016